SH

He smiled, 'You weren't assigned to me because we need diplomats around here.'

'What do you want me to do?' I asked.

He regarded me sadly. 'I want you to spy on one of your own kind.'

'One of my own kind?'

'A British Officer, John. A guy with an outstanding military record . . . in France, before Dunkirk; in the desert against Rommel; in Sicily; in Italy. Goddam it, he's been decorated twice for bravery in the field!'

The reason for Hibberd's distaste was now plain. I wasn't exactly enchanted by the odour myself.

'Why?' I asked. 'What do you suspect him of?'

'At the best, stupidity. At the worst, treason. But, one way or the other, *we've got to know*.'

Also in Arrow by Douglas Scott

THE ALBATROSS RUN
CHAINS
DIE FOR THE QUEEN
EAGLES BLOOD
THE HANGED MAN
IN THE FACE OF THE ENEMY

SHADOWS

Douglas Scott

ARROW BOOKS

Arrow Books Limited
62–65 Chandos Place, London WC2N 4NW

An imprint of Century Hutchinson Limited

London Melbourne Sydney Auckland
Johannesburg and agencies throughout
the world

First published by Martin Secker & Warburg Limited 1987

Arrow edition 1988

Printed and bound in Great Britain by
Anchor Brendon Limited, Tiptree, Essex

ISBN 0 09 958500 6

CONTENTS

Prologue

The dug-out where the Major slept was both damp and draughty. He awoke to the sound of the wind buffeting at the canvas flap of doorway. He sat up, shivering, and unrolled himself from the grey blanket that had been wrapped round his body. The blanket was damp and clammy to touch. Meagre grey light filtered through cracks at the doorway, partly relieving the tenebrous interior of the dug-out.

The roof was too low to permit the luxury of standing erect, being uneven rock – part of the natural grotto that the Major had converted to his use. A shelf of flat solid stone, stepped above the earth floor, provided his bed. He sat now on its groundsheet covering, head bowed to avoid the roof. He had been sleeping fully – clothed. Swinging his booted feet off the bed and swivelling into a more comfortable sitting position, he reached for a cigarette and matches.

The cigarette from the cylindrical Churchman's tin was dry but the matchbox was sodden. After several attempts to light the cigarette, he threw the matchbox away in disgust. Moving his feet, he found that water had seeped into the dug-out. The weight of his boots on the earthy floor was pressing up dark little puddles. He peered down at the mud, hating it; loathing its obscene ubiquity. It insinuated itself everywhere in these benighted mountains.

The Major glanced at his watch and sighed. Gritting his teeth, he divested himself of battledress blouse, pullover, shirt and singlet and shivered anew at the exposure of his flesh to the raw cold. Picking up a towel and soap-bag, and remaining stooped to avoid contact with the roof, he manoeuvred himself to the end of the dug-out. He paused briefly, bracing himself before pushing aside the canvas flap and facing the elements.

The Major grimaced as the sleet-laden wind gusted at him and dewed his bare chest and head with freezing droplets. The sound of voices drifted from the Command Post, a roomy cavern close to his private grotto. There was the clank of a metal dixie: promise of fresh-brewed tea. He suppressed a deep craving to taste hot sweetened liquid in his gullet. Self-denial was the source of his strength. Hot tea was the priority of weaker men, not his. He strode briskly down the winding gully where most of Three Company were encamped.

Here, high in the Apennines, Three Company and the small Panzergrenadier rearguard facing them were – it seemed – fighting the war all on their own. Most of the German forces had retired behind formidable defensive positions further north, where they had constructed their Winter Line. With the British armoured divisions slowly bogging down near the coast and the foot divisions pausing for breath as the Italian winter set in with a vengeance, the major battles of the summer had given way to isolated hand-to-hand actions at company strength and less.

The battalion to which Three Company belonged had led the looping advance of the British into the mountainous interior, by-passing a spiny range of heights that speared into the Eighth Army line like a thorn. The German withdrawal to their Winter Line had been orderly and it was clearly not their intention to hold on indefinitely to this spiky salient, which projected south from their prepared defence. For all that, the Germans were in no hurry to abandon their occupation of the craggy fastnesses and commanding ridges of this last

8

narrow salient. They would concede the ground according to their own timetable and at their own price. The terrain was such that a small rearguard, skilfully deployed, could exert an irritant pressure on the enemy that was quite disproportionate to the modest size of the force required.

Three Company had been assigned the task of removing the irritant. Detached from Battalion, the Company had back-tracked for five miles and climbed higher into the mountains. Infiltrating by night behind the spiky projection, they had by day overcome the most southerly German positions and secured a foothold on the high narrow salient. Having clipped off the sharp tip of the 'thorn', they then turned face again to the north and began the thankless task of rolling the enemy positions up from the side.

On the flag-pinned map at Divisional HQ, Three Company's task looked straightforward enough. They had a two-to-one advantage in men and were contesting the narrowest of fronts, where the enemy's superiority of altitude had been neutralised. What the map at Divisional HQ did not show were the ravines and gullies of the high Apennines, nor the succession of dips and ridges that faced them.

The Panzergrenadiers occupying these mountains had given early intimation that, if they were going to be dislodged, it would be one bloody ridge at a time and, even then, only when it suited them. In four days of relentless slogging, Three Company had advanced barely half a mile and each day of lashing rain and flurrying snow was taking on a pattern of unbridled misery that was a repeat of the day before.

Today promised little in the way of change for Three Company. They occupied a high gully in the lee of a high ridge, from which their forward posts looked out across a shaly depression to a similar ridge occupied by Panzergrenadiers. At night, they had heard the Germans singing – strange plaintive love-songs mainly – and the sweetness of the enemy voices had been profoundly disturbing. Why could the enemy not be silent in the misery of these mountains instead of haunting them with the reminder that German soldiers were human, too?

Now, the unreality of the night had given way to the harsh reality of another day. And in its first light, Three Company's commanding officer strode half-naked down the gully encampment. The Major picked his way round glutinous pools of mud, using the bare rock of mountain as a foothold where the morass was worst.

Primitively sheltered along both sides of the rocky fissure, like cave-dwellers of another age, were the 'resting' infantrymen of Three Company. Gaunt, tired faces stared out impassively at the Major.

Although the cold of the sleet on his skin was so intense that he wanted to cry out from the pain of it, the stern-faced officer gave no sign of its biting torture. No more did he acknowledge the stares of his men, turning his head neither to right nor left as he progressed below them. Yet he was as keenly aware of the watching eyes as he was of the cold. He sensed an awe, a grudging respect, in those gaunt tired eyes – and it pleased him. The awe was his due.

These men did not give their respect readily. It had to be extracted from them like an unpopular tax: prised from them. It was not enough for the Army to put insignia on his shoulders and proclaim his superiority to the lower ranks. That superiority had to be made visible in other ways. The major's crown, on its own, could not provoke the awe that inspired instant obedience. The man who wore it had to be seen to be of a superior fabric.

The Major drew an almost masochistic pleasure from the acute discomfort of the ritualistic parade to his dawn ablutions. No other man in the Company voluntarily exposed his body to the wintry air of these inhospitable mountains. It gave him satisfaction, therefore, that he

alone had the endurance and self-discipline to be unde-
terred by climate or circumstance from what he believed
to be the essential habits of civilised man.

Reaching a small waterfall at the lower end of the
twisting gully, the Major set a mirror on a rock and
shaved with almost leisurely fastidiousness. Then he
stripped to his underpants and splashed his head, body
and legs with icy water from the fall. As he towelled
himself vigorously, he interspersed his drying actions
with a variety of exercises to stimulate bodily warmth:
running on the spot, swinging his arms, jumping.
Throughout, he emitted little barks of sound, that might
have signalled either joy or self-encouragement.

His public ablutions at an end, he gathered his trousers and his boots in his arms and jogged up the gully
towards his dug-out. Halfway up the gully, his path
crossed that of a bulky figure on the way down. The
figure – eyes peering from beneath lowered helmet and
enshrouding cape – made a token semblance of coming
to attention.

'Morning, sir.'

'Morning, Sergeant-Major,' the Major called brightly,
without altering his stride. 'Jerry's late this morning,
eh?'

'Yes, sir,' the other confirmed, and stared after his
departing commander with eyes that were faintly
contemptuous, faintly pitying. 'Mad bastard,' he
muttered softly to himself. There was more sorrow than
rancour in the observation.

As the Major disappeared behind the flap of his dug-
out, the first mortar shell of the morning came whining
down from beyond the ridge to explode harmlessly at
the low end of the gully. It was followed at irregular
intervals by more. The bombardment, like the Major's
ablutions, was part of the daily pattern of events that
Three Company had come to expect. And the one, like
the other, was repeated for psychological effect. The
morning bombardment was less an exercise to inflict

11

casualties than a reminder from the German line that today would be every bit as unpleasant for Three Company as yesterday.

In the event, the day that had newly begun was to prove more unpleasant than all the yesterdays that Three Company had endured. An inkling of its horrors began to permeate the minds of the platoon commanders as the Major divulged to them his immediate intentions.

Three Company, since it had gained its foothold on the heights, had gained no ground that the enemy had not abandoned of his own volition. This state of affairs could not be allowed to continue. Three Company had to seize the initiative and, having taken it, hold it until the small force of Germans facing them had been driven all the way back to their Winter Line. The terrain prohibited any possibility of enflanking the enemy – the standard two-horned attack that pushed and sought to encircle simultaneously – so the assault had to be frontal, vigorously pressed home so that by sheer weight of numbers, Three Company would sweep over the thirty or so Panzergrenadiers in its path.

From the ridge that Three Company held, Charlie Platoon would provide covering mortar and machine-gun fire while Abel and Baker Platoons swarmed across the intervening space to the next ridge and stormed the German positions.

If the platoon commanders were uneasy, none voiced his concern. Exhorting them to silence, perhaps, was the ribbon of the Military Cross on the Major's tunic. All knew he had won it in the Western Desert, personally leading a bayonet charge on an enemy machine-gun position. He was asking no more of them than he had asked of himself.

Snow was falling in big heavy flakes when Three Company launched its attack in mid afternoon. At first, it seemed that its suddenness had caught the German line unready. Fire from Charlie Platoon had certainly

12

forced the Panzergrenadiers to keep their heads down – as the Major had said it would – and all of Abel Platoon had been committed before there was any reaction from the Germans. But when it came, it was deadly. The front ranks of the British attack were across the shaly hollow and halfway up the slope at the far side when they ran into withering fire. By this time, Baker Platoon – slithering on the shale below the British ridge – were not far behind. Their ranks, too, were swept by bullets. The attack faltered and halted as men threw themselves to the ground and sought cover behind every friendly rock and boulder that could be found.

The Major watched in dismay from the ridge above. His exhortations brought no response from the foot soldiers worming and wriggling for any protection that offered itself in the killing ground of no man's land.

The Major screamed and shouted. Unavailingly, he urged the men who were pinned down in the depression between the ridges to rise and renew the attack in spite of the flying bullets. When they did not do so, a fury seemed to grip him. Drawing his revolver, he rose to his feet and stood for a moment atop the ridge from which he had watched the slaughter of perhaps forty of his men. Then he plunged down into the shale, carving an erratic path towards the German line. Every half dozen paces, he stopped to exhort men flattened in the sparse cover to follow him. He cursed them as cowards and ran on alone when none followed. At first, he led a charmed life amid the bullets streaming from the German positions. Then the German guns ceased firing, as if the Panzergrenadiers had paused, awed by the spectacle of the crazy dervish-like figure running and stumbling towards them. He fired from his revolver as he came but, his arm waving wildly, the shots presented no danger to human life: blazing harmlessly high towards the leaden sky.

Reaching the far up-slope, he kept on going, slipping and falling to his knees several times but doggedly continuing upwards and still trying to fire his revolver although the hammer now clicked on empty chambers. Snow coated him, augmenting his wild wraithlike appearance. The Panzergrenadiers let him come.

Finally, with a cry of triumph, he clambered over the ridge, dislodging some slabs of rock in the process, from the roof-covering of a sharp-shooter's nest. The German wriggled free of his post to defend himself but the act was unnecessary. A Panzergrenadier, his helmet and body cloaked in white, rose from a nearby crevice of rock to fell the madly shouting intruder with a single blow from a trenching tool.

It was dark when the Major came to his senses. He was lying flat in the open and could see stars twinkling in a ribbon of sky overhead and hear the sough of the wind. He seemed to be at the bottom of some kind of ravine. Hearing movements nearby he turned his head to see moving shadows and the flickering reflection of firelight on rock wall. One of the shadows materialised to become the figure of a man shrouded in white over-clothing. The man shone a weak battery light into the Major's face.

'Ah, so you are awake, Herr Major?' a voice said from behind the light. The Major sat up slowly and discovered that his head was bandaged. Then he realised that the English-speaking German was pushing a mug of bitter-smelling coffee into his hands.

'Do I need to tell you, Herr Major,' came the voice, faintly mocking, 'that you are a very brave man but a very stupid one?' Then came the great cliche: 'For you, the war is over.'

In the light of events to come, nothing could have been further from the truth.

ONE

Temporary Assignment

I had just completed the text of yet another leaflet – designed to lower the morale of the German civil population when one of the clerks stuck his head round the office door and said the Prof wanted to see me. I dropped my finished text into the Translation Department on my way along the corridor to the Prof's office. I found him standing at the window looking out at the Seine. He looked worried. But that meant nothing, he always looked worried.

Although the Prof carried the rank of colonel, there was no formality in our outfit. I parked myself on the chair in front of his desk and waited for him to acquaint me with the reason for the summons.

'How are you getting on with that radio script?' he asked, turning to face me with his sad spaniel-like eyes.

'I'm not,' I replied. 'I've jotted down a couple of rough ideas but that's all. You said to give the air-drop leaflets priority.'

'You can forget the radio script,' he said flatly. 'I'll take care of it myself. You've got your marching orders.'

I stared at him in dismay. My marching orders? I had been with the PWD for the best part of five years – sincejust after the outbreak of war – and had established a comfortable niche for myself. I had no wish for a move now, when the end was almost in sight. I forced myself to voice a sudden dread.

'I'm not being sent back to the Army, am I? Not

15

after all this time?' The Prof goggled at me, affecting astonishment.

'Good grief John. You know as well as I do that the Army wouldn't have you back as a gift. It's a disciplined institution with no place in it for square pegs. You'd undermine the entire edifice.'

I sagged back against my chair, limp with relief. One week as a raw recruit – after I had volunteered in 1939 – had made me realise that the Army and I were philosophically incompatible. It had taken the Army a little longer to arrive at the same conclusion because, although I had passed a selection board for officer training, I had only been a fortnight at OCTU when I found myself back in civilian clothes and a member of the infant Psychological Warfare Department. I never did discover who was responsible for the invitation which resulted in my transfer but, as far as I was concerned, it was an inspired one. Quite apart from my intense dislike of parades, route marches, saluting and the necessity of doing everything by numbers, I had secretly begun to fear that at the first sight of enemy Panzers, I would turn and run a mile.

The PWD had provided a much more agreeable environment for me, being staffed largely by free and easy mavericks who believed that all authority existed to be questioned. Even the Prof – whose right arm I had become in devising dirty tricks to play on the Germans – had a delightfully loony side to him. He had almost as many degrees as a centigrade thermometer but he had an outrageous sense of humour, which he never betrayed by actually smiling or affecting jollity. He knew more about Freud and Jung and their works than either of these two gentlemen knew about themselves and he could unravel a person's psyche with the facility of a sous-chef peeling an onion. He was an authority on chess, bridge and crossword puzzles, and his conversation about human behaviour was peppered with terms such as 'mother fixation', 'psychosis', 'anti-hedonism', 'ethnocentrism', 'authoritarianism', 'sexual deviation', 'motivation' and so on. The human mind to him was like a clock mechanism to a jeweller and he seemed to know exactly what made it tick. Indeed, with his knowledge of the human animal, he would have made an excellent Fleet Street features editor – which was what I had been aspiring to become when Hitler had so inconsiderately interrupted the aims and aspirations of all my generation. Working with the Prof had been an education, but now he was telling me I had got my marching orders.

'It's not a permanent move, John, but when the request to have you on temporary assignment comes from the great white chiefs at SHAEF, there's not a hell of a lot I can do about it. You're to report at Versailles tomorrow morning at eleven. To an American called Hibberd. Does that ring any bells?'

Hibberd? The name triggered a positive peal of bells. The last time I had been called on to do field work – in London, during the late summer of '43 – the officer in charge of the American military intelligence team with whom I had worked had been a major called Hibberd. I remembered him as a quiet reserved man, who thought long and hard before opening his mouth and who invariably made a lot of sense when he did have anything to say.

'My six weeks chasing shadows,' I said. 'The big spy hunt. The number one Yankee shadow-chaser was a Major Hibberd.' The only reason I had been roped in was because the spies and traitors being sought in the massive security operation had been controlled by German psychological warfare experts: people like the Prof and myself, only they wore SS uniforms and thought Hitler was the Messiah.

'We never did crack the dreaded *Schatten Gruppe*,' the Prof said, with a slightly mocking air. 'Maybe your Major Hibberd is now chasing shadows here in France?'

The same idea had occurred to me and the prospect

of working again with Hibberd and his investigators by no means displeased me. At the best, it would get me out altogether from the same old four walls that I occupied or, at the worst, give me a change of office for a few weeks. I had enjoyed playing at detectives in 1943. *Schatten Gruppe,* I should explain, was a rather sinister wing of the Nazi intelligence service, which resorted to all manner of ingenious schemes to plant its agents on the Allied side of the fence. With about ten thousand civilian fugitives and escaped prisoners of war getting out of Occupied Europe every year, it was not too difficult for it to infiltrate spies and informants.

Three very capable and dangerous agents, who had eluded our screening, had slipped through our security net in 1942/43 and caused considerable damage before they had been eliminated. Indeed it had been as a result of information extracted from one of these spies that the big operation to track down members of *Schatten Gruppe* (Shadow Group) had been mounted. We had checked up on thousands of escaped prisoners of war and fugitive Europeans and attempted to verify that they were who they said they were. It was rather like looking for needles in haystacks and, to my knowledge, very few spies were unearthed but I certainly enjoyed searching for the enemies within as a change from dreaming up fiendish ways of hoodwinking the enemy without. I learned enough about *Schatten Gruppe* and its devious ways to put the knowledge to use when I returned to work with the Prof. I organised a series of broadcasts for our black propaganda people with the aim of shattering Nazi confidence in any of their agents who might still be at large on our side of the line.

'Where do I find Major Hibberd?' I asked the Prof.

'The Trianon Palace Hotel, Versailles. And, John . . . Remember, will you, that the place is the Supreme Headquarters of the Allied Expeditionary Force? Wear your best uniform and see that your socks match. They're very fussy about dress. I don't want you turning

18

up there with your tie in your pocket and looking like you've just woken up from celebrating the liberation of Paris.'

I smiled. 'You're the boss. I'll make a special effort although I've told you before, you can't make a silk purse out of a sow's ear.'

'Just try to look like an officer and a gentleman,' he pleaded, 'even if you have no pretensions to being either. You'll be rubbing shoulders with real officers and you will save yourself a lot of grief if you don't let them suspect that your commission is strictly an honorary one. Try to give the impression that you're one of them.'

I sprang smartly to attention. 'Yes, sir, All present and correct, sir. Will that be all, sir?'

He stared at me with the weary tolerance of one who must humour the insane.

'No, you'll need this to gain admittance to the Palace of the Great White Chiefs.'

He handed me what seemed to be a passport. It folded open to reveal a photograph of me, looking like a wife-murderer who was still in shock from hearing the judge pronounce sentence of forty years. It identified the holder as John W. Abernathy, Captain (Acting), Special Service Corps, and it was endorsed by no less a personage than Air Chief Marshal Tedder, the Deputy Supreme Commander.

'How do I get to Versailles?' I asked.

'Be at the Gare du Nord before nine and report to the RTO. There's a regular motorised shuttle to Versailles. Oh, and your Major Hibberd, that's not strictly correct . . . He's Colonel Hibberd now.'

'He's gone up in the world?'

'The Americans don't believe in keeping a good man down. They reward enterprise and efficiency with promotion. So, get your skates on, John, he could be a one-star general by the time you get to Versailles. Just hand everything over to Watkins and get on your way.

You'll have to pack a few things. You could be gone a week, a month I just don't know. . . .'

'I get the sudden feeling I'm not wanted. You'll miss me, you know.'

The Prof frowned. 'Oh, yes, I shall miss you as I miss my nagging wife in Cambridge. I love her dearly but find that my life has a peaceful tenor when she's not around. I shall miss striking sparks on your lively, if somewhat inferior, intellect. I shall miss your cheerful disrespect for my authority and your unashamedly philistine outlook on life. I shall miss your coarseness and your vulgar honesty. I shall also miss having you at hand to indulge my craving for nicotine. I shall now have to cadge cigarettes from Watkins and he lacks your generosity of spirit. He grudges every fag I prise from him. Oh, yes, I shall miss you, John, but I shall struggle manfully on and make every endeavour to reconcile myself to your absence. So, be a good chap, will you, and bugger off so that I can get on with my work. Give my regards to Ike, if you bump into him at Versailles.'

It was not the most sentimental of dismissal speeches, unless you knew the Prof as well as I did. The dear old sod didn't hand out glowing testimonials like that every day. I dropped an unopened pack of cigarettes on his desk.

'That'll keep you off Watkins' back until lunch-time,' I said cheerfully then drew myself to attention in best military fashion and barked: 'Abernathy, J., buggering off now, sir!' I did a smart about turn and buggered off.

Getting into the Trianon Palace Hotel in Versailles was like trying to get into the vaults of the Bank of England. There were so many guards and check-points around the place that it came as a surprise not to be hauled into one of the many guard-houses and given a lie-detector test. There were red caps, white helmets and white webbing everywhere, and even my identity passport signed by the Deputy Supreme Commander was examined with the greatest suspicion. One burly redcap sergeant read the details on it as if it gave off a particularly foul odour.

'What's the Special Service Corps, sir?' he asked, eyeing me as if the photograph was a likeness of Himmler, which it could have been. 'Never heard of the Special Service Corps.'

'Neither have I,' I said with a disarming smile. 'But it sounds impressive, doesn't it?'

My answer surprised him. He wasn't sure how to take it. His perplexity did not last. He threw me a look that seemed to say there was one smart-Aleck officer he'd like to have drilling on the parade-square as a means of straightening him out.

'Are we taking the mickey, sir?' he enquired icily.

'Wouldn't dream of it, Sergeant,' I replied. 'Are you querying my credentials or merely trying to satisfy your ignorance of my service function, which I am not at liberty to disclose?'

'Sorry, sir,' he said, his face reddening. 'Please pass through.'

An American military policeman, built like a Sherman tank, escorted me to the office of Colonel Hibberd, eventually. A plaque on the door said 'External Communications', which made me smile. Anyone who believed that would believe anything. Hibberd's function was counter-espionage. I supposed, however, that even in a ritzy headquarters like this, which was bursting at the seams with brass hats, spy-catchers liked to operate with a degree of anonymity.

The American Colonel greeted me like an old friend, although I was scarcely that. I had exchanged less than a dozen words with him in the past and my contributions had been limited to 'Yes, sir' and 'No, sir'. Now, he was calling me 'John' and apologising for spiriting me away from the flesh-pots of Paris. Working

21

nearly eighteen hours a day, seven days a week, in a poky little office near the Gare d'Orsay, had left me little time for riotous living, but I did not correct Hibberd and reveal the limitations of my social life. Instead, I waited with some trepidation for him to reveal why a big wheel in the US Military Intelligence Service was being so chummy with a very minor cog in PWD. The thought crossed my mind that all he had to do now, to convince me that something unpleasant was in store for me, was offer me a cigar.

He promptly produced a leather case from an inside pocket and invited me to sit myself down and have a Havana.

I needed the seat – and a stiff brandy wouldn't have gone amiss – but I declined the cigar. I smiled at him inanely and waited for the worst.

'We've got a rather delicate little job for you, John,' he said.

'External Communications, sir?' I enquired politely, tongue in cheek. He smiled.

'More inter-service relations,' he said. 'Or even more precisely, Anglo-American relations. That is where the delicacy is involved.' He was watching my face for the slightest reaction. Seeing none, he went on: 'You come highly recommended for the job. And, of course, we remember you from London . . . when you were on the team before. You impressed us then, John, as a guy who was remarkably free of prejudice.'

'Oh, did I, sir?' I said, pleasantly surprised that I had made any kind of impression at all.

'Yeah, you did,' Hibberd confirmed. 'You may not know it but we wanted to keep you on the strength. You never seemed to take yourself too seriously but you were conscientious at your work and you were damned good at it.'

'It's kind of you to say so, sir,' I said, and looked him straight in the eye. 'Are you by any chance trying to soft-soap me?'

Hibberd laughed out loud. 'Hell, no,' he replied mirthfully, and added triumphantly: 'We *were* right about you. There's no side with you. You're direct. You come right out and say what's on your mind.'

'I know some people who don't look on that as a virtue,' I said, a trifle ruefully.

He smiled. 'You weren't assigned to me because we need diplomats around here. That isn't our line of business.' He frowned, as if he'd had a second thought. 'I'm not saying there won't be any call to exercise tact. I said this was going to be a delicate kind of job. But it's a job for a guy who isn't blinkered by prejudice . . . a guy who isn't going to be blinded from the truth because maybe it's unpleasant.'

Here it comes, I thought. We've had the sugar coating, now we get the pill. But Hibberd was in no hurry to get to the point.

'We've got a lot of mighty touchy guys here in Versailles,' he said. 'We've got British guys who don't like goddamned Yanks and we've got goddamned Yanks who can't stomach goddamned Limeys. You and me, John, and the guys in our kind of work . . . I hope we're different. The only guys we want to score points off are goddamned Nazis. Do you go along with that?'

'A hundred per cent,' I said, and meant it.

'Good,' he said. 'Because, that understood, it makes it easier for me to spell out what I want you to do.'

'What do you want me to do?' I asked.

He regarded me sadly. 'I want you to spy on one of your own kind.'

'One of my own kind?'

'A British Officer, John. A guy with an outstanding military record . . . in France, before Dunkirk; in the desert against Rommel; in Sicily; in Italy. Goddamn it, he's been decorated twice for bravery in the field!'

The reason for Hibberd's distaste was now plain. I wasn't exactly enchanted by the odour myself.

'Why?' I asked. 'What do you suspect him of?'

'At the best, stupidity. At the worst, treason. But, one way or the other, *we've got to know.*'

'I see,' I said, although I didn't see at all. I had expected to be assigned discreet screening work, like I had done in London: checking on the backgrounds, personalities, habits and so on of escaped POWs and other fugitives from Occupied Europe, in order to establish that they were genuine escapers. This had a slightly different smell to it.

'It's possible,' said Hibberd, 'that the guy we want you to watch is as pure as the driven snow. Some of his own brass have tried to block any investigation at all, because they believe that the idea of him selling out to the Germans is unthinkable.'

'But you don't think it's unthinkable, sir?'

'I find it as hard to stomach the idea as anybody else. What I can't afford to do is take a chance on the possibility, however remote, that any guy in this headquarters – of whatever nationality – has been subverted by the goddamned Nazis. And I'm not alone in this. My British colleagues are in complete agreement and my authority to mount an investigation has come right from the top. The condition is that we keep everything unobtrusive. Not even Internal Security are being let into the secret. That's why you have been brought in from outside. You're not known here and it was agreed that, whoever our plant was, it would be better if he were British.'

Hibberd told me then about the man, whose innocence or guilt had to be established: Major Henry Cotter. He had come into the picture as the result of a flap over the disappearance of highly secret documents, to which some fifty officers – both British and American – had access. In the course of a check with all these officers, Cotter swore that he had never clapped eyes on the documents and insisted that he had no reason for even wanting to borrow them. During a search, however, some of the missing papers were found in an

24

unlocked stationery cabinet in Cotter's office. Cotter consequently changed his story. He remembered seeing the papers after all but thought they had been returned. He had forgotten all about them.

'Very embarrassing,' I murmured to Hibberd.

'Very embarrassing indeed,' Hibberd agreed. 'The Internal Security boys didn't find him very convincing. They got the impression that the Major was trying to cover up. . . .'

'Incompetence or a guilty conscience?'

'They thought it was inefficiency. And we got the same impression from a different quarter, although it was just scuttlebutt. It seems that Cotter's chief − a colonel − has been quietly trying to get rid of him, because he was drinking too much and never seemed to be around when he was needed.'

'But you're not convinced that that's just what it was, that the major was incompetent?'

'He's too bright. Not the kind of guy you expect to fall down on the job. And his chief, Colonel Vardon, is one of the prickliest customers you're likely to meet in a day's march. He's a real fire-eater, who's known to give his subordinates a hell of a rough ride. There's no doubt that there's been a personality clash between Cotter and the Colonel, although you wouldn't think so now.'

'Why?'

'When it was suggested that Cotter should be shipped back to a combat unit, Vardon nearly raised the roof. He's one of those touchy guys I mentioned who froths at the mouth if he thinks the British are having to dance to an American tune. What I should explain, John, is that here at SHAEF we have a unified command system and that Colonel Vardon's immediate senior is an American general. When the General suggested moving Cotter back to a fighting unit, Vardon dug his heels in and said that whether Cotter stayed or went was for the British to decide. And he wasn't going to be pressurised into sacking Cotter on American say-so just because some papers had been accidentally mislaid.'

'So Cotter has been allowed to stay'

'Where we can keep an eye on him.' Hibberd paused meaningfully.

'Where *you* can keep an eye on him, John. I want you to stick so close to him that he doesn't do a goddamned thing without you knowing about it. If he goes to the little boy's room, I want you to know what he's doing there!'

'How am I supposed to accomplish this without making him suspicious?' I asked.

'It'll be made easy for you, up to a point. You'll be working with him and you'll be billeted right alongside him. If anything comes up which you feel you can't handle – like staying close to him when he's off duty – you'll have a number to phone for help. But, most of the time, you'll just have to use your ingenuity in not making things too obvious.'

'What kind of work will I be doing with him? I'm not Army

'No, John, you're the guy who's been sent down from PWD, Paris, to sift through a whole range of Army intelligence reports – interrogation of German prisoners, that kind of stuff – so that you can garner material for propaganda broadcasts. It's the kind of stuff that Cotter has been collating and he's been told you're coming. He has also been told to give you all the help you need.'

Hibberd could sense that I was still uneasy – and not just because there was an inbuilt element of distaste in spying on a veteran soldier who had distinguished himself in battle. He asked me what was on my mind that was troubling me. So I told him.

'I've got to say it, sir. You're going to a hell of a lot of trouble to investigate a man who may not be the world's best office manager but who may never in his life have entertained an unpatriotic thought. There's a hell of a difference between being sloppy with official papers and passing them over to the Germans. Surely, you've got more to go on than you've told me?'

'There is one thing I haven't told you about Cotter, which is significant,' Hibberd admitted. 'He was taken prisoner in Italy and spent nearly three months in German hands, most of that time being moved from one hospital to another. He escaped into Switzerland.'

'Schatten Gruppe?' I didn't mean to whisper the question but that's how it came out.

'There's a chance they got to him. Just a chance. We know he's not a ringer . . . He is the real Major Cotter. There's one person who has left us in no doubt on that score: his wife. But there are others who would never have been fooled, including his dentist. We're pretty thorough now in the way we debrief guys who make a home run.'

'But you still have a doubt?'

'He was hazy about his movements when he was a prisoner, says he was drugged a lot of the time, and he was certainly in pretty bad shape. *Schatten Gruppe* operate with drugs. There was a sea-captain they tried to break but couldn't. He was the guy who gave us our first real lead on *Schatten Gruppe's* existence

'The Chisholm case?' I asked, interrupting Hibberd. He nodded. 'You were shown the file in London?'

'It was prescribed reading when we were shadow-hunting. The Germans used Chisholm as a false quarry to draw you away from the real thing.'

'And they damned near succeeded,' Hibberd said with a touch of bitterness.

'Maybe Cotter's been set up the same way,' I suggested.

Hibberd stared at me thoughtfully. 'That possibility has been giving me nightmares,' he said. 'It gives us another reason for having you watch Hibberd from cover. If he has been passing on secrets, he hasn't been doing it solo. Somebody has been controlling him —

although how you subvert and control a man with his record of service to his country is beyond my imagination.' He sighed. 'Maybe we're sending you on a fool's errand, John. If we are, it'll be me who ends up with egg on his face.'

I got the impression then that Hibberd almost hoped that he would wind up with egg on his face, that such an outcome would be preferable to the discovery of a viper in the bosom of SHAEF. My initial distaste for the role that had been allotted to me was already wearing off. In its place came a heady excitement at the challenge of working undercover.

In the afternoon, I was whisked off to a spired country chateau overlooking the Marne. This, I gathered, was the true nerve centre of Hibberd's cloak-and-dagger empire and here I was intensively briefed by one of Hibberd's men: an ex-New York cop called Calvin T. Thorn. Thorn was agreeably surprised to find my PWD training had included everything from parachute-jumping to weaponry and unarmed combat.

'You keep yourself in trim?' he asked me.

'Only if you count brushing your teeth as physical exercise,' I said. 'I've been office-bound.'

Thorn shook his head sadly. I had clearly gone down in his estimation.

'A pity we don't have time to give you a few work-outs and get you into shape,' he said.

I shuddered at the thought. 'I'm only going to be working in another ruddy office,' I told him. 'I'm not going on a commando raid.'

'You may finish up thinking that a commando raid would have been easier,' he said, and he wasn't joking. He was deadly serious. 'You haven't done much field work, have you?'

I admitted that it was all quite new to me. Again, he shook his head.

'Looks like I'll be playing mother again,' he said. He explained that while I was busy watching Cotter, he

28

would never be far away. He would be watching me.'
If you get out of your depth, for Christ's sake, holler!'
he advised me sternly. 'I'll come running.'

I told him thanks but could not imagine what kind
of difficulties would necessitate such an SOS. I was
beginning to think that Captain Calvin T. Thorn was a
bit of an alarmist. After all, carrying out close-quarters
surveillance on a suspect British officer within the armed
camp that Versailles had become did not seem to me to
be an assignment redolent with danger. Yet Thorn
seemed to be treating it as if I was being parachuted
into the headquarters of the German High Command.

The crunch came when Thorn led me down to a cellar
in the chateau that housed a small armoury and target
range. He fitted me out with a 45 Colt Automatic and
holster.

'You don't really think I'll need this?' I said to him.

He glowered at me. 'There's one thing you'd better
understand,' he said. 'I've met up with *Schatten Gruppe*
before and, like everybody else, I kind of underestimated
them. They don't play games. Anybody who managed
to get close had a nasty habit of winding up dead.
There's a chance you may never have to use this Colt,
Mr Abernathy, but there's also a very good chance that
you'll find it's the only goddamned friend you have left.'

Thorn's words sobered me like a douche of cold
water. My heady glow of excitement vanished, as did
the clouds of unreality that had cluttered my brain for
the past few hours. I was back with my feet on the
earth and suddenly wondering what I had let myself in
for. Perhaps it was just as well for my peace of mind
that I did not know.

The Pension Charleroi was almost as old as Louis the
Fourteenth's magnificent Palace of Versailles but a lot
more difficult to find in the wintry murk of a November
afternoon. I drove round in circles for half an hour
before I finally found the place that was to be my new

billet. Once, perhaps, the pension had been an elegant town-house with stables to the rear, but now it needed a coat of paint. It was one of a terrace of three-storeyed buildings that had all seen better days.

Between the wars, the Pension Charleroi had catered for the bed-and-breakfast tourists who had thronged into Versailles to gawp at the ostentatious complex of palace, park and fountain where the Sun King had housed his court in comfortable decadence. In November 1944 there weren't too many tourists around – apart, that is, from the steel-helmeted foreigners on expenses-paid overseas duty, who, if the truth be told, would rather have been somewhere else. Like Little Rock, Arkansas, or Solihull, Warwickshire, or wherever it was they came from.

I, certainly, was wishing that I was somewhere else as I stood at the door of the Pension Charleroi with my finger on the door-bell. I was on my own now, flying solo, as it were, and far from confident that I knew how to land.

The 'concierge' who answered my ring was a Catering Corps corporal with an accent that located his origins as close to Bethnal Green. He was chief factotum of the small staff who cooked and scrubbed for the pension's officer residents. The corporal had materialised from the basement, where he and his minions lived.

'We've been expecting you, sir,' he said. 'You're billeted next to Major Cotter. That's Room Thirteen. Hope you ain't superstitious.'

'Not at all,' I said. 'Thirteen's my lucky number.' He grinned when I knocked on the wood of the door and added: 'Touch wood.'

The corporal eyed the jeep standing at the kerb. It had come to me courtesy of the US Army – a perk with certain strings attached.

'That your transport, sir?'

I confessed that it was.

'Wouldn't leave it there too long,' he advised. 'The

soldiery around 'ere will nick anything that ain't riveted to the floor. We got a yard round the back where it'll be safer. I'll show you when you've seen your room.'

The interior of the pension was spotless, almost anti-septically so. Everything – walls, ceilings, stairs, doors – was painted white. Room Thirteen had the same sterile decor.

'It ain't the Ritz, sir,' the corporal said, as I eyed the spartan furnishings, 'but it's clean.' He deposited my suitcase, which he had carried from the jeep, and waited. I wondered if he expected a tip, like a hotel porter – but, no, he was waiting to quote the house rules at me. They were as numerous as the regulations laid down by the landlady of a seaside boarding-house, and their source was 'The Colonel'.

'No pin-ups to be stuck on the walls, sir,' the corporal informed me. 'That's the Colonel's orders. Breakfast is at seven-thirty prompt and dinner's at seven in the evening.' The corporal frowned. 'The Colonel doesn't like anybody to be late for dinner, sir. So try and make it on time. Oh, and if you'll be out any evening and won't be needing dinner, you've to let the mess orderly know before nine in the morning. Colonel's orders. That's Colonel Vardon, sir. He's the SAO in residence.'

There was more to come. If I wanted a front-door key, I had to get one from the SAO. Otherwise, the front door was always locked at 10 p.m. A provost patrol was responsible for the security of the premises between ten at night and six in the morning.

The corporal showed me where to park the jeep and told me that there was a mixture of both British and American officers resident in the pension's fourteen rooms. They all commuted between the pension and Allied Headquarters nearby, where they carried out their various functions. Like good bureaucrats, they usually managed to hold to regular office hours.

'What's my neighbour like?' I asked, as casually as I

31

could. 'Is he the Major Cotter who got a gong from Monty a month or two back?'

'The one and the same. He's got a chestful of medals, does our Major Cotter. It shows, though.'

'What shows?'

The corporal gave me a sidelong glance. 'I didn't mean no disrespect for the Major, sir,' he said, 'but you can see he's had a basinful of fighting. He ain't exactly twitchy, but he clearly ain't the man he was. Not bomb-happy, but kind of haunted. Like his mind is somewhere else most of the time.'

The corporal's summation of Cotter proved to be shrewdly accurate. At least, it coincided with my own first impression when I met the Major a couple of hours later. He seemed to be a man haunted by private devils. His mind – as the corporal had said – seemed to be somewhere else most of the time. He had the athletic build and face of a young man – he was only twenty-nine – but there was a hollowness around the eyes, a tiredness of expression, that made him look old.

A whole world of sadness stared out at me from those weary eyes and my reaction was not the one I anticipated. I had come ready to dislike the man who might be a traitor. Instead, I felt an inexplicable compassion for him. It was like gee-ing yourself up to run a race against a formidable sprinter and discovering that he only had one leg. I didn't want to be the one who did him down. I didn't want to be the instrument of more hurt and suffering than he had already endured. Much as I reminded myself that my job was to expose either Cotter's treachery or his incompetence, I found that the objectivity I needed was deserting me after a few minutes in his company.

The corporal must have told Cotter of my arrival, because he came to my room to introduce himself within minutes of his own arrival from SHAEF. I had just started to unpack.

'I believe you're going to be working with me,' he

said. 'It'll be good to have a new face in that dreary office.'

'It can't be any drearier than the one I've just left,' I said, and added lightly, 'Do I take it that you're not very happy in your work, Major Cotter?' The sad eyes became even sadder.

'Happy?' he echoed, and his thoughts seemed to settle in the distance, on a plane far removed from that small room. 'Happy? What is happy?' He seemed to have forgotten that I was there at all, so remote was his preoccupation. It was disconcerting. I had to repeat myself to get his attention.

'Headquarters work must be a change for you,' I said. He looked at me blankly. I nodded at his battle-dress front. 'Those ribbons you're wearing . . . You didn't get those flying a desk.'

He seemed not to have heard what I had said. Only one word had registered.

'Headquarters?' he asked, emerging from his distraction. 'Headquarters? You're new to headquarters work, are you?'

'Yes,' I replied. 'I've led a pretty sheltered service life, I'm afraid.' He half smiled. 'The important thing to remember about any Headquarters, Captain Abernathy, is that they are all temples for the preservation of fragile egos. Forget about your own and massage balm into the egos of those in authority above you and yours will be a serene and peaceful life. Rub 'em the wrong way and you will have a life of unmitigated hell.'

'Is that what you do, Major?' I asked mischievously. 'Rub them the wrong way?'

'There might have been a time,' he said, regretfully. 'What I do now, Captain, is yearn for the quiet life. There's scarcely a day passes but that I wish I was back in the Western Desert, where all I had to contend with was the heat . . . And the flies, and the scorpions, and the Afrika Korps. Life wasn't nearly so complicated there.'

I smiled, although I'm damned if I knew what I had to smile about. Major Cotter was not going to make my job easy for me. I liked him.

Dinner at the Pension Charleroi was an uncomfortable experience for the uninitiated. Although I was almost to get used to it in the week or so I spent at the pension, I never once enjoyed a meal there. And my first dinner, I enjoyed least of all.

Five small tables, pushed together and covered by overlapping linen cloths, served as one long dining-table. The food came up from the kitchen by means of a lift and a small hatch in the wall. It was dispensed by an orderly in a high-necked white tunic with regimental buttons.

At the top of the table sat the SAO and Mess President, Colonel Hubert Macaulay Vardon. I soon found out that he always referred to the pension dining-room as 'the Mess' and that he became extremely annoyed if anyone called it anything else. He conducted the meal with some of the formality of a regimental mess but, in practice, it seemed to owe more to the disciplines of an English public school than to military custom. In this Vardon fulfilled the role of watchful housemaster while the rest of us were cast as unruly schoolboys who had to be made to respect his authority.

Such niceties as which way to pass the port did not arise. Vardon was a strict teetotaller and did not permit anything stronger than water to be served at table. A small ante-room bar was opened before and immediately after dinner – which the residents seemed to eat with indecent haste – but Vardon himself never darkened its doors. Indeed, he seemed to pretend that the ante-room did not exist.

During dinner, as soon as the first course was served, the Colonel would rise and formally invite us to charge our glasses and toast 'His Majesty, the King'. This done, he would invariably invite one of the Americans to

34

propose the health of the President of the United States. It has to be said that he never managed to make the invitation without sounding like he was doing the Americans an almighty favour.

I wasn't alone in thinking that the toasts were a bit of a joke. The American officer on my right would offer the water-jug with the advice to drink sparingly. Water, he warned, was the most notorious typhoid carrier around and was really unsafe without alcohol added to kill the bacteria.

The dinnerware was railway-café standard – no regimental silver here – and the food was not much better. My American neighbour put it in perspective.

'Well,' he drawled, 'I suppose it beats K-rations.'

Although I consider myself to be a fairly inoffensive sort – I tend to make friends more quickly than I make enemies – it is fair to say that Vardon took an instant dislike to me. Although, as far as I knew, I was a total stranger to him, he treated me from the outset as if I personally encapsulated all that was odious. With my usual objectivity, it took me all of half an hour to realise that I reciprocated his sentiments. That's how long it took me to discover that if the Colonel had any good qualities, he managed to conceal them with an effortlessness that bordered on genius.

An indication of things to come appeared before we sat down to dinner on my first evening in the pension. Cotter took it upon himself to introduce me to Vardon. The Colonel pointedly ignored my proffered hand – maybe he expected a salute – and made only the most perfunctory acknowledgement of my existence. The snub was so deliberate that Cotter flushed with embarrassment for me.

'I get the impression that he thinks I don't wash too often,' I said to the Major, and laughed it off.

I was, however, in no way dismayed to be allocated the seat at the table furthest from Vardon: the end position at the bottom. I was far enough below the salt to feel reprieved from the necessity of polite conversation with the Mess President. The distance between us was not to inhibit the Colonel.

The coffee stage had been reached when Vardon suddenly boomed out in his hee-haw voice that there was a civilian interloper at the table. The way he was glaring the length of the table at me left the company in no doubt whom he meant. He seemed to be waiting for me to make some kind of denial, and I felt myself going rather red about the ears. Everyone was staring at me expectantly.

'I'm not exactly a civilian,' I protested feebly in my own defence.

'You are not exactly an Army captain either!' Vardon boomed back at me. 'Although the uniform you're wearing might give that impression.' I felt my face go redder.

'The uniform goes with the job I do,' I replied.

'Does it?' Vardon came back. 'Does it, indeed? And a regiment with it, I suppose? What's your regiment, *Captain* Abernethy? Do they let you wear a badge in your cap?'

I ignored the mispronunciation of my name and his sarcastic emphasis on the word 'Captain'.

'I wear no regimental badge,' I said.

The admission seemed to delight Vardon. He tried to make me wriggle some more.

'Tell us why,' he prompted me.

I stared at the faces, staring at me. I did not like this attention one little bit.

'Tell us why,' Vardon repeated, enjoying my discomfiture. 'We all want to know why you wear no regimental badge. Don't we, gentlemen?'

I looked around helplessly. 'It's embarrassing, sir,' I prevaricated. 'I feel rather ashamed . . .'

'Tell us,' commanded Vardon.

'Well, sir,' I answered, as solemnly as I could, 'I didn't really want it to get out . . . But there's a good reason for not wearing any regimental identification. You and these gentlemen might make me feel I was unwelcome in this Mess That I didn't belong. The truth is that my name is really Scheuerpflug and I am a Hauptsturm-führer in the Waffen SS.'

There was a moment of stunned silence. It preceded an eruption of unrestrained mirth from everyone around the table, except Vardon. I thought my American neighbour was going to choke to death. His paroxysms of laughter seemed to be exerting alarming stress on his respiratory system.

Vardon sat at the table-top looking like he had been struck by lightning and a slow fire had taken hold in the region of his back collar-stud. His eyes bulged with outrage and his bristly moustache quivered on a trembling upper lip.

'Silence!' he roared, and had to repeat the admonition before the merriment subsided to a respectful hush. By then he was on his feet. 'You're behaving like mindless children,' he rebuked the company at large.

'Aw, c'mon, Colonel, where's your sense of humour?' chided my American neighbour, who was still weak from laughing. 'Can't you take a joke?'

Vardon glared at the American. 'If any of you had faced the Waffen SS in the field – as I have done on several occasions – you might find that *Mister* Aberne-thy's idea of a joke is in singularly bad taste,' he declared coldly. His eyes fixed on me. 'As for you, Abernethy, it is bad enough to have a glorified civilian in this Mess – and a non-combatant at that – without having to tolerate your smart-Aleck remarks.'

'Gee, Colonel,' protested my American sympathiser, 'you were needling the poor guy. You kinda asked for it.'

Vardon looked like he might explode, but he controlled himself.

'If that is the majority view – and your faces would indicate that it is – then there is no more to be said on the subject. If you will excuse me, gentlemen, I propose you finish your dinner without me. I bid you goodnight.'

With a final glare at me, he marched out, tight-lipped.

'Pompous son-of-a-bitch!' my American friend commented as the door closed behind the departing Colonel. The others voiced similar sentiments and, as they broke from table, seemed eager to congratulate me for taking the wind out of Vardon's sails. Clearly, he was less than popular.

Only Major Cotter hung back from the rush to express satisfaction at what had happened. He had not joined in the general hilarity as whole-heartedly as the rest and now he seemed glumly apprehensive. 'A bad start, eh?' I enquired, when he confronted me, looking disapproving. 'I haven't been in the place ten minutes and already I'm rubbing egos the wrong way.'

'You've got to make allowances for the Colonel,' he said, his eyes reproachful. 'Maybe I should have warned you . . . He's got a low boiling point and he can be rude as bloody hell – but it's just the way he's made.'

'What about the way I'm made? Does that count?' I asked Cotter. 'He picked on me for no reason and tried to make me look small. And he was enjoying it . . . if I'd been a fly, he would have had me on a pin, hauling my wings off. . . .'

'He's very touchy about the Germans.'

'I'm very touchy about me,' I replied testily. 'And I don't like bullies who use their rank as if it gave them some God-given right to trample over other people.'

'You don't understand,' Cotter said. 'OK, so you got a laugh with your crack about the SS – but it wasn't that bloody funny. You wouldn't have done much laughing if you'd been strung up and tortured by the Gestapo, like old Hubert was . . .'

'The Colonel?' I interrupted. 'The Gestapo tortured him?'

'You weren't to know,' Cotter said. 'He doesn't broadcast it.'

I felt totally deflated. 'I had no idea,' I murmured.

'Just make allowances,' Cotter advised, sympathetically. 'I do.'

In silence, I nursed a small pang of guilt over Vardon and wondered why I found it easier to make allowances for Cotter's battle-weary disillusion than the Colonel's bullying rudeness. Vardon was just plain unlovable and, overriding any guilt I may have harboured, I felt a sudden curiosity about the man. I wanted to know the how, the why and the when of his rough treatment at the hands of the Nazis. But Cotter had stopped being talkative. When I asked him to tell me about Vardon, the words just bounced away into space. I think if I had shouted it would have made no difference. His mind was already away on some distant cloud of thought.

Like a man who had suddenly remembered urgent business elsewhere, he pushed past me with a polite 'Excuse me' and made for the door, still absorbed. I was more than a little perplexed. I was coming to the conclusion that Hibberd had made a mistake in briefing me to keep an eye on Cotter. He should have called in the MO and got him to run the rule over both the Major and his chief. In my humble opinion neither man should have been holding down important jobs at SHAEF. They should have been on sick leave.

TWO

Go Directly to Gaol!

The official address of Allied Headquarters in Versailles was No. 1, Boulevard de la Reine. They should have spelt it 'Rain'. The boulevard was constantly awash from the torrents emptying from the low stratus overcast that was encamped permanently over the town. The weather was typically English November, only wetter. After a week of it, I was convinced that Thorn had made an error of judgement in equipping me with a revolver. An umbrella and a pair of sea-boots would have afforded better protection. Fortunately for me, Cotter did not spend much time out of doors, so I was not obliged to trail after him around the rain-swept streets.

Every morning, Cotter and his colonel were driven to SHAEF in Vardon's dun-coloured staff car. Cotter did suggest to the Colonel that, since we were all going to the same place, I should ride with them but Vardon was having none of it. As far as the Colonel was concerned, I would be doing everybody a favour if I walked to HQ and back every day and took a long time doing it. He was as peeved as hell to discover that I had a jeep and would not have to trudge in the rain. The result was that, every morning, when Vardon and Cotter drove off to the Boulevard de la Reine, I was waiting in my jeep; ready to tag along behind them.

I cultivated the acquaintance of Thomson, Vardon's driver, so that I wouldn't be caught out by any change in their routine. Thomson was a friendly sort, who thought that I just wanted to keep in the Colonel's good books by keeping abreast of his movements. He became very good at tipping me off about his orders for the car, so that I was always forewarned. By slipping Thomson the odd tin of cigarettes in appreciation, I made the driver a discreet and loyal helper.

Vardon and Cotter operated from a suite of offices at the rear of the former hotel on the Boulevard de la Reine. The main entrance was near the eastern boundary of the magnificent park where the historic Trianon palaces were situated. Vardon's offices looked the other way, south-east, towards the seventeenth-century church of Notre-Dame and Versailles town.

Gauging the precise function of Vardon's department was not easy for a new boy like myself – and it was made no easier by the Colonel making me only slightly less welcome than a visitor from Hitler's OKW. Vardon himself rejoiced in the title of 'Contingency Planning Co-ordinator', which could have meant anything and probably did. He and Cotter seemed to spend a long time at a huge map, locating and relocating reserves and replacements for the battle-fronts although, I gathered, this was largely a paper exercise. They did not actually move men and vehicles around France and Belgium like chess-men. Rather, they kept tabs on a fluid situation and enumerated choices of action for the real decision-makers higher up. The top brass adopted or rejected their department's projections as they saw fit.

The department also had a number of ancillary functions and, of course, it was one of these that had supplied my pretext for temporary attachment. Cotter made periodic analyses of enemy unit movements from the information coming back daily from the various Army Groups. Much of this information came from the interrogation of German prisoners and, ostensibly, it was my job to sift the interrogation transcripts for material that could be used in the propaganda war.

41

There was no need for me to pretend interest because I found much to fascinate me in the transcribed interrogations and wrote screeds of notes for despatch to the Prof in Paris. I was left very much to my own devices while I worked and, sitting at a table in the corner of what Vardon called his Operations Room, I had ample time to study not only Cotter but Vardon, too, as well as the clerks, stenographers, and signal personnel who made up the team. Vardon flitted around like a busy moth, retiring every so often to his own little private sanctum or going off to briefings or conferences elsewhere in the building.

It struck me that Cotter was the real brains in the department and carried Vardon. Indeed, the more I saw of Vardon, the more I was impressed by the man's incredible stupidity. He could be stubbornly pig-headed and his intelligence was far from being the brightest I have ever encountered. He had a genius for separating the significant from the trivial and then confusing the two, with the result that he devoted much energy and passion to the irrelevant. Indeed, it astonished me that he had reached the dizzy rank of colonel without it being found out how limited was his intellect.

Perhaps – in the light of my own brief skirmish with Army ways in 1939 – I should not have been even mildly surprised that Vardon had made colonel. Then, I had reluctantly concluded that the dimwits in any new Army intake rapidly became NCOs and that those who weren't bright enough to make lance-corporal were either earmarked for officer training or doomed to peel potatoes and dig latrines for the rest of their lives. It was only because I was glad to escape from the latter fate that I did not feel too insulted at being selected for officer training.

Cotter, as far as I could see after a week's observation, led a blameless life. In spite of his disturbing habit of suddenly switching off in the middle of a conversation, he seemed to work hard and conscientiously and he had

42

no social life worth talking about. At the pension in the evenings, I saw him once make up a four at bridge with three of the Americans but usually he disappeared up to his room soon after dinner and that was him for the night. Because of the allegation about his drinking, I wondered if he was tippling away in private. Twice, with the excuse that I was on the scrounge for books, I disturbed him to find out. On both occasions I found him sober and writing long letters to his wife in England. He seemed to write pages and pages every day, with the result that I started wondering what on earth he had to say.

I kept in touch constantly with Thorn. He always contrived to phone me mornings and afternoons at SHAEF. We talked obliquely in a kind of code we had pre-arranged, so that our conversations would have an innocent normality to anyone who overheard them.

We also met nightly, usually after I had satisfied myself that Cotter was tucked up safely in bed. The arrangement was that I should take a late-night stroll as far as the Avenue St Cloud and that Thorn would pick me up somewhere along my agreed route. Sure enough, sooner or later he would materialise from the shadows and fall into step beside me. I never once managed to spot him before he actually appeared.

It irked me that I never seemed to have anything of value to report and that the weather was not conducive to late-night strolls: invariably wet and cold. Thorn did not seem to mind the weather or the negative nature of my reports. He exhorted me to patience and warned me repeatedly not to relax my vigilance because nothing was happening. He was also patient in another respect. I seemed to spend much of our time griping about Vardon. Thorn's counsel was not to let him distract me from the job in hand.

The Colonel, however, was becoming a real pain in the neck. He never lost a chance to make me aware how much he disapproved of having a 'non-Army type' foisted on him and installed in *his* operations room. He got a kick out of talking about me to Cotter in a very loud voice, knowing that I was listening. Everybody in the room was listening.

He seldom referred to me by name. I was either the 'psychology wallah' or the 'PWD johnnie'. Such species, he was fond of declaring, were not to be confused with real soldiers. The PWD were a thoroughly disreputable lot and their existence was an affront to any right-thinking Englishman with a pride in the glorious traditions of the British Army. They were just a gang of unprincipled charlatans.

'They're not like us,' he told Cotter one day, as he aired his prejudices. 'Just a bunch of long-haired intel-lectuals and ruddy fortune-tellers that they've pulled in off the street. All they're interested in is keeping as far from the front as possible and all they're good for is lying and cheating and bamboozling. Take my word for it, there's no underhand trickery too despicable that they wouldn't turn their hands to!'

Vardon's ranting tended to boomerang, inasmuch that the more he went on about me and the PWD, the more sympathy I got from his minions. He treated all of them, including Cotter, with a rudeness that was quite appalling.

At first I thought that perhaps he made life miserable for his subordinates because he got a rough ride from his superiors – but I saw no evidence to support the view, even though I heard Vardon frequently maligning the 'senior management' in front of Cotter. The Colonel did not have the reputation of being a yes-man with the higher-ups – Hibberd had described him as 'difficult' and 'prickly' – but he was always affable in a gruff formal kind of way if a general dropped in on the department. He reminded me on those occasions of a particularly 'awkward' managing editor I had known. He was almost devoid of journalistic talent but had risen the ladder of command through a capacity for saying 'no' to every idea and enterprise that came up for consideration. Even the newspaper's proprietors went slightly in awe of him because they interpreted his wholly negative rigidity as prudence. In fact, it stemmed from a mind that was barren of creative thought. He had absolutely nothing to offer, so he said 'no'. The proprietors did not connect a continuous drain to other papers of their brightest young men to the stifling obduracy of this one man. It was not until the negative one retired that the paper began to recover from a steady slump in circulation. By then, the paper had been overtaken by rivals who were riding high on the talents of defected employees.

Vardon impressed me as being negative in the same way as that much-feared managing editor. The strange thing was that, although Cotter suffered more than most at his hands, the Major frowned on it if anyone said a word out of place about his insufferable chief. It was possible, of course, that Cotter was prepared to make unlimited allowances for the man who, he had said, had been tortured by the Gestapo. This was an aspect of Vardon's past that had aroused my curiosity, but Cotter was reluctant to enlighten me. It was something Vardon didn't talk about, so Cotter wouldn't. Maybe it was because of this that I was less inclined to be as generous as Cotter in making allowances for Vardon. Being ill-treated by the Nazis did not, in my book, give anyone the excuse to behave like one.

I found myself regretting that Cotter was my quarry and not Vardon. If it had been the Colonel who had come under suspicion, I would have had a much stronger appetite for my secret task. Indeed, I would have relished it – and said as much to Thorn on one of our nightly trysts. He was amused.

He knew that Vardon was regarded as a king-sized 'pain-in-the-ass' by many American officers at SHAEF – a 'real boil on the backside of Anglo-American relations' – but he reckoned that just because a man was obnoxious it did not follow that he was a traitor. I reluctantly had to agree. Vardon was much too unsubtle to play a double game. Cotter, on the other hand, had depth – and he was a troubled man. The way he closed himself off mentally was more than the automatic escape mechanism of a man who had suffered too much of the stress of battle. It was a sign perhaps that he was burdened by complex pressures that he had to conceal.

Was it possible that a surfeit of battle had effected a profoundly radical change in Cotter's entire personality and outlook – in a way that made him turn all his former loyalties upside down? What had been right before, now became wrong – and vice versa. Strange things happen to the human mind. Had he experienced something like Paul's conversion on the road to Damascus, only in reverse?

It was the kind of theory I longed to discuss with the Prof. Was there such a thing as the Judas syndrome? Could a man betray all he held dear because of complete disillusion?

Thorn, the one person with whom I could discuss such notions, was not strong on theories. He was a facts man. Facts were what mattered. Facts were evidence. No cop ever got a conviction by producing theories in court and, according to Thorn, it was time I started thinking like a cop. If Cotter was our man, he would make a move sooner or later – and when he did I had better be on my goddamned toes!

The admonition delivered, Thorn promised to do some checking on Vardon – just to keep me happy. In the meantime, I was to keep my eye on the ball. By ball, he meant Cotter. I was not to allow myself to be sidetracked by Vardon. Unfortunately, nobody told Vardon.

I had no inkling what was in store for me at SHAEF the following morning. The day started in precisely the same fashion as the preceding days, with Vardon and

46

Cotter going off to attend the first ritual of the morning: the G–2 briefing, at which the overnight intelligence information from the Army Groups was disseminated.

The second ritual was celebrated with the reverence of early Mass, soon after the pair returned at 9.30: the dispensation of tea and coffee from a trolley that parked outside the Operations Room. The empty mugs were being collected for the trolley when Vardon emerged from his inner sanctum.

'Abernethy,' he called, 'I want to see you in my office. At once!' He marched back inside his room, leaving the door open. Cotter grinned across at me.

'The master calls,' he murmured.

'He's not my bloody master,' I said, with some feeling. However, I did not think it would be politic to keep Vardon waiting. I entered his office to find him already behind his desk. There was an upright chair for visitors to the sanctum, but he did not invite me to use it. He had a glint in his eye that I didn't like – the look of a hanging judge who enjoys his work. The desk was bare but for a telephone and a big buff-coloured envelope, which he kept tapping with the swagger cane held lightly in his right hand.

'I want you to know that I have your number, Abernethy,' he began, without preamble. 'I had you twigged right from the start. I knew you were a wrong 'un.'

'The name is Abernathy, sir,' I corrected him. 'Not Abernethy.'

'I know your damned name,' he snapped, but he held his sudden anger in check. 'Abernethy,' he said more softly, as if savouring the word, 'takes the ruddy biscuit, don't you think?' He smiled icily at his own feeble joke. 'Abernethy, Abernathy what's the difference? Not a name one forgets, eh? Not a name that I'm ever likely to forget. Not as long as I live!'

It was an odd thing for him to say and I felt vaguely uneasy at the way he said it. He was staring at me like a cat contemplating the sparrow it has pinned with a forepaw.

'I have a long memory, Abernethy,' he went on, mysteriously. 'I put two and two together as soon as I saw your name on the docket they sent down from the HQ Commandant's office telling me that you were to be inflicted on us.'

'I'm sorry if you find my presence a burden, sir,' I said, but my mind was locked on his boast that he had put two and two together. What the hell did he mean? Why should my name mean anything to him *before* I had even arrived at SHAEF?

'I find your presence more than a burden, Abernethy,' he replied.

'I find it an unforgivable insult! To me! To the memory of my father! To the British Army!'

I was mystified. 'You've lost me, sir,' I said. 'I just have no idea what you're talking about.'

'Don't come the innocent,' he snapped. 'I knew from the start that it was too much of a coincidence to expect that there was more than one John Alexander Abernethy, and God knows one is enough

'The name is Abernathy, sir,' I pointed out again, not that it made any difference. To Vardon, I was Abernethy – and Abernethy I would remain. He was tapping away with his swagger stick at the envelope sitting on his desk.

'Do you think that I wouldn't take the trouble of checking up on you?' he demanded imperiously. He tapped the big envelope some more. 'I've been waiting a week for this. It arrived from London this morning. And it confirms that you are exactly who I thought you were.'

'May I ask who it is you think I am?' I asked patiently.

He put down his stick and extracted some sheets of paper from the envelope.

As he shuffled them into the order he wanted, he said: 'The psychology wallahs in London weren't very helpful. My friends at the War Office were none too impressed with your employers. They found them very secretive and very reluctant to say anything about you.'

'How unfortunate,' I observed.

'Oh, they weren't totally unco-operative,' Vardon said, with a cold smile. 'They did say that you had come to them from the Army. My friends had only to turn up a few records to tell me all I wanted to know about you.'

'The Army were probably happy to be rid of me. I could have told you that without you going to the bother of getting in touch with the War Office.'

He ignored that. He now had the papers in order.

'You are John Alexander Abernathy, born fourth of August, nineteen hundred and fourteen . . .?'

'Yes . . .'

' . . .and you appeared before a War Office selection board on November ninth, nineteen thirty-nine? By God, they must have been hard up!'

'I won't dispute that,' I said cheerfully. He glared at me.

'Then you will not dispute that your civilian occupation was that of journalist with a gutter rag called the *Daily Graphic*?'

'The *Graphic* was a good little paper. I've worked for much worse . . .' I broke off puzzled by the triumphant glint in Vardon's eyes.

'So, Abernethy . . . You will not deny that you are the J.A. Abernethy – I beg your pardon, Abernathy – whose name appeared under the most scurrilous catalogue of lies that has ever been printed, even in that ragbag of a so-called newspaper!'

'Scurrilous' is not the word I would have chosen to describe my journalistic excesses. Lurid, perhaps, or sensational – like my ghosted confessions of an axe-murderer's bride – but not scurrilous.

'I think you've got the wrong Abernathy,' I said to Vardon. 'If I had written anything scurrilous, I would have remembered the lawyers' letters. There is such a thing, you know, as the law of libel.'

'It did not prevent you libelling my father and some of the finest officers in the British Army!' Vardon roared, rising from his seat.

The penny dropped instantly. Now I knew what he was talking about. It had been published to coincide with the Somme anniversary of 1937: a double-page spread called 'Butchers in Brass Hats'. But it had been no catalogue of lies. What it had catalogued had been the blunders of a few mindless generals who had caused the untold suffering and deaths of tens of thousands of their own men between 1914 and 1918. Men like my own father, one of the thousands who had died at the Siege of Kut – sacrificed at the altar of military incompetence. I had expiated a duty to my father with that piece. There wasn't a single word in it that I would take back. But had there been a Vardon in it? I was certain he wasn't one of Haig's staff and I was pretty sure he wasn't one of the lot I had dubbed 'the Bagdad Bunglers', whose campaign in Mesopotamia had been so notoriously mismanaged.

'I'm afraid I don't remember writing anything about your father,' I told Vardon.

'Well, I damned-well remember!' Vardon shouted at me. 'And, by God, my mother remembers. Have you any conception of what it was like for me? My life at Sandhurst became a bloody hell! Not that your calumnies went down very well there, Mr Abernethy. You made enemies of more than me. I'm not the only one who'll never forgive you . . .'

'I'm sorry,' I said, 'I still can't place your father . . .'

'Because you were afraid to name him, you scum!'

A light dawned. 'Gallipoli?' I looked to Vardon for confirmation. 'Your father was one of the Gallipoli crowd? The one the Aussies called King Kookaburra?'

Vardon reddened. 'You dare say that hateful name to my face!' he shouted.

'I didn't bring the subject up,' I said, surprised that after just having been called scum, I could still behave with reasonable cool.

'It's all past history now. Bringing it up isn't going to change anything.'

'Isn't it, by God! We'll see about that!' he declared fiercely. 'If you think I'm going to keep quiet about having an Army-hating pacifist at headquarters, you're very much mistaken! God knows what damage you're capable of doing here – but you're not going to get the chance. You're going out on your ear!'

'I wouldn't be too hasty about that, sir,' I cautioned him reasonably – the pompous fool could ruin everything – 'I didn't ask to be assigned here. My orders were issued under the authority of the Deputy Supreme Commander and until he countermands them . . .'

'I am terminating your attachment!' he roared. 'D'you think that the Deputy Commander won't back me to the hilt? D'you think that I have no authority to run my own damned section?'

'I think you're making a mistake . . .' I began, but he didn't let me finish. He cracked the swagger stick down on the desk.

'Making a mistake!' he shouted, eyes bulging. 'Making a mistake! The only mistake I'm making, Abernethy, is in not thrashing you to within an inch of your life!'

He looked and sounded like a ham actor from a Victorian melodrama who had escaped into the twentieth century with the lines of his script intact and was playing it for real. I didn't know whether to laugh or cry, and the little bubble of sound that escaped from my throat was a compromise between a giggle and a sob of despair.

'Oh, go boil an egg!' I said, for no other reason than it made me feel better. It was the wrong thing to say.

'You impertinent upstart!' he screeched, and there was such savage hate in his eyes that I realised he really

51

was crazy enough to lay about me with his stick; his threat had not been empty rhetoric. And, not only had he meant every word, he was big enough and strong enough to injure me most painfully. He was also surprisingly fast on his feet. He came at me round the desk, reaching for me like a crazed orang-utan.

I don't think he intended to do more than grab me, but that is speculation on my part. I didn't wait for his outstretched hand to fall on me but side-stepped with some alacrity. Vardon made a short but spectacular journey into space, his left ankle momentarily arrested by the cable from the telephone on the desk. I winced as he crashed all his length, cracking his head hard on the chair that he had not invited me to use. The telephone went flying across the room, propelled by his cable-snagged leg. The noise of his fall could have been heard in Paris.

It was certainly heard in the Operations Room and the corridor beyond. In no time the room was suddenly full of clerical staff and military policemen. Major Cotter led the invasion. He stared at me with eyes like saucers.

'I didn't do a thing,' I said.

Vardon was not badly hurt, apart from his dignity, that is. He had a cut above his right eye, where his head had hit the chair. He submitted to first aid from Cotter, breathing fire and fury and insisting that the room be cleared. I was told to get out with everybody else but my dismissal was accompanied by the threat that he would deal with me later. I retired to the Operations Room to contemplate what that meant. Cotter emerged from the inner office a few minutes later and a provost officer went in.

'What the hell was that all about?' Cotter asked. 'He's in a hell of a temper and he's got it in for you. From the way he's talking the best you can expect is a firing squad at dawn.'

'The man is a maniac,' I said. 'He came at me like a mad bull. I didn't lift a finger . . .'

'You must have done something!' Cotter accused.

'I told him to go and boil an egg. That's all.'

'Oh, my God!' Cotter groaned.

The provost officer was very polite and asked me to accompany him. I said I would if it made him happy and I was going to say a lot more but he cut me short. If I had anything to say, he advised me, I would be given the opportunity later. In the meantime, I was to say nothing.

I decided to go quietly. I was escorted along the corridor to a small room, where I was left to cool my heels in solitude for fully quarter of an hour. Then the provost officer returned. With him were two stony-faced redcaps. I was to go with them, the officer said. I asked where, but I was again cautioned to silence.

I was marched right out of the building and into a waiting jeep.

As it whisked us along the Rue des Reservoirs, I found the temerity to ask the MP at my side where we were going.

'Well, sir,' he replied, 'we call it the Bastille.'

His name for the establishment was chillingly apt. We drove through an archway into a complex of buildings that had once been barracks or stables, or both. It may not have been the Bastille but the place could have been the work of the same architect; the period was pre-revolutionary. The premises lacked the grandeur and comforts of the royal palaces not far away: more the kind of place where the Sun King might have chained up his revolting peasantry or, in later years, the revolting peasantry might have accommodated the Bourbons.

I was handed over to some more military policemen, who relieved me of my side-arms and belt, and led me down a dimly lit subterranean stone-Ragged walkway to a row of stoutly doored cells. They fitted perfectly

53

with my image of the nether regions of the Chateau D'If. One of the cell doors was opened and I was invited to enter. The furnishings were a single bed and a zinc bucket.

'Don't I get an iron mask?' I asked the turnkey. He stared at me without comprehending.

'I'll have to ask the Sergeant,' he said. 'What was it you said you wanted?'

'A bottle of whisky and a box of cigars will do,' I said.

He looked at me blankly while he tried to work out whether or not I was being serious. From the look on his face it was clear that his final conclusions did not fill him with amusement and that my levity was the result of possible mental abnormality. He shook his head and went out, locking the door after him.

Alone in that wretched cell, the reality of my predicament bore down on me in a most depressing way. I was tempted to bang my head against the stone walls in sheer despair – but it would only have proved that my head was equally as thick. Thorn, Hibberd and company were not going to be the least amused when they discovered I was in pokey – but I was determined not to scream to them for help except as a last resort. I had to get word to the Prof in Paris that I was the innocent victim of a mad colonel who thought the PWD was staffed by dangerous subversives. Somebody had to lean on Vardon from above and point out to him the error of his ways – and the Prof was just the man to arrange that kind of pressure.

I was sure that I wouldn't be left to rot forever in my dungeon but, after two hours, I was beginning to have my doubts. My stomach was telling me that it was lunch-time when the cell door was finally opened. The turnkey led me out nearer to the fresh air. Our destination was an interrogation room. Its furnishings were a table and two chairs. A captain was seated at the table.

He looked up joylessly at my entry but waited until the turnkey had departed before he spoke.

'We have a problem . . .' he said.

'The one I'm stuck with is more pressing,' I told him. 'I want out of here.'

'It's not so simple as that,' he said. 'We are not quite sure what your status is . . . If it were a straightforward matter of military discipline we would have no hesitation in charging you . . .'

'Charging me with what, Captain? I haven't done anything . . .'

'That's not quite the way that Colonel Vardon puts it.' He produced a notebook from a pocket in his battledress and consulted it.

'Gross insubordination . . . Threatening behaviour . . . Assaulting a senior officer . . . Inciting disobedience and disaffection of military personnel . . . Illegal possession of a US Army vehicle . . . Oh, and there's the matter that you pose a risk to military security in general and to Allied Headquarters in particular. What do you have to say to that little lot?'

I was almost speechless, but not quite.

'It's a load of absolute tosh!' I protested. 'The man is not just a liar, he's off his bloody head!'

'That may be your opinion,' the Captain retorted sharply. 'But you're talking about an officer who has distinguished himself in the field and happens to be one of the most respected British staff officers in Versailles.'

'Captain,' I said, 'I don't care if he's a candidate for canonisation, he's off his bloody chump – and the sooner he's awarded the bowler hat and star and shipped to a rest home, the better!'

'Making intemperate remarks about Colonel Vardon is not going to help your case . . . Mr er, Captain . . . Abernathy. If anything, it will make things worse.'

'Can the Colonel support any of his crazy allegations with witnesses?' I asked heatedly.

'Does he need to? If it comes down to his word

against yours, whose word, do you think, is the most likely to prevail? Did you assault him?'

'No. If anything, it was the other way round. He said something about thrashing me to within an inch of my life. I'm afraid I didn't take his threat seriously.'

'What happened?'

'I told him to go and boil an egg.'

The captain stared at me, eyes wide. He could not keep his face straight. I thought he was going to burst out laughing but he recovered himself quickly.

'That was not very . . . er . . . courteous,' he said.

'Downright disrespectful,' I agreed. 'But, before that, he had called me scum, liar, and a few other things . . . I'm not used to people talking to me like that. Anyway, he came charging round his desk at me and he went all his length on the floor. He caught his foot in the telephone cable. I didn't touch him.'

'I'm tempted to believe you,' the Captain said.

'It's the truth,' I assured him. I fished in a pocket for my SHAEF identity passport and other documents, which the military police had allowed me to retain. I pushed them across the table. 'These will tell who I am,' I said. 'You'll find I have documented authority for the jeep, plus a load of requisition warrants that allow me to draw as much petrol as I like from the Americans.'

'They're very free with their vehicles . . . and their petrol. Why should you come in for this kind of bounty?' he asked, studying the papers.

'They're interested in the work I do at SHAEF. They're very generous people.'

'What exactly is your work at SHAEF?'

I smiled. 'That is privileged information, Captain. In general terms, let's say that I examine enemy morale and consider ways and means of weakening it.'

'I see,' he said. 'Colonel Vardon says you are a pacifist. Are you?'

'No. Hitler's philosophy is the philosophy of violence, not reason. You can't reason with violence. You give

56

in to it or you fight it. That's why I volunteered for this war. That's why I am in France now.'

'Why should Colonel Vardon think otherwise? He seems to think that you are politically motivated, anti-military . . . That you are only interested in undermining confidence in the armed forces . . .'

'Captain,' I interrupted, 'Colonel Vardon hates my guts because, in the happy days of peace, I wrote a newspaper article condemning one or two Great War generals whose stupidity caused hundreds of thousands of British casualties. I didn't know it, but one of those generals was Colonel Vardon's father. My article was not politically motivated. Nor was it the advocacy of pacifism or any other 'ism'. It was a lament for lives wasted by the idiocy and incompetence of a few vain-glorious men who never showed an iota of remorse or regret for the suffering they caused.'

I spoke with a rare burst of passion. The captain was not unmoved. He acknowledged what I said with a bird-like nod of his head.

'Yes,' he murmured, almost inaudibly, 'yes . . . I see.' He smiled wanly. 'I lost my own father at Wipers, as they called it, and an uncle at Passchendaele, another uncle at Cambrai . . .'

'Does that make you a pacifist?' I asked gently. He smiled.

'It made me think twice about which regiment I joined. Fortunately, I didn't land in the infantry.' His smile widened. 'Not that Field Security doesn't have its problems. I don't know what the hell I'm going to do with you. I can't let you out . . . I hope you realise that.'

There was one thing he could do, however, and I persuaded him to do it. He could get a message to the Prof. I was returned to my dismal cell with his promise to contact Paris, my one and only consolation.

By three in the afternoon, I was impatient. By seven in the evening, I was pacing the floor of my cell in a near-demented state. I was not worried by the fear that Vardon could make any of his idiotic accusations stick. What really stirred me up was my frustration at not being able to fulfil the brief that had brought me to Versailles. I had been assigned to watch Cotter twenty-four hours a day, and I had done so faithfully – but now, thanks to that clown Vardon, I had been absent from duty for nine hours. I was convinced that if Cotter was up to any monkey business he would make his expected move when there was nobody around to observe the fact. It was not that I believed he had an inkling of being under observation. I am sure he did not suspect me. It was simply an unhappy certainty I had that that is the way things happen in life: like fishing a river for days for the monster that you know is there somewhere. It goes gliding by when you have taken off your waders and packed up your fishing gear.

I was almost frenzied when the cell door opened and there, standing beside the turnkey, was the Prof. He looked around the cell, his nose wrinkling with distaste.

'Rather primitive lodgings, John,' he observed.

'The cuisine is pretty hellish, too,' I told him.

'Come on then, let's be off,' he said briskly. 'I've settled your bill with the management. At some inconvenience, I might say. I had to go to the Great White Chief himself'

I was so overjoyed that he had worked the oracle and secured my freedom that I could scarcely speak coherently. He fidgeted impatiently as I signed for the return of my side-arms and went about the formalities of my release. I welcomed the feel of drizzle on my face when we were at last outside and he was ushering me into the tiny two-seater roadster which, he said, he had 'requisitioned in the name of the Liberation'. My liberation.

He drove very badly, grinding the gears and with an excess of caution that did not endear him to other road-

58

users. He professed a profound distrust for all things mechanical.

'I've spoken to your friend, Hibberd,' he told me. 'He says that, in the light of today's events, you're to abandon your in-house surveillance or whatever it is you've been up to.'

'I'm all washed up then?' I said dispiritedly.

'Oh, no. Hibberd's man will meet you as usual tonight. He'll put you in the picture.' The Prof was smiling, which was unusual for him.

'You find all this amusing, do you?' I asked. His smile broadened.

'I would have loved to see your set-to with Hubert Vardon,' he said. 'Worth ten guineas of anybody's money, I reckon.'

'You know Vardon?' I was astonished.

'I know of him, let's say. Bit of bad luck, wasn't it, that you should run into the son of one of the generals you massacred in print?'

'You know of that, too, do you?'

'Oh, I know all about that, John.' He ignored the driver of a Citroen, who went past us furiously sounding his horn. 'I doubt if you've written anything better than that *Graphic* piece, before or since.'

'You've actually read it?' I blinked at him. The Prof was positively full of surprises tonight.

'Have you never wondered why you were recruited for the PWD?' he asked, as he dangerously cut the corner into the Rue des Reservoirs.

'Often,' I said.

'Well, now you know,' he said. 'Whether you believe it or not, John, that newspaper essay of yours contained some quite brilliant psychological insights. It was a splendid analysis of the psychotic thinking that sometimes results from the conditioning of the mind from exposure to the less desirable conventions that are concomitant with the military caste system and peculiar to it.'

'Oh?' I said. One of us knew exactly what he meant, but it wasn't me. I was glad that he had found anything I had written so meritorious but I wondered why he had taken until now to tell me.

'I was telling Ike about it,' he went on. 'He said he'd like to meet you some time.' I stared hard at him. I could never be sure when he was being serious or sending me up.

'My engagement book's pretty full,' I said.

'So is his,' said the Prof. He pulled into the kerb. I wondered why.

'Well, get out and get back to work, damn you,' he said. 'This is where you get off.'

I climbed out of the roadster and was about to thank him for coming to my rescue but he gave me no chance. 'See you,' he said, and drove off

I stared after the departing car in a daze. There were a thousand and one questions I had wanted to ask the Prof. Now, the opportunity was gone.

He had dumped me only a short distance from SHAEF and that, at least, was a happy fortuity. My jeep was still in the compound at the back of the former hotel. I made my way there. To my surprise, I spotted Vardon's car parked nearby. Thomson, his driver, was leaning against the wing, puffing away at a cigarette. I went over. 'No home to go to tonight?' I greeted him.

He straightened up and then sagged with relief when he recognised me.

'Oh, it's you, sir. Just having a quiet drag, I was. The Colonel and the Major are working late.'

'An emergency?'

'No idea, sir. All they told me was to be here at eight and to make sure the tank was full. They could be going somewhere.'

'That's a bit of a bind for you,' I sympathised.

'All part of the job,' said Thomson. 'I expect Major Cotter wants me to run him up to Paris again. The Colonel hardly ever goes out at night.'

I felt a small surge of excitement. Maybe I hadn't missed the boat after all.

'What does the Major get up to in Paris?' I asked. 'Got a lady up there, has he?'

Thomson laughed. 'Not the Major. No, I think it's an old Eighth Army chum he meets. A Canadian, I think. He's with Monty's lot up in Belgium or Holland and he nips down to Paris every so often. Don't say I said so, sir, but between you, me and the gatepost, I think it's all semi-official and that Monty is at the back of it.'

'What do you mean?'

'I served with Monty. I know his tricks. Cunning old bird, he is. Has his blue-eyed boys all over the place, keeping him posted on what the Yanks are up to. D'you think he wouldn't give his back teeth to know what the Yank generals are getting up to in Versailles? It's not exactly a secret that some of them would like to get shot of him. They think he's too big for his boots. Jealousy, I reckon.'

'I wouldn't have believed it,' I said. And, indeed, my mind was boggling. 'Fancy Major Cotter getting involved in something like that.'

'Us old Desert Rats stick together,' Thomson said proudly. The smile suddenly left his face. 'Look, sir, for the love of God, don't say anything about this to anyone. I've just been putting two and two together, see, and I wouldn't like the Major to think I was a blabbermouth. It's not the sort of thing I'd as much as mention to anyone I didn't trust.'

'You can rely on me,' I assured him.

He had to dash off then to collect his passengers. I drove out of the compound, not far behind him. He joined a queue of three staff-wagons, waiting near the entrance to Headquarters. I parked on the opposite side of the Boulevard de la Reine, some distance away, and waited.

Eventually Cotter and Vardon emerged and got into

the back of the staff car. When Thomson drove off, I was already cruising. I kept at a comfortable distance and followed.

Thomson followed a familiar route, back to the pension. I saw Vardon get out alone and then the dun-coloured car was on the move again. I followed at a distance of about two hundred yards. Thomson did a circuit of the block and kept south until he was once more on the Boulevard de la Reine. There, instead of going left towards Headquarters, he turned east, where all roads led to Paris.

There was not a lot of traffic but what there was was mainly military – with enough jeeps about to make my own reasonably inconspicuous. I had no difficulty keeping the staff car in sight. I was concentrating so fiercely on the car ahead that I was scarcely aware of the miles. A bridge loomed up. It was guarded by French Army but nothing was being stopped at the check-point. The river was the Seine, but I wasn't sure where – somewhere near the apex of the big loop the river takes to the south of the Bois de Boulogne.

The road was straight and I began to recognise it when we had passed through the Porte de St Cloud and we hit what I knew to be the Avenue de Versailles.

Thomson obviously knew his way around Paris, because he kept going north and east at a speed that made me fearful of losing him. I had no problem as he hugged the north bank of the Seine, but when he branched off through narrower streets I had to put my foot down to catch up the distance between us. The leafless chestnut trees on the Champs-Elysees had a spectre-like quality, lit only by the masked lights of the traffic that hurried below in the drizzle. I had my bearings again but Thomson did not stay long on the famous thoroughfare, shooting off to the left and maintaining his north-easterly course. I gave up trying to figure where exactly I was.

The traffic had thinned to nothing by the time the

car in front slowed and turned off into a quiet side-street, lined by a stone wall with overhanging trees on one side and a row of shuttered shops and dark apartments on the other. The car stopped two hundred yards ahead of me. I turned sharp right into an alley that was barely wide enough to take the jeep. It was a cul-de-sac, with nothing at the end but a patch of bare ground and a corrugated-iron structure with big double-doors: a lock-up of some kind. I turned the jeep and reversed against the doors. Then I made my way along the alley on foot.

The staff car was parked in the side-street, almost hard against the wall that skirted its far side. Hugging the shadows of the shop-fronts, I edged nearer. I froze when a figure moved near the car. A match flared as a cigarette was lit. It was Thomson. There was no sign of Cotter.

In the deep shadow of a doorway, I waited: wondering what the hell to do next. I scarcely heard the motor of the long, sleek vehicle that came purring along the side-street, passing close, and then stopping behind the staff car. Three figures emerged and I heard one of them speak to Thomson. I saw Thomson follow them through a wrought-iron gate in the wall. The gate clanked shut and an eerie silence descended on the deserted street.

THREE

Missing

Ten, fifteen, twenty minutes passed, while I lurked in the shadows and indulged in too-late wishes. I wished I had brought a top coat. I wished I'd had something to eat. I wished that Thorn had given me a hot-water bottle to strap on my hip instead of a revolver. The narrow back-street remained as quiet as the grave.

I kept asking myself questions to which I did not know the answers. Why, if Cotter was meeting an old Canadian chum, had he picked such an out of the way rendezvous? Why not a bar or café in a more convivial part of Paris? And who were the three recent arrivals? Had the Canadian brought some friends and they were all having a regimental reunion somewhere beyond the stone wall on the other side of the street?

At least the newcomers had shown more consideration for Thomson than Cotter had. They had not left the driver outside in the cold. Did that mean that the meeting beyond the wall was likely to go on for some time? Or did it just mean that Cotter was not too concerned whether or not his driver froze through to the marrow?

After twenty-five minutes, I had reached my boredom threshold and was getting very wet in the icy drizzle. My feet were like blocks of ice, my hands were frozen and I was developing a drippy nose. I decided it was time to reconnoitre and take a closer look at the wagon parked behind the staff car. As it had glided past me, I had been too startled to take much in other than its shape. It had looked like a hearse.

Closer inspection revealed that it wasn't a hearse. It was a field ambulance: big-engined and of American make. Although it was almost impossible to tell in the dark, I reckoned that the paintwork was dark military green. It had US Army insignia but these and the red cross markings had been rendered almost invisible by the coating of mud and grime that covered the bodywork. The ambulance looked as if it hadn't been washed since it left the assembly line in Detroit.

I peered through the grilled gate where Thomson and the three occupants of the ambulance had disappeared. Flights of steps led upwards through a jungle-like garden to a house that was a mere shadow beyond the untidy clutter of trees and shrubbery. I went in, taking care to close the gate quietly after me.

The stone steps were treacherous with fallen leaves and moss. On both sides the overgrown garden looked as dense as the Tasmanian bush. From the top of the third flight of steps, I could discern the house more clearly. It was narrow, three storeys high: odd-shaped, inasmuch as it seemed all height and no breadth. On either side of the heavy front door the windows seemed to be boarded up. No lights showed anywhere.

I crept closer. The steps levelled on to a flagged terrace that was badly overgrown with weeds. I investigated one of the boarded windows, peering through the cracks in the warped planking for any sign of light within. There was none. I was straightening, puzzled by the absence of any indication of life, when a sudden sound almost made me jump out of my skin. It came from the front door. Someone was rattling the handle from the inside.

From the noise, I had a clear mental picture of the kind of handle it was: one of the big brass knob variety and temperamental, unless you happen to know the secret of opening them smoothly. The person trying to get out obviously did not know the combination. The rattling went on for some seconds before the door finally jerked open. I used those seconds to back into the depths of an overgrown hydrangea bush and pretend I was part of the vegetation.

A man, wearing what looked like a high-collared flying jacket, went past me and down the steps. I heard the clang of the gate and the bang of a car door. The man returned, carrying what, at first, I took to be skis. As he passed, I saw it wasn't a pair of skis but a neatly rolled stretcher. Of course! From the ambulance! The speed of thought with which I made the deduction gave me no cause for self-congratulation. I did, however, feel faintly pleased that my mind was still capable of any function. Fear of discovery had rendered me almost witless with fright and the hydrangea bush was the source of a number of bodily discomforts that made me want to yell in anguish. Icy water was trickling down my neck from somewhere and spiky twigs held me in an impaling embrace. My centre of gravity was in the wrong place and I was sure that, if I as much as batted an eyelid, the bush would collapse under me with a horrendous noise.

When the man went back into the house, I debated the possibility of making a dash for the street. I took much too long in making up my mind or, alternatively, plucking up the courage to abandon my uncomfortable hiding place. Before I could move, there was more activity from the doorway and the sound of voices in whispered conversation. Little was said but I couldn't have been more jolted by sudden shock if a high-voltage charge had been shot through me. The owners of the voices had spoken in German!

Until that moment, I do not think I honestly believed that Cotter was engaged in anything truly sinister. It was possible that my own observations of the man – and the conversation with Thomson – had lulled me into a false sense of security I suspected that, at the end of the day, I would find him guilty of nothing more reprehensible than passing on headquarters gossip to his old commander. The discovery that he was hobnobbing, not with just one German, but a positive swarm of them, was traumatic. While I stood neck-deep in dripping-wet vegetation, too scared to blink lest I was seen, I was astonished at the number of people emerging from the house. I knew five had gone in — but at least nine came out. Several had flashlights, which they used to illuminate their path down the narrow steps to the front gate. Two were women. Their high-powered scent nearly knocked me over at five paces. The women were close on the heels of two men carrying a stretcher. There was a blanket-wrapped body prone on the stretcher. The last pair to leave paused only an arm's length away from me, and the way one of them was flashing a light around I felt that discovery was inevitable.

It is possible that I have a face not too unlike the withered head of a hydrangea flower. At any rate, the two men standing close to me were unable to tell the difference. Maybe their eyes were not so attuned to the dark as mine were. One seemed to be staring straight at me. The other seemed more intent on finding the top of the steps with the flashlight. Thanks to the way he was waving it around, I saw enough of the pair for several significant details to register.

The one with the light was Cotter. There was no mistaking his rather battered Army cap and the light camel fabric of his three-quarter length British 'warm'. The man nearer me was coatless and wearing what I took to be a US officer's uniform: a dark 'Eisenhower' field jacket and the piped forage cap which the Americans called the 'overseas cap'. There was a Medical Corps flash on his left shoulder. Incongruously for a medical man, he sported a holstered hand-gun on his thigh.

There was no conversation between the two other

than a grunt from Cotter as he found the steps and shone his light so that the path for both was lit.

I remained stock-still, wondering if the exodus from the house was over. Down the street, doors banged and a motor spluttered into life. I reckoned it was high time I came to life, too. I emerged from the depths of the sodden bush, shedding water and dead petals like a dog. I was as stiff as an arthritic Airedale. Beyond the wall, a vehicle reversed and accelerated away with a roar of throttle. I took the fastest route down the last flight of steps. I fell. It was not intentional. In my haste, I took too little care on the wet leaves and greasy stone and damned nearly went head-first through the grilled gate in the wall. From the pain, I was sure I had broken a leg and dislocated a shoulder at the very least, but I managed to get to my feet. Resisting the temptation to sit down and cry from the hurt, I hobbled out to the street.

The ambulance was gone. But the staff car was still there, with no sign of Cotter or Thomson. For the second time in the space of a minute, I wanted to sit down and cry. I should have been ready with my jeep to stay on that ambulance's tail, but now the chance was lost; it could be miles away. And the chances of finding it again were zero. I had bungled it.

One thing, however, gave me hope. The presence of the staff car was surely a sign that Cotter's absence was only temporary. He and Thomson would have to come back for it if they were going to be on duty at Versailles in the morning. They were unlikely to roll up there with an ambulance full of German-speaking chums. Then, for the first time, the question of Thomson's role occurred to me. I was acutely disappointed by the thought that the driver must be in cahoots with Cotter and his friends. Unless . . . My blood ran cold at the memory of one of the party making his exit from the house on a stretcher. My dread was made worse by the realisation that I had not identified Thomson among

68

the shadowy figures who had poured out of the house. Thomson *might* have been amongst them. I just did not know.

I had another thought. *Was there still anyone left in the house?* The need to know suddenly seemed to assume importance to me. With hindsight, my impulse to investigate the house was not a very bright idea, but at the time it seemed the right thing to do. I limped back up the steps with a great deal more care than I had come down and made a circuit of the house – there was a surprising amount of ground at the back – but there was no sign of life from within. To my surprise the door with the big brass knob for a handle – I was right about that – was not locked. I wrestled with the handle for fully thirty seconds, recklessly ignoring the noise and, to my surprise, the door opened. I went in.

The place was in pitch darkness. Eventually I found a light-switch but flicking it up and down had no effect so I had to resort to a box of matches – which wouldn't last me long as it contained only half a dozen matches. My investigation of the ground floor drew a blank. The rooms were bare, not a stick of furniture. Upstairs, there were an uncommon number of tiny bedrooms, not much larger than cubicles. Each contained a narrow bed and an uncovered mattress and very little else. The uncarpeted floors were littered with stamped-out ciga-rette-ends.

I was running out of matches by the time I got to the top floor. Perhaps, in the light of subsequent events, it is just as well – because it governed my course of action at the time. I had one match remaining when I reached the top landing and, when I struck it, I was already three-quarters of the way to the conclusion that my search of the house would be fruitless. I was unprepared for the sight that greeted me in the light of that match. The hairs on the back of my neck stood on end as the flickering light revealed a pair of naked legs, dangling in front of me, several feet off the floor.

The body of a man, suspended from the ceiling by electric light cord, was clad only in underwear. The face was distorted, eyes bulging, and there was no doubt that he was quite dead. I recognised the face as the match burnt my out-held fingers and dropped, leaving me in darkness.

I had found Thomson.

I still have nightmares about the grim discovery I made in that house in the Rue du Bourrelier. I have told myself a thousand times that my subsequent actions were governed by the absence of light and the futility of remaining in the house. The truth, however, is that my immediate reaction was one of sheer panic. The simple act of striking a match can still awaken the trembling horror that gripped me.

I can see again with terrible clarity what was revealed to me in the brief light of a spluttering match that night: the grotesque face, the swaying body and the taut flex, which seemed to be fastened to a hook or bolt some-where in a sky-light recess above. Then the darkness as the match died. My hand brushed against Thomson's naked leg, and the touch of that icy flesh galvanised my terror. I recoiled in revulsion and sheer fright. I thought that I was going to be physically sick but that reaction was overtaken by the more potent compulsion to escape from the obscenity of that swaying corpse. My instincts were ruled by the single desire to get out of that house as fast as my legs would carry me. I groped my way blindly down the stairs and out into the night.

The drizzle had now given way to rain that was descending in torrents from the inky sky — but the fact scarcely registered with me. I reached the front gate ready to collapse; gasping like an asthmatic. I leaned my hands against the bars, head between my arms, and fought waves of nausea. It took me moments of conscious effort to overcome my shivering tension and face up to the reality that had prompted my cowardly flight.

Thomson was dead in there. No matter how much my mind wanted to reject that terrible fact, it remained. Thomson – cheerful, smiling Thomson – was dead. Murdered. Murdered in cold blood and callously strung up like a side of beef. As my mind came to terms with the unacceptable, so my fright gave way to outrage and anger. Not all of that anger was directed at Cotter and his German-speaking friends. I was angry with myself: at my weakness; at my incompetence; at my failure to appreciate that Thomson was even in danger; at my failure to raise a finger to help, while those thugs had been garotting that blameless young man.

Why had they done that to him? Why? Because of what he knew? Or just because he had been there and, perhaps, had seen faces that he should not have seen? It galled me to think that I had watched Thomson go into the house in the belief that he had been shown kindness, that the occupants of the ambulance had taken pity on him waiting outside in the cold. How wide of the mark I had been!

One thing now seemed fairly certain to me. Cotter, surely, would not now be returning to the scene of the infamy in which he had had a hand. I thought it inconceivable that he would have the nerve to collect the staff car and show up at Versailles in the morning as if nothing had happened. Even allowing for his possible ignorance of my interest in him, what story could he use to explain the disappearance of his driver? He would have a hard enough time explaining why he had gone to Paris. The conclusion that I found difficult to avoid was that Cotter, alerted by the security flap over the 'mislaid' papers, had been planning to run for cover ever since. Now he had done so and, by eliminating Thomson, he had silenced the one man who might have been able to throw any light on his previous excursions to Paris.

My problem was: what did I do next? My responsibility was to Hibberd and Thorn and the role they had given me. I could not be the one to raise a general alarm over Thomson's murder without revealing why I had trailed a SHAEF officer from Versailles to a shuttered house in Paris. My job, until I received orders to the contrary, was to stay in the shadows. I hated the thought of leaving Thomson strung up there in that house, but I squared my conscience on that point by convincing myself that my duty left me no choice. I did not realise that, in making this decision, I would owe my life to it. Nor did I realise that, as a result, two men would die.

If I had been heedless of the rain when I had fled the house on the Rue du Bourrelier, that ceased to be the case by the time I had recovered a semblance of composure and begun to think rationally about my predicament. I did not immediately return to the jeep. Indeed, I had only the vaguest notion of where in Paris I was and did not even know the name of the street where I was steadily getting wetter and wetter. So, my first rational act was to walk to the corner and ascertain the street name. The name meant nothing to me but it was vital information if I hoped to find that shuttered house again.

I hurried down the alley to the jeep in a state of considerable misery – soaked through to the skin and shivering with cold. I was only marginally more comfortable at the wheel of the jeep: dripping water everywhere and with a soggy awareness of the seat of my pants. Wherever I moved against the leather upholstery, I squelched. I drove around for ten or fifteen minutes, trying to get my bearings. Emerging from a maze of back streets into a wider thoroughfare, I got lucky. The feeble headlights picked up a sign directing military traffic to the Gare du Nord. I followed the pointing arrow. The main-line station had a large military presence and, possibly, a land-line to SHAEF. My number-one priority was to get a message to Thorn and tell him that I needed help. I could also have used a large glass of brandy, but I reckoned that might have to wait.

Inside the railway station, I gave the Military Police post a wide berth and scouted around until I spotted an American army sergeant with a 'Transport Control' arm-band. I told him I worked at SHAEF and that an emergency had cropped up, which made it imperative that I call Headquarters immediately. My half-drowned appearance must have given verisimilitude and a degree of urgency to my request. He could not have been more helpful. I was invited to use the telephone in the 'depot' commander's office, which was hooked directly to the HQ exchange in Versailles.

The duty officer was even more hospitable than the sergeant. I showed him my Special Service Corps identification and he vacated his comfortable office in the administration block so that I could make my call in privacy. He told me to help myself to coffee from the stove and excused himself saying it was time he was 'out on the tracks' anyway.

Thorn was not at the Headquarters number in Versailles, which I had been given for emergencies – but Hibberd was. His first words were: 'Where the hell have you been?'

I told him, and from the barrage of questions, not to mention expletives, with which he punctuated every sentence of my account, I did nothing for his blood pressure. The nearest he came to expressing relief was when I told him I had not raised a general alarm and brought in the military police or the gendarmerie and that I was making the call from the American rail-road control office at the Gare du Nord, without giving reasons. I was happy to feel that I had at least done one thing right.

His orders on what I should do next were quite explicit. I was to stay exactly where I was, speak to nobody about the events of the night, and do nothing until Thorn arrived and took charge of me. I was left with the impression that it had probably been a mistake to let me out at night without a keeper.

I was drying my clothes at the stove and enjoying my third mug of coffee when Thorn arrived. He had been driven from Versailles by Hibberd's personal chauffeur and Hibberd had told the man to hurry. Thorn was still white-faced from the experience. His first words to me were: 'Where the hell have you been?'

It transpired that he had been hanging around near the pension, waiting to intercept me on my release from the Bastille. He had seen me roar off in pursuit of Cotter and had tried to wave me down – but I had raced past without seeing him. He was not too pleased with me.

After I had told him of all that had happened at the Rue du Bourrelier – at least twenty times – he was still not too pleased with me.

'Goddamn it, John, you shouldn't have lit out for Paris the way you did,' he rebuked me. 'You shoulda called, tried to get a message to me.'

'I didn't get the good-looking chance,' I protested, edgily. It was two o'clock in the morning. I was tired. And I'd had a very trying day. 'If you saw me taking off after Cotter, why didn't you take off after me? You were supposed to be watching me watching him, remember?'

'You were gone too goddamned quick,' he replied angrily. 'I spent half the goddamned night looking for you!'

'Well, now you've found me. Where do we go from here?' 'You're going home to bed,' he said. 'I got work to do.'

'Am I finished?' I asked. 'My old chief was talking to Hibberd and he was told that the in-house surveillance of Cotter was being discontinued, or words to that effect. I took it to mean I was being shunted back to the PWD.'

'Is that what you want?' Thorn asked.

'No, it isn't!' I snapped. 'I want to get the bastards who strung up Thomson. That's what I want!'

He grinned. 'Then go and get some sleep, Johnnie boy. You gotta be at your desk at Headquarters at nine in the morning, just like nothing happened.'

'What about Vardon?'

'Maybe it's time I straightened out Vardon,' Thorn said. 'In the meantime, just don't you rub him the wrong way. Say you're under orders to carry on as usual.'

'What about Thomson? Are you going out to that house?'

He shook his head sadly. 'No, John. You did the right thing not to disturb anything out there. Somebody else will have to find the stiff.' I winced at his choice of word. 'Nobody knows we were watching Cotter,' he went on. 'We keep playing it that way. The hornet's nest has been stirred up now it'll be time for us to show when we can be sure of wiping out the whole goddamned swarm. Not before.'

'You're not even going to look for that ambulance?' I asked, incredulous.

Thorn smiled. 'I didn't say that, John. I told you I had work to do. Before sun-up, I intend to see that every check-point and mobile patrol in France has a description of that wagon, and Cotter, and your gun-toting medic. The word will be that they've got anthrax or bubonic plague aboard, or something of the sort. The vehicle is to be stopped and isolated, by force if necessary, until a decontamination team can be rounded up. That's us.'

I overslept the next morning, missed breakfast, and it was nearly ten before I got into SHAEF. I was frankly worried about encountering Vardon, because I did not share Thorn's equanimity about my continued presence in his section. After his performance the day before, it was on the cards that he would start foaming at the mouth the moment he clapped eyes on me. At the least, I expected to be ejected bodily.

My fears proved groundless. Vardon was nowhere to be seen and his operations room was in a state of quiet uproar. By that I mean that very little work was being done but there was much scandalised whispering, while a pretence of intense activity was maintained. I pretended to work, too, for a few minutes, guessing that Cotter's non-appearance must be partly responsible for the atmosphere.

'What the hell's going on?' I asked one of the telegraphists.

'We didn't think we'd see you again after yesterday,' he replied.

I asked him if that was why everyone was creeping around as if the typing pool had just heard that the three senior secretaries were pregnant. He looked at me in surprise.

'But you were matey with the Major . . . Haven't you heard?'

'Heard what?'

The telegraphist lowered his voice.

'He's skinned out. Took a bundle of classified papers with him. Pinched the Colonel's car – and his driver! You missed all the excitement. Colonel went bananas. He had the security boys in here at eight o'clock this morning. They gave the place a right old going-over.'

'Are you trying to tell me that Major Cotter is a spy?' I asked, affecting surprise.

'That's the buzz,' he said. 'But you know the Colonel. He does get a bit worked up, don't he? Yesterday, it was you was the spy.'

I had to admit that there was a certain logic in what he meant.

Half an hour later, Vardon walked in from wherever he had been. As he crossed the operations room towards his office, he saw me. His lips tightened and he looked at me very hard, but he said nothing. He walked on, into his room. I waited and wondered. Ten minutes passed before Vardon appeared in the doorway.

'Captain Abernathy, a word, if you please.'

He had called me captain, got my name right, and said please. It was almost too much. I entered his room with some trepidation. I became even more wary when he invited me to take a seat. I had never seen him so subdued. He found it difficult to look me in the eye.

'I have been taken to task for what happened yesterday,' he said, still avoiding my eyes. 'But I want you to know that it changes nothing between us. I dislike you and I dislike your kind – and nothing will ever change that.'

'Are you . . . Are you trying to make some kind of apology, sir?' I asked politely.

His head swivelled and he gave me the full glare of his eyes.

'I am making no apology to you,' he snarled. This was more the Vardon I knew. He drew in his breath, as if controlling himself. 'All I am saying is that I shall offer no impediment to your work in this section unless you give me cause to do so. I had no idea that you had been sent here to spy on Major Cotter and that your sanction came from the very top.'

'I see,' I said, although I did not. 'Someone has told you that my job was to spy on the Major?' I was surprised. The note of disbelief in my voice was not feigned.

'I'm not a fool, Abernathy,' he said. 'I didn't need to be told in so many words. Do you deny it'

'I'm just a humble psychology wallah,' I said blandly, as if the idea of me spying on anyone was ridiculous.

'Have it your own way,' he said. 'I find it regrettable that the Army wasn't left to sort out Cotter in its own way. We might have done if you hadn't come poking your nose where it wasn't wanted. Do you think I didn't have my own suspicions about Cotter? Thanks to you and the rumpus you caused yesterday, I was completely distracted – and he took his chance and bolted.'

'There may have been a rumpus yesterday, sir,' I replied, 'but it wasn't me who started it. As for Major Cotter and whatever he has done, you seem to know a lot more about it than I do.'

He eyed me, as if trying to ascertain whether or not I was being serious.

'Are you saying that you don't know Cotter has absconded?'

'There was talk next door. I didn't pay much attention.'

A smile broke on his face. 'They kept you all night in the cells?'

'Not quite all night,' I said, letting him read that any way he wanted.

'Your faceless masters won't be very pleased about that,' he said, and there was malice in his voice. 'My superiors appreciate that when I had you removed yesterday, I did so because of my grave concern for the security of this section. Your superiors may be less charitable to you when they come to consider why it was that Cotter got clean away. They may conclude that, if you had aroused my suspicions, you also put him on his guard. If it was your job to keep an eye on Cotter, Abernathy, it seems to me that you have botched it.'

'That's your privilege, sir,' I said. As far as I was concerned, he could go on speculating all day. I intended to give away nothing. 'Will that be all, sir?' I asked.

'There's just one more thing I want to say,' Vardon said. 'I find it regrettable that those in the know did not see fit to take me into their confidence when you were attached to my section. I consider that an unforgivable oversight – but I trust they are now regretting it. The outcome might have been very different if someone had had the courtesy, if not the wisdom, to tell me what was going on.'

Vardon turned and stared out the window with an air of deep pre-occupation. I returned to my desk in the operations room. I suddenly had a lot to think about too.

The Colonel, clearly, was unaware that I had tailed him and Cotter from Headquarters the previous night. He was equally unaware that I had spoken to Thomson in the vehicle compound. When Cotter had dropped him at the pension, Vardon surely must have known that Cotter intended to go on to Paris. Thomson had known, and Thomson took his orders from Vardon. It troubled me, too, that Vardon had been told enough about my activities to guess the real reason for my attachment to his office. Had that been the price of getting the Colonel off my back? Someone in authority had obviously put pressure on him to lay off me – but it was a pity that, in applying that pressure, someone had hinted too strongly to Vardon that I was working undercover and that Cotter was my target. I distrusted Vardon with every instinct I possessed and nothing that had happened, so far, had disappointed my belief that he was capable of any treachery. In spite of Cotter's desertion, I was not ready to leap to the conclusion that he was the only rotten apple in the barrel. On qualifications of sheer nastiness, Vardon had always seemed the much stronger candidate of the two and I was not ready to discount the possibility that he was putrescent to the core. He went out soon after our little interview and he did not come back. A little after mid-day, Thorn called me.

'Hard at work?' he enquired.

'Sure,' I said. 'I'm sitting here watching an empty chair. Some people might think I'm wasting my time. That includes me.'

'It's unanimous. We're pulling you out.'

'Back to my Paris treadmill?'

'Nope. You and I have work to do. You know the Cathedral of St Louis? There are some gardens close by, the side near the royal parks. Meet me there in twenty minutes.'

'I'll find the place,' I promised him.

I was there inside fifteen minutes and found he had beaten me to it. He looked tired.

'I've just come from the Prefecture,' he said. 'Your SIB police had your pal, Vardon, along to identify an automobile they found in the Rue du Bourrelier in Paris. They let me sit in on the questions and answers.'

'They interrogated Vardon?'

Thorn snorted. 'Hardly that! They sorta held his hand and said they needed to know a few things for the record. They were thorough but they went easy on him. Maybe because he's a colonel but maybe on account of the shake he got when they told him that it wasn't just an auto-theft they were investigating but a triple murder

'A triple murder?' I broke in, almost shouting the words.

Thorn regarded me steadily. 'Let's take a walk, John. I've got news for you that might come as a bit of a shock.'

He kept me in suspense until we had walked some distance along the edge of an ornamental pond.

'The angels were sure on your side last night,' he began. 'The mobile patrol who found the Colonel's buggy found his driver, too – only they don't know it was the driver. . . .'

'He'd been stripped. But surely . . .'

Thorn cut me short. 'He could have had a placard round his neck, saying who he was . . . it wouldn't have made any difference, John. They don't have a body anymore.'

I stopped and stared at him. His tired eyes studied me from a face that was bleak.

'John, the guys who found the body called their head-quarters and asked for an ambulance and an investigation team, but they didn't wait for help to arrive.

80

They must have decided to cut down the driver. That's the theory anyway. . . .'

'And . . .?'

'They reckon the body was booby-trapped. Not just an anti-personnel bomb . . . but a big charge . . . Maybe as much as a hundred pounds of explosive, with a phosphorus attachment . . . One of the British guys reckoned it was the hollow-charge kind of bomb that the Heinie paratroops use to blow their way into armoured fortifications. It blew the roof clean off the house. What was left became a furnace . . . There's not much left . . . of the house, of the driver, of the two guys from that patrol.'

I felt sick. Thorn put a hand on my shoulder.

'You look like you could use a shot of cognac,' he said. He produced a flask from his hip pocket, unscrewed the top, and invited me to take a swig. I did and handed the flask back, then gave vent to a shuddering sigh.

'Another?' asked Thorn, holding out the flask.

'No, thanks,' I said. The shock of realising how close I had come to death passed quickly. It was replaced with sorrow for those two unknown military policemen and an angry, raging bewilderment. 'What kind of monsters are these people, Cal?' I cried. 'Why did they go to such lengths? Why, for God's sake?'

'I don't know, John,' he said softly, 'but it sure helps me to hate better. We'll get the sons-of-bitches, I promise you that. We'll get the sons-of-bitches!'

'Have you told the Special Investigation boys that it was Thomson's body?' I asked. 'That I can give positive identification?'

'No. They're already assuming it was the driver, so we keep you out of it. They know my outfit is interested in Cotter but that's as far as it goes. They'll be making their own investigation and it'll be up to Hibberd and his British opposite number to decide on how much information is passed down to the guys on the ground.'

'They didn't take long to find Vardon's car,' I remarked.

'You can thank your pal Vardon for that. He called out everybody but the Marines this morning when he found out that he had no car, no driver and Major Cotter hadn't come home all night.'

'There's something about Colonel Vardon that doesn't add up, Cal. And he's no pal of mine! I wouldn't trust him further than I could throw him!'

Thorn smiled sideways at me. 'I'd be sore at him, too, if he'd had me wheeled off to the slammer. Forget him, John. From what I hear, somebody took him aside and told him a few facts of life. They say he took it, meek as a kitten, and promised to be a good boy.'

'He knows I was put in to watch Cotter,' I said.

Thorn showed surprise. 'They told him that?'

'To quote the man himself, "not in so many words". He worked it out for himself. Told me so this morning, amongst other things. I played it stupid . . . made out I didn't know what he was talking about.'

'So what's new?' Thorn said with a grin. I ignored the good-humoured gibe.

'Vardon's a head-case, Cal,' I said. 'One of the dangerous kind. He's top-heavy with prejudices and his mind runs on a narrow-gauge track like a roller-coaster. His idea of the truth is what he happens to be saying at the time. The criterion is that it has to fit in with his self-delusions and galloping egomania. He's the kind of man who could commit any crime in the book and still justify himself in his own eyes that he had acted like a saint. The whole world could be wrong but not him . . . never him!'

Thorn smiled. 'Have you been talking to his shrink? Sure you ain't maybe kinda prejudiced yourself?'

'I'm not joking, Cal. He's a bloody colonel in the Army. Men's lives could depend on the state of that bastard's liver. It's frightening.'

'Cotter's the one that skipped, John.'

I nodded grimly. 'Yes. Cotter's the villain. But did you know that Vardon suspected him all along? And Vardon and the Army would have sorted Cotter out if we hadn't interfered. That was what Vardon was saying today That Cotter had tumbled me as a plant and that was why he bolted.'

'He's being wise after the event,' Thorn said. 'He's protecting his position. He told the SIB guys that he hasn't trusted Cotter since some missing papers turned up in the Major's desk. He said he'd been keeping a special eye on him ever since.'

'And last night, he gave Cotter his car and his driver to go buzzing off to Paris! How did he explain that, Cal? Thomson knew that Cotter was going to Paris. Last night wasn't the first time. You're not going to tell me that Vardon knew nothing about these trips. It was his car, his driver. Damnit, they dropped Vardon off at the billet!'

Thorn considered this, as if accepting the validity of my argument.

'The trouble is,' he said, 'that Vardon's story fits with what you saw. He told the SIB guys that Cotter caught him on the hop last night. He said he'd had a bad day at Headquarters. Yeah, I thought that'd amuse you . . . And the only thought on his mind last night was a hot bath and early bed. He said that if it hadn't been for that, he would have realised last night that Cotter was up to something. The driver was only supposed to be running the Major round to the Field Post Office. He shouldn't have been gone for more than half an hour.'

'But Thomson *knew* he was running Cotter to Paris, Cal. He told me. And all that other stuff about Cotter keeping Montgomery genned up on the inside politicking at SHAEF.'

'Cotter must have told Thomson some kind of story if the Paris trips were a regular thing, John,' Thorn said. 'You yourself were keeping that driver in cigarettes to keep him sweet – but I bet you a month's pay you didn't tell him why you were doing it. There's nothing to suggest that Vardon knew anything about what was going on.'

'I still don't think Thomson would have taken that car anywhere without Vardon's permission,' I contended.

Thorn shrugged. 'Maybe you're right,' he conceded, 'but there's not a hell of a lot we can do about it. The one guy who could tell us for sure is dead.'

'Which is very convenient for Vardon.'

Thorn regarded me wearily. 'And goddamned convenient for Major Cotter. He's the one that keeps strange company, John. He's the one who leaves corpses around instead of calling cards and wires them up so that they go off with a big bang. He's the bastard we've got to find. And we've got to find him goddamned quick!'

He was right, of course. I was becoming paranoid about Vardon.

Thorn had other things to tell me. The most important was that I was to clear my desk at SHAEF, collect my belongings from the pension and report later in the day to the chateau that looked down on the Marne. Hibberd would be there some time in the evening and he wanted to see us both.

'Any idea why?' I asked Thorn.

He shook his head. 'Nope. The only thing I know for sure is that he's hopping mad that Cotter got away. He sure as hell won't be pinning any medals on our chests.'

My desk at SHAEF did not need much tidying: some notes to collect and a few interrogation reports to be parcelled up for return to G–2 files. It was about three when I got to the pension and started packing my case. I was in the midst of it when there was a knock at the door. It was the corporal who had quoted the Colonel's rules at me on the day I had arrived.

'Will you be missing dinner tonight, sir?' he asked. 'The cook kept something for you till nine last night, but he had to throw it out . . .' He stopped when he saw my suitcase open on the bed. 'Are you leaving us then, sir?'

I told him I was and that I would not be needing dinner. I would have closed the door but he was determined to gossip.

'Right schemozzle about Major Cotter, weren't it?' he said, all but putting his foot in the door. I said I knew nothing about it, but that was a mistake. He insisted on telling me all about the Major going absent. The redcaps had taken Cotter's room apart, even lifting the floor-boards.

'Did they find anything?' I asked.

'Only his things.'

'His things?'

'His clothes, and the rest of his gear. They took it all away. Funny him skinning out like that, don't you think, sir? Didn't even take a clean shirt nor a change of socks. Not like the Major at all. Very fussy about a fresh shirt in the evenings, he was. Don't understand it at all.'

I agreed that it was all very strange. And indeed it was. It showed that Cotter's break had been spontaneous, not planned in advance. Perhaps he had simply seized his opportunity on the spur of the moment. But when? When had he decided to burn his boats? Was it when he had arranged with Thomson to go to Paris? What had frightened him off? What had made him run?

The corporal offered to take my case out to the jeep and I was happy to let him do so, if only to be rid of him. I followed him down the stairs. In the hallway, I stopped out of habit to see if there were any letters for me in the rack near the front door. I don't know why I did it, because there never were any letters for me. Nor was there a letter for Abernathy on that occasion. There was, however, a letter addressed to Major Cotter. I wondered why the redcaps had not removed it when they had taken away the rest of the Major's possessions. The oversight seemed downright careless to me.

It was one which I felt should be remedied. I picked the letter out of the rack and popped it into my breast pocket. When I got outside, the corporal was standing at the door of the jeep, looking as if he expected a tip for his porterage. I didn't give him one.

FOUR

House of Ill Repute

After SHAEF and the Pension Charleroi, there was a pleasant absence of military formality about the American MIS station in the château above the Marne. The proper name of Hibberd's operational base was the Château Beauséjour but that had been corrupted by its temporary occupants to Fort Boozey-Joe and I never heard it called anything else.

The gracious oak-floored *salle-à-manger* had been converted into an American-style cafeteria, and 'chow-time' – with both officers and men queuing in the same line – was in startling contrast to dinner at the pension. If the pension dinners had been railway-buffet fare disguised as *haute cuisine,* the château meals were unashamedly 'Joe's Diner'.

Thorn and I queued for our meatballs in ketchup, followed by apple pie ('like Mom used to make') and we ate our repast at one of the small foldaway tables provided for that purpose. We sat beneath a magnificent stained-glass window, circular in shape and ten feet in diameter: a central feature of the wall that divided the dining hall from the Terrace Room next door. The window owed much in artistic inspiration to the huge Rose Window in Chartres Cathedral, being a kind of free translation in miniature. Some miniature! Its ecclesiastical grandeur was inhibiting and Thorn and I felt obliged not to raise our voices above a conversational whisper for fear of irreverence. Reflected colour from the window tinged our meatballs with green and blue highlights, with the result that they tasted more appetising than they looked.

It was after nine when Hibberd showed up at the château. He had had no food since breakfast and he bade us wait for him in the Terrace Room, while he went off in search of the last of the meatballs. He must have been successful because, while he dined in solitary splendour on one side of the stained-glass window, we shuffled around for half an hour on the other side, speculating on the cost of the window as opposed to the installation of central heating. Most of the Terrace Room's furniture had been removed and what remained was lost in the emptiness of the long uncarpeted chamber. It had the cosiness of a church hall, an impression in no way diminished by the stained-glass window in the inside wall. The other walls were bare. The paintings that had once adorned them had, like most of the furniture, been removed and only large rectangles – lighter in shade than the areas around them – showed where they had hung.

At one end of the room was a huge Italian-marble fireplace – but no logs blazed below the great chimney-piece. Instead, looking decidedly out of place, a kerosene heater in the centre of the hearth emitted pungent oily fumes that scarcely took the chill off the air.

When Hibberd joined us, he pulled the room's solitary arm-chair close to the heater and invited Thorn and me to do likewise with the only other serviceable piece of furniture: a rather worn chaise-longue. We perched on this – our backs exposed to a draught that curled under the doors – while Hibberd spread the contents of his brief-case on his knees.

To our relief, Hibberd wasted little time lamenting the fact that Cotter and the US Army ambulance seemed to have vanished from the face of the earth. Clearly, he was not a man to cry over spilled milk nor bolt the doors of emptied stables. He was much more concerned with how Thorn and I were to go about the task of picking up the scent of our quarry.

'You're the cop,' he said to Thorn. 'Got any ideas?'

Thorn had. He said he didn't want the Colonel to kid himself that there were any short cuts. When a trail went cold, you went back to the place where you lost it and you quartered the ground like a bloodhound. You knocked on a lot of doors and you pounded a lot of sidewalk. You asked questions – lots of questions – until you started getting some answers that made sense. You went back all the way you'd come, to where you'd started if necessary – and you looked for all the things you must have missed.

'OK,' Hibberd said. 'Now to be more specific.'

'I don't think we'll find any answers in Versailles,' Thorn said. 'The one thing we've got now that we didn't have before is this house in Paris . . .'

'What's left of it!' put in Hibberd. Thorn patiently rode the interruption.

'The house is where the trail went cold,' he went on. 'And, sure, it got blasted all to hell . . . but it can still tell us a lot. John says there were cigarette-butts all over the place and lots of mattresses and beds – which suggests that the guys Cotter saw must have been meeting there often, maybe living there. The place was maybe set up as a safe house before the Krauts quit Paris, I don't know . . . But there are things we can find out that might give us a lead. Who's the owner? Or who rented it last? Maybe there's another house just like it and Cotter and his pals are holed up in it right now . . . maybe only two blocks away . . .'

Thorn would have gone on but Hibberd stopped him.

'Hold it, Cal. I'm ahead of you. Maybe you've got me thinking like a cop, too, but I stopped off at the Sûreté in Paris on my way here from Versailles and I've fixed up for you and John to meet with a guy there.' Hibberd told us that at the Sûreté he had conferred with senior French officers about the explosion and fatalities

at the Rue du Bourrelier. The French had no intention
of taking a back seat in any investigation of an outrage
that had taken place in their capital, even though the
case bristled with sensitive issues affecting Allied military security. Indeed, that aspect seemed to have made
them doubly determined to get to the bottom of it.

'Who do you want us to meet?' Thorn asked.

'The guy the French have put on the case. He's one
of their best criminal investigators. By morning, he may
have the answers to some of those questions you were
wanting to ask. He hasn't been letting the grass grow
under his feet.'

'You met him, sir?'

'No, Cal, but I can tell you that you were right about
that house. It seems it does have a history.'

'What kind of a history.'

'I don't know. All I know is that Joubert – he's the
guy I want you to meet – has been digging around there
all day and that he smells Nazis. That was all the Chief
Commissioner got out of him when he phoned in, earlier
in the evening. Seems this Joubert has a reputation for
playing things close to his chest. But I want you to find
out what the hell it is that he's found out!'

Thorn frowned. 'How do we play it?'

'Any which way you can,' Hibberd said. 'I've said
you'll be at the Sûreté first thing in the morning. He'll
be there.'

'He'll co-operate?' Thorn sounded doubtful.

Hibberd smiled. 'He has been ordered to do so –
although I gather he may need a little coaxing. Like
I said, he has the reputation of being a little close-
mouthed.'

'Great!' said Thorn. Hibberd glowered warningly at
him.

'I'm banking on you hitting it off with him, Cal. He's
your kind of cop. Twenty years on the force . . . and
most of it on homicide detail.'

'Does he speak English?' Thorn enquired.

'I don't know,' Hibberd said. 'That's something else you'll find out in the morning.'

The morning revealed that Inspector Guillaume Joubert did speak English of a sort: a rather fractured sort, and only when he chose to speak. He was not the most communicative of men. Furthermore, he welcomed the interest of two English-speaking strangers in his investigation with the joy he might have reserved for the application of a hot mustard poultice to his anatomy.

Thorn and I reached the Sûreté at 8.30 a.m. and were shown to a tiny interview room next to Joubert's office. Joubert – a swarthy thick-set man in his late forties – walked in at nine. Twenty minutes of laboured conversation produced little from him in the way of information and certainly imposed no strain on the policeman's English vocabulary. It was like drawing teeth to extract from him a response that went beyond *'Oui'* or *'Mais non'* or *'Possiblement'*.

It fell to me to make the great break-through after he had shrugged off a question from Thorn with a show of Gallic petulance, in which he lamented to heaven something about having his working life cursed by interfering foreign amateurs. He made the declaration with much rolling of eyes and waving of hands and, although Thorn did not get the gist of his rapid-fire French, I read him loud and clear – and I took grave exception to the insult. On Thorn's behalf, not my own.

In my best French – which was better than the average – I remonstrated vehemently with the Frenchman. He was talking *merde,* I told him. Captain Thorn was no amateur. He had probably caught more crooks in his day than the entire French gendarmerie had caught colds. Did the Inspector not know that Captain Thorn had been one of the finest detectives ever to work for the New York City police? The Inspector could call me anything he liked but I wasn't going to stand idly by

91

and allow him to describe such an illustrious professional officer as an amateur.

Joubert's jaw dropped and he goggled at me, astonished, if not at the passion of my outburst, at least at the coarseness of my language. Then a broad grin spread across his face. Not only did he find my gutter terminology endearing – being on his own wavelength – but my revelation, that Thorn had been a New York cop, opened a deep well of emotion in the Frenchman that could not have been more gushing with benevolence for us if we had been long-lost brothers. The change in Joubert was almost metamorphic. His taciturnity and hostility vanished. He became positively effusive in his warmth.

It transpired that one of the high spots of Joubert's life had been an exchange visit in the United States, when he had spent a month at a precinct office on New York's east side, studying American police methods. It had left him with an undying admiration for the city of New York and its law-enforcement officers. The chunky Frenchman raged at us for our failure to have enlightened him straight away on Thorn's credentials. He now became as talkative as, before, he had been uncommunicative. He and Thorn became so thick that, because I had never pounded a beat nor shot it out with bootleggers, I began to feel that my education had been seriously neglected. I finally had to prise them apart.

'Look, fellows,' I pointed out, 'it would be a great thing for international relations if you two decided to get married, but we've got a job to do. Isn't it time we started talking about that house in the Rue du Bourrelier?'

The intrusion did not go down too well. Two heads and two pairs of eyes stared at me as if I had popped out of a hole in the woodwork. Thorn had the grace to shrug.

'John's right,' he said. 'We should be getting down

to business.' Joubert gave a disdainful toss of his head. Not too graciously, he acknowledged my presence.

'What do you want to know about the house in Rue du Bourrelier?'

'Anything you can tell us,' I said. 'Who lived there . . . Who owns it . . . We were told it had a history – a Nazi connection.'

Joubert looked at me sharply.

'It also has English and American connections, monsieur. The woman who lives above the *boulangerie* on the corner told me that she saw an English soldier prowling around the street on the night before the explosion. She saw him drive off in a jeep.'

'How strange,' I said, poker-faced. 'Did she see anything else?'

'Oh, yes, monsieur. On several occasions over the past two or three months, she saw men coming and going from the house – although it was boarded up, empty.'

'What kind of men, Inspector?'

'They wore uniform . . . English, American. Officers, she thought.'

'Did she report these . . . goings-on?' I asked.

'To the police, Monsieur? No.' Joubert shrugged. 'She is *parisienne*. She likes to see what is going on. She watches from her window like a sparrow on a roof – but it is none of her business, so she does nothing.'

'The Nazi connection is the one that interests us, Inspector Joubert,' Thorn broke in. 'What can you tell us about that?'

Joubert swung his head round to face Thorn.

'During the Occupation, the house was always full of SS.'

'There were Germans quartered there?' Thorn asked, his eyebrows arched in surprise.

Joubert laughed uproariously. 'You could say so, Capitaine,' he agreed, and seemed to find the idea highly amusing. 'The house was a . . . was a . . . He groped for the English word but could not find it. '*Un bordel* . . . How do you say . . . *Une maison de débauche?*'

'A brothel?' I roared.

'*Oui*, Captaine Abernathy,' he agreed delightedly.

Thorn was staring at the Frenchman, askance.

'You're telling us that it was a whore-house? What happened to it? Did your guys close it down?'

'*Non, non* . . .' Joubert shook his head fiercely, as if the idea of closing down a brothel was unthinkable. 'The woman who owned the house cleared out when your armies were getting close to Paris. The girls who knows where they went? Disappeared, all of them. They knew that the Resistance would take revenge on them.'

'The woman who owned the house? She sold out?'

Joubert did not instantly understand Thorn's choice of idiom.

'Ah, the property, Captaine? No, she did not sell the house. She is still the owner. Her name is Fabienne Lans.'

'Can she be traced?' Thorn asked.

Joubert shrugged. 'Perhaps,' he said. 'It will be difficult. She is believed to have gone somewhere up north. She is Belgian, not French. She had many friends among the Boches and they would have made it easy for her to get away. Perhaps she is out of the country altogether.'

Thorn frowned. 'Too bad. I don't suppose there's much hope of tracking down her girls either,' he observed gloomily.

Joubert got to his feet. 'There is always hope,' he contradicted Thorn. 'If we are to find the brutes who laid that bomb, the *prostituées* are perhaps our only hope. Because we know the names of every one!'

Joubert excused himself and went through to his office. Through the glass partition we saw him talking to a uniformed policeman, who had been typing industriously at the big upright machine on the desk before him. Joubert returned, holding sheets of paper which he had obtained from the typist.

'*Voila!*' he said.

The closely typed sheets contained the names and particulars of some two dozen prostitutes who had worked at No. 65, Rue du Bourrelier. The French police maintained a register of known prostitutes but Joubert's list – he told us – had not come from that source. He had unearthed it from files left behind by the Germans when they had quit Paris iii August. They, too, had kept a register of prostitutes, with a comprehensive dossier on each woman. The dossiers contained identification photographs, background details, a record of medical examinations and health particulars, employment history, special characteristics, and so on.

'The Boches are very thorough in such matters,' Joubert said. 'They saved me many hours of search in our own archives.'

Thorn, perusing the list which Joubert had given to him, gave a sudden grunt of surprise.

'You have found something interesting?' Joubert asked.

'Perhaps,' Thorn replied, and passed the list to me. I ran down the names, wondering why on earth one of them should have any significance for Thorn, or me. Then I saw it – the name Violette Brochant. The name itself meant little, it was the entry alongside it that leapt out at me.

It said: '*Née St Cyr des Bains, 15 Janvier 1920.*'

I looked up to find that Thorn was studying my face intently.

'St Cyr des Bains?' I murmured.

'It hit you, too, eh?'

'What is so important about St Cyr des Bains?' Joubert wanted to know.

Thorn smiled enigmatically. 'That makes two SS connections, Inspector,' he said. 'First, there's your whore-house in Paris . . . The SS also had a kind of rest-camp in St Cyr des Bains – one where murder and mayhem went with the therapy. Maybe they didn't lay on girls for the customers, but my money says we've got a connection . . .'

St Cyr des Bains . . . the name had made an instant connection for me. The coastal village had figured prominently in the casebook material that had been prescribed reading when I had worked for Hibberd in London: the file on the entrapment by *Schatten Gruppe* of a sea-captain called Chisholm. But was the birthplace of a Paris prostitute enough to tie in Thomson's murder and Cotter's desertion with *Schatten Gruppe*?

'Maybe it's just coincidence,' I suggested to Thorn.

He stared at me hard-eyed. 'There ain't no such thing,' he declared uncompromisingly. 'I stopped believing in coincidences when I found out about Santa Claus!'

I don't know at what tender age it was that Thorn found out about Santa Claus, but I began to think that we would have been more fruitfully employed scouring Greenland's barren wastes for a red-suited man with a white beard than we would have been searching Paris for a young lady of questionable morals with the name of Violette Brochant. Thorn and I toured the seamiest quarters of the French capital, seeking a lead on the whereabouts of the elusive prostitute whose birthplace just happened to be St Cyr des Bains. Joubert proved an able guide and took us to places which I resolved never to approach on a dark night unless accompanied by a battalion of paratroops. Our undertaking was not a job for anyone who had enjoyed a sheltered upbringing. Even the unshockable Thorn went pale with astonishment at the depravity of some of the bizarre vendable services being marketed in the twilight zones of Paris.

We drew a complete blank at all the haunts and addresses which the Germans, with bureaucratic fastidiousness, had so kindly listed for us in the dossier on Violette Brochant. We did not, as Thorn had envisaged, do too much pounding of sidewalks – we drove around in Joubert's Citroen – but we did climb countless stairs to countless attics and ask countless questions, all to no avail. At the end of three days, we were no closer to locating Violette Brochant than when we had started. It was Joubert who suggested that, perhaps, the girl – fearing retribution from the Resistance in Paris – had fled to her native village and the familiar territory of childhood.

Thorn agreed, but was reluctant to abandon the Paris hunt until the name of every girl listed as being on the pay-roll at 65 Rue du Bourrelier had been checked out. The outcome was that I was elected to go to St Cyr des Bains and rake up anything I could about Mademoiselle Brochant. In the meantime, Thorn and Joubert would continue the search in Paris.

The prospect of a trip to the seaside did not dismay me. Three days of poking into the least salubrious corners of Paris had been enlightening but had left me longing for a whiff of clean fresh air. A breath of sweet ozone would be welcome.

Hibberd who had been becoming more agitated by our lack of progress daily – wanted to see me at the Chateau before I left for the coast. When I duly reported, he handed me a fifty-page file on the former SS establishment at St Cyr des Bains. It had been updated since I had seen it before, during the *Schatten Gruppe* flap in London more than a year previously. Hibberd wanted me to make myself thoroughly familiar with the happenings at St Cyr des Bains in late 1942 and early 1943.

In particular, he drew my attention to the account by the sea-captain, Hector Chisholm, of his escape with several Canadians from the Nazis' so-called 'rehabilitation unit' at St Cyr des Bains. It contained another of those curious coincidences that Thorn did not believe in. The Nazis had employed a French collaborator to pose as a member of the French Resistance group which had organised the escape of Chisholm and the Canadians: a young woman known only by her first name – Violette.

Having pointed out the coincidence, Hibberd warned me not to build too high hopes of finding Violette in St Cyr des Bains.

'If the Violette in the report is the same Violette Brochant that you've been looking for in Paris, you're not going to find her in St Cyr,' he said. 'Because St Cyr is about the last place on earth she'd run to. The local Resistance group was wiped out by the Nazis – and if she wasn't the one who actually betrayed them, she sure knew all about it. There's a lot of people in St Cyr who've been waiting for that young lady to show her face there again, so they can put a bullet in her head.'

'But you still want me to go there anyway?' I asked, surprised.

'Why not?' said Hibberd. 'You may dig up something. Up to now, we've left the French to hunt out their own traitors. We've been more interested in the Nazis who hired them. Your job in St Cyr will be to find out one way or another if there's any link at all between that blown-up whore-house in Paris and that stinking rat-nest that the SS were operating on the coast.'

I was about to go when I remembered the letter addressed to Cotter, which I had purloined from the hall-rack in the pension. I had passed it on to Hibberd, unopened, and heard no more about it. So now I asked Hibberd if the letter had revealed anything important. He seemed faintly embarrassed to be reminded of the letter.

'Nothing really,' he replied. He seemed reluctant to talk about it and I wondered if it had anything to do with his surprise when I had passed on the letter without reading it. He had seemed to think then that my lack of curiosity stemmed from admirable scruples about reading other people's mail. In fact, I had been restrained only by the knowledge that theft of HM

Royal Mail is a serious criminal offence and that a colonel had more authority for that kind of larceny than a mere acting captain.

'Maybe I shouldn't have pinched that letter,' I said to Hibberd. 'but letters can often tell as much about the person who gets them as they can about the sender.'

'It was from Cotter's wife,' Hibberd said. 'And I wish now I hadn't seen the goddamned thing! All it's done has made me feel sorry for the wretched woman and what that bastard has done to her.'

'She was in the dark about everything, you think.'

'I'm sure of it. Goddamn it, John, she worships the guy. It made me squirm to read what she said. I'm afraid I don't get a kick outa reading how a guy's wife is counting the hours until she can hold him in her loving arms.'

'Like that, was it, sir? All love and burning passion.'

'She's going to get a hell of a shock when she finds out that he's taken a powder and gone over to the Krauts,' Hibberd said. 'Cotter must have told her that he had a chance of home leave at Christmas. She was sure built up about that . . . All the things they were going to do.'

'Will she be told he's done a bunk?' I asked.

'She'll have to be, in due course.' Hibberd peered at me from under a furrowed brow. 'Did Cotter ever say anything to you about the baby?'

'Baby?' I goggled. 'I didn't know there was any family.'

'There isn't, yet,' Hibberd said. 'It's not due until the spring. And that poor sap of a woman is gonna be left holding it.'

'You think Cotter knew about the baby?' I asked.

'He knew all right. The letter is full of the answers to questions he must have asked. He had even mapped out the school for it, if it was a boy. It seems he set a lot of store on the kid being a boy because his wife tries to warn him not to get carried away . . . that a little girl ain't such a bad thing. She wants to know if a smaller version of herself would really be all that much of a disappointment to him. She sounds so sensible and so trusting that I could have goddamned cried.'

'Cotter kept a photo of her beside his bed,' I told Hibberd. 'Nice smile, and pretty.'

'Did he ever speak about her?'

'No, not to me. But he was always a very private kind of man, not the kind to blab about things that mattered to him. The odd thing is that I got the impression that his wife was the most important thing in his life. He spent hours on end writing to her . . . And I saw the way he looked at her photograph. It doesn't make any sense . . .'

'What doesn't make any sense?' Hibberd asked, with a frown.

'Cotter doesn't,' I replied. 'He was worried to hell about something but I'm sure he wasn't eaten up with conscience . . . the way he should have been at the enormity of the thing he was doing. He hasn't just betrayed his country and thrown in his lot with a gang of murdering thugs, he has betrayed that girl back in England and his own unborn child . . . He's destroying everything that matters to him . . . Why, for God's sake, why?'

'The charitable view is that he's crazy — battle-fatigued . . . that he's all so twisted in his mind that nothing makes sense to him any more.'

I shook my head, perplexed. 'There has to be more to it than that,' I said. 'Battle fatigue doesn't make a man destroy the most precious things he's got left. It's more likely to make him run to them and cling to them — anything to escape the killing and the whole bloody business of war. It doesn't make him run to the other side in the killing match. They can't offer him any kind of comfort at all.'

Hibberd allowed a grim little smile to play about his face.

'Is this your psychology training speaking?' he asked.

'It's just common sense, sir,' I replied, a little needled. His expression hardened.

'Don't waste your time feeling sorry for Cotter,' he advised me sternly. 'You're the only one who has seen his playmates. And,' he reminded me, 'you're the only one who saw what they did to that driver. Maybe you'd better remember that every time you start feeling a little bit of sympathy for Cotter and wondering about his motives. Our job is to catch the son-of-a-bitch. We can start trying to understand him when we've got him behind bars.'

'Yes, sir,' I said stiffly.

'Well, don't let me keep you,' he said. 'You got work to do.'

That was my dismissal, but he called me back before I had reached the door.

'Oh, John,' he said, and his smile was conciliatory. 'If you try to stop worrying about why Cotter turned rat, I'll try to stop feeling sorry for the son-of-a-bitch's wife.'

Buff McLennan stood six-feet-four in his socks and was so thin that I reckoned the wind would blow him away if he emptied the loose change out of his trouser pockets. He was the man – both Hibberd and Thorn had been emphatic on the point – whom it was imperative that I contact and consult before I made my investigations in St Cyr des Bains. He was in charge of a special intelligence unit and had been based in Rouen since the city's liberation on the last day of August, six days after the Allies had reached Paris. His present responsibilities covered a territory that took in the entire coastal strip between Le Havre and Rouen in the north and Caen and the beaches of Normandy in the south.

I ran McLennan to earth in Rouen after a slow but uneventful six-hour drive from Château Beauséjour. He was a very intense man who seemed to have the worries of the world bearing down on his beanpole frame, but he could not have been more attentive and welcoming if I had been the personal emissary of Winston Churchill. A man in his early forties and a commander in the Royal Canadian Navy, McLennan had landed in Normandy as part of the Advance Head-quarters staff of the Canadian First Army. He seemed to regret having been detached at Rouen and missing the rapid push up the Channel coast into Belgium. As far as I was concerned, he proved to be hospitality personified: wining and dining me and supplying a bed for the night in his own roomy quarters, a huge farmhouse some miles south of battered Rouen. The city had taken a terrible pounding from our bombers before the Normandy landings and during the three months following, while it had remained in German hands.

At the most, I had only expected information from McLennan and a speedy send-off on my way. It didn't work that way. He insisted on dropping everything and accompanying me to St Cyr des Bains and showing me around personally. I tried to tell him that I had no wish to drag him away from his normal duties – St Cyr was a good seventy miles from his base in Rouen – because I doubted if I could fulfil my brief in a day, but he was adamant.

'If you are, as I suspect you are, on the trail of the Nazi filth who ran the old sanatorium in St Cyr, and I can help,' he said, 'there is nothing more important I could be doing.'

'I'm just looking for connections,' I told him. 'There may not be any. We could both be wasting our time.'

'That's a possibility,' he conceded, 'but I'm coming with you just the same. If Colonel Hibberd has sent you all the way from Paris, it must be because he's finally got a line on *Schatten Gruppe* or that pox doctor, Keitler. That means that, for you, I pull out all the stops. I want those bastards wiped off the face of the earth. I want that badly.'

'You know about *Schatten Gruppe*?' I asked him.

'Most of what there is to know,' he said. 'Let me tell you something, John. I was at Dieppe in 'forty-two, on a destroyer. I saw the cream of the Canadian Army chewed up like mincemeat on the beaches. I'll never forget the things I saw. That was bad enough. What I'm not going to forget either, nor forgive, is what Keitler and his rat-pack at St Cyr did to some of those poor guys who made it off the beach. You know about Keitler?'

I nodded. It had all been in the Chisholm file.

'I've read about him. He was the doctor who ran the SS hospital in St Cyr des Bains?'

'Yeah,' McLennan confirmed, almost snarling the word. 'Keitler was the guy who specialised in trying to bend the minds of our guys who'd had legs and arms blown off . . . tried to make them into Nazis by taking advantage of the shock and confusion they'd suffered . . . Can you imagine anything more obscene? Anything more vile?'

I admitted that I could not. Exploiting the psychological traumas of maimed prisoners-of-war in order to indoctrinate them politically was a crime that reached a new low in inhumanity. The fact that the first known instance of the crime had been committed against Canadians – mostly Dieppe survivors – filled Buff McLennan with a deep and passionate longing to see the perpetrators caught. He had landed at Juno Beach in Normandy, inflamed by the hope that he would be personally involved in tracking them down.

Knowledge of what a fanatical wing of the German *Sicherheitsdienst* had been doing at the former sanatorium in St Cyr des Bains had prompted the Canadian to attach himself to the infantry battalion charged with the capture of St Cyr, when the armies had broken north from Caen. It was a source of pride to McLennan that he had actually been the first man to enter the sanatorium after its abandonment by the Germans.

'Colonel Hibberd and Cal Thorn came to have a look at the place about a week after we took it,' the Canadian told me. He shrugged his shoulders in a way that expressed unhappy resignation. 'We didn't find much. Nothing that we didn't already know about. All the files had been removed, or burnt – but I'll show you the hell-hole tomorrow. You should see it.'

I said I was looking forward to seeing the notorious sanatorium. I had heard enough about it to be filled with curiosity. At first light the following morning we were on our way to St Cyr des Bains.

The village, with its picturesque little harbour, was one that I could easily have fallen in love with – in high summer. In the grey gloom of winter – with rain squalls rolling in from the sea like tumbleweed and obliterating the views – its ability to enchant was less forceful.

I brought the jeep to a halt at the doors of the harbour-front inn. Waves were splashing over the quayside and sending spray across the broad cobbled thoroughfare that fronted the inn. A tall-masted yawl was moored at the quay. McLennan pointed at the yawl.

'That's the *Thérèse*,' he said. On the way from Rouen, we had been talking of how the sea-captain, Chisholm, and some of the Canadian prisoners had escaped from St Cyr – and now he reminded me of the conversation. 'That's the fishing boat that Chisholm and the other guys stowed away in. They hid in the hold overnight and then went out with the boat in the morning when she sailed for the fishing grounds.'

'I thought their boat sank,' I said, trying to recall details of the Chisholm saga.

'Not the *Thérèse*,' McLennan said. 'The *Thérèse* just took them far enough out to be out of sight of the shore. When they were out at sea, the six guys who made the break were unloaded into a little sail-boat that the *Thérèse* used to carry on her deck . . . no size at all, just a dinghy. But they made it to England. All six of them!'

'More dead than alive, if I remember correctly,' I said. 'A minesweeper picked them up somewhere near the Isle of Wight.'

'I'll show you where they were held,' McLennan said. 'The sanatorium's not far.' He indicated the way the jeep was facing. 'It's straight on and up the hill to the left.'

I had to stay in low gear on the steep twisting road that led to the sanatorium where the infamous Dr Keitler had used prisoners-of-war as guinea pigs in his psychological experimentation. The long low main building sat on a plateau looking out to sea. The lawns that had once graced the front had been churned up by the wheels of many vehicles and had a sorry, abandoned look. The sanatorium was relatively intact structurally, only one end having been damaged by shell or bomb. Most of the glass from the terrace of sea-facing windows had gone. I parked the jeep and we got out.

'The French paid fancy prices to come and convalesce here before the war,' McLennan told me as we walked along the front terrace. 'When the Germans were here, they used this part – the main building – as a nursing home for their own seriously wounded troops. SS troops, that is. The prisoner compound is round the side, in the grounds.'

We skirted the end of the main block and came to a complex of barracks-like huts, still surrounded by the remains of a tall wire fence. The huts were derelict: windows and doors broken, green paint peeling from the timber frames. They had a ransacked look.

'This is pretty much how we found things,' McLennan said, and led the way inside one of the deserted huts. 'This is the place the Canadian prisoners called 'The Pavilion' – although God knows why. It was where they lived, like rabbits in a cage.'

I explored the long narrow interior: the main ward,

into which two dozen hospital beds had been crowded; the shower and washroom; a number of cramped two-bed cubicles. The false ceilings – no more than thin boarding – had been torn down in places, exposing yards and yards of overhead electrical cabling.

'The entire joint was wired for sound,' McLennan explained. 'Dummy ventilators in every goddamned compartment. The guys in here couldn't cough or scratch their backsides without the sounds being picked up in the listening hut across the yard. The Jerries listened in on every goddamned thing they said or did. Nothing happened that they didn't know about.'

I shuddered. 'The Pavilion', with its ghosts, gave me the creeps. I was not sorry to get out into the wet grey morning. My tour of inspection had been educative, inasmuch as it had given me an insight into the devilry of which *Schatten Gruppe* were capable, but I wanted something much more solid than phantoms to pursue. And only phantoms were to be found within these rotting walls.

We returned to the village. It was still before midday but the inn was open and customers were drifting in for a glass of wine. We joined them. It was as good a place as any to start asking questions about Violette Brochant. In my most optimistic hopes, I did not expect to be rewarded quite so quickly and so fully as we were.

The most casual of enquiries was enough to elicit that the name of Violette Brochant was not only known in the village but positively reviled. The mere mention of the name was enough to stir the locals into passionate loquacity. They vied with one another to bombard me with the venom-laced recollections of a girl who had been born and brought up in the village but had sullied its name with her shameless collaboration with the hated Boches.

It did not take me long to establish without doubt that the Violette who had worked for the German SD at the sanatorium on the hill above St Cyr was the same

Violette, surname Brochant, who had sold her body to the SS clientele of the brothel at 65 Rue du Bourrelier in Paris.

I asked, perhaps naively, if Violette had been a nurse at the sanatorium – because it was as a nurse that she had figured in the escape of Chisholm and the Canadians, an escape orchestrated and monitored by the Germans with great cunning. My innocent question was greeted with scoffing ribaldry.

Sure, the girl had worn a nurse's uniform and had worked at the sanatorium one old timer informed me – but she was no nurse. She spent more time in bed with healthy Boche officers than she had ever spent at the bedside of the sick and wounded. She was a whore and had been a whore from the time she was old enough to peddle her fanny. Long before she left the village school, there wasn't a boy of her age who hadn't had a turn in the bushes with her at fifty centimes a time.

'Where is she now?' I asked the old-timer. He pulled a face.

'She cleared out at the same time as the Boches. Went to Paris, they say.'

'Do any of her family still live around here?'

'Only her witch of a mother,' the old man informed me sourly. 'She has a cottage up on the road to Deauville. But you'll stay away from her if you have any sense. She's half-mad. Nobody around here will have anything to do with her.'

'Because of her daughter?' I asked.

The old man shrugged. 'That's reason enough. She spawned the whore, did she not? We do not forget, monsieur, that when our grandchildren had not enough to eat, that old cow was eating red meat – thanks to the Boches and her slut of a daughter.'

McLennan and I lunched at the inn, on grilled white fish that had been line-caught only the previous day. It was both delicious and cheap and saved me broaching the iron rations which I'd loaded up at the château. Our

107

next stop was at the cottage on the Deauville road, where the widowed mother of Violette Brochant lived in reclusive solitude.

Although we saw the woman peer at us from behind curtains as we wrestled to open her heavy dilapidated front gate, she did not at first open her door to our repeated knocking. She finally relented, however — perhaps because she could no longer stand the furious barking of her dog. The animal was going demented every time we renewed our hammering.

The woman, who opened the door to us at last, was a shrew-eyed creature, with straggly red hair that showed grey where the henna had worn off. She wore a drab heavy cardigan over a faded print dress and her legs were encased in thick woollen stockings. Brass hoops, like curtain rings, hung from her ears and the rings festooned on her fingers made it look like she was sporting knuckle-dusters on both hands. Her cheeks were rouged like a pantomime dame's and the crimson blur that was her mouth suggested that she had trowelled on her lipstick blind-folded. If I had drawn her in a blind date, I would have shot myself on the spot. She glared at me with hostile, beady eyes. In no uncertain terms, she told us to clear off or she would set her dog on us.

Summing up my most winning smile, I told her that we meant her no harm; that we only wanted to speak with her. She was unimpressed and repeated her threat to put the dog on us. I assumed a look of injured disappointment and let her see the Heinz beans cardboard box that I carried in my hands. I expressed regret that she should turn away the bearer of gifts. Her greedy eyes lit up. She told us to wait where we were while she tied her dog round the back.

She disappeared within and I winked at McLennan. He nodded appreciatively, acknowledging the success of my stratagem. I had anticipated from all we had been told that the widow Brochant would not be welcoming

108

and I had armed myself with peace offerings, all purchased at the PX store at the Château Beauséjour.

'A little bribery works wonders,' McLennan murmured. 'What made you think of it?'

'Instinct,' I told him, 'developed as a reporter who has knocked on many doors. Getting a foot in the door is the easy bit. The tricky bit will be getting her to talk.'

The woman returned and invited us into the kitchen. The interior of the cottage was like its owner: ageing, garish and rather unkempt. The kitchen table was covered by a wax cloth in need of wiping. It was littered with crumbs. A wine bottle, a cracked cup, a greasy plate and the end of a loaf testified to a recent meal. I placed my package on the table.

'Some coffee, sugar, soap and a few chocolate bars, madame,' I said. 'It must be difficult for you living on your own.' I spoke in French.

'I manage,' she said. But she snatched up the goodies and stored them away in the cupboard. She locked the cupboard and popped the key into a cardigan pocket. She offered no thanks.

'What do you want of me?' she demanded, and her glare suggested that whatever it was we were not going to get it.

'I've come from Paris,' I said. 'Because I need your help. I want to get in touch with your daughter, Violette. She has moved away from the house in Paris where she was living.'

'I do not know where she is. I cannot help you.'

'That's a pity, madame,' I said. 'We were counting on you. Her life may depend on us finding her.'

The beady eyes showed alarm. 'You are lying,' she accused.

I regarded her with regretful reproach. 'Madame, I have no reason to lie. There are people who would do harm to Violette if they find her before we do . . . People who think she was too friendly with the Boches. We can protect her . . . if we find her first.'

She stared at me distrustfully. 'I will tell you nothing.'

I shrugged my shoulders. 'I had hoped, Madame, that you still cared for her. But it seems that she has no friends. In the village, they say that she is a bad girl . . . I had hoped that her own mother . . .'

She interrupted me angrily. 'They can say what they like in the village! They do not know Violette! She has always been a good daughter to me.'

'A good daughter, madame? Who runs off to Paris? Who deserts her mother and leaves her to fend for herself in these hard times?'

'Violette is a good girl. She has never deserted . . .' The denial was out before the woman suddenly seemed to regret her reply. She pursed her mouth shut. I tried a long shot.

'We know she has sent you money, madame,' I said.

'No,' she screeched, but the sudden fear in her eyes was enough to tell me that she was lying. She darted an anxious look towards the high sideboard that stood against one wall. I took a step towards it and the fear in her became acute. If she had shouted out loud that there was something on the sideboard that she did not want me to see, she could not have drawn my attention to the fact with greater certainty.

I walked round the table to examine the sideboard at close quarters. On it sat a number of hideous ornaments – the kind that are given away at fair-grounds – and one, in particular, caught my eye. It was a bright-red jug, its neck stuffed with papers. The woman screamed at me as I reached out and extracted the papers. Then she flew at me, hands clawing: trying to retrieve the papers from my hand. I fended her off and put the table between us.

Most of the papers were household bills – years old, by the look of some of them. The exception was a fresh-looking blue envelope. The front bore Mme Brochant's name and address, penned in a child-like scrawl. A Belgian postage stamp had been franked with the town

110

of origin and date. The letter had been posted in Spa on the 5th November 1944. But the envelope was empty.

I held it up so that Mme Brochant could see my discovery. She stared at it in despair. Her whole face seemed to quiver and huge tears rolled down her rouged cheeks. She threw herself into a chair and her weeping was piteous to behold. I found myself feeling sorry for her.

Having failed to sustain the lie that Violette had not sent her money, the weeping woman tried to make amends by throwing herself on our mercy and telling us all she knew. She seemed to sense that we were, perhaps, the only lifeline Violette had if she were to be saved from French revenge, and she tried to paint a wholly different picture of her daughter from the one we had been given in the village. Mme Brochant cooperated, too, from self-interest. It became clear that she dreaded the possibility that because she had tried to conceal that Violette kept her in funds we might be instrumental in cutting off that income.

She told us that she had not seen Violette since February, when the Germans had started to scale down their use of the sanatorium. It had been closed as a hospital in March. Violette had gone to Paris 'to work in another military hospital, an officers' hospital'. I made no comment on this. There seemed little point in enlightening Mme Brochant on the kind of nursing services her daughter might have provided at the establishment on the Rue du Bourrelier. Not that Mme Brochant would have revised her opinion of Violette. She begged us to believe that Violette was not the wicked girl that she was painted in St Cyr des Bains. She was a good loyal daughter whose only crime had been to work in a hospital run by the Boches. Was it a crime to work at such a noble calling as nurse, in order to ensure that her poor mother did not starve? A nurse made no distinction between nationalities and it made no difference to Violette whether her patients were

111

German or French or Chinese. Her only duty was to the sick, the wounded and the dying.

It was because of Violette's abilities as a nurse that the Germans had offered her work in Paris. She would have been a fool not to have accepted the job, her mother believed. The pay was good and, dutiful daughter that Violette was, she had sent money home regularly – as she had promised she would. There was never a letter with the money – Violette was never one for writing letters – but it came from Paris regular as clockwork: just bank-notes in a plain envelope.

Mme Brochant had received ten such envelopes from Paris between February and June, when the Allies had landed in Normandy and everything had been disrupted. The payments had stopped until only a few weeks ago, when an envelope containing ten twenty-franc notes had arrived. She had only kept the envelope because the stamp was so unusual. She had never seen one like it before.

McLennan and I were on the road back to Rouen soon after dark. I did not feel too dissatisfied with the fruits of my excursion to St Cyr des Bains. Indeed, in many respects, I thought I had struck lucky. I was not returning to Thorn empty-handed. I had established a definite link between *Schatten Gruppe's* 1942 operation at St Cyr and the house on the Rue du Bourrelier. The connection was Violette Brochant. And Violette Brochant had been in Spa, in Belgium, only a week or two ago. Had she gone there for her health? McLennan intruded on my thoughts.

'You handled that old biddy pretty well, John,' he said. 'But one thing's been puzzling me. How were you so all-fired sure that her daughter had been sending her money in the mail?'

'I wasn't sure at all,' I said.

'But you told her we *knew* the girl had been sending

her money. Goddamn it, even I believed you! I thought you *did know*.'

'I was guessing,' I confessed. 'It was something somebody said at the inn . . . the inn-keeper's wife. They were all going on about how they wouldn't sell eggs and fish and that to the widow Brochant, because of the girl. But the inn-keeper's wife said the shop-keepers in Deauville weren't so fussy. They didn't turn her away. She'd seen the old crow coming back from Deauville last week with a brand-new coat − and she wondered where the woman had got the money. I wondered, too − and then put two and two together.'

The Canadian concluded from all this that I was one hell of a smart operator. I knew better. I had just been lucky. I dropped McLennan at the farmhouse near Rouen and pressed on towards Paris, wondering if Thorn and Joubert had turned up anything in my forty-eight hours' absence.

It was midnight before I reached Paris and getting on for two in the morning before I got to the château. In the hope of a cup of coffee, I made straight for the kitchen. The access was via the big *salle-à-manger* with the stained-glass window. To my surprise, I found both Thorn and Hibberd there. They were standing over a map, which they had stretched over one of the small tables, and they were deep in earnest conversation. I thought they would be bursting with curiosity to find out how I had got on at St Cyr des Bains but the barrage of questions I expected did not immediately materialise. Thorn and Hibberd had other things on their mind. In my absence, there had been developments and now things were happening all over the place.

FIVE

Points North

It was a bit deflating to be upstaged by a map of north-west Europe. There I was, simply bursting to tell Hibberd and Thorn about my discoveries in St Cyr des Bains; and there they were, absorbed over that wretched map. They acknowledged my arrival in a manner that could have been no more off-handed if I had popped out momentarily to the toilet, instead of having driven halfway across France.

'Oh, so you're back?' Hibberd greeted me, exhibiting no anxiety to learn the outcome of my excursion to the coast. He returned his attention immediately to the map. Thorn merely grinned at me.

'Come and take a look at this, John,' he invited me, referring to the map. I peered over their shoulders to see that somebody had been busy on it with wax pencils. It was dotted with blue crosses, some of which had been circled in black, and a heavy red line had been drawn across it like a diagonal.

'A work of art,' I observed tartly.

Hibberd threw me a withering look. 'I've spent the whole day in Versailles plotting this out,' he said. 'I don't want any goddamned wisecracks outa you!'

'Sorry, sir,' I apologised, 'the labour speaks for itself. What all the crosses are for is not quite so obvious. I take it they're not kisses but something much more important.'

'Tell him, Cal,' Hibberd said to Thorn. 'Tell him what it means.'

Thorn grinned at me again. 'I'm sure John didn't know just how much work you put into it, sir,' he said to Hibberd. To me, he said: 'The Colonel's been going cross-eyed reading through G–2 flimsies and field reports just to put these noughts and crosses on this map. He's come up with some mighty interesting findings. Look, I'll show you.'

He ran a fingernail down the thick red line that had been pencilled on to the map. It extended from mid-Holland to the Vosges Mountains and coincided, for a lot of the way, with the border of Germany.

'This is the front line,' Thorn said. 'You can see that most of the little blue crosses the Colonel's put on the map are on our side of the front, between a place called Elsenborn in the north and Luxembourg in the south ... the city of Luxembourg, that is. The crosses mark the locations of incidents that have occurred during the past six or seven weeks.'

'What kind of incidents?' I asked.

'Ambushes,' Thorn said. 'Where our guys have been jumped by Krauts.'

'It's good ambush country,' Hibberd chimed in. 'Very hilly, lots of forests and steep valleys. And it's the thinnest part of the line between Holland and Switzerland. We got no more than four divisions strung out along maybe eighty miles of front.'

'And the ambushes have some significance for us?' I said.

'Some of them,' said Thorn. 'The ones the Colonel has circled with blue.'

A glance at the map showed me that, whereas there must have been more than fifty crosses plotted on the map, only half a dozen had circles drawn round them.

'You'll notice,' Thorn went on, 'that the circled crosses are all inside our territory, anything up to thirty miles. The others are all much closer to the front. We reckon they're the work of Kraut patrols infiltrating our lines at night and then dodging back to their own side of the line. For the past couple of months, that's the kind of war it has been up there. No big plays that made the headlines but lots of patrols and the odd little skirmishes that nobody takes much notice of.'

'But you don't think the circled incidents fit in with that?' I suggested.

'They could. The country up there lends itself to deep penetration. A specialist outfit could work deep inside our territory, hiding out by day and operating by night. But there's been a pattern to them. The guys the Krauts have been taking out in what would normally be considered 'safe' areas haven't been fighting men but non-combatants – medics mainly. More than that, the Krauts didn't just stop at ambushing guys, who were unarmed, and killing them . . . They stripped the bodies and left them lying there. . . .'

My mind flashed immediately to my discovery of Thomson's body in the Rue du Bourrelier. He had been stripped of his uniform, too. And Cotter's German companion had been dressed as an officer in the medical fraternity. Their transport was an ambulance The connections were piling up. Hibberd was watching my reaction, and now he produced the clincher.

'Remember you saying, John, that one of the guys you saw with Cotter was an Army doctor – or dressed up as one – and that he was wearing a gun?'

'That's just what I've been remembering,' I said.

'Take a look at this then,' Hibberd said. He handed me a document that he had fished from his brief-case. 'This is what made me sit up and take notice the minute I read it.'

It was a copy of a report from a G–2 officer attached to the US Ninth Armored Division and had been relayed from General Bradley's HQ in the city of Luxembourg. The report had been compiled from interviews with three officers in the Ninth Armored, who were stationed in a reserve position not far from the Luxembourg capital.

The three tank officers had been on their way to eat in the hotel that had been taken over as their mess when they had encountered, in a nearby street, three fellow-American officers in the company of two expensively dressed women. The officers, who were escorting the women, comprised a lieutenant-colonel and two majors. Their helmets and uniform sleeves carried the red cross emblazonments that identified them as medical officers. The Ninth Armored men saluted the other group and received salutes in return. It was not until the tank officers were inside their mess-hall and about to sit down that, simultaneously, it clicked with all three that there had been something distinctly wrong about the apparel of the medical officers. All three had been wearing side-arms – in direct contradiction to all medical corps tradition.

The tank officers had run out into the street to search for the suspect 'Americans' and their lady friends. But the five could not be found.

Even as I read the report, I was understanding all too clearly why Hibberd's excitement had been raised by the document. I stared at him.

'The three officers with the women, sir. . . The same people I saw in Paris, with Cotter?'

Hibberd shook his head. 'No, John. The time factor rules it out. The guys you saw in Paris were a different bunch.'

'How can you be sure?'

'Because we know exactly when and where the phoneys in Luxembourg got hold of their American uniforms. A lieutenant-colonel and two majors were ambushed and stripped up near Diekirch only three days before the phoneys were spotted by the three tankers. That was *after* you met up with the other phoneys in Paris. That's what started me off looking back through six weeks of battle-front reports. I wondered if there were other ambushes like the one at

117

Diekirch or if it was just an isolated thing that guys were being killed and their bodies stripped.'

I looked at the circled crosses on the map and counted them. There were seven.

'It's happened seven times,' I said.

'And you can see the pattern,' Thorn said. 'The Diekirch ambush was the furthest south and the nearest of the seven to the actual front . . . only eight or nine miles from the line. The other six were all a long way from the front.' He tapped the map with his finger. 'In this part of Belgium they call the Ardennes.'

'Seven times they hit us, John,' Hibberd put in. 'And seven times they stripped the bodies . . . a total of twenty-eight dead Americans in all. Twenty-eight uniforms taken – and every time from non-combatants, medics mostly.'

I stared at the other two. 'Why should the Jerries want to collect medics' uniforms? Twenty-eight of them?'

'That, John, is the sixty-four-thousand-dollar question,' Hibberd said, with feeling. 'They sure ain't doing it for fun! How many guys have they got running around in our uniforms? When phoney medics turn up in Paris to collect a renegade staff officer and God knows how many SHAEF secrets, we got a situation that may not worry some people but sure scares the life outa me!'

'Our guess is that the Krauts must have some kind of base on our side of the line, up there in the Ardennes, and it's there that Cotter has gone to earth.' The contribution came from Thorn.

'He could be anywhere in France,' I pointed out. 'He could still be in Paris, for all we know.'

'What you don't know, John, is that Joubert and I got lucky while you were away at the seaside playing with sea-shells on the sea-shore. We found ourselves one of the hookers on that list of Joubert's. We've run us down a cutie who did a lot of horizontal collaboration with the Krauts in that Bourrelier Street whore-house – and you'll never guess what!'

'What?' I prompted him.

'She knows where the boss-lady hightailed it to when Paris was getting too hot for her and her SS whore-masters. Not only the boss-lady but most of the girls, too.'

'Don't tell me where they've gone,' I said. 'Let me make an educated guess.' I bent over the map and found the town of Spa, in Belgium, in the north of the region known as the Ardennes.

'How about here?' I asked innocently, and put my finger on Spa.

Both Hibberd and Thorn looked at me as if I had just demonstrated how to turn water into wine with a pass of the hand.

'How the hell did you figure that out?' Hibberd demanded to know.

'Elementary deduction, sir,' I said modestly. 'Spa is the town where Violette Brochant has been plying her trade. At least, she was until two or three weeks ago. And, just for the record, I can confirm for you that there's only one Violette. The girl we were looking for in Paris and the girl who did tricks for *Schatten Gruppe* at St Cyr des Bains are the same girl.'

I told them, then, about my St Cyr investigations. Hibberd heard me out with impatient eagerness.

'That does it!' he said. 'We've gotten ourselves three leads now and they all point one way – up north! Now we've got to figure out just what the hell's going on up there.'

He was quite charged up and, in spite of the lateness of the hour and my own fatigue, I felt a surge of adrenalin myself. We returned to study the map with a definite sense of quickening excitement. All the answers to the mystery confronting us seemed to be located somewhere among the forested hills and twisting rivers of that region, embraced by four countries, and known as the Ardennes. None of us had an inkling at that time of the storm that was about to break over the Ardennes and transform its hills and forests into one of the bloodiest battle-grounds in the history of the war.

At three in the morning, Thorn, Hibberd and I retired to our cold and draughty bedrooms in the chateau's west turret to sleep the sleep of the just. A mood almost of elation gripped us. We were buoyed with a rosy optimism that we were on the verge of solving the riddles of Cotter's defection, Thomson's murder and the mysterious killings of Army medical personnel in the Ardennes. We had no doubts that all were connected and that the common factor was *Schatten Gruppe*.

Of all the jig-saw pieces of information that we had gathered, one perhaps had excited us most of all. It had emerged from Thorn's and Joubert's questioning of the prostitute, whom the pair had cross-examined in a Paris hospital.

The girl had described in detail a high-ranking Nazi officer, with whom Madame Fabienne − the owner of the house in Rue du Bourrelier − had been on the closest of terms. The description tallied, almost word for word, with the description − provided almost two years previously by the sea-captain, Chisholm − of Colonel Keitler, the evil genius who had presided over *Schatten Gruppe* operations at St Cyr des Bains. The girl had even described, as Chisholm had done, the single sleeve chevron on the Nazi's uniform. This rare emblem was worn only by a few of the SS elite as a special entitlement. It signified service to the Nazi Party before its coming to power.

In 1943, Chisholm's recall of that chevron on Keitler's uniform sleeve had identified the doctor as an intimate of the Nazi hierarchy in general and of Heinrich Himmler in particular. This had been borne out subsequently by the discovery that *Schatten Gruppe* was a highly secret offshoot of the *Sicherheitsdienst,* or SD, as the secret security service founded by Himmler was known.

As Hibberd had said, all our clues led north. They pointed, in particular, to the Belgian health resort of Spa, which was now the headquarters town of the US First Army. Was it possible that a Nazi group, who dared to venture abroad in stolen US medical corps uniforms, was operating from a clandestine base within the Allied line at or near Spa?

The more we considered that grim possibility, the more we became convinced that it was a very real likelihood. Therefore, it followed that we now had to concentrate our enquiries on Spa. It was perhaps too much to hope that Keitler himself was still directing Nazi operations from Allied soil, but that remote possibility was enough to fire Hibberd with the belief that any investigations undertaken by Thorn and myself would be greatly reinforced if we took along the one person who could positively identify Keitler, Madame Fabienne, Violette Brochant and any other fugitives from 65 Rue du Bourrelier. That person was Danielle Roussillon, the prostitute, who was in hospital in Paris but who was due to be released next day.

Thorn had nearly fallen off his chair when Hibberd made the suggestion – but his counter-arguments had made little impression on Hibberd. If it had gone to a vote, Hibberd would have been for, Thorn against, and I – on the grounds of uncertainty would have abstained. As it was, the decision was unanimous, because Thorn and I had no franchise and what Hibberd said, we did.

I went to sleep that night wondering about the journey that lay ahead of us and about the prospect of Thorn and I playing chaperon to a prostitute. I had met prostitutes before, professionally – my profession, that is, not theirs. I tried to convince myself that the experience in prospect would be educational.

I was still rubbing sleep out of my eyes when I emerged into the frosty cold of morning to find that

Thorn had been up and about for an hour. His jeep was standing in the stable yard at the back of the chateau and he was putting the finishing touches to loading it – for a trans-Siberian expedition, it seemed. The back was packed with cases of K-rations, assorted weapons, ammunition, and jerry-cans of gasoline.

'Good afternoon, John,' he greeted me.

'It's still the middle of the night,' I complained. 'Couldn't we have waited until it got daylight?'

'We got to go into Paris,' he reminded me. 'We'll be goddamned lucky to be on our way north by noon.'

'Where's the girl going to sit?' I asked, staring at the loaded rear of the jeep, from which the back seats had been removed to make way for cargo.

'We'll all pile in the front,' he said. 'It's cosier that way.'

'What's in the big canvas bag?' I enquired, with foreboding. 'A tent?'

He laughed. 'Maybe we'd be glad of one, but no, it's not a tent. It's some of the latest cold-weather combat clothing. Boots, too. For you, me and the girl. They've had snow up north.'

'Great!' I said. I was wishing I'd stayed in bed. 'Have you tried to get hold of Joubert yet?'

'I spoke to him on the blower.' Thorn grinned. 'He was still in bed. And he's sore that he's not going with us. He'll fix everything though and meet us at the hospital. We pick the girl up at ten.'

'How does she feel about all this? What if she doesn't want to go?'

'She'll go,' Thorn promised. 'She plays ball with us and gets herself a merit mark – or Joubert throws her to the wolves. My guess is that she'll play ball.'

Again, I found myself wondering about Danielle Roussillon. I had an image of a hard-bitten trollop with a mind like a cash register and the tongue of a fishwife. That, somehow, was the picture that had evolved

122

from what Thorn had told me. He and Joubert had given her a real grilling the previous day.

At first, she had tried to deny that she had been one of Madame Fabienne's girls at 65 Rue du Bourrelier, but once she had made the admission she had been extremely frank about all that had gone on there and the extent of the establishment's German sponsorship. The latter had come about, she said, because of Madame Fabienne's close association with the Nazi officer who – we now believed – was the notorious Colonel Keitler. In the past, Madame Fabienne had performed special services for the Nazi – Danielle Roussillon had no idea what these services were – and, consequently, she had been held in high esteem by the Germans. She had enjoyed privileges and protection that had come the way of very few during the Occupation.

When it had become clear that the Occupation was coming to an end, the Germans had gone out of their way to help Madame Fabienne escape the wrath of the Allies. She had announced the closure of the house early in July and – with promises to her girls that they would not be abandoned – had driven off in a big limousine with her Nazi officer friend. That was the last Danielle Roussillon and the girls had seen of Madame Fabienne.

Earlier, on the day of Madame's departure, a large pantechnicon had collected a load of furniture and several trunks holding her possessions. It was generally believed that Madame – a good-looking woman, not yet forty – had fulfilled her boast of early retiral to her native Belgium and a life of some style. She was reputed to be extremely wealthy, having invested the profits of her lucrative enterprises in land and properties. Some of these properties were believed to be in the Belgian highlands, near Spa: a part of the world she talked about frequently.

The rumours – that Madame had settled in Belgium – were given some substance when all the girls had been given the opportunity of continued employment in Spa, where the Germans had established a leave centre for SS officers recuperating from wounds. Violette Brochant had acted as intermediary and recruiting officer and had made all the arrangements with the Germans and, although Madame Fabienne had not been seen again by the girls, they believed that hers was the unseen hand behind the move.

Some of the girls had elected to get out of Paris and go their own ways but most — fearing retribution as collaborators — had accepted the offer of moving to Spa. They had been driven north in a German Army truck and installed in a large villa overlooking Warfaz Lake.

Danielle Roussillon had not taken kindly to life in these new surroundings. She had missed the city and had resented the lack of freedom at the villa. The girls had been compelled to function like automatons for the German officers, who had arrived in car-loads from Spa, many of them the victims of hideous disfigurement and permanent disablement. It had all been very different from the gaiety and party-like atmosphere that had prevailed at Rue du Bourrelier. Things might have been better, Danielle Roussillon believed, if Madame Fabienne had been in charge, but Violette Brochant had been elevated to the post of house-mother and general superintendent and she ran the villa like a concentration camp.

Danielle Roussillon had deserted at the first opportunity. On a rare day off to go shopping in Spa, she had fallen in with a truck-driver who had proved an easy victim for her charms. She had persuaded the man to take her with him into Brussels, where she had promptly ditched him. She had been among the cheering crowds who had welcomed the liberating British Army into Brussels only a week later and, returning to her old trade, had found no shortage of customers among the liberators. The British, however, did not throw their money around, and tales of the fortunes being made by girls in Paris, off free-spending American soldiers on leave, made Danielle hungry for her old haunts in Montmartre.

She had succeeded in making her way back to Paris in late November, only to be recognised immediately in a bar which she had frequented much in the past. A street rival had spat on her and denounced her as a collaborator. She had been pursued and set upon by a mob, who might well have killed her but for the intervention of a passing SP patrol. As it was, her hair had been hacked off with a knife and her face had been slashed before her rescuers had stepped in and rushed her to hospital.

Now she was to be released into the custody of Thorn and myself and I was much less apprehensive about the arrangement than perhaps I should have been. Thorn, I knew, had misgivings aplenty, but I was content to let him worry enough for both of us. There was a piquancy about the prospect, a novelty, that filled me with anticipation. It was like setting out on a voyage of discovery without being sure if the world was round or flat. It might be painful finding out, but I wanted to *know*.

The hospital was a few blocks away from the Place de la Republique. Because of the supplies in the jeep, I had to sit guarding it while Thorn went off to collect the girl. A good half hour passed before he returned. Joubert was with him and between the two walked a slight figure who was dressed up like the juvenile mascot of an American regiment. The bundle of clothing that Thorn carried into the hospital had obviously been utilised: Danielle Roussillon was kitted out like a miniature infantryman. She wore greenish-coloured weatherproofed trousers tucked into brown boots that laced over her ankles. Her upper half was lost in a voluminous winter combat jacket, which was several sizes too big for her, and a woollen cap had been pulled down over her head. Part of her head and most of her face was

125

hidden by the khaki-brown scarf wound round her neck. A pair of wide brown eyes peered out over a fold of the scarf. I came under their scrutiny as I climbed out of the jeep.

'Say hello to Captain Abernathy,' Thorn told the phenomenon at his side. He grinned at me. 'John, meet Private Danny.'

The brown eyes stared at me with cold hostility.

'Fuck you!' she said from behind the scarf.

I was taken aback but rode the shock and beamed her a big smile.

'Hi Danny,' I greeted her. 'They didn't tell me you could speak English,'

'Goddamned *anglais*!' she said, with contempt.

'Watch your goddamned mouth,' Thorn rebuked her sternly. He threw me a look. 'Her English is kinda limited. I think she learned it in a saloon.'

'Fucking goddamned Yankee son-of-a-bitch!' she spat at Thorn. He scowled down at her from his superior height.

'I told you to watch that mouth of yours, young lady. If you got nothing nice to say, you just keep it shut, you hear?'

Joubert, who had been watching in silent amusement, weighed in to lecture her severely in her own tongue. He warned her with some severity of the fate that would befall her if she gave any trouble to Captain Thorn. He, Joubert, would personally arrange for her to be handed over to some people who did nasty things to cheap little tarts like her, who preferred German pricks to French. She had a choice. She could behave herself and do what she was told or she could take her chances with the scavenger squads of the Resistance. If she chose the latter option, then God help her, because he, Joubert, would not.

The warning seemed to chasten her. Blinking resentfully at Joubert, she obeyed Thorn's instruction to get into the jeep. We shook hands with Joubert and climbed in on either side of her. She sat between us, hunched up in angry silence, then withdrew her woollen-capped head deeper and deeper within the neck of her over-sized jacket, in the manner of a tortoise retiring into its shell. There she remained in dejected resignation.

'*Bonne chance, mes amis,*' Joubert called, and raised his hand in farewell as Thorn eased the jeep away from the kerb and across the traffic flow into the Avenue Richerand. At the foot of the avenue, he swung right along the canal quay and headed north. We kept going north across the city.

We were speeding along a main arterial boulevard when an elbow poked fiercely into my side. The woolly cap emerged from the jacket beside me and two brown eyes stared appealingly into mine.

'*Cigarette? Vous avez cigarettes?*' The voice was plaintive.

I fished in my pocket and extracted a pack of Chester-field. I popped a cigarette out for the girl. She had to roll back a sleeve to free a hand for the cigarette and she had to emerge fully from the jacket to complete the operation of placing it in her mouth. I was holding out my lighter, ready to spark it with my thumb, when she dropped the scarf down over her mouth to reveal her face for the very first time. I caught my breath at the sight. Down both cheeks were raw ugly weals of purple-red flesh, from which the stitch-marks had not disap-peared. A single four-inch scar disfigured one cheek. An uglier Y-shaped double scar marked the other. The eyes stared at me defiantly.

'*Regardez bien!*' The words were flung at me, and she plucked the cap from her head to reveal a scalp that had been shorn of hair. There was an uneven overall growth of perhaps quarter of an inch: not enough to conceal livid red marks where the skin had been hacked. '*Regardez bien!*' she repeated with that edge of defiance in her voice that made the invitation a challenge.

The sight of what they had done to her filled me with

127

a devastating sadness. And anger. Scarred as she was, there was a gamine prettiness – a sweetness – that the ugly weals and crew-cut hair had failed to destroy.

'*C'est belle, la figure?*' she cried. '*C'est belle, non?*'

I shook my head. '*C'est tragique,*' I said. '*C'est criminel . . . Le fait des monstres . . . Le fait des betes . . . des barbares!*' And it *was* criminal, the work of mindless beasts.

My reaction was not the one she had expected. Perhaps she had expected me to recoil from her, to be repelled by the wounds to her femininity. She may even have expected a gloating pleasure of approbation at the brutal justice that had been meted out to her. Whatever reaction she may have expected, my roused sense of outrage clearly came as a surprise. I realised that, perhaps, until that moment, she had experienced little in the way of sympathy for her injuries.

She studied me, the brown eyes wide and watchful.

'I am ugly,' she declared, and the word she used – *laide* – seemed to have its meaning embodied in the jarring dullness to the ear of its sound.

'No,' I said, returning her stare. 'You are not ugly. You have been marked but you are not ugly.'

She wrinkled her little button of a nose and shrugged her head slightly to one side – as if, although she wanted to believe me, she could not bring herself to do so.

'I am not beautiful,' she said, glancing at me coyly, inviting my agreement but desperately hoping to be contradicted. I lit her cigarette and grinned at her.

'I've seen worse,' I said. 'You've got nice eyes. And your hairstyle's rather cute. Short hair suits you.'

'Fuck you, *anglais,*' she said, but there was a twinkle in the brown eyes that had not been there before. I detected no rancour in her remark.

'Fuck you, too, *française,*' I replied cheerfully. I had the feeling that we were going to get along just fine.

Clear of Paris, the jeep began to eat the miles. Danielle Roussillon showed little interest in the scenery and then, after much fidgeting, snuggled down with her head against my shoulder. Within seconds, she was sleeping with the innocence of a child. Thorn glanced sideways and caught my eye.

'You'd better watch out, John,' he warned. 'I think she's taken a fancy to you.' He was grinning all over his face.

The comment I made in reply was succinct, in the advice offered, and as obscene as it was succinct.

'See what I mean?' Thorn said. 'You're beginning to talk like her.'

Anxious to use all the daylight available to us, Thorn and I shared the driving: making stops only to change seats. We kept starvation at bay by eating candy from our supply of rations in the back of the jeep.

Danielle Roussillon's delight at being given a large bar of chocolate amused us both. Such luxuries were unknown to her and she made a theatrical production out of unwrapping the confectionery and drawing out the consumption of each small square. She drooled with pleasure as she rolled her tongue around every melting morsel, prolonging the performance and giving us a running commentary on the bliss to her taste buds.

By early afternoon, we were two hundred miles north of Paris and had crossed the border from France into Belgium. It was all new territory to me but, as we drove north, I found myself reading off the place-names on the road-signs with a sense of rediscovery. Many had a poignant familiarity, taking me back to grown-up conversations I had overheard as a youngster and to books and articles I had read. The sign-posts pointed the way to towns and villages with names that had become household words thirty years before – in the war that had taken my father and so many of his gener-ation. The names awakened in me the awe I had known as a boy for that other war and its awful carnage. They conjured up, in my mind, shell-torn landscapes and legions of marching ghosts. Our haste to hurry by seemed almost profane in its heedlessness of sacred ground so close — like careering across a graveyard on a motor cycle as if it were just another field.

At one road junction, where we stopped so that Thorn and I could swap seats, I paused for a moment to stare up at a direction sign pointing the way into Flanders. It told me that Mons was twenty-eight kilometres distant. The name was as powerfully evocative as that of any of the battlefields we had passed and it stirred my imagination as it had done when I was a boy. Then, a picture in a book had imprinted itself on my mind: a lone soldier standing on a mountain of rubble and, beyond him, rubble and desolation as far as the eye could see. Mons was the place where the great senseless slaughter had all begun in August 1914 — where a squadron of spike-helmeted Uhlans had ridden slap-bang into advance elements of the British Expeditionary Force and where, after initial astonishment on both sides, the armies had locked horns and got down to the serious business of killing.

'Are you going to stand there all goddamned day?' Thorn bawled at me from the jeep.

I was jerked back to the present. The ghosts we sought were not at Mons. The road to Mons was left, to the west; we forked right, to the east — along the road that ran parallel to the slag-polluted River Sambre to its confluence with the sweeter Meuse.

The rivers meet at Namur. The pink-brick town, nestling in the shadow of its giant craggy citadel, is also the meeting place of six roads. It is one of several gateways into the high forested uplands of the Ardennes. We found our way barred at the bridge over the Meuse by a squad of Belgian fusiliers in British-style battledress. We pulled in before the check-point to ask their advice on the best road to Spa.

The Belgians debated the matter furiously but were of one mind. We could — they agreed — chance the hilly by-ways that criss-crossed the Ardennes, but if we did we would probably get ourselves lost. Far better, they said, to take the road along the south bank of the Meuse and keep the river company all the way to Liège. From Liège, we could loop round towards Spa, a short run that should take us no more than half an hour.

We took the river road. And snow, flurrying in the bitterly cold breeze, seemed to confirm the prudence of our choice. The sky was leaden-grey and if, as it promised to do, the weather deteriorated, the low valley road seemed a better bet than hilly tracks at the back of beyond.

Darkness overtook us on the last stretch of an uneventful run down the Meuse valley into Liège. Snow still fluttered fitfully against the windscreen as we entered the ancient city, but the flurries were light and the blizzard we feared had not materialised. I had read somewhere that Liège with the river at its heart, its islands, its canals, its surrounding hills – was a city of great natural beauty and had once been known as 'the Venice of the North'. Its charm escaped us on that cold December evening. It was probably there all right but it wasn't on show. Liège was much too near the fighting war and proclaimed that proximity to us with a force that left no room for other impressions of the place to be absorbed. Here we left behind a zone of comparative tranquillity and crossed the border into another where every nuance of life was conditioned by the nearness of the battle-front.

The darkened city bustled with prodigious activity: workers hurrying homewards, soldiers everywhere and the streets log-jammed with military trucks of every shape and size. At a crawl, we threaded a way through the congestion, frustrated by the slowness of our progress but all our senses quickened by an awareness that this was where the war zone began. As if to emphasise the latter fact, there was an eruption of gunfire from batteries sited all around the city but hidden from our

131

view. It came so suddenly and with such surprise that the three of us in the jeep almost expired on the spot with fright. But all we could do was to sit tight, hemmed in as we were by traffic, and wonder nervously why no one else in Liège was paying the slightest attention to the sudden racket. Was it an exercise, which took only us unawares? Or did the local anti-aircraft guns just blaze away at any old time in a manner to which the citizenry were accustomed?

The distraction was probably responsible for us missing the turn-off to Spa, with the result that we saw more of Liège than was our intention. Not that the black-out permitted much sight-seeing. The lasting impression that we had was that the town had been converted into a gigantic arsenal. It was, of course, a major supply centre for the US First Army and wherever room could be found for them along the waterway quays, vast quantities of materials had been stock-piled. All the appurtenances of war were there: ammunition, fuel, food, crates of medical supplies, spare parts, and line upon line of vehicles.

We got caught up in a big convoy of trucks heading for Aachen before we realised we were on the wrong road. We had remedied the error and were back-tracking through the town when we became aware of another phenomenon: aerial activity. We heard a jet-like rasp of engine noise overhead before, once again, there was an eruption of gunfire and we saw streams of tracer shells ascending into the black overcast. It dawned on Thorn and myself simultaneously what the unseen target of the guns was.

'Doodle-bug!' I proclaimed, in the same instant as Thorn was crying out: 'It's a goddamned buzz-bomb!'

We waited to hear the explosion, which would have announced the flying bomb's fall to earth. But there was none and the AA guns fell silent as suddenly as they had burst into life. The absence of any explosion on the two occasions that the guns had fired prompted us to the conclusion that the target of the bombs had not been Liège but Brussels, which lay fifty miles to the west. We drew no comfort from the fact. It gave us an uncomfortable feeling to realise that the missiles had been launched from German soil, only fifty miles to the east. Any lingering doubts we may have had, that we were in a war zone where people actually got hurt, now fled.

We drove on towards Spa with alertness sharpened and pulses beating that little bit faster – like frontiersmen who know they're in Indian country. The road climbed and twisted out of Liège and our headlights sparkled on banks of snow in the verges, although the road itself was clear. The wind had dropped to nothing and, the higher we climbed, the thicker became the banks of mist that swirled across our path from the dark swatches of fir and spruce flanking our route.

Because of the mist and the amount of slow-moving traffic on the road, it took us more than an hour to reach Spa. There, our immediate destination was the Hotel Britannique, Headquarters of the US First Army. Hibberd had warned us that, before we started turning over stones in the First Army's bailiwick, it would be politic to let Headquarters know we were in the neighbourhood. We would be dependent on them for communication with Hibberd at SHAEF and there were other reasons why we should keep sweet with them. Quite apart from the help that the US Counter-Intelligence Corps HQ staff could afford us in the way of local knowledge and conditions, it was essential that our freedom of movement was not curtailed by ignorance of routine security procedures – such as the daily password changes – or by failure to equip ourselves with up-to-date 'trip tickets'.

Hibberd had been anxious to impress on us that our investigations should be conducted unobtrusively. He did not want us to get in anybody's hair nor tread with our size eights on anybody's toes. We were to remember that the guys at Spa were fighting a land battle, which had a preoccupying effect. They were unlikely to jump up and down with excitement over our mission, which they would likely consider a side-show and something of a nuisance.

That said, Hibberd had foreseen no difficulties for us. Compared with other parts of the European battle-front, the Ardennes front was relatively quiet: so much so that it was being used to 'rest' battle-weary divisions or to give line experience, of a not too harsh variety, to raw troops who had never seen action.

What Hibberd had not warned us about was that First Army Headquarters was even more of a madhouse than other Army headquarters. I admit that I am a bit cynical about all such establishments. They have much in common with the head offices of all large corporations, where the pursuit of power is the only true religion. Status is all-important and vanity, which demands its worship, rules – with the consequence that head offices, military or commercial, become hotbeds of corridor politics and inter-departmental rivalries.

At the Headquarters of the First Army in Spa, the feuds and jealousies bubbled away with such ferocity that the staff had earned a notoriety which was the talk of other Army headquarters throughout the European theatre. Unfortunately, Thorn and I were blissfully ignorant of this when we cruised out of the mist to present our credentials at the Hotel Britannique. It did not, however, take us long to discover that freelance operators like ourselves could not expect the most cordial of welcomes.

Thorn went inside to report our arrival to the CI Corps duty officer but was immediately buttonholed by a busy-body colonel who demanded to know why Thorn had been sent from Paris, who had sent him, and what the hell did he want from the Counter-Intelligence section? Did Thorn not know that this was a goddamned Army headquarters and that all headquarters visitors had to check through the office of the headquarters commandant? Did Thorn think that any Tom, Dick or Harold could just march into the goddamned place with the idea he could see this, that or the next person as if it was open night?

While Thorn was being educated *ad nauseam* on HQ protocol, I was stretching my legs beside our jeep and enjoying a quiet smoke. At least, I was until a voice rudely demanded to know who the hell owned that goddamned jeep.

'Who the hell wants to know?' I asked, peering at a group of great-coated figures who had emerged from the hotel. A white-helmeted military cop loomed out of the mist to inform me that it was General Somebody-or-other who wanted to know and that I had better move the jeep pretty goddamned quick. The outcome was that I moved the jeep pretty goddamned quick.

Half an hour passed before Thorn reappeared in the company of a husky giant, whom he introduced as Lieutenant Joe Kinneally. The Counter-Intelligence Corps lieutenant peered at me through steel-rimmed glasses in a strangely anxious way, as if his close inspection would reveal that I was a carrier of plague. There was nothing timorous about his handshake, however. He seemed unaware of the crushing strength in the great paw that enveloped my hand.

'Glad you're on our side,' I murmured, nursing my fingers and wondering how many were fractured.

'Nice of you guys to drop by,' he said, without convincing me that he meant it. He seemed decidedly uneasy and he became more so when Danielle Roussillon hailed him cheerfully from the jeep.

'You must be ... Danny,' he said, with a nervous gulp. He greeted her politely in French and stood there nervously moving his weight from one foot to the other. I got the impression that he either had prostate trouble or was inordinately shy. The truth of the matter was that to Joe Kinneally – the most amiable of men – the three of us were an almighty embarrassment.

It was bad enough to have Thorn and me descending on him out of the blue. Danny added an extra dimension to his embarrassment. Females were about as welcome at First Army headquarters as devil-worshippers in a monastery. The fact that Danny was not only a female but a female who had co-operated – bodily, if not spiritually – with the enemy, did not enhance our standing.

It was nothing personal, Kinneally tried to assure us. First Army Headquarters just did not take kindly to visitors of any kind. True, they had put out the red carpet for Marlene Dietrich and they were getting ready to lavish hospitality on a troupe of star baseball players – but these were the kind of public relations exercises that every headquarters had to put up with now and again. We had to admit, did we not, that Danny did not quite have Hollywood star status and that nobody was going to be asking Thorn and me for our autographs? The sad truth was that Thorn and I represented a branch of the service that was so despised by the First Army brass that the best thing we could have done would have been to give Spa a wide berth and gone somewhere else. Joe Kinneally didn't want us to get him wrong; he would do everything he could to help us. But he was consumed by one burning anxiety in the meantime: the need to get us away from the environs of the Hotel Britannique as speedily and as discreetly as possible.

All the time he was talking to us he kept glancing over his shoulder towards the main doorway, with the dread of one who fears being seen in the company of known malefactors by vigilant proctors. Happily, he felt obliged to make sure that we were not abandoned to walk the streets of Spa during the night. His solution was that we adjourn to the requisitioned school which served as both barracks and office premises for the CI

Corps team and a provost company. Accommodating Thorn and me was no problem – we could put our bed-rolls down anywhere – but Kinneally was in something of a sweat wondering what to do about Danny. We were unsure whether he wanted to protect Danny from his licentious soldiery or vice versa.

The requisitioned school sat in its own grounds about a mile and a half the other side of Spa. Kinneally led the way in his jeep, with me keeping him company. Thorn and Danny followed behind in ours. Every yard we travelled away from headquarters brought about visible relaxation in the big lieutenant.

'You gotta understand that outfits like mine don't rate a goddamn back there,' he told me. He explained that the presence of the small Counter-Intelligence Corps staff at First Army HQ was only barely tolerated. They were there on sufferance.

The Army Commander, General Hodges, and his G–2 chief – a Colonel Benjamin A. Dickson, with the nick-name 'Monk' nursed a profound dislike of cloak-and-dagger operators. There had been an OSS detachment at First Army HQ in Normandy but the brass had kicked them out 'because of undue demands placed on the Army's communications system'.

'That's the official reason,' Kinneally told me, 'but there were others that nobody talks about if they know what's good for them.'

He told me that a wag in his own outfit had written a spoof report that had soured relations in a big way. The report – purporting to be the results of interrogating a German prisoner who had been Hitler's personal lavatory attendant – had found its way to Army Group HQ, where nobody had seen the joke. It had been taken seriously. First Army had been ordered to fly the non-existent prisoner back to SHAEF immediately for more interrogation. There had been many red faces at First Army Headquarters.

The G–3 staff at First Army had taken advantage of

the incident to strengthen their power base at Headquarters.

'They run the show,' Kinneally declared. 'And they don't give a goddamn for anybody else. They go their own sweet way. That colonel who gave Captain Thorn a bad time back at Headquarters was one of them.'

Kinneally did not have a very high opinion of G–3, the staff elite who planned operations. The G–3 at Spa tended to look down their noses at the military intelligence section, G–2, accepting their estimates and advice only when it happened to coincide with their own preconceptions of a given situation. And the G–3 positively abhorred the more clandestine wings of the intelligence service, with a distaste that Kinneally thought was all too typical of certain military staff officers: the kind who treated the deployment of fighting divisions as ego-trips whereby they might exercise their Napoleonic propensities.

The unhappy state of affairs at Spa was aggravated by a G–2 section which had a track record that was far from lustrous and which possessed an unconcealed contempt, not only for the G–3 planners but for all other branches of the intelligence apparatus.

When he learned that I had been engaged on black propaganda work in Paris, Kinneally warned me not to reveal my PWD connections to anyone at First Army HQ – especially the G–2 section. Black propagandists were anathema to the intelligence section because of a recent gaffe.

The G–2 boys had become very excited over a radio intercept. Believing that they had hooked in to a station inside Germany, they had trumpeted the sensational 'news' that Germany was caving in; Rundstedt, the enemy commander, had started disarming the SS; and Rundstedt wanted to talk peace with the Allies. There had been much chagrin at First Army HQ when it was discovered that an American black propaganda radio outfit, operating in northern France, had broadcast the misinformation. The broadcast had been designed to spread alarm and confusion and it had – but not in the German rear, where it had been aimed.

In the days when Spa had been a playground for the idle rich, the school where Kinneally was quartered had been a finishing establishment for the daughters of wealthy Europeans: seldom housing more than thirty pupils. It had been run by nuns, and the ascetic nature of their order seemed to be stamped into the stonework of the edifice, which was as stark and severe inside as it was outside. It must have turned out spartan young ladies.

The cell-like accommodation and the dressed-stone interiors of the larger rooms in the main building had been converted, without effort or imagination, to the uses now required of them by the military police in occupation. The Counter-Intelligence Corps occupied a small and more modern annexe. Only one part of the annexe was not in use: a small science laboratory and ancillary store.

'It's the best I can do as a guest-room,' Kinneally said, and blushed. 'You'll have to sort out the sleeping arrangements yourself.'

'It's better than camping out,' Thorn told him. 'You can sleep in the store-room, Danny. OK?'

Danny had a look in the store-room and was clearly unimpressed.

'OK,' she said, keeping any misgivings to herself. We had soared high in her estimation by stopping at the PX in Spa to buy her some lip-stick, face powder, scent, a couple of bars of Lux toilet soap, and a carton of Lucky Strike. She was not going to rock the boat now by holding out for five-star accommodation.

Her 'room' had a tiny window, a sink with running water, a gas burner that worked, and Kinneally even installed a camp bed for her. He also found a kerosene heater which I managed to get going and which warmed up the meagre space in no time. We were so solicitous about her comfort that she reacted in the last way we expected. She tried to tell us that she was grateful but was overcome by emotion in the process and burst into tears.

I tried to console her and staunch the flood whereupon she flung her arms around my neck and clung like a fretting child, weeping copiously. Thorn just stood there and grinned, enjoying my discomfiture. I could have crowned him.

'She's scared half out of her mind,' I told Thorn, with defensive anger. 'How would you like it if you'd been through what she had and got suddenly shanghaied to this damned place?'

Thorn went on grinning and Danny stopped snivelling long enough to stare up at me through tear-filled eyes, with adoration shining there. She seemed to think that I was some kind of white knight.

'Come on, soldier,' I coaxed her. 'Dry those pretty eyes of yours and show that American simian over there what a touch of lipstick will do for French morale, eh?'

The reminder of the recently acquired cosmetics seemed to do the trick. She allowed me to disentangle her arms from my neck, but not before she had reached up and kissed me lightly on the mouth. Then she ran off to her store-room boudoir.

'It's just her way of saying thanks,' I snarled at Thorn, whose face beamed with joy.

'I didn't say a word,' he absolved himself. I glared at him.

'Goddamned Yankee son-of-a-bitch!'

'Through and through and all the way down to my cotton socks,' he agreed, with what I thought to be an uncommon degree of delight.

We dined picnic style on the laboratory bench, while our jug of coffee brewed nicely on the Bunsen burner on the bench top. The repast was not elaborate – Spam and dehydrated potatoes, followed by tinned peaches –

but it was satisfying. Danny had rejoined us, having applied lipstick and powder over-generously to her face. We congratulated her uncritically on her appearance, aware of her sensitivity concerning her scars, and she rewarded us by exhibiting absurd happiness at our compliments – accepting them as sincere rather than tactful. Indeed, she had softened, if not obliterated, the livid marks, and her joy in combating those affronts to her femininity was touching. She had a candour that some might have found shocking but it was allied to an impish humour that was totally refreshing. She was good company and even Thorn responded in a way that showed he was enjoying himself as much as I certainly was.

Kinneally – who had returned to Army HQ and left us to our own devices – had promised to look in about eleven to discuss our plans for the morrow. It was nearer midnight when he showed up, soon after Danny had gone off to bed. He apologised for being late but something had come up at HQ, which he thought might interest us.

From his document case he took a couple of sheets of closely-typed foolscap and passed them to Thorn.

'Take a look at that,' he said. Thorn held the sheets out so that I could read over his shoulder.

'What is it' I asked.

'It's a straight translation of a German divisional order,' Kinneally replied. 'We took it off a Kraut officer who was captured by one of our patrols. They've still got the guy up at our interrogation centre at Herbesthal.'

'The date on this is third October,' Thorn observed.

'That's the date of origin,' Kinneally said. 'The day when the Kraut divisional commander issued it.'

The two-months old order instructed English-speaking personnel to report to Obersturmbannführer Otto Skorzeny, HQ Panzer Brigade 150, at Friedenthal, near Oranienberg, by 1 November 1944. Thorn read aloud for my benefit:

'The Führer has ordered the formation of a special unit for special tasks on the Western Front. Volunteers from the Waffen SS will be accepted who are physically fit, mentally alert, have strong personalities, and are fully trained in hand-to-hand combat.' Thorn turned to look at me, wide-eyed, before continuing: 'A knowledge of English is essential and volunteers must be acquainted with American dialect and technical terms used by the military. Captured American clothing, equipment, weapons and vehicles are to be handed in to equip these volunteers, and divisional quartermasters are ordered to arrange the collection and despatch of such materials by 1 November.'

Thorn stared at me and then Kinneally.

'Where the hell is Oranienberg?' he asked.

'Near Berlin,' Kinneally told him. 'But that doesn't mean a damned thing. Oranienberg, Friedenthal . . . is, or was, only a mustering point – and Skorzeny wanted his volunteers there on 1 November. We're now nearly halfway through December and that means that Skorzeny's had a month to lick his outfit into shape and two weeks to put it in the line anywhere between Holland and Alsace. My bet is that he's waiting to go right at this minute.'

'With what objective in mind?' I enquired.

Kinneally frowned at me over the steel rims of his glasses.

'Knowing Skorzeny and his reputation for the spectacular . . . and remembering that he's mustering a goddamned Panzer brigade the target could be Paris and Eisenhower's headquarters – SHAEF itself!'

Thorn snorted in disbelief. 'Go easy, Joe,' he cautioned.

'OK,' conceded Kinneally. 'Maybe going for SHAEF is too ambitious, even for Skorzeny. But how about another headquarters? Bradley's, say, down in Luxembourg. Or here? How long do you think it would take a Panzer brigade to bust through our line and hit us here in Spa? My guess is that they could be rolling down that road out there inside twelve hours. Especially if they were dressed in GI uniforms and driving captured Shermans!'

We were looking for thirty or so Nazis, who drove ambulances, toted guns and dressed as medics. The possibility of an entire Panzer brigade, chewing gum and charging down on Spa in Shermans opened up a new dimension that made the mind boggle. Thorn's mind was already boggling.

'I wonder if they'll be here before breakfast?' he mused aloud.

SIX

The Sapphire Line Connection

I went to sleep with Panzer brigades on my mind but my dreams, unaccountably, were filled with images of Danny Roussillon. There was a nightmarish quality to my dreaming. Freud might have been able to explain why my sub-conscious should keep casting Danny as a bride in flowing white – with Hibberd as the clergyman and me as the eager groom but I certainly could not. The wedding ceremony kept repeating and ending at precisely the same place: with me removing the veil from Danny's face and recoiling in gibbering terror from the sight. The face was corpse-like, waxen-white, with blind staring eyes from which blood flowed like tears. I woke each time it recurred, shaken and sweating, and vowing never to eat Spam for supper again.

On the final occasion, I awoke with a shout to find that the light had been switched on and someone had entered the room. The stranger – enveloped in a great-coat that reached almost to his ankles and with an American helmet framing his gaunt, sallow face – still had his finger on the light-switch at the doorway. Thorn was half out of his bedroll and in his hand, pointing firmly at the intruder, was his 38 Police Positive.

'Sorry if I startled you guys,' the man at the door apologised.

Thorn did not lower the gun – not until the newcomer had twice earnestly identified himself as Major Ben Goldman and assured Thorn somewhat indignantly that he was the C-I Corps Area Commander. Even then Thorn did not seem totally convinced.

'Lieutenant Kinneally said you were in Herbesthal,' Thorn said.

The Major glared at Thorn down his aquiline nose.

'I was,' he said, and glanced at his watch, 'until an hour ago.'

'What time is it now?' I asked, wondering what was so important that it merited wakening us in the middle of the night.

'It's time you guys were showing a leg. It's getting on for noon.'

Thorn and I exchanged looks of consternation and scrambled from our bedrolls. Goldman watched our frantic activity with amusement before his conscience got the better of him.

'I was kidding, fellas. I didn't mean to panic you.' He chuckled. 'Truth is, it's just gone seven.'

I sank back on my bedroll, pulling on my trousers; and if looks could have killed, Goldman would have dropped dead at my feet. Thorn continued dressing unflustered. He eyed Goldman impassively.

'Is this a social call, Major?' he asked.

'I want to know what you guys are doing in my yard. Forewarned is forearmed as they say. Maybe you don't know it, but you cloak-and-dagger boys ain't too popular at Headquarters. I get a hard enough time without outsiders rockin' the boat for me.'

'We've got a job to do,' Thorn said.

'Sure you do,' Goldman agreed, 'and if I can help, all you got to do is say the word. Only, keep me in the picture. I'm due at headquarters in half an hour and I don't want to be walking into something that I don't know about because nobody told me. That's why I stopped in to see you and get my card marked. That's why I was on the road from Herbesthal at some god-awful hour this morning instead of getting my beauty sleep. All I know about you guys is what Kinneally told

145

me on the phone last night – and that wasn't much. Maybe I dreamed it, but I coulda sworn he said you had a dame with you.'

Thorn briefly enlightened the Major on the nature of our mission to Spa. Thorn may have understated things but Goldman did not seem to attach any earth-shaking importance to our investigation. Indeed, the Major seemed relieved that our enquiries did not indicate to him the likelihood of clashes with eager-beaver staff officers at headquarters. He became relaxed, affable.

'Did Kinneally tell you that Skorzeny's been dredging the SS for English-speaking volunteers and rigging them out in GI uniforms?' he asked us.

Thorn gave a tight little smile. 'He told us. He seemed to think that the yard out there would be full of Panzers before breakfast. That's what made me kinda jumpy when you woke us up like you did, Major. You'll never know how near you came to getting a thirty-eight slug between the eyes.'

Goldman laughed. 'Kinneally's a panic-monger. He should leave the worrying about Skorzeny to G–2.'

Thorn arched his eyebrows. 'Doesn't Skorzeny worry *you*, Major?'

'No more than the next guy.' Goldman shrugged. 'It ain't my job to worry about Skorzeny and his Panzers and come up with fancy theories. That's for G–2. And you know somethin'? I think that maybe they got it right for once.'

'What *do* the G–2 boys make of it, Major?'

'They know Skorzeny's reputation,' Goldman said. 'How he rescued Mussolini outa that mountain prison and all that. He's the Kraut's number-one commando – a soldier, not a subversive. G–2 thinks the Krauts are planning a counter-attack up near the Roer dams and that Skorzeny's outfit could get the job of being the sharp end.'

'Why the American uniforms?' Thorn wanted to know.

'Shock tactics. To take our guys off guard . . . create confusion. There's only one thing bothering me. The Krauts have a nasty habit of not playing their cards the way our G–2 say they're going to. Only one thing I'm sure of . . . The Krauts ain't licked yet. And they sure are building up for something.'

'How do you know that?'

'Because the sons-of bitches have been telling me so for days!' Goldman said in an aggrieved tone. 'I got plenty on my plate without interrogating PW's up at Herbesthal all the time, but you try telling that to the guys at Headquarters. You'd think Ben Goldman was the only German speaker this side of the Rhine. Ben'll get the goods, they say. Ben'll make the bastards talk. But what's the good of making the bastards talk if they ain't gonna believe any of it!'

Thorn was perplexed. 'How come they got you interrogating prisoners?'

'Because I speak their lingo,' Goldman replied bitterly. 'Goddamn it, I should – I was born in Berlin! I'm Jewish – but until I was eight years old I thought I was a Kraut like all the other kids. I'm still Kraut enough to know when another Kraut's telling me the truth or lying through his goddamned teeth!'

'And others aren't?' I prompted.

Goldman favoured me with an unhappy stare.

'All the Kraut prisoners I've been quizzing say that von Rundstedt's going to attack in a big way before Christmas.' He sucked his breath in sharply before adding vehemently: 'And I believe 'em, goddamn it! They don't sell Ben Goldman no moonshine!'

'But G–2 thinks they're feeding you crap?' Thorn commented.

'It's their prerogative,' Goldman said, with a weary shrug. 'Their divine right! The Krauts are too far gone to stage a big offensive, they say. They don't have the men, the fuel, the guns. The trouble is that most of the PWs are deserters – and G–2 says that deserters are

147

trash . . . that they just ain't reliable. Deserters'll say anything that'll make 'em look important to the guys that have captured them. anything to cover up the fact that they're yellow-bellies and have run out on their own buddies . . .'

'What makes you so sure they're telling you the truth?' I asked.

'I've looked into their goddamned eyes,' Goldman said, fixing me with his own diamond-hard stare. 'And me? What do I see? I see a lotta frightened guys . . . guys who have taken a lotta war and just can't take any more. It ain't us that's put the fear of God in 'em. It's their own officers that's scared them. They were terrified of their own officers and what those officers were geein' 'em up for. Once more into the breach and all that crap. That's what these guys couldn't face – the big offensive before Christmas, the big one that's going to push the goddamned Amis back to the Seine . . . Victory or death – that's what this one's about Only they've heard it all before and they don't buy it. The guys I spoke to reckon the Führer will get the victory, if there is one, and they'll get death . . . Every way they look, that's all that's in it for them – death. Death if they attack, a firing squad if they don't. Who wants these options, when going over the hill gets you a PW camp, three square meals a day, and the chance to live to a ripe old age? I've said my piece about it until I'm blue in the face. That's the way it is.'

'A voice crying in the wilderness?' I suggested, with sympathy.

'Not even that,' Goldman declared bitterly. 'I've been told to shut up . . . keep my opinions on deserters to myself . . . not make a case for them. Because our own guys could get the same idea.'

'G–2 must have a pretty low opinion of our guys,' Thorn said.

'G–2 have a pretty low opinion of anything that

walks on two legs,' Goldman said sourly. He changed the subject. 'What do you guys aim to do today?'

Thorn told him that we first wanted to find the house overlooking the lake where Danny had been kept. We also wanted to find a local realtor or estate agent who knew about land or property-registration deals: someone who might throw light on the acquisitions of a Madame Fabienne Lans from Paris. We would also be looking for a woman called Violette Brochant, of whom we had an indifferent photograph but whom Danny could identify for us.

The property expert was no problem, according to Goldman. A lawyer called Theobold Bech was our man. He had an office in Spa and he had been a big help to the First Army's requisitioning officers. Bech could be trusted, too. He was a 'White Army' man: a local Resistance leader who had helped organise the escape of many Allied airmen during the Occupation. Indeed, Bech had helped the Belgian police round up more than a dozen 'collaborators' who were currently in the local gaol, awaiting trial. They might be worth interrogation by Thorn, he suggested. Thorn agreed that they might be.

'Don't this house by the lake have a name?' Goldman asked.

'Not that we know of,' Thorn said. 'But Danny knows how to get to it from Spa. We'll find it.'

'All the houses have names,' Goldman persisted. 'Sounds to me like it's one of them fancy places up on the ridge, the place they call 'Balmoral'. The houses up there all have lake views.'

'We can always ask Danny,' Thorn said. 'Maybe she mentioned the house having a name but it didn't register with me. She described the joint inside and out, but she didn't know the road it was on or anything.'

'Let's ask her,' said Goldman. 'I'd like to meet this dame.' I went over and knocked on the store-room door.

'Danny, are you awake? We've got somebody here wants to ask you something.'

A few moments later, Danny emerged, bleary-eyed. She was wearing an army shirt, which came down to her knees, and nothing else. She stared at us and then retreated into the store-room again, returning with a blanket draped round her shoulders.

'It's cold,' she explained. She had not fetched the blanket on account of modesty. 'What do you want?'

'This is Major Goldman,' Thorn said, and she acknowledged the Major's presence without enthusiasm. 'Danny, did that villa by the lake have a name? The house where the Germans took you and the other girls?'

Danny looked at Thorn blankly. He had spoken to her in English. I translated his question for her.

She thought deeply for a moment and nodded brightly.

Le Bocqueteau.' Yes, that was the name of the house. She repeated it: *'Le Bocqueteau.'*

For a moment, I thought Major Goldman was having a seizure. His jaw sagged open, his eyes widened and then he staggered about as if he was choking. He was choking – with uncontrollable laughter. The reasons for his helpless hilarity eluded the rest of us.

Thorn felt impelled to go to his assistance, steadying him while enquiring what was so funny about the name of a house. It was a moment or two before Goldman could answer coherently, declaiming mirthfully that it was the richest thing he had ever heard.

'Do you know the place?' Thorn asked, with some exasperation. The Major nodded, still trying to control his laughter.

'Know it! Everybody at headquarters knows it!' he roared. 'It's the Army Commander's house! It's where General Hodges lives! Holy God! And it used to be a cat-house!'

Since its heyday in the seventeenth and eighteenth

centuries – when its thermal waters and gambling casino had made it the playground of Europe's aristocracy – Spa had slipped steadily in eminence as an international resort. It had enjoyed a brief notoriety in 1918 when Kaiser Wilhelm had established the German High Command there and constructed a huge concrete shelter at the Neubois château.

'Everybody who was anybody has stayed here at one time or another,' Joe Kinneally informed us as we drove through the town in his jeep. Goldman had assigned Kinneally to us as a guide and chauffeur and he was taking the job seriously, although Thorn and Danny – riding in the back – did not seem to be taking much interest.

'The place sure has a history,' the big American went on enthusiastically. 'Did you know that Peter the Great stayed here? And one of your English kings, too – King Charles . . . I think it was the Second. And there was the great Swedish queen . . . Christina . . .'

'Now, they'll put up a plaque to say Joe Kinneally slept here,' I suggested mischievously. He grinned at me good-naturedly.

'For the General, maybe. Not me.'

'It's a pretty obvious place for a general to make his headquarters,' I said, with a touch of cynicism. 'If it's good enough for half the crowned heads of Europe, it should be good enough for a general. They like their creature comforts, don't they?'

'Oh, Hodges is OK,' Kinneally assured me, detecting a side-swipe at the First Army's commander. 'He had his share of the trenches in the last war. No point in holing up in a barn if you don't have to. Besides, he ain't the first American general to stop off in Spa.'

He was going to enlighten me anyway, so I waited for him to tell me.

'Black Jack Pershing came here back in 1918,' he said, enjoying airing the knowledge. 'I reckon he wanted to mosey around the Kaiser's bunker.' Kinneally cocked

151

an eye at me. 'Do I get the impression, John, that you don't like generals?'

'Don't pay any attention to me, Joe,' I warned him. 'I'm just as suspicious as hell of anybody who sits in authority and tells everybody else to do this and do that and do the next thing.'

'Somebody's got to give the orders.'

'That's what Hitler said when they burned down the Reichstag. Look what happened.'

Kinneally laughed. 'You're a funny son-of-a-bitch,' he said, and made it sound like a compliment.

'Flattery will get you nowhere,' I told him.

We left the comparatively busy Rue Royale for a quiet tree-lined street where Kinneally halted the jeep in front of an unpretentious two-storey block of offices. At the side of an arched entry, a brass shingle announced the chambers of Messrs Servais, Lemmonier and Bech, with the legend, *Avoués et Notaires*.

Theobold Bech looked startled when his somewhat deaf and doddery old clerk ushered us, unannounced, into his first-floor office. He seemed unable to take his eyes off Danny, at whom he stared with unconcealed dismay, to the exclusion of Thorn, Kinneally and myself.

Even when Thorn spoke to him, the lawyer seemed reluctant to divert his attention from the girl. No one was more acutely aware of the hostile scrutiny than Danny, who had removed her woollen cap and was clearly disconcerted by the effect of her appearance on Bech. I could see her resentment rise. She tilted her jaw pugnaciously and, returning Bech's stare, invited the lawyer to have a really good look. Lip curling, she asked him if it would help if she took off all her clothes. If not, he could put his pig eyes back in his head.

Bech reeled back indignantly and, assuming an air of outrage, demanded to know why his office had been invaded. What did we mean by bursting in on him with this creature of a collaborator?

Kinneally — to give him his due — met the lawyer's bluster head-on. He told Bech to come down off his high horse and think carefully before throwing around any more wild accusations about collaborators. Just because Mademoiselle Roussillon wore her hair short and didn't like being stared at did not mean she was a collaborator, certainly not the kind of collaborator Bech thought she was. The only kind of collaborating Mademoiselle Roussillon was doing was with the Allied authorities and the object of that collaboration was the identification and arrest of a gang of Nazis, who might or might not be holed up right here in Spa.

Bech was suitably chastened by the Lieutenant's homily and insisted that his willingness to co-operate with the Allied authorities was, as the Lieutenant knew, whole-hearted and without reservation. He regretted if he had jumped to conclusions at the sight of our companion but the Lieutenant must know what scars on the face and a shorn head usually meant. It was the brand of Cain ... et cetera, et cetera. Although he still kept glancing suspiciously at Danny, we finally got around to the business that had brought us to his office. First, there was the question of ownership of the villa called 'Le Bocqueteau', where General Hodges was living.

'The owner has not been in Spa since before the war,' Bech told us. 'He has mining interests in the Belgian Congo. When the Boches came, they requisitioned the house and there were officers living there during most of the Occupation. When the Boches pulled out, the Americans moved in.'

'We're interested in the last months of the Occupation,' I said. 'There was a bunch of girls living there, we believe.'

Bech shook his head, puzzled by the suggestion.

'I do not know of this,' he said. 'The Boches never allowed us civilians near the house, especially after the SS took it over. They took girls there, we know — but they were never local girls. Tarts from Brussels and Paris . . . For the amusement of officers on leave . . . Spa was a leave centre . . . Many wounded were brought here to recuperate, before being sent back to the front.'

'Have you heard of a Madame Fabienne Lans?' Thorn asked.

Again, Bech shook his head. 'I know of no one of that name,' he said.

Thorn produced the tiny passport-style photograph we had of Violette Brochant.

'Do you recognise this young lady?'

Bech studied the photograph. He took such a time that I felt a sudden welling of hope.

'There is something vaguely familiar about the face,' he said, and handed the photograph back with a shrug. 'But it could be anybody. I'm sorry . . . I could say even that there is a likeness to my own sister . . . But it is the photograph . . . It is not good, no?'

Thorn did not quite succeed in concealing his disappointment. He turned to the subject of properties around Spa: properties that might have been acquired by an agent dealing for a Paris client – perhaps over a period of years. This brought another shrug of helplessness from Bech.

He declared that people who speculated in property frequently used agents in order to preserve their anonymity. There had been a slump in the value of land and properties before the war and the war had made things even worse. A number of estates had changed hands very cheaply as a result but he, himself had no knowledge of a purchaser acting for anyone in Paris. Did Thorn have no more to go on than that?

'The Paris client I have in mind was a woman, aged between thirty and forty and possibly quite rich,' Thorn said. 'According to our information, she came to live in Spa – or somewhere in the area – during the summer. July probably. And, according to our information, she's the kind of person who would have been noticed –

bionde, attractive-looking and not averse to the company of Nazis. Her boyfriend was an SS colonel.'

Bech shook his head yet again. He seemed perplexed.

'If I did not know better, I would say that you were talking about a very good friend of mine. But it is unthinkable. Sonya would never . . .'

Thorn did not allow Bech to finish. He reacted like a dog pouncing on a bone.

'Tell us about this friend of yours, Monsieur Bech.'

'Sonya . . . Sonya Zinoniev . . . My friend came here in July. She came to these parts when the old man died – her uncle, that is. She is good-looking . . . middle thirties . . . not short of money. But she did not buy the Zinoniev estates, not as far as I know . . . She inherited them. She was the old man's last surviving relative . . . And she is no friend of the Boches. Never! She was one of us!'

'One of *you*?'

'The Resistance,' Bech said, with a touch of hauteur, clearly proud of belonging to an organisation that stamped him as a patriot. 'She was part of a Paris cell before she came here and her uncle was a key member of our group. When the old man died and she came here to live, she took over his link in the escape line we ran and she operated it very successfully.'

'This escape line,' I chipped in. 'It was for Allied bomber crews who had been shot down?'

'About ninety-nine per cent of the escapers were airmen,' Bech agreed. 'Occasionally, we had escaped prisoners. We were only part of a chain that stretched from Holland to the Pyrenees.'

Thorn changed tack yet again. 'This old man . . . with the Russian name – Zin . . .'

'Zinoniev,' supplied Bech. 'Anton Zinoniev. He was Russian by birth, an aristocrat – although he never used his titles.'

'This Zinoniev,' Thorn went on. 'How did he die?'

Bech shrugged. 'It was an accident. He fell down the

stairs in his home. The result of a heart-attack. It is thought he was overcome by a heart-attack and took a tumble down the stairs before he could take one of the special pills that he always carried. The pills were scattered all over the stairway when his housekeeper found him. His neck was broken.'

'He could have been pushed down the stairs,' Thorn said.

'He was alone in the house,' Bech said. He regarded Thorn sceptically. 'Who would have done such a thing?'

'Somebody who wanted him dead,' Thorn suggested, with a certain logic.

'The only people who might have wanted him dead were the Boches – but even they had no motive. They did not know of his anti-German activities. Besides, they had their chance. They could have shot him. They certainly had no need to go to the trouble of making his death look like an accident.'

'What do you mean they had their chance?' Thorn asked.

'They arrested Anton three weeks before he died. But they got nothing out of him and they let him go after twenty-four hours. He knew they had nothing on him.'

'They must have had their suspicions,' Thorn persisted. 'Why arrest him?'

'It was their way.' Bech replied. 'They did not need suspicions. They used to go round picking people off the streets and grilling them for no reason at all. Random security checks, they called them. And God help you if your papers weren't in order or you didn't have good answers for the questions they asked!'

Thorn was still not satisfied. 'This old man Zinoniev was a key man in your Resistance group and the Germans just let him go after questioning him for twenty-four hours?'

'I have told you so,' Bech said testily. 'And if you want to blame anyone for his death, blame the Boches. He was never the same after his arrest He said they did not hurt him but it must have been a dreadful ordeal for a man of his age. The doctor said that although the Boches did not put a bullet in Anton, they did the next best thing. The stress he suffered almost certainly strained his heart and hastened his end.'

This answer seemed to provide Thorn with food for thought. I took advantage of his silence to question Bech some more about his Resistance group. He said that, in the early days, they had indulged in fairly minor acts of sabotage but, as a result of direction from London, the Resistance networks and their operations had become more sophisticated and rather better organised. Latterly, his group had concentrated on staging Allied escapers north-to-south through their sector of what was known as 'The Sapphire Line'.

Most of the escapers came south from Holland. They would be handed along the line by Dutch groups as far as Maastricht, whence they were smuggled into Belgium to the next Sapphire link. Bech's group would pick the escapers up from a group that operated from Verviers and would pass them on to another group in the Liège area. Because each group only came in contact with its immediate neighbours, no single group knew the precise route of the Sapphire Line – but Bech understood that it extended all the way to Paris and, from there, to southern France.

Thorn emerged from his thoughtful silence to show that he had been listening to all that had been said but still had Zinoniev on his mind. He wanted to know precisely what contribution the émigré Russian had made to Bech's set-up.

'He was vital to it,' Bech said. 'Anton not only provided a safe-house, where the escapers could lie low while they were in our area, he was also responsible for transporting them to Liège and beyond. His sanatorium was perfect cover for . . .'

The mere mention of 'sanatorium' – shades of St Cyr des Bains – was enough to provoke instant and simultaneous interruption from Thorn and myself. The lawyer stopped in mid-sentence as we strained across his desk with the same question bursting from us: 'What sanatorium?'

Bech told us then how Zinoniev had repaid the country that had given him asylum after the Great War. He had converted his forty-room mansion – or part of it – into a sanatorium for Belgian coal-miners suffering from chest diseases, such as silicosis and tuberculosis. 'Sanatorium' was perhaps too grand a name for the establishment; it was more of a holiday home, where sick miners could spend two or three weeks breathing good air. At any rate, the regular coming and going of miners to and from the coalfields of the Borinage had provided a perfect cover for Allied escapers travelling amongst them, even if most of them had usually looked too healthy for the part.

Bech smiled. 'We used to encourage the escapers to cough a lot,' he said. 'If they were stopped and asked for the identity papers we provided for them, nothing discouraged the Boches more than being coughed all over by somebody who was supposed to be tubercular.'

'What happened after the old man's death?' Thorn asked. 'You said his niece took over.'

'It was much more difficult for her. Anton died in March and it was the middle of the summer before Sonya arrived from Paris. By then, the Germans had taken over the big house and were using it as a convalescent home for their own casualties – mainly men who had lost limbs in the Normandy fighting. They let Sonya live in the hunting lodge – it's on the estate and it was there that Anton was living latterly – but it made things ten times more risky. We couldn't pass the escapers off as miners anymore and we couldn't unload more than two or three at a time on Sonya – but she was determined to keep on Anton's work. And she did! Right under the noses of the Boches! She was an inspiration to us all.'

Thorn caught my eye and treated me to a meaningful look.

'I think, John, that you and I had better meet this remarkable lady,' he said. I agreed. I was sure that his suspicious mind and mine were on identical tracks. It was possible that Bech was the Belgian patriot he said he was and innocent of any connivance with the Nazis, but the more he had expounded on the subject of the Zinonievs and 'The Sapphire Line', the stronger had become the whiff of *Schatten Gruppe* in my nostrils.

From the time we had left Paris, Thorn had not concealed from me his belief that Danny was an encumbrance to us. By the time we left Bech's office, I had reluctantly come to the same conclusion. Until we produced someone whom she could identify for us, she was going to be more of a hindrance than a help in our enquiries. We solved the problem by unloading her on to Joe Kinneally.

Neither Kinneally nor Danny was enchanted with the arrangement but our need for room to manoeuvre was – we decided – more important than their feelings on the matter. We collected our jeep and despatched Kinneally and Danny to view General Hodges' villa, so that Danny might confirm that it was the place where she had been installed by the SS. Thereafter, we wanted Kinneally to try to find a small hotel where Thorn, Danny and I could be accommodated. Much as we appreciated his hospitality, we felt the old science laboratory left much to be desired.

Thorn and I headed for the Hotel Britannique, where Major Goldman was less than overjoyed to see us. However, we were able to assure him that we had not tangled with any unfriendly staff officers on the way in. Army Headquarters was awash with the spirit of goodwill – Christmas was less than a fortnight away – and everyone we met was so welcoming that it was almost unnerving. When he realised that no one else

159

resented our presence, Goldman overcame his initial unease and fell over himself to be of help. We made no mention of the fact that a deferential desk sergeant had identified us to the duty officer as 'two staff officers from Supreme Headquarters in Paris' and that we had done nothing to correct that inaccurate description.

Mindful that the First Army had booted out its resident OSS detachment because of the strain it had imposed on the Headquarters communications system, Thorn and I tried not to feel too guilty by the demands we made on it. We had agreed, however, that our interview with Theobold Bech had raised a number of questions to which we wanted quick answers before we called on the mysterious Sonya Zinoniev. Hibberd, in Versailles, was unable to supply all of these answers immediately but he must have lit a few fires under the people who could. In response to our first lengthy communication, the answers started arriving within the hour. They continued to reach us at regular intervals throughout what was left of the morning.

A little after one, Thorn and I were bucketing along in the jeep, heading for the Zinoniev estate. According to Bech, who had given us directions, it was a good twelve miles south-east of Spa and – although it extended to something like a hundred acres – was not the easiest of places to find. Swirling mist enveloped the landscape – as it had done the previous evening – and this made our task no easier.

The Zinoniev mansion had been modestly named 'L'Abri' – The Shelter – and it was not sign-posted. Nor was it visible from the road. Perhaps, as a result of this and the persistent mist, we missed the turn-off. When we realised that we had gone too far, we back-tracked at a crawl until we found a path that looked promising. It had been invisible to us on our former approach, cutting back from our line of travel at an acute angle. Approaching from the opposite direction, the steep track through the forest presented itself more as a fork to the road and we decided to chance it. The path twisted upwards through banks of spruce that all but shut out the light. On higher ground, it looped round through a hundred and eighty degrees so that we were travelling parallel in the opposite direction to our first line of a scent from the road. Suddenly, the track led sharply away from the main road, somewhere below us, and meandered down through high-standing pines, before levelling off and following a less tortuous route. On the flat, the trees were less densely crowded, and weathered stumps dotted the clearings like head-stones in a misty graveyard.

We came at last to the grey mansion building, with its dark-red eaves and buttressed walls. Our first view, through the trees, was of the rear – hidden at its lower level by outhouses that encompassed a yard. The track circled in towards a gaunt gable which shared a broad surround of sparsely-gravelled open ground with the front of the house. Thorn drove slowly past the stark gable and halted the jeep in the middle of the broad forecourt. The house front, with the tall ground-floor windows painted the same dark-red as the eaves, was solid and forbidding in appearance. Aesthetically, it was about as exciting as a Lancashire cotton mill. It had a drab, bleak, neglected air.

Parked close to the front door was a dark-green military ambulance of American make. The bonnet was raised and an overalled figure was bent over the engine. I stared at the ambulance and was aware that my heart-rate had slipped a gear and was positively racing. I had seen an identical ambulance before. On a dark wet night in Paris that I was never likely to forget.

'That ambulance!' I croaked at Thorn. 'It's the same as the one in the Rue du Bourrelier.'

'Maybe we've hit pay dirt,' Thorn murmured. As he spoke, the man in the overalls looked up and saw our jeep sitting fifty yards away across the puddles and pot-holes of the forecourt. The mechanic abandoned his work on the engine and ran into the house with unseemly haste.

'We could be outnumbered, Cal,' I warned. 'Maybe we should go back and get reinforcements.'

Thorn smiled. 'We got no cause to get jumpy, John,' he said softly. 'All we're doing is paying a social call on the lady who owns this barracks. Look . . . Here comes somebody to see what we want. Leave the talking to me.'

A tall figure in an 'Eisenhower' jacket had emerged from the house and was striding towards us.

'Well, goddamn!' Thorn burst out. 'Will you look at that? A medic!' The information did nothing for my jangling nerves. As he neared, I could see that the man wore a major's insignia as well as the red cross tab.

'Hi,' he greeted us. 'You guys lost?'

'We're looking for a lady called Sonya Zinoniev,' Thorn replied. 'We were told she lives hereabouts.'

'She does,' the man said. 'Nearly a couple of miles on through the woods – in the old hunting lodge. This mausoleum belongs to her, too, but it's being taken over by the US Army.'

'I didn't know we had anybody here,' Thorn said.

'Not many people do. We're an advance party and been looking for a base. We reckon this'll be as good a place as any to set up our stall.'

'A hospital?'

'Yeah. We got to get it ready before the Division moves up. Half of it is still in England.'

'What division is that?' Thorn asked.

The man grinned. 'We ain't supposed to say. But since you asked, it's the Seventy-Fifth.'

Thorn grinned back. 'We won't tell the Krauts.'

'What do you want to see the lady about?'

'Headquarters is throwing a Christmas shindig for the local bigwigs. The General is hoping she'll come along. How do we find this hunting lodge?'

The man pointed to a track that led off from the

162

forecourt towards deep woods and told us that, if we followed it, we would come to the lodge eventually. He assured us that it was wide enough to take the jeep but to take care because it was mighty rough in places.

The track through the wood was indeed very rough in places. As we bumped along it, I confessed to Thorn that maybe I had jumped to conclusions about the ambulance. The American major had seemed very genuine to me.

'Me, too,' Thorn said. 'There was just one thing bothered me. If the guys in the house are an advance party for a hospital, how come they had a couple of riflemen up on the roof?'

I stared at him, eyes popping. 'They had what?' I burst out, trying not to shout. 'I didn't see them!'

'I just got a glimpse,' Thorn said. 'There were at least two. I saw one guy duck down behind a chimney breast at one end of the roof. And there was another on that parapet just above the main door. Did you not notice how the guy who was talking to us stood well to one side so that he wasn't in the line of fire. He only had to give the sign and we could have been dead men.'

I confessed that all of this had escaped me and that perhaps it was just as well. I doubted if I would have remained quite so cool as Thorn had done. It sent a shiver through me just to realise that, moments before, a sniper might have had me lined up in his sights.

'If that major was a phoney, do you think he swallowed all that baloney you gave him about why we were calling on the Zinoniev woman?' I asked.

Thorn smiled grimly. 'I sure hope so, John. If he didn't, we might find it tricky getting out of these goddamned woods.'

That gave me plenty to think about as we followed the holed and muddy track ever deeper into the forest. The lodge, when we reached it, came as a surprise. I had expected something not much grander than a log cabin. It turned out to be a barn of a place, looking out over a small lake. The exterior was a combination of rounded logs and weather-boarding with verandahs all the way round at the first and second-floor levels of the main central building. Single-storey wings extended out from the central structure in what I can only describe as ranch-house style. Some distance away, through the trees beside the lake, we could see outbuildings of the same timbered character, which were possibly stables or staff quarters.

We parked the jeep and were making for the front verandah steps when a figure came up through the trees from the lakeside. The figure was worth a second look. It belonged to a woman who might have stepped from the pages of *Country Life*. She wore breeches that emphasised her slim hips and knee-boots that fitted snugly against the calves of her long shapely legs. Her woollen sweater was tucked in at the waist-band of her breeches, causing her ample breasts to thrust against the fabric. At her neck, she wore a yellow kerchief, knotted at the collar of her open lumberjack shirt. Her hair was blonde and swept up to complete a sleek, elegant appearance. I would have put her age at about twenty-eight but for a darkness and slightly lined quality in the flesh below her eyes – and the eyes themselves. There was a maturity in those eyes that suggested they had seen more life than could be gauged by observation of the youthful complexion alone.

'I have been expecting you,' she greeted us in accented English. 'Theo said you would come. Shall we go inside? Perhaps you will take a glass of wine?'

Whether she took in the astonished expressions on our faces, I do not know – but she did not wait for an answer. She swept past us and led the way into the house. We followed her into a spacious room that reminded me of the reception area of an olde-worlde country inn. Boars' heads adorned the walls, a log-fire blazed in the centre of a cavernous stone hearth, and

164

the dark wooden furnishings and various skin rugs had the durable simplicity of another age.

'Theo?' queried Thorn.

'Theo Bech,' she said, and I saw anger register briefly on Thorn's face. 'He said you were asking all sorts of questions about me. He had some absurd story about you looking for Nazis in Spa.' She smiled disarmingly at Thorn. 'I was absolutely fascinated.'

'I thought our conversation with Monsieur Bech was confidential,' Thorn said. 'It seems I made a mistake.'

She looked up from the task of filling three glasses with wine from a bottle and emitted a tinkling little laugh.

'You made a mistake if you believed that Theo would keep from me anything that he felt concerned my welfare.' She stared at Thorn, eyes wide and questioning. 'Didn't he tell you that he hopes to marry me?'

'No,' Thorn said, 'he didn't tell us.'

Her eyes were bright with amusement as she handed us each a glass of wine.

'How like Theo!' she said, and again gave that tinkling little laugh. 'He has asked me three times to marry him and he is too proud to admit that I'm being serious when I say no. He finds it difficult to accept that much as I like him, I haven't the faintest desire to be his wife. I enjoy my freedom far too much. Marriage is a kind of bondage, wouldn't you agree, Captain?'

'Thorn, ma'am,' and he nodded in my direction: 'And this is Captain Abernathy.' She acknowledged my presence with a slight inclination of her head, but her frank coquettish gaze returned to Thorn.

'Well, Captain, do you agree . . .? That marriage is a kind of bondage?'

'I suppose it could be, ma'am,' he said.

'I can assure you that it would be with Theo,' she said emphatically. 'And I have no intention of becoming his plaything. Although I do not believe for a moment that bodily lust for me as a woman has much to do with his devotion. He won't admit it, even to himself, but he is much more attracted to my bank account than he is to me.'

'You are a very attractive woman, ma'am,' Thorn replied gallantly. 'Call me Sonya, please,' she invited, with a purr in her voice, and seemed to be inviting a lot more than first-name familiarity with the treatment she gave Thorn with her dark, seductive eyes.

'It's a nice name,' he murmured, as if he was melting under her sultry come-on. I thought he was really falling for it. But his voice hardened perceptibly as he added: 'It makes a change from Fabienne. Or should I say Madame Fabienne? That's what they called you back in the Rue du Bourrelier, wasn't it?'

She was taken completely off guard and recoiled so sharply that half the wine in her glass sloshed over the rim on to the floor at her feet. But she recovered quickly, drawing herself up haughtily.

'I am Sonya Zinoniev,' she declared.

'And you're looking remarkably good,' Thorn agreed, with a smile that was all icy sweetness. 'I sure hope I look as healthy as you after I've been dead for six months.'

SEVEN

Such a Good-Looking Corpse

In the moments after Thorn had made his startling statement, the only sound in that spacious olde-worlde room was the ticking of a wall-mounted grandmother clock. The woman who called herself Sonya Zinoniev was not the only person stunned by the American's blank observation that she looked remarkably healthy for a six-month-old corpse. I was more than a little staggered myself. Thorn had given me no advance warning of this bombshell approach.

Both he and the woman seemed to have forgotten my existence, but I was quite happy to take a back seat and watch the eyeball-to-eyeball confrontation. It was like spectating at a high-stakes poker duel between two seasoned professionals. I was glad not to be in the woman's shoes because Thorn – with deceptive mildness – had seized a psychological advantage and looked like he meant to keep it. I realised I was watching a formidable player in action. He certainly had nerve.

Thorn's calm suggestion to the woman that she was really Fabienne Lans had been his testing shot, to gauge reaction. The woman had shown shock, outrage the expected things but she had shown more. For an instant, she had shown stark *fear*. I had seen it. Thorn certainly saw it. And it provided all the encouragement he needed to stake everything on his instinctive judgement. Having been convinced that the woman had lied once – with her declaration that she was Sonya Zinoniev he invited her to lie again or explain a miracle. How could she

167

be Sonya Zinoniev when he, Thorn, *knew* that Sonya Zinoniev was dead and had been dead for six months?

Thorn waited for an answer with the confidence of a man who held all the aces and also knew in detail the pitiful weakness of his opponent's cards. Only I knew differently. I knew he had no aces.

For a man who had done a lot of preaching to me on the value, in police work, of supportable fact as opposed to theories, Thorn was showing a startling disregard for the shortage of facts in his armoury. Yet, there he stood, giving the impression of omniscience: a man whose authority sprang from the veritable arsenal of incontrovertible facts at his finger-tips.

Hibberd and his OSS contacts in Paris had furnished us with much interesting information about Sonya Zinoniev, the 'Sapphire Line', and the Resistance Group in Paris with which Sonya Zinoniev had been active – but they had not said that the lady was dead. Our information was *that she had not been seen in Paris for more than eight months and that her present where-abouts were unknown*. We had been advised that it might take some time to trace her because most of her friends in the Resistance had been rounded up and shot by the Germans after the Group had been penetrated and, eventually, forced to scatter. Hibberd had been unable to say, one way or the other, whether Sonya had made good her escape or if she had suffered the same fate as most of her comrades. If she had been executed by the Germans, the fact had gone unrecorded.

Ignorance of what had actually happened to Sonya Zinoniev did not inhibit Thorn, however. He brushed aside the blonde woman's indignant protests that his accusations were absurd and meaningless.

'Tell us about your second coming, ma'am,' he invited her. 'Medical science would sure be interested in the details. Me, too!'

'What you are saying is preposterous!' she retorted fiercely. 'What do you want of me?'

168

'The truth would help,' Thorn said, with the air of a reasonable man. 'Tell us why you're passing yourself off as somebody we know you're not. Or why that big house back through the woods is full of guys who're dressed up like genuine American GIs when they sure as hell ain't!'

Again, fear showed in her eyes as Thorn spoke, but she tried to cover it with haughty indignation.

'What authority have you to bully me in my own home like this?' she demanded imperiously. 'Are you police? Are you arresting me?'

Thorn patted the .38 at his hip. 'This is my authority, ma'am – the only one you need worry about. As for your second question, the answer is yes. We're taking you into Spa.'

'This is monstrous!' she protested.

'Sure it is,' Thorn agreed. He glanced across at me. 'John, this place seems empty, but make sure, will you? Have a good scout around. And watch how you go.'

I climbed the broad open stair to the first floor, waiting until I was out of sight before drawing my Colt .45. It seemed a reasonable precaution. Only two upstairs rooms showed any sign of occupation.

One of them was clearly Madame's bedroom. A suit-case containing female garments lay open on the big double bed. Two coats – one an expensive fur – lay on the bed beside the partly packed case. A large leather handbag had been thrown on top of the fur coat. I opened it. The contents took my breath away. If the bag had been mine, I would not have left it lying around. An inside pocket that opened with a clasp was crammed with paper money: Belgian currency, French francs, and US Military Authority dollars. It added up to a small fortune. Equally interesting was the tiny handgun nestling at the bottom of the bag. It was of Spanish make: a .25-calibre Astra Firecat automatic.

I took the dinky little weapon out and examined it. It was loaded. Somewhere, sometime, I had read about

169

an Astra Firecat automatic. Such a gun had figured in the Chisholm case – the first encounter with *Schatten Gruppe* – but the precise circumstances of that occasion eluded my memory. I removed the bullets and slipped them and the gun into my pocket.

Taking the leather bag with me, I continued my search. The other bedroom that showed signs of occupation was smaller and more sparsely furnished than the first. It, too, was obviously a woman's room. But whose, and where was she? My guess was that the absent occupant was not far away. A packed suitcase – it had been locked – stood ready at the door. A fur coat and matching hat had been laid out on the bed.

The rear stairway took me down to a roomy kitchen, which had a tidied look. The fire in the wood-burning stove had been lit earlier in the day but it was now almost dead. Only a coffee-pot showed signs of recent use. All the other utensils had been cleaned and stacked away. The big larder could have been Old Mother Hubbard's for all it contained: the end of a loaf some cheese and half a flagon of milk.

I returned to my starting point and briefly reported my findings to Thorn. He turned to the woman, who was sitting stiffly in a wooden armchair, glowering at Thorn as if she would like to cut his throat.

'Planning to leave, were you?' Thorn asked.

'It's Christmas,' she answered tartly. 'I intended to spend it with friends.'

'Where?'

'I have no intention of telling you.'

'Who has the other bedroom upstairs?'

'The girl who works for me. My servant.'

'Where is she?'

'I don't know – and I wouldn't tell you if I did.'

Thorn made a face at me. 'She's not being very co-operative.' He eyed the handbag, which I had laid down on a chair. 'Is that hers?'

'Yes. Interesting contents. There's a small fortune in

170

notes inside. And there was a gun, which I've confiscated. Dinky little thing – an Astra Firecat.'

'Surprise, surprise,' Thorn said brightly. 'Those Spanish pea-shooters must be standard equipment for the broads who work for *Schatten Gruppe*. The cutie who put a bullet in my old friend Chizz Chisholm used a Firecat.'

He turned back to the woman and regarded her quizzically: 'You 'pack a gun, eh?'

'I know how to use it, too,' she said. 'And I know who I would like to use it on.' Her glare at Thorn made enlargement on the remark unnecessary.

He smiled. 'Now, now, Fabienne. That sounded awfully like a threat. Don't you realise that we got enough on you to hang you? The only chance you've got is if you tell us things – like why you carry a gun in your bag?'

'For my protection,' she said stiffly. 'I *did* fight for my country with the Resistance . . . I risked my life a hundred times during the Occupation saving *your* airmen! Theo must have told you. . . .'

'Oh, yes,' Thorn agreed, and shook his head sadly. 'Theo told us how you took over for Uncle Anton. Only, he wasn't your Uncle Anton, was he? He was just a poor old guy in the Resistance that your Nazi friends got wise to. Pity they had to bump the old guy off so that you could hot-foot it up here from Paris and get in on the act. It must have been a real wrench for you leaving that whore-house in Paris, Fabienne – but that was just a side-line anyway, wasn't it? A front for your real work. For the Reich, I mean. How long were you in partnership with Doctor Keitler, Fabienne? Does it go way back? Does it go back to another name? The one you had before you were Fabienne?'

Thorn was way ahead of me. For a man who didn't hold with theorising, he was either reasoning intuitively from his familiarity with how *Schatten Gruppe* operated or he was guessing wildly. One look at the woman, however, was enough to tell me that, if Thorn was guessing, his arrows in the air were hitting bulls'-eyes every time. She was staring at him, positively ashen-faced with fear. Thorn did not relent.

'You say you fought for your country, Fabienne . . . But what country? And as for all those airmen you rescued . . . Strange, wasn't it, how none of them ever got beyond Paris? That was where the Gestapo always picked them up . . . until, that is, the Gestapo had to get out of Paris themselves. Strange, wasn't it?'

She made no answer. 'Are you not going to tell us why Paris was always the end of the line for our guys that you sent there, Fabienne?' Thorn prompted and, still getting no answer, prodded some more. 'I'm talking about the Sapphire Line, Fabienne. You must have known all about the Sapphire Line, because you were part of it. Your Nazi friends knew all about it, too, of course. That's why Paris became the terminus – the end of the line. How long were your German chums working the line to suit their own tricky little ends, Fabienne? They could have pulled up the tracks any time it suited them, couldn't they? They could have taken Theo, the guys in Verviers and Liége – the lot! But they just let these poor saps keep going like clock-work as if nothing was wrong. Why Fabienne? Why?'

'I am telling you nothing,' she said, her voice almost inaudible. And, much as she tried to hide it, she was trembling with fear.

'You'll talk,' Thorn said. 'Believe me, you'll talk.' He glanced across at me. 'Maybe this ain't the best place. Maybe the ride into Spa will loosen her tongue. Besides, we got somebody there who knows her.'

Thorn's final remark drew another terrified glance from the woman in the chair. The elegant assured woman who had invited us to drink her wine seemed no longer to exist. Her place had been taken by a haggard stranger, whose eyes were bleak with the despair of hopelessness.

We delayed only long enough to collect the dispirited woman's case and fur coat from her bedroom. Thorn bundled woman and case into the back of the jeep and climbed in after her. Producing a pair of handcuffs, he snapped one bracelet on to her wrist. He fastened the other to his own.

'You drive, John,' he ordered. 'I'm not taking any chances on this baby walking out on me.'

I started the engine and was reversing in a half-circle when, with some consternation, I saw a small saloon car come bumping towards us down the track from the big house. It braked to a halt fifty yards away on open ground. A girl got out, followed by the driver. The man wore a leather flying jacket, a woollen cap and khaki-green trousers. The pair were halfway towards us when the woman behind me suddenly screamed something in German. The warning was cut short as Thorn, without ceremony, uppercut his prisoner and knocked her cold – but the damage was done. The approaching pair stopped dead in their tracks.

With a sudden cry to her companion, the girl turned and bolted back towards the woods. The man reached inside his jacket and produced a dark object, which – when he levelled it at the jeep – left me in no doubt as to what it was. The pistol shot and the crack of a bullet drilling a hole in the windscreen were almost simultaneous.

How the shot missed me I do not know but the fright galvanised me into action. I ducked and rolled out of the jeep in one movement, tugging frantically for my heavy Colt as I tumbled. I would have won no prizes at the Wyatt Earp school of fast-draw. Another bullet shattered through the windscreen. A third screamed off metal and ricocheted God knows where.

When I finally got my own gun out, I wondered briefly if I would be able to get my hand to stop shaking long enough to fire the damned thing, but a seething fury pushed doubt to the back of my mind. The realisation that flying jacket was actually intent on killing me filled me with blazing anger. I was almost beside myself with rage. Using the jeep as cover, I edged round the front wheel on my belly. Flying jacket was backing slowly towards his car and peering towards the jeep, as if waiting for a target to appear. Still on my belly and using my elbows to steady my aim, I fired.

Flying jacket jerked round as if an unseen angler with an invisible rod had hooked him by the shoulder and pulled violently. He went spinning four or five paces like a drunk before losing his balance and falling heavily in mud. He hit the puddled ground with a splash and then dragged himself up on to one knee. He had dropped his gun and the side of his face and the collar of his jacket were dark brown with adhering mud. He tried to crawl towards his car but kept collapsing, emitting great bubbling gasps of sound.

'Leave him!' a voice screamed at me from the jeep. 'We'll come back for him and his pals later.' Thorn had raised his head to see what was happening and the sound of his voice was sweet music to my ears. Until that moment, I had feared that one of the bullets through the windscreen might have hit him. But both he and our passenger were unhurt.

The young woman who had been with flying jacket was watching us from behind a tree, at a safe distance. She ducked out of sight when she realised I had seen her but she need not have bothered. She, too, could keep until we returned with reinforcements. I climbed back into the driving seat.

'There must be another way out through these woods,' Thorn shouted as I manoeuvred the vehicle over rough ground in front of the lodge. 'Down there, John – by the lake . . . There's another track. Let's try it! The way we came in might be unhealthy.'

He was alternately thumping my shoulder and waving a hand in the direction he wanted me to go. I needed no persuasion. Any road off the estate that avoided the big house was, in my opinion, the prudent one. I jogged the jeep down a grassy bank towards the lakeside. The track I was aiming for was one which seemed to loop from the hunting lodge, via the outbuildings we had seen, and come down to skirt the lake shore. The terrain from the front of the lodge, across the base of the loop, was bumpy and boggy in turn but as soon as our wheels hit the firmer track I was able to accelerate sharply.

We soon left the lake behind and were bucketing along through thick forest that was unknown territory. The track's surface was no better but no worse than the rough trail we had previously travelled between the big house and the hunting lodge. Thorn tried asking our prisoner where it led but she was still dazed and half-stupid from his heavy-fisted anaesthetic. She probably would not have told us anyway.

We must have covered a couple of miles before the path suddenly straightened and the trees began to thin out into pleasant parkland. In the distance, straight ahead, we could see a wooden gate at the track's end.

As we approached, three figures emerged from what looked like a hide, close to the gate. The makeshift shelter had been constructed from branches of firs. The three men wore combat clothing and looked like Americans. Each carried a carbine. I did not like the way they took up a stance across our path.

'Trouble!' I warned Thorn, who was already taking an interest. He was hunched forward, peering over my shoulder through the shot-up windscreen.

'Whatever you do, John, don't stop for them!' he instructed, bellowing in my ear.

'They look American,' I cautioned.

'We're not taking chances. Ram that goddamned gate if you have to but we don't stop for anybody in these woods.'

'You're the boss,' I said.

As we closed on the three men, one of them started waving an arm and indicating we should stop. I did not even slow down. Another of the three started raising his carbine with unmistakable menace. I accelerated.

The man with the raised carbine was the first to realise that a bullet at close range was not going to stop a forty-mile-an-hour jeep from flattening him. He was the first to make a dive for the side of the track. He was only fractionally quicker off the mark than his two comrades.

We must have been doing fifty when we hit the gate. I was bracing myself for the impact but it still came with a shock. Although it all happened in the space of less than a second, I was aware of the gate springing open on one side while the other remained momentarily anchored by stout hinges. The hinges resisted only briefly: just long enough to dictate that the splintering gate was catapulted to that side of the track, on my right. I was wrestling to hold the wheel as we shot through between the gate-posts to find that the continuation of the track went straight downhill for a hundred yards or more. We were careering down this gradient when we came under fire. I heard the crack of carbine shots and, amid the noise of our racketing progress, might not have identified them for what they were but for the whine of a bullet, which zinged off a metal roof-strut somewhere behind me and exited via the windscreen on the passenger side. It splintered the glass and left a hole big enough to accommodate a fist.

The hail of bullets from behind did not terrify me half as much as the steepness of the track and the speed of our descent towards a horrifying bend. All my wits and all my strength were concentrated in regaining control of the quarter-ton monster, with its racing 54-horse engine, which seemed intent on hurling itself to destruction on the trees beyond the bend. Thorn – for a reason that was not immediately apparent to me – was pressing down on my shoulders from behind and making it almost impossible to control the wheel. Only by thrusting back with my shoulders and throwing him off was I able to get steering room and slam down hard on the brakes as we hit the bend. The jeep took the bend sideways, sliding in a slow spin for twenty or thirty yards, before coming to rest facing back up the track. I reversed up a steep bank, and shot forward on course to negotiate a second bend with more circumspection. To my surprise, the second bend opened dramatically to join with a good metal road, which was narrow but spectacularly benign after the forest tracks we had left. I was congratulating myself on our good fortune when I realised that all was far from well with Thorn. The woman, to whom he was handcuffed, was screaming at me hysterically and I was slow to appreciate the reason. Thorn had been hit and was bleeding all over her.

I brought the jeep to a screeching halt.

'Keep going, goddamn you!' Thorn shouted at me, as I turned to inspect the damage. He was slumped back against the seat, grey-faced and wild-eyed, and trying to struggle free of his combat jacket. He was sweating with pain from the effort. His left arm – the wrist handcuffed to his charge – was hanging limp against her and her hands were bloodied where she had come in contact with the scarlet wound below his left shoulder. 'Keep going!' he snarled through gritted teeth. 'Get me to Spa!'

I hesitated, torn by dilemma. My instinct was to ignore what he was ordering me to do and give him the attention he obviously needed.

'Get me to Spa,' he ground out again and, as if to show me that he could cope, he reached out with his free hand and grabbed the kerchief from around the woman's throat. He thrust the kerchief inside his shirt and growled at the astonished woman: 'Give me a hand, damn you!' He turned glazed eyes towards me again. 'For Christ's sake, John, get moving! Do what I goddamned tell you!'

Against my better judgement, I acquiesced. The

sooner I got him expert medical assistance the better. I just hoped he did not bleed to death in the meantime. I put the jeep into motion and tramped down hard on the gas pedal. Below my breath I prayed fervently that the road we were on went somewhere near Spa. I had not the faintest idea where we were in relation to the town.

Thorn had difficulty keeping up his stoic front. Fearful that his prisoner might attempt desperate tricks, he unsheathed his .38 and dropped it on to the passenger seat beside me and told me to put it out of her reach. He was taking no chances. He promptly passed out.

He probably did the wise thing in passing out because, although he was taking no chances, I was. There is no saying what traumas he might have suffered if he had remained awake and seen the way I was driving. It had everything to do with my state of mind. The dread that he would bleed to death before I got him to help induced in me a maniacal urge for speed that was made all the more frantic by my total ignorance of where the road was taking us.

Thorn's precaution of passing me his gun seemed unnecessary as we hurtled sideways round hairpin bends. His manacled companion was totally preoccupied with fear for her life, as she made plain to me with piercing screams and repeated entreaties to slow down. She kept her loudest scream of all for our sudden egress on to a wider road.

This was a veritable highway – broad enough to allow two vehicles to scrape past each other – and the way our road just fused with it took me by surprise. So did the sight that greeted me. Straddled right across our path was an army bulldozer, backing out from a cleared edge of forest.

With the woman behind me hitting high C in terror and the hairs on my head standing on end, I thrust down on the brake with all my weight and waited for the inevitable to happen. The tyres squealed as we slid head-on towards the leviathan and, as the distance narrowed, its huge frame seemed to grow before my eyes until it blotted everything else from view. Wheels locked, the jeep slithered – first right, then left – before hitting the monster full amidships with a resounding crack.

Thorn and the woman finished on the floor and I was pitched over the steering wheel – but the impact of the collision was much more gentle than I had any right to hope. A yard less of braking distance and we should have ended up like corned beef. As it was, I was able to back the jeep off relatively undamaged.

The sound of the crash and the lurid profanities issuing from the driver, sitting high on the 'dozer, brought half a dozen soldiers running from the forest verge where a heavy truck was parked amid stacks of cut timber. The men were American Army engineers engaged in logging operations.

I quickly explained to them that I had a wounded American officer on board and that the woman handcuffed to him was a German agent whom we were taking into Spa. The engineers produced a Corpsman, who was soon expertly applying a field-dressing to Thorn's wound. The others were much more interested in the woman, around whom they clustered, regarding her with great suspicion after I had released her from Thorn and snapped the empty bracelet on her other wrist.

The Corpsman reported that Thorn would live but that we had to get him to hospital fast.

I gladly accepted his offer to ride with us into Spa.

'Think nothing of it,' he said, with a cheerful grin. 'Nothing much ever happens in this goddamned place.' He led me to believe that treating a genuine gunshot wound made an interesting change from the mashed fingers and squashed toes that usually cropped up on logging detail.

The hospital – on the outskirts of Spa – would have been difficult to miss. Its existence was well advertised by numerous direction signs, erected at the roadside. Following a succession of route arrows, we came to a complex of single-storey buildings which had huge red cross symbols adorning the white-painted exterior walls. I was speedily relieved of my casualty.

Thorn was borne away on a stretcher with a swarm of medics and nurses in attendance. My relief that he was in good hands was enormous, but I did not hang around. I had things to do.

I drove straight to Army Headquarters, with my hand-cuffed prisoner sitting stiff-backed and silent in the passenger seat beside me. She had recovered from her earlier hysteria and was now sullen and uncommunicative. In front of the Hotel Britannique, two 'snowdrops' of the Praetorian Guard approached the jeep as I cut the engine. They bore down on me like Sumo wrestlers in search of a grudge match.

'Whaddya want?' one of the white helmeted MPs demanded, with a typical absence of circumlocution. His jaw dropped slackly when I told him. With some uncertainty, they took custody of my still-sullen but docile prisoner. The sergeant in charge of the 'snowdrop' detail was more suspicious of me and my funny limey talk than he was of my prisoner and he was not mollified until Goldman had been summoned and was able to vouch for me.

Goldman did not exactly jump for joy when I unfolded the tale of our adventures. He was positively dismayed when I told him that it was now a matter of priority that we returned to the Zinoniev estate immediately and rounded up the unknown number of Germans who were in occupation there and masquerading as Americans.

'How many of them do you reckon there are?' he wanted to know.

'Your guess is as good as mine,' I told him. 'Maybe

a dozen. Maybe twenty or thirty. They could hide a whole regiment in those woods!'

He groaned like a cow in labour. 'Holy Toledo! Do you think I'm Joshua and all I gotta do is blow a horn and I got an army! Where am I gonna get enough men for a stunt like this? You think maybe my name is Eisenhower and all I gotta do is snap my finger at the General and say I want two companies of riflemen to clear up a little mess we got. 'Cause the way you're talkin', that's what we're gonna need! Hell, a battalion of infantry mightn't be enough!'

'How about the Belgian Army, then?' I suggested. 'From what I hear, they've got plenty of men and they're fed up because all they get to do is guard ammo dumps and the like.'

Goldman's pained look told me what he thought about that suggestion.

'You think life isn't complicated enough without we drag the goddamned Belgians in?' he demanded sourly.

'This is Army Headquarters,' I reminded him. 'If we can't rustle up enough men here, for heaven's sake, where in creation are we going to get them?'

'I didn't say we couldn't do it,' he came back. 'All I'm saying is that it isn't gonna be easy. What with Christmas coming up and one thing and another, it sure as hell ain't gonna make me the most popular guy in this command.'

'My heart bleeds for you,' I said bitterly. 'Captain Thorn's lying with a bullet in his shoulder and all you can do is talk like you're running for President.'

'You watch your tongue, you son-of-a-bitch. I don't have to take that from you. You're not the one who's got to face the General and tell him about this goddamned hornets' nest he's got on his doorstep.'

'I'll tell him!' I promised angrily. 'He doesn't frighten me!'

'Well, just you do that,' Goldman invited. 'Only you'd better hurry, 'cause the last I heard he wasn't feeling so hot and was heading for an early bed. Just you wait right where you are, Captain Abernathy, while I call his office. I'm sure meeting you will make his day!'

General Hodges told me to sit down and say my piece. He volunteered the information that his gut had been giving him hell all day but that if my business with him was as important as I seemed to think, the state of his intestines was of no consequence. He made no mention of it but also seemed to be suffering from a cold. His eyes were rheumy and his soft Georgian voice sounded hoarse.

He listened to all I had to say, interrupting only occasionally to seek clarification on a point of detail. Given the answer, he would nod gravely and tell me to continue. At the end of my recital, he sat contemplatively, considering folded hands with the air of a family physician who has heard the patient's symptoms and must now proffer a diagnosis. He looked up suddenly.

'Two questions, Captain Abernathy,' he said crisply, eyeing me solemnly. 'One – this woman. What can she tell us?'

'A great deal, I suspect, sir. But I don't think she will talk voluntarily. If we get anything from her at all, it's going to have to be dragged out.'

'I see. So, we can forget for the meantime that she'll tell us what the hell's been going on at the country estate?'

'Yes, sir. She'll play for time, I'm sure of it. She's no amateur . . . She's not going to crack easily.'

'Second question,' said the General. 'You said this phoney American medic at the big house claimed his outfit was part of the Seventy-Fifth Division. If these guys are Krauts – and I've only got your say-so that they are – how in hell did they pick on the Seventy-Fifth to use as cover?'

'I've no idea, sir. He said that most of the Division was still in England. Is it important, sir?'

182

'It's goddamned strange!' the General said softly, but with feeling. 'They either know a hell of a lot that they shouldn't or they're clairvoyant! You may not know it, Captain, but for the last week we've been trying to convince von Rundstedt that the Seventy-Fifth Division is moving into the line up near the Luxembourg border.'

My face must have shown my puzzlement.

'The Seventy-Fifth doesn't exist as a fighting division, yet,' he explained, as if I were extremely dense. 'It's nowhere near ready for line duty. Like your phoney medic said, half the Division is still in England and the other half is in transit. So your phoney is either very well informed or he's goddamned psychic!'

I was obviously very dense. I could not yet see just what it was that the General was driving at. I dared a tentative question.

'Sorry if I seem stupid, sir, but why should you be anxious to convince von Rundstedt that the Seventy-Fifth Division is in the line when it isn't?'

'Because,' said the General, with a hint of impatience, 'we're going to attack near the Roer dams. Not in Luxembourg! All we got going in Luxembourg is a rubber-duck operation.'

'A rubber-duck operation, sir?'

He smiled at me. 'Haven't you ever gone duck-hunting, Captain?' he asked.

'No, sir.'

'It happens to be one of my favourite sports,' he revealed. 'If you knew anything about duck-hunting, you'd know it sometimes fools the ducks if you sit a rubber duck down in the water among the reeds and make noises like it was a real duck.'

'A decoy, sir?'

'Precisely. That's why we got a detachment of Special Troops with sonic gear and inflatable tanks up on the border. They've been making noises like we had the whole Seventy-Fifth Division up there . . .' He broke off and arched his eyebrows at me. 'Is something bothering you, Captain?'

'Yes, sir,' I confessed. 'I appreciate that you've got this deceptive operation going, up in Luxembourg . . . and I can see why. You want to make the enemy think you're going to attack in one place, while you attack in another . . . But, sir, what I am wondering is who is fooling who?'

Even as I spoke, the General was nodding his head fiercely in agreement. He stood up.

'That,' he declared, 'is what bothers the hell out of me!' He bunched his lips, bristling the thin grey moustache on his upper lip. He ran a finger along the line of the moustache, thoughtful, once more doctor-like in demeanour: his expression severe, the diagnosis formed in his mind. Now, the treatment had to be pronounced. He glanced at his watch.

'Six hours!' he enunciated. 'I want a hundred men in position and ready in six hours! We move in on that house in the woods at midnight. And then, by God, I want to know who's been fooling who!'

The group to which I attached myself was ahead of schedule. With midnight still fifteen minutes away, Three Platoon had disembarked from their trucks and were assembling in sections on the steep track that led off the main road to the Zinoniev estate. It was biting cold and I shivered as I hung about, waiting, anxious to be on the move. The commander of Company K – a slow-spoken major from Athens, Georgia was giving a last-minute pep talk to the young officer in charge of Three Platoon, a Lieutenant Platt. This tête-à-tête over, Platt hurried up the slope, calling for his sergeant. The Major strolled over to join me.

'I'm making my CP in the radio truck,' he said. 'I'll take it up the hill a piece as soon as you guys have moved. You're set on going with the Lieutenant?'

184

'Yes,' I said. 'I know the way. And it's better than freezing to death here.'

'I got no choice,' he replied, teeth gleaming in the dark. 'My orders are to stay close to the road until we get some kind of picture. We're ahead of time. One and Two Platoons have still to report in.'

We had found that there were three routes in to the mansion: the way in and the way out that Thorn and I had taken earlier, and another, an old logging trail. Ironically, the best map of the neighbourhood to be found at headquarters had been a 1934 Belgian publication put out for campers.

Three Platoon was to approach the mansion on foot along the inward path that Thorn and I had taken with the jeep. One Platoon was to approach along our former exit route from the estate. Two Platoon had drawn the old logging trail.

'Ten minutes,' said the Major, and marched off to the radio truck, which was parked at the foot of the track, near the road. I was chatting inconsequentially with Lieutenant Platt when, a few minutes later, he returned.

'Number One Platoon's in position,' he announced. 'They found that gate you busted off its hinges and they checked out the guard post you said was there. It was empty. Nobody there.'

'Any word from Two Platoon?' Lieutenant Platt asked. Like me, he disliked the waiting and he was impatient to be on the move.

'One of their trucks got bogged down,' the Major told him. 'But they're on their start point and waiting for me to give them the word. You can move out anytime you like, Lieutenant. Keep your radio man close beside you. I want to know what you find up there.'

'Yes, sir,' Platt said brightly. He tapped me on the arm. 'Let's go, pilgrim!'

Three Platoon moved out in three sections, a short distance apart: walking in single file, with weapons at the ready. The Lieutenant, his radio man and I tagged on to the first squad.

'No more talking,' the Lieutenant ordered, as we moved up the steep track. It was unnecessary advice as far as I was concerned. I needed all my breath for the punishing climb. I was sweating by the time we completed the twisting ascent from the road.

The forest was eerily still, with mist wisping in the trees. Patches of days-old snow, that had survived from the first fall of winter, quilted the ground here and there, but the track was muddy and soft under our feet; deadening our footsteps. In places, the darkness was intense, making it easy to blunder off the path; but in others a ribbon of starry sky overhead shed a channel of light along our way.

The tall silent men with whom I marched were a comforting presence, providing me with a courage that I might not otherwise have felt. They had complained a lot at being plucked at short notice from their comfortable billets in Chaudfontaine, where they had been enjoying a few days rest out of the line, but the grumbling had been of short duration. The cheerful resignation that seems to go with the rifleman's lot had taken over. I admired the philosophical way they quickly accepted that this rather strange emergency operation had to be done and that, because they had been available, it had fallen to them. The philosophy seemed to stem from the fact of life that every infantryman knew to be true: that whenever there's dirty and dangerous work to be done, the foot soldier will get the job ahead of all other candidates. These men belonged to the division known as the Big Red One and perhaps a third of them had fought and marched with the Division through Tunisia, Sicily, Normandy and across France to these Belgian forests on the border of Germany. They took pride, if no comfort, from the fact that they were the Army's most vital commodity and – perversely and paradoxically – its most expendable.

186

With Thorn in the jeep, the distance between the road and the Zinoniev mansion had seemed short. On foot, through the darkness, the journey seemed interminable. The luminous hands on my watch showed almost one o'clock when, ahead, the great inky shadow that was the big house loomed across our path.

Lieutenant Platt halted our section and detached two men to scout ahead and report back. They were gone no more than five or ten minutes, returning to say that the mansion was entirely in darkness and that there was neither sight nor sound of human life. It looked to me that General Hodges' prediction was about to be proven true. He had gloomily forecast that, alerted by Thorn's and my activities, the Germans would have cleared out. He had, nevertheless, insisted that – because the size of the German intrusion could not be calculated – our probing force had to be big enough to take care of itself. Mounting that force had, of course, meant using up valuable hours and giving the enemy time to disperse, but to forestall that eventuality a number of road-blocks had been immediately set up at strategic locations. No one had been optimistic, however, about the Germans taking to the roads. In the forests, they could evade detection and capture indefinitely.

Lieutenant Platt deployed his platoon into cover to the rear and on one side of the mansion. His radio operator, meantime, raised the Command Post. The other platoons were not yet in position, facing the far side of the mansion and its front, and Platt was instructed to hold and wait. It was close to one-thirty when all three units were in place. The soldier with the radio set called softly to Platt that the CP wanted to speak to him. The Lieutenant was crouched beside me, surveying the dark gable of the house. He disappeared momentarily from my side and I heard his low-voiced conversation with the CP and the other platoon leaders.

When he returned, he said: 'The Major wanted us to

blast a few rounds into the house to see if anybody was awake. I talked him out of it.'

'What are you going to do?' I whispered.

'Get inside and see if the goddamned place is as deserted as it looks. There's no point in shooting up an empty house. Do you know where the main door is?'

'Yes,' I told him. 'Just forty, fifty yards beyond the end of that gable.'

'Like to show me where it is?'

'You mean, take you there?'

'How else you gonna show me?'

I was going to say I would have drawn a little map but I think he might have got the impression I was dragging my feet.

'Follow me,' I said.

He detailed two men to keep us company. With them at our heels, we left the cover of the trees and splashed across the puddled open ground towards the mansion. Hugging the gable, we made our way round its end to the front of the house. Nothing stirred along its length. The main door was on a portico that jutted out nine or ten feet from the line of the building. I led the way towards it.

The portico was stepped above ground-level within a semi-circle of paved steps. Platt tried the handle of the heavy door. Predictably, it was locked.

'I don't think there's anybody at home,' I said. 'We'll soon find out,' Platt said. He turned to one of the soldiers. 'You got a grenade?' he asked.

The man produced a grenade from a pouch on his belt and handed it to Platt. The Lieutenant palmed it and told us to get the hell out of it and hit the deck. We scuttled to a safe distance, staying close to the front of the building, and watched while he broke a panel window in the side of the portico. I heard the grenade rolling around on the stone floor of the portico and, seconds later, Platt was throwing himself on the ground beside me. There was a roar of sound and the heavy

188

door was blasted twenty yards across the forecourt. The sides of the portico blew out, showering us with masonry and broken glass.

We waited. I was deafened, ears buzzing. Nothing happened. No sound came from within the house. I was unsure if I had gone permanently deaf or if there was nothing to be heard. Then Platt spoke.

'Let's take a look,' he said.

We clambered through the ruins of the portico into a high-ceilinged reception area with two broad stairs leading up to a gallery and several doors leading off. We only glimpsed some of this in the light of a hand-lamp that Platt had unhooked from his belt and was flashing around. Clouds of dust from the explosion were swirling everywhere, looking for a place to settle. It got up our noses, in our mouths. I choked on the stuff coughing uncontrollably. The more I coughed, the more dust I seemed to gulp into my lungs and the more I tried to keep my mouth closed, the more I choked. I could not breathe.

Platt was not much better. He guided me back out into the fresh air, where I sat on the front steps, convinced that I was going to expire. I was coated in the wretched dust and declined when Platt asked me if I wanted to give the house another try.

'Give me a couple of minutes,' I said. I could scarcely speak and was convinced my pulmonary system was damaged beyond repair. I could only marvel at Platt's powers of recovery.

'Take your time,' he advised sympathetically. 'I'll have a mosey round inside and when you feel up to it, maybe you'll whistle up the rest of the section to check the place out good. I got the feeling we ain't going to find a goddamned thing.'

I was inclined to agree with the Lieutenant and, to my everlasting regret, I made no attempt to dissuade him from his intentions. He called to the two soldiers and went back inside the house. Still feeling utterly miserable and hawking and spitting like a consumptive, I staggered towards the side of the house where the men of Three Platoon were waiting and probably wondering what on earth was happening.

I located the radio man and the rest of the section. They were agog to know what the bang had been and were relieved to learn that no resistance had been encountered and that a grenade had been needed to unlock the front door.

We were on our way back when one of the men who had accompanied Lieutenant Platt met us at a run. It was me he was looking for.

'The Lieutenant wants you to come quick,' he blurted out breathlessly. 'He's found this dame – naked as the day she was born, she is. She's been hung!'

My blood ran cold. 'Where?' I screamed at the man. 'What is he doing?'

'He's trying to cut her down. In one of the corridors at the top of the stairs . . .' He said more but I was already past him and running. I scrambled through the portico and ran slap-bang into the second soldier who had been with Platt. We both fell in a heap. I disentangled myself cursing him, took the flashlight that I had knocked out of his hands and made for the nearest stairs. I leapt up them, shouting at the top of my voice: calling Platt's name and telling him to wait.

The explosion came as I reached the top of the stairs. An eruption of smoke, dust and superheated air rushed in a wall along a corridor at the top and blew me backwards down the staircase. The world seemed to be collapsing around my ears.

EIGHT

A Taste of Ashes

Consciousness never fully left me. I was aware of tumbling through the air and falling in untidy somersaults to the foot of the stairs. It was like being churned at high speed in the revolving drum of a cement-mixer and then being suddenly ejected, with legs and arms in all directions. My mind took in the whirling violence to which my body was subjected but what was happening to me was beyond the comprehension of the whisked-omelette confusion of my brain.

Later, much later, it was possible to marvel that my neck – and a lot more besides – had not been broken. At the time, I felt that my entire anatomy had shattered. I remember lying there in a well of aches and pains: seeing nothing, hearing a bewildering confusion of meaningless sounds, and powerless to protect myself from the rain of debris that showered all around me. I was engulfed by chunks of powdering plaster, crumbling brickwork and creaking spars. Wreckage rolled slowly over me, flowing down the stair like lava. I was unable to move and the only coherent thought that I could assemble was a hopefully rising suspicion that I might not be dead. It was not strong enough to be a certainty. A disturbing element of doubt remained.

I do not know how long I lay there, but it could only have been minutes. I became aware of figures moving ghost-like amongst the rubble. I could hear exclamations and shouted profanities, and groans and grunts as pieces of fallen masonry were man-handled and pushed aside. There was light, too: light that flickered and danced with the suffocating clouds of dusk that hung in a fog, enveloping everything.

I called out and shapes solidified in the shifting mist, reaching for me, clearing obstacles, casting aside what looked like part of a gate but was more likely a section of banister. I was dragged clear of the weights that pressed down on my legs and borne out into the cool fresh air of night.

'Stretcher-bearer!' a voice called. Another – a drawling voice, close to my ear – spoke across me as a hand groped along my limbs and felt for injuries:

'At least he's alive. And I can't feel no breaks.' I do not know whom this was meant to reassure but it greatly reassured me.

'I'm OK,' I said, but with difficulty, because my mouth and throat seemed full of gritty sand. The words came out through my dust-caked lips like a frog's croak.

'Sure you are,' the drawling voice said comfortingly. 'Try moving your legs. Have you got any life in your legs?'

I found I could wiggle my legs, and my arms. But I seemed devoid of strength.

'I'm OK,' I said again. 'A bit groggy, that's all. What happened?'

'Don't you remember? You went chasing into the house after the Lieutenant, shouting like a madman. You were trying to warn him, I guess.'

It all came back. Suddenly. Terrifyingly. I tried to sit up. 'Lieutenant Platt!' I cried out. The man gently restrained me.

'Take it easy,' he soothed. 'You did your best. But there ain't a thing you can do for the Lieutenant now.'

I wanted to scream in protest. The knowledge of what had happened was like a knife in me.

'You don't understand,' I cried out hoarsely. 'It was a booby-trap . . . that body he found . . . It was booby-trapped!'

192

'I know, I know,' the soldier said. 'We figured that much. Don't you worry about it. The Lieutenant musta gotten careless . . . It ain't like he hadn't seen plenty of booby-traps before. He was usually mighty careful . . . A nude dame, though! That's a new pitch! Usually, it's just a photo of a nude. Never heard of the Krauts wiring up a real nude before! The guys say she was hung. Shame about the Lieutenant. He was a real good guy.'

A real good guy! I had no doubt that that was what the Lieutenant had been — a real good guy. Nor did I have any doubt that he would still have been alive if only I had ignored the discomfort of a little dust in my lungs.

My recollections of the rest of that night are hazy. It was not without further incident. My interest in what was going on, however, was curtailed by the concussion I suffered in the blast that had killed Platt. Considering the size of the explosion and my proximity to it, I got off lightly: more cuts and bruises than I could count and, of course, the effects of the concussion, which left me feeling like a punch-drunk zombie. The fact that I was able to walk away relatively unscathed after the event was a near miracle.

Two medics had carried me to the far end of the forecourt, so I did not immediately appreciate that the explosion had started a fire on the first floor of the mansion and that the conflagration was being watched with some awe by most of K Company, who had now converged on the scene. There was little they could do to save the house. The roof went up spectacularly and flames, leaping high in the air, lit up the faces of the medics, who provided me with a running commentary while they sponged blood and grime from my face.

They were distracted from the blaze by a new explosion somewhere in the woods. This remained unexplained for some time, but an indication that something was wrong was conveyed by a lot of coming and going in our vicinity and the despatch of a squad to investigate. They returned with the news that a truck, sent through the woods from the road, had struck a land-mine.

At precisely what hour the decision was taken to abort the fruitless operation and withdraw K Company, I do not know, but I was feeling sufficiently recovered, when it came, to insist that I was going out as I had arrived: on my own two feet. I remember little of the march back through the woods other than that two medics supported me for most of the way. We came upon the smouldering remains of a three-ton truck a mile up the track but the image that I retained was blurred, like the memory of a dream.

I declined transport to the military hospital in Spa for no reason that makes sense. The idea was fixed in my mind that 'home' was Kinneally's barracks – why, I do not know – and it was there that I insisted on going. My arrival – reeling like a drunk who had switched over to auto-pilot on getting lost – caused something of a stir.

Kinneally, roused from his bed, bombarded me with questions which, in my befuddled state, I was unable to answer coherently. Poor Kinneally did not know what to make of me. He was torn between concern for me and an anxiety to know what had happened – and I did nothing to help his predicament. I was simply unable to cope with explanations. I was so physically and mentally exhausted that I would have had difficulty telling him what my name was. All that I wanted to do was lie down before I fell down.

When it dawned on Kinneally that I was on the point of collapse and that there was no hope of getting any sense out of me, he did not press me further. His concern was solely for me. I have no memory of him installing me in his own bed, but that is what he did. Nor do I have any recollection of conversation between us as he undressed me and covered me with blankets, but he

194

told me later that I kept thanking him profusely and assuring him that I was all right and that all I needed was sleep. I must have gone out like the proverbial light. I did not fall into gentle slumber so much as surrender to deep coma – an oblivion as black and dreamless as death.

Waking was slow and painful. I emerged from the long journey through darkness, aware of my eyes and feeling that weights were pressing down on them. I blinked my eyes open and immediately regretted it. The mere movement of my eyelids triggered pains in the head. I gradually became aware of the rest of my body and, with it, a host of nagging aches so distributed throughout my frame that the least movement made me want to cry out loud.

I must have made some sound as I sought orientation in waking because it brought an immediate response from close at hand. A crooning French voice made comforting noises and cool gentle fingers caressed my forehead. I recognised the voice.

'Danny?' I murmured. It still hurt to keep my eyes open and, as I dared to do so at longer intervals, all that I could make out was a shadowy figure close to me. I made a determined effort to keep my eyes open and focus them. The only light in the room came from the edges of a curtained window. It seeped from beyond the curtains. Daylight.

I surfaced slowly from the depths. Danny continued to make sympathetic noises and stroke my forehead in the best Florence Nightingale tradition, although I doubt if old Flo would have soothed a patient with such terms as 'my poor little cabbage'.

It took me a little time to work out where I was, how I had got there and why I should be feeling like someone who had lost an argument with a brick wall. The events of the previous night came back to me in a flood, but it was Danny who told me that I was in Kinneally's room. I could not remember returning to the former school or talking to Kinneally at four in the morning. Nor could I think why I had chosen to return to the school. I could remember seeing the Zinoniev house in flames and walking through woods – but everything after that was a complete blank.

Danny was unable to fill in the gaps. Kinneally had taken her back to the school the previous evening after the C-I Corps lieutenant had failed to find other accommodation for her, Thorn and myself. She did not know, until I told her, that Thorn had been wounded, and the first she had known about my misadventure had been at eight that morning when Kinneally had wakened her and asked her to keep an eye on me.

'He was very worried about you,' Danny said. 'He telephoned the hospital about you and he said a doctor would be coming . . . but to let you sleep . . . not to let you out of bed.'

I was in no tearing hurry to get out of bed, but the mere suggestion that I should be kept there sparked that contrary side of my nature which resents interference with my freedom of choice. Neither Kinneally, Danny, nor any doctor who chanced along was going to keep me in bed against my will.

I told Danny to draw the curtains and let in some light; I was getting up. She threw back the curtains to let in the light of a cold, grey day but tried to persuade me to remain in bed.

'There's not a damned thing wrong with me,' I yelled at her, so ferociously that I thought she was going to burst into tears. Recoiling as if I had hit her, she made no attempt to stop me as I threw aside the blankets and eased myself painfully out of bed.

The desire to immerse my aching flesh and bones in a hot bath became so strong that I would have committed murder to achieve it. Not only did a luxurious soak present itself to me as the one sure balm to my screaming muscles, but I also realised that the hygienic necessity was equally pressing. The medics had done their best to sponge away the mortar and grime that had coated my face but I was still smeared grey with ash, like an Aborigine in mourning, and my hair was matted with the stuff. Indeed there were few parts of my body that the clinging dust had not reached. I was positively filthy.

Investigation revealed a bathroom, two doors along the corridor from Kinneally's room. Unfortunately, the water supply to the heavy cast-iron bath – which stood on four squat legs shaped like the spread paws of a lion – was icy. Danny and a civilian kitchen-hand came to the rescue. They portered large cauldrons of boiling water from the kitchen stove to the bath, while I stood about, shivering.

The boiling water seemed lost in the bottom of the long narrow tub, but by the time I had topped it up with cold from the tap there was an adequate eight inches into which I lowered myself.

I settled down to enjoy the restorative luxury of the water's warmth. It was sheer bliss – but my hopes of enjoying it in privacy were short-lived. I had soaped myself from head to toe and was wallowing at the bottom of the tub when Danny bustled in with another huge pan of steaming water. I had to hunch up at one end of the bath to avoid being scalded as she tipped it into the tub.

I waited for her to leave but, instead, she rolled up her sleeves in a business-like manner and told me that the cuts on my head needed better attention than I was capable of giving them. To prove her point, she dabbed with a flannel at a smarting scalp wound and thrust the greyed cloth in front of my nose so that I could see what a poor job I had made of cleaning it. She proceeded to investigate other abrasions on my anatomy, with the zeal of a mother cat cleansing a kitten. I submitted without too much resistance to her gentle ministrations, which I might have found embarrassing but for the

197

candour and complete absence of coyness with which she went about the task of soothing my hurts. I might have begun to enjoy the therapy if the water hadn't cooled so rapidly. Having lowered myself into the bath like a rheumatism-stricken nonagenarian, I emerged with the frisky vigour of a spring lamb.

Kinneally's promised doctor did not show up at the school and I had no intention of hanging around to see if he would, being eager to make amends for the shambles that our investigation had become. I was still haunted by a sense of failure but, rested and refreshed, I was determined not to be defeated by events. If I were to ease my conscience over Lieutenant Platt's death, the best way was to keep on after the perpetrators as doggedly as I knew how. The fact that I no longer had Thorn around to lean on and make most of the decisions' merely strengthened my resolve. It was all up to me now.

A telephone call to the military hospital elicited the news that Thorn had spent a comfortable night and that his condition was not considered critical. He had come through surgery well and in another twenty-four hours – it was hoped – would be sitting up and taking nourishment. I was vastly relieved.

Decked up in fresh American togs, courtesy of a black quartermaster sergeant from the deep south – and looking more like a combat-ready GI than a semi-civilian Brit – I walked with Danny into Spa, to the Hotel Britannique. We could have scrounged a lift but the walk loosened up my aching muscles.

Our jeep was still parked at Headquarters, where I had left it the previous night, and the surly sergeant was again in charge of the guard detail. He eyed Danny with eyebrows arched so high that they disappeared below the rim of his white MP's helmet. He recognised me.

'You again,' he said, and jerked a thumb in Danny's direction. 'Who's the broad? What's up with her face?'

He made the enquiry with all the subtlety of a dance-hall bouncer confronted by two street-corner yobboes.

'The lady happens to be on special assignment from SHAEF – so, careful what you say, Sergeant,' I warned him. 'It'll go right back to Eisenhower.'

'Straight up?' he asked, seemingly impressed. Perhaps the memory of seeing me hob-nobbing with General Hodges, only the previous evening, had inspired him to treat me with cautious respect.

'Straight up,' I confirmed.

'What's she doin' here?' the sergeant wanted to know. I told him.

'As a matter of fact, she can identify the female prisoner I brought in yesterday. Where have you locked her up? We'd like to see her.'

'She ain't here no more,' he said.

I stared at him in consternation. 'What have you done with her? Where is she?'

The MP shrugged his broad shoulders. 'My guys can't look after civilian broads. The dame was handed over to the Belgian police. She's in the local slammer.'

'But she's not a civil prisoner,' I started to complain.

'That ain't nothing to do with me,' the sergeant interrupted. He growled, with an air of indifference: 'You got any grouse, you better take it up with the Commandant's office. I don't give the orders around here. I just see they get done.'

I got Danny to wait for me at the jeep. Back inside Headquarters, I located Major Goldman. He was surprised to see me.

'Kinneally said he was getting you hospitalised. There was an ambulance coming for you at noon. Didn't it show up?'

'I didn't wait to see,' I said. 'I'm OK . . . and I've got a mess to clean up.'

'You can say that again!' he agreed, rather too vehemently. 'I'm carrying the can for that foul-up last night. Some of the brass around here ain't too happy about a rifle company being taken off R and R to do a police job.'

'The General didn't see it that way,' I protested.

'So I keep telling them,' Goldman said unhappily, 'but it hasn't stopped the flak. And I gotta sweep up the pieces. Nobody's beefin' about you. You're sitting pretty. You covered yourself with glory. I heard all about it.'

'I got a good officer killed. I'm not proud of what happened last night,' I said bitterly. 'Did you know that the Zinoniev woman had been handed over to the Belgians?'

'She's in the local jug with the other Belgies who played footsie with the Nazis. She'll keep there as good as any place else. I've had other things to think about besides her.'

I waited for him to elaborate. He did.

'First thing this morning, I got Kinneally to take a squad out to that house you burned down. He radioed in half an hour ago. They made an interesting find in the basement.'

'They found something?'

'Bodies,' Goldman said. 'They found bodies in a cellar.'

'Identifiable?'

'They ain't burned, if that's what you mean. But they shoulda been. They were stinking of kerosene and they should've gone *pfoot* when the cellar light was switched on but they didn't. The blaze that took the house burned up all the wires and junction boxes and shorted everything . . . There wasn't any juice in the cellar light.'

'Does Kinneally know who they are . . . the bodies?'

'Nope. He said there were five stiffs, all female, white caucasian, aged between twenty and thirty . . . They all died the same way. One bullet in the back of the head, fired at close range.'

I digested the horror of what he was telling me.

'What is he going to do . . . with the bodies, I mean?'

'I'm sending a wagon over to collect them,' Goldman said. 'But it'll have to wait until engineers have cleared the estate road of mines. You know about that, of course. The outfit you were with lost a truck. The road's been closed since it happened and it'll stay closed until the engineers give it the OK,' Goldman paused, regarding me thoughtfully. 'You got any ideas on who these dead women might be?'

'I may be wrong,' I said, 'but I've got a feeling that Danny will be able to tell us who they are. We never did find out what became of her friends . . . the girls the Jerries shipped up here from Paris as comforts for the troops. My guess is that they outlived their usefulness to the Third Reich.'

'That's what I'd figured,' Goldman said. 'What I can't figure is just what these Kraut bastards are up to.'

'Neither can I,' I admitted, 'but, if it's the last thing I ever do, I mean to find out.' I got up to go.

'Where'll you be if I need to get in touch?' asked Goldman.

'My first stop is the Zinoniev place,' I told him. 'I'll be with Kinneally. After that, you'll find me in the local jail with a certain blonde, who's going to do a lot more talking than she's done so far!'

The road from Spa to the Zinoniev estate was beginning to exert a monotonous familiarity as I flogged the jeep at speed along its twisting length. Danny sat beside me. She was in good spirits: inordinately pleased that, today, I was not palming her off on someone else, as we had done the day before. I tried to break it to her gently that we were not embarked on a picnic and that what I had in store for her was likely to be extremely unpleasant. I did not go into details.

We were challenged at the entrance to the Zinoniev estate, where several Army vehicles were parked close to the main road and a check-point had been set up. The GIs on guard let us through, with the warning that we might not get all the way to the house. A mine-clearing detail was on the track and we would either have to stay behind it or run the jeep off the track and go on to the house by foot.

In the event, we did not overtake the engineers. They had swept the track through the woods all the way to the house before we got there. They had found no more mines – an indication, perhaps, that the mansion's former occupants had had just enough time to booby-trap the house and lay only the one mine on the access track before making a hurried departure.

Long before we reached the burnt-out shell of the mansion, we got the stench of smoke. The heavy atmosphere was pungent with the unmistakable smell. It was again a windless day, with low cloud hanging close to the surface of the earth and wreathing the forest with clinging mist.

We found Kinneally at the rear of the house. I hailed him and went to meet him while Danny followed at a slower pace, gazing at the roofless walls, from which the hollow window gaps stared back like sightless eyes.

Kinneally was blackened and his clothes marked from exploration of the mansion's charred interior. The fire had long since burned itself out, but tendrils of smoke still drifted up here and there from embers that smouldered stubbornly. Like Goldman had been, Kinneally was surprised to see me. I asked him about the bodies. He pointed to the far side of the yard. The five corpses had been laid out on the ground in a row covered with pieces of sacking.

'We're waiting for a truck to take them to the morgue,' he said, low-voiced. 'I see you got company. Maybe it would be better if Danny don't see them. They ain't covered right. All we could find was some burlap out of one of the sheds out back. They ain't a pretty sight – although they must have been good-lookers . . . before . . . all of them . . .'

'They could be friends of Danny's,' I explained, and

found that I, too, was keeping my voice low. 'That's why I brought her along . . . So she could tell us one way or the other.'

'I hope she's got a strong stomach,' he said unhappily.

'She'll be OK,' I assured him with more confidence than I felt. 'The sooner we get it over with, the better.'

Danny strolled towards us. I saw her eyes go uneasily to the far side of the yard, beyond us. Then her eyes met mine and she forced a weak smile.

'It must have been a big fire,' she said. She gave a tilt to her head. 'Over there on . . . the ground . . . those unfortunates . . . They are the men who did not escape?'

I took her hand. 'They're not men, Danny. They're women . . . young women. They were not burned in the fire. They were shot. I think you know some of them. I want you to look at them and tell me.'

Her eyes widened. She nodded grimly.

'What you want me to do, I shall do,' she said.

I led her across the yard and, while Kinneally watched from a distance, uncovered the face of each corpse in turn. Danny said nothing but her hand, clasped in mine, tightened fiercely.

'Enough?' I asked softly.

She nodded, mouth pursed shut. I led her away, giving her time to compose herself.

She wrinkled her nose. 'That smell . . . what is it?' she said.

'Kerosene. Whoever killed them doused the bodies in kerosene. They intended to burn them.'

'The Boches did this?'

'Yes.'

'They are monsters! It is too horrible! Why have they done this? Why?'

I ignored her question. 'Did you recognise any of these girls, Danny?'

'All of them,' she said, with a sob, and recited the names: 'Lucille, Marie, Andrée, Jacqueline and Celeste.' She turned to me with tears in her eyes. 'They were my friends, Johnny! Some would say they were bad girls – like me . . . But they were not wicked girls. They gave men pleasure . . . They did not deserve this.'

'I know, I know,' I murmured, and held her as she sobbed against my chest. 'When did you last see them, Danny? Was it in Spa, at the villa you ran away from?'

'Yes,' she sobbed.

'Then you're lucky, Danny. Running away was the best thing you could have done. If you hadn't, you could have been lying there beside them.'

'Why have the Boches done this, Johnny?' she cried. 'Why? Why?'

'I don't know why, Danny,' I said, 'but I'm not going to rest until I find out. And you can help. There's one person in Spa who knows some of the answers. Someone you know.'

'Who is this person?'

'She has more than one name, Danny. But I think you knew her as Madame Fabienne.'

Danny stared at me, astounded. 'If she has done this, I will tear her eyes from her head with my fingernails,' she vowed passionately. 'I will tear the heart from her body with my own hands!'

I nodded grimly. 'And maybe I'll let you,' I promised. 'If she doesn't talk, maybe I'll let you.'

The uniformed police chief to whom I introduced myself at the prefecture in Spa was of red-necked peasant stock: moon-faced, overweight, and possessed of watchful avaricious eyes. He was, in turn, obsequious and struttingly self-important and getting a straight answer from him on anything was like trying to eat soup with a fork. The more you dipped, the less you got.

I got nowhere with him, initially – perhaps because I sold myself a bit short and he mistook my excessively polite approach as deference to one whose patronage is sought. I quickly corrected any false impressions on this score by making it clear that I was seeking no favours but, given the right kind of co-operation, was in a position to grant them. I implied that I carried a great deal more authority than was actually the case, and I was not above injecting a little threat to emphasise that authority. I told him that I had been sent from Paris as General Eisenhower's personal trouble-shooter and that I had only to lift my finger to ensure early retirement without a pension for anyone who obstructed me in my duty.

He got the message and became all fawning co-operation. He had to be careful, he kept saying. The woman he knew as Sonya Zinoniev was a very important person in the district and she had many influential friends. Already, the Mayor and other notables, such as the lawyer, Bech, had made representations about her detention – which, they said, must be a mistake – and it had taken him all his time to handle the unfortunate situation without offending these dignitaries. He had played for time in the matter because he was equally anxious not to offend the US Military Authorities, who had said that Sonya Zinoniev was to be held in custody until charges could be brought against her. Unfortunately, no one had specified these charges and he was completely in the dark as to what they might be. Were they serious?

I told him that he could make his own mind up on that but they were likely to include: aiding and abetting the enemy, conspiracy to murder, fraud, procurement for immoral purposes, operating a vice ring, and a lot more besides. He was shocked and disbelieving. Nevertheless, his shock enabled him to overcome his earlier reluctance to allow me to interrogate his prisoner without him or her lawyer being present. He agreed to have her brought to an interview room immediately. He even volunteered to entertain Danny in his office until such time as I might require her. From the lascivious glances he kept darting at Danny, I was none too sure about entrusting her to his mercies. However, in an aside she assured me that she could handle the slob. That may not be the precise translation of the French word she used, but it is close enough to capture accurately her independent assessment of the police officer.

A night in a cell did not seem to have done much harm to the woman who claimed to be Sonya Zinoniev. Her hair was combed differently, she was wearing fresh make-up, and she had secured a change of clothing from somewhere. Most notably, however, she had shaken off the utter despair of the evening before. She was no longer the dispirited creature whom I had handed over to the snowdrops. She was brimming with self-confidence – no doubt from convincing the Mayor of Spa and her lawyer-friend, Bech, that she had been wrongfully arrested.

Well, there was a lot about Sonya Zinoniev that Bech and the Mayor did not know – and I intended to wipe the smug smile from her face. However, I gave her the chance to make things easy for herself by making a full confession. She laughed in my face and made an unprintable suggestion.

I pretended to be much more amused by her coarseness than I was.

'Let's start again, shall we?' I proposed. 'Let us consider that mansion, which you claim to own. I spent an interesting night out there, last night – and I've been out there again today. Aren't you curious to know what happened to your friends?'

'Friends?' she mocked. 'Or do you mean tenants? The place was taken over by the American Army – your friends, not mine. They said I would be compensated. This is the thanks I get, I suppose.'

I could not make up my mind whether she was deliberately trying to provoke me or if she honestly believed that she could brazen things out.

'What,' I asked, 'can you tell me about Lucille, Marie, Andrée, Jacqueline and Celeste?'

The glazed smile on her face did not waver.

'Nothing,' she replied.

'They tell me a great deal about you,' I said.

'Do they? The names mean nothing to me.'

'They should. They were all former employees of yours, Madame Fabienne. So why waste time telling any more lies? They condemn you – all five of them.'

'Do they?' she repeated. Her eyes hardened. 'Then let them condemn me to my face. Or is that not possible?'

Her defiant stare told me something which, until that moment, I had not even suspected: that Danny's five friends had been murdered – or their deaths ordained – *before* Thorn and I had even set foot on the Zinoniev estate. This woman *knew*. There was no need for me to tell her that all five were dead. Even if she had not actually fired the bullets, she was as guilty of the murders as the bogus Americans in occupation of the mansion. I realised something more. Thorn and I had not frightened off the occupants of the mansion. Their departure had been planned before we got there – as this woman's had certainly been. The packed suitcase was evidence enough. We had interrupted the departure, not caused it. The decision that the five girls were surplus to requirements had already been made.

'Do you think that only the living can testify against you, Madame Fabienne?' I asked softly. 'Do you think that the dead cannot accuse you?'

'They are not renowned for telling tales,' she said, with a smugness that made me want to hit her. 'And neither am I,' she added. 'So, why don't you give up this nonsense? Theo came to see me today and he told me that I have nothing to fear from you. He will get me out of here by tomorrow. He is making a court application for my release.'

'He won't get it,' I promised. 'He's a bigger fool than I took him for if he still believes you're Sonya Zinoniev. And you're deluding yourself as well as him if you think we can't prove otherwise. Theo can't save you . . . And

207

civilian law isn't going to save you either – because it doesn't count for two beans in a war zone. You won't even get the luxury of a jury. You must know that, for what you've done, you can be shot out of hand . . .'

She stared at me, saying nothing. The sneering smile, however, was a lot less certain. She was having difficulty maintaining its permanent fixture on her face. I beamed her an encouraging smile of my own.

'Tell me,' I invited her, 'what did you tell Theo about the shooting out at the lodge yesterday? How did you explain Captain Thorn stopping a bullet from your chums? A little misunderstanding, was it?'

Her lip curled. 'I had nothing to do with it. He was shot by American soldiers . . . You saw them. It was your fault. You would not stop for them.'

'They were genuine Americans, of course? Like the one in the car, with the girl. He was an American, because he was wearing an American flying jacket. That's why you shouted to him in German. And because he was American and he wasn't used to getting shouted at in German, he started shooting at us. I must have been very dim not to have understood at the time. He must have thought that *we* were Germans. What an unfortunate misunderstanding.'

She was looking at me as if it would afford her pleasure to cause me grievous bodily harm.

'Am I not getting things right?' I asked her. She made no reply.

'OK,' I said, 'put me right. Let's start from the very beginning . . . how it was that a pretty young thing like you came to be working for the Nazis . . . How you became involved . . . How you met Keitler . . . What you did for him . . . Everything . . . I want the lot.'

'I am telling you nothing,' she said emphatically.

'I had hoped we could do it the easy way,' I said. 'However . . . you leave me no choice. Looks like we'll have to do it the messy way.'

A dour-looking gendarme was stationed just outside

the door. I asked him to step inside and keep an eye on the prisoner. In the police chief's office, Danny was sitting, looking bored, while he – looking equally bored – was behind his desk, busily sharpening a pencil over a waste-paper basket. Both looked relieved to see me.

The chief was disappointed to learn that my interview with the prisoner was not over. I told Danny that I wanted her to meet the prisoner because I believed she could identify her. She was about to accompany me back to the interview room when I had an idea. I asked the police officer if I could borrow the discarded blade with which he had been whittling at the pencil on his desk. He looked at me in surprise. I patted my breast pocket.

'For my own pencil,' I explained, untruthfully. 'I am making notes of everything.'

'Watch you do not cut yourself' he advised me, and carefully folded the blade into the paper wrapper beside it before handing it to me.

On the way back to the interview room, I stopped off in the washroom to purloin a roller towel from a rail beside the wash-hand basin. I had decided that Danny, on her own, might not be enough to frighten the truth out of our stubborn prisoner. A little bluff, with the right props, might increase her candour.

The woman who called herself Sonya Zinoniev looked encouragingly shaken when I walked into the interview room with Danny at my heels. The gendarme, in whose charge I had left her, threw a puzzled glance at the towel in my hands but made no comment as I showed him the door. Danny, meanwhile, had taken up a position in front of the seated prisoner, staring at her. Indeed, the pair of them seemed engaged in a contest to outstare one another. No words were spoken. Danny's gaze was resolute: demanding that sign from the other that was an acknowledgement of recognition. The older woman's was defiant, refusing to concede that acknowledgement. I decided to hurry things along.

209

'You two seem to know each other,' I said.

'I have never seen her before in my life,' the seated woman cried out.

'*Menteuse*!' Danny hurled in her face.

'Just tell me who you say she is, Danny,' I said.

'Her name is Lans,' Danny said, spitting out the words. 'Fabienne Lans.'

I gently eased Danny to one side and pushed a chair under her. But her stare remained locked on the other woman.

'That's all I wanted to know, Danny,' I said. 'Just you sit there for a moment and think about Marie and Jacqueline and Celeste and the others and what you would like to do to the woman who promised to see that they'd be all right. Fabienne's memory isn't as good as it used to be. It needs a little jogging.'

I turned to the other woman. 'I told you yesterday that we had someone who knew you,' I said. 'Didn't you believe me?'

'I've never seen her before!' the woman persisted.

'Your voice is shaking,' I said. 'Are you afraid?'

'No!' she cried. 'Take this creature away! Her face repels me. Tell her to stop staring!'

'Are you going to talk?' I asked.

'No! Never!'

'Show her your face, Danny,' I said. 'Let her have a good look at it. Let her see what they did to you because they thought you were too friendly with the Boches.'

Danny got out of her chair and thrust her face in front of the other woman's. Fabienne Lans half fell out of her own chair in her attempt to escape a close-up view of Danny's scars. 'No!' she screamed. 'Stay away from me!'

I called Danny off. Fabienne Lans regained the security of her chair but refused to look at Danny. She kept her head averted.

'How would you like to look in the mirror and see scars like that on your face, Fabienne?' I asked softly.

'Don't you think it's unjust that Danny is scarred and you're not? God knows you're the one that deserves cutting up. Danny thinks so, too. She saw Marie and Jacqueline and Celeste and Andrée and Lucille . . . She saw them only a few hours ago . . . saw what your butchers did to them . . .'

The woman turned, hesitantly, staring at me with fear bright in her eyes. Knowing that I had her full attention, I tossed her the towel I had taken from the wash room.

'Better wrap that round your neck, Fabienne,' I advised her airily. 'It'll keep the blood off your clothes.' Her eyes were wide with alarm.

'What are you going to do?' she stammered, her voice almost inaudible.

'I'm not going to do anything,' I told her. 'I'll leave that to Danny. I'm just going to hold you.'

'You wouldn't dare,' she said, scarcely able to raise a whisper. I took the wrapped razor-blade from my pocket and removed the paper.

'Gillette,' I said. 'They make good blades but this one's a bit hacked from sharpening pencils. It's a bit dirty too. I hope you don't get lead poisoning.' I handed the blade to a surprised Danny. 'Watch you don't cut your fingers,' I said, as she grasped it gingerly. Fabienne Lans was out of her seat and backing towards the wall. She was very, very frightened.

I moved towards her, without hurrying.

'You'll make things worse if you struggle,' I warned her. As she shrank from me, I pinioned her arms behind her back with my right arm and grabbed her hair with my left hand. Danny, holding the razor-blade as if it was a grenade that might go off in her hand, was scared stiff.

'You want me to cut her face?' Danny croaked. She was ready to do it if I gave her the word but she was clearly horrified.

'Not until I say so,' I warned. 'I want Fabienne to

have one more minute to think about her pretty face and what it's going to look like when she wakes up tomorrow. She can still save herself a lot of grief. She can start talking. She can start telling me everything she damned well knows.'

I twisted her face round, so that she could see the razor-blade in Danny's shaking hand. Whether it was the sight of one, the other, or the terrifying combination of both that did the trick, I do not know, but to my undying relief she cracked. Quivering in my grip, she let out a long pleading sob.

'Please, please, no!' she wailed. 'I'll do anything, tell you everything – but please do not cut me. Please, not that!'

I nodded wordlessly to Danny, who backed away. I was unable to speak. If I had opened my mouth, I think I would have been sick. The contents of my stomach had risen in my gorge at my nearness to a deed that I would never have undertaken. I just wasn't cut out for Gestapo work. Danny, too, was sagging with relief. In spite of her brave words, earlier, about clawing Fabienne's eyes out, she was as big a softie as me when it came to it.

Fabienne Lans sagged into a chair when I released her, hiding her face in her hands and sobbing. I was thankful for the moment to get a grip on myself and try to assume once more the stony-faced calm of a brute who had no qualms about carving up women. I did so by reminding myself that the doe-eyed blonde shedding crocodile tears over the near loss of her looks was a murderous bitch with God knows how many deaths on her conscience.

I told Danny to leave us and return the razor-blade to its rightful owner. There was no need for her to hear Fabienne's tale of misdeeds. What Danny did not know could not hurt her. She went without protest, seeming a little uncertain of me – as if she had seen a side to me that she had not hitherto suspected, and she had not liked what she had seen. I turned grimly to Fabienne Lans, and found that I did not have to simulate anger edged with cruelty.

'All right, you bitch,' I snarled at her, 'start talking!'

NINE

Confession

To anyone who had just come up the Mersey in a banana boat, the account by Fabienne Lans of how she became involved with one of the most sinister eminences of the Nazi Party might have been extremely moving. To a hardened newspaper hack like me – who had heard more hard-luck stories than a counter clerk in a parish welfare office – sympathy had to be squeezed like the juice from a lemon. She extracted very little from me.

Mendacity came so easily to her that I did not delude myself for one minute that the story I got from her was the whole truth and nothing but the truth. I am satisfied, however, that I got the bones of the truth. The skeleton was somewhere behind the extravagant clothing of words with which she dressed her sanitised version of events. I shall, therefore, make no attempt to cloud the issue by repeating her self-portraiture as a trusting innocent. Perhaps she hoped to bring tears to my eyes with her picture of a motherless waif who was more sinned against than sinning, but the more she sought to present herself as an angel who had fallen from grace due to a combination of cruel fate and bad luck, the more she strained my credulity. She was no angel.

If she had ever been a trusting innocent, it must have been when she was about five years old – because precious few of her activities from pre-puberty onwards bore the mark of innocence or would have encouraged me to trust her further than I could throw her.

She had been born Hilde Gronbach in Aachen, the daughter of an itinerant con-man, who had – when he was not in prison – moved around the border areas of Germany, Belgium and Luxembourg, fleecing the more gullible gentry of their bank-rolls. Her mother had run out on the family when Hilde was three and her father had shamelessly used his fair-faced child as a sympathy-catcher in his nefarious enterprises. By the time she was seven, she was his active partner in crime. Young Hilde was in her middle teens when she realised that she was better at the bunco game than her old man and that she could be pocketing all the profits instead of the miserly pittance he allowed her. She promptly shopped her father to the gendarmerie and, while he was being put away for ten years, she went solo.

She had drifted into casual prostitution, when funds were low, before realising that a desirable body and the promise of sexual favours were formidable weapons in the business of extorting money. When used in combination with her extensive repertoire of tricks in separating ingenuous males from their cash, she found that her sexuality was the key to untold riches. She set her sights high and operated with some style. No street-walking for Hilde. With a little capital accumulated, she dressed in the finest clothes and haunted the best hotels; moving continually between the capital cities and the most fashionable resorts in Europe. Her victims seldom complained to the law after being taken for large amounts of money or expensive jewellery. Most preferred to take a loss and write it down to experience rather than have their folly exposed. Hilde prospered.

In Berlin in 1937, however, one intended victim had cottoned on to her game at the outset and had let her play it out before revealing that there was not going to be a pay-day and that she had been caught to rights. It was an unhappy awakening for Hilde. She was completely at the man's mercy and realised that, for the first time in her life, she faced a long prison sentence.

It was no consolation to discover that the man she had tried to fleece was a prominent member of the Nazi Party. He also happened to be a doctor: an expert on psychology and anthropology, who had done considerable research into sexual motivation in human behaviour.

The doctor's name was Keitler.

To Hilde's surprise and relief Keitler had not had her arrested. Far from bearing her any malice, he had confessed admiration for her artistry in exploiting human weakness. He, himself was engaged in a variety of psychological experiments which included ways of manipulating the human mind by exploitation of the subconscious sexual fears and desires of the chosen subject. He saw in Hilde someone who could not only be invaluable to him in his research but someone who might be used as a tool in bending unwilling minds into service of the Nazi cause.

He had had little difficulty in bending Hilde Gronbach's mind to his own will. She had become his mistress, and during two years under his patronage had discreetly performed special services to the State which, in any other country, would have earned a stretch in a penitentiary. According to her, Keitler had exploited his hold over her to ensure her acquiescence and total obedience but, nevertheless, she seems not to have shrunk too violently from the bizarre but well-rewarded chores that he and his Nazi friends put her way. She also procured for SS officers, providing carefully recruited women, who doubled as playmates for the Party faithful and lures for enemies they wished to compromise.

Hilde Gronbach professed to having no political beliefs but, under Keitler's irresistible indoctrination, claimed to have been drawn more and more deeply into the Nazi fold. It had been to escape his influence – she maintained – that she had accepted his suggestion to work for the SD's embryo foreign department. After training, she had been assigned to Paris with the identity

216

of Fabienne Lans. She had not wanted to become a brothel-keeper but, under cover of that activity, she had cultivated the patronage of French government officials and built a reputation for discreet service and the ability to provide for a wide variety of sexual appetites and tastes.

She had done no actual spying, she claimed, and had extorted no government secrets. All that had been done by others. She had merely provided the ancillary services, such as the girls and the premises with mirror windows, hidden cameras, etc.

Without being aware of how sanctimonious she sounded, Hilde Gronbach insisted to me that she had been in almost all respects a model French citizen: paying her taxes, giving generously to worthy charities, and employing dozens of girls who, otherwise, would have become victims of disease and their own shortage of business skills. She attributed it more to the respect accorded her by the French authorities, rather than to their total ignorance of her Nazi connections, that she was allowed to continue in business as usual after the outbreak of war in 1939. The Occupation of Paris by the Germans had caused no great upheaval in her provision of social services. A fall-off in the French clientele frequenting her establishments had been more than compensated for by an increase in the number of German customers.

All this she told me with a little prompting and only the occasional reminder that the loss of her facial beauty would be the price of anything less than complete candour. Perhaps because I could no more have resorted to my threatened barbarity than fly to the moon, it was necessary to conceal from her my feelings of relief — and, I must admit, astonishment — that my threats to damage her looks were so effective. So great was her fear of disfigurement that promise of it terrified her much more than the prospect of a firing squad or the hangman's rope: ends for which she was a prime candidate.

This phobic dread – rooted in vanity rather than fear of physical suffering – was all the more surprising in a woman who, in every other respect, was as hard as nails. It was a strange defect in someone whose mental strength was otherwise formidable, and finding it was like chancing upon the vulnerability of Achilles' sensitive heel or Samson's attachment to his glorious mane of hair. She would have walked on hot coals if it had meant saving her looks. Death, with her looks intact, was to her a much more welcome prospect than a single day of life with them blemished.

Fear may have loosened her tongue but talking seemed also to provide a release for her: an escape at last from the tensions of living a double life. She seemed to need to unburden herself or, at least, to try to justify herself. I am sure that she talked about things that, until that moment, she had not divulged to another living soul. But it was her immediate past that interested me most and it was noticeable that her answers to my questions became more guarded whenever I tried to focus her attention on to recent events. The reason, I believe, was that Thorn had probably given her the impression, the previous day, that we knew a great deal more about her than we actually did. Thus, the chances of me catching her in a lie were greater when her more recent activities were in the spotlight. She could embroider like mad on her dim and distant past, but the closer we got to the present day the more warily she felt she had to tread. I doubt if she would have talked half so freely if she had suspected how much in the dark I was.

I could see that she thought I was testing her veracity when I pinned her down to the succession of events surrounding her abandonment of the house in the Rue du Bourrelier and her move to Spa under the name of Sonya Zinoniev.

218

She persisted in trying to impress on me that she was innocent of anything sinister in assuming Sonya Zinoniev's identity. She had been manoeuvred unwittingly into the deception by Keitler. He had played upon her unconcealed ambition to retire one day to the Ardennes and own a château, where she could live like a lady.

She had never met the real Sonya Zinoniev – she insisted – nor known that anyone of that name had existed. When Keitler – whom she saw occasionally in Paris – had come to her and told her that it was time to move north, nearer home, she had believed that the move was for her protection: that it was a reward for services rendered to the Third Reich. She thought she was being provided with a manufactured identity, behind which she could hide and live out a comfortable retirement, no matter how the war went. She had been convinced that the impressive array of documents supplied by Keitler, confirming her title to the Zinoniev estates, were watertight enough to withstand any amount of scrutiny. It was not until just before she·left for Spa that Keitler had intimated that certain strings went with the safe haven she was being offered.

She had been told for the first time that her new identity was that of a woman whose activities with the Paris Resistance had been known to the Gestapo for some time. That was the bad news. The good news was that the woman in question was never likely to contest her claim on the late Anton Zinoniev's estate. She had disappeared, permanently.

I questioned Hilde Gronbach, alias Madame Fabienne, on this point. She denied all knowledge of the fate of Sonya Zinoniev. Pressed, however, for a possible explanation she admitted that her assumption was that Sonya Zinoniev had been eliminated by the Gestapo or the SD.

Hilde's instructions on the role she was to play in Belgium were explicit. She was to cultivate people such as Theo Bech, the lawyer, who was known to be leader of the Resistance cell to which Anton Zinoniev had belonged. She was to offer her services to Bech, making it clear to him that she had been active against the Germans in Paris and wished to continue the fight in Belgium. She was told that any checking Bech cared to do would not put her in jeopardy. So extensive was German infiltration of the Resistance networks that the English agent directing their activities from Paris was, without being aware of it, being controlled by the SD's Paris headquarters. His reports to London were even vetted for him by the SD before they were transmitted.

Hilde Gronbach's biggest fear was that someone who knew the real Sonya Zinoniev might give her away, but Keitler had played down the risks. The real Sonya Zinoniev had never set foot in Belgium and was unknown there. It had also worried Hilde that she perhaps bore little physical resemblance to the woman: there was a five-year discrepancy in ages. Keitler had assured her that such fears were groundless: an intimate – and there was no record of Sonya Zinoniev having any – might have spotted differences, but it was because of a striking similarity in appearance that the whole idea had taken shape in Keitler's mind.

'But the girls from the Rue du Bourrelier knew you as Madame Fabienne,' I pointed out. 'Surely they were a danger to you?'

She made a woebegone attempt at a smile.

'The one that got away, you mean?' she said, alluding to Danny. She shrugged. 'The others were too afraid to be a danger. When the war came to Spa, they were only too glad to be given a place to hide and do as they were told.'

'You hid them on the estate?'

'It was as good a place as any. The big house needed cleaning from top to bottom. There was much work to be done. Anyone who asked questions, and not many did – visitors were not encouraged – was told that staff had been recruited from Brussels.'

'What about the men in American uniforms?'

'I know nothing about them.'

'Nothing?' The disbelief in my voice was enough to make her reconsider her answer.

'Next to nothing,' she amended. 'There were only half a dozen of them at first. They came across the border by night. They weren't dressed as Americans then. They were dressed as civilian workers and they had papers and permits issued by the American Army. They were supposed to be carpenters, bricklayers, things like that. I had been told to expect something of the sort. I was dreading it, in fact. . .'

She turned all the appeal she could muster into the look she gave me.

'You must believe that,' she said, with emphasis on the 'must', and she managed to sound sincere. 'Germany is losing the war. I've longed for it to end . . . to be free of the trap I'm in.'

'You haven't told me why those men were brought over the border to this side of the line.'

'Because I don't know why!' she protested, her voice rising. 'I was told to do all I could to help them stay out of sight but for the most part, I was to keep out of their way and ask no questions. Their leader was a man I knew only as Frederick and any orders for me would be relayed to me through him. He left me in no doubt what would happen to me if I did not do exactly as he said.'

'How were you supposed to explain away all these strangers?'

'I wasn't. I was staying at the lodge and they took over the big house. I was told to keep away from them and, if necessary, to make out that I had nothing to do with their being there . . . that they were workmen who had been sent by the American military to prepare it for occupation. Frederick had papers to show that they had been contracted by the military . . . by your own High Command.'

'When did they acquire American uniforms?'

'I don't know . . . maybe five or six weeks ago. Frederick came and told me not to be alarmed if I saw American soldiers on the estate, that they were his men. The next day, he turned up at the lodge dressed as an American colonel. He spoke like one, too. His accent was perfect . . . He said I was to take no notice if I heard things at night . . .'

'What kind of things?'

'Vehicles on the move, motor engines . . . that kind of thing. There was a lot of coming and going after that. More men arriving . . . others leaving. I hardly saw a soul during the day . . . But at night, there was always coming and going.'

'How many of them were on the estate?'

'Maybe twenty . . . Maybe thirty . . . I just don't know.'

'You were about to clear out when Captain Thorn and I came to the hunting lodge. Where were you going?'

'Germany.'

'How did you intend to get through the lines?'

'There are dozens of ways. We were going to cross near Bleialf.'

'What about Frederick and his crew up at the house?'

'They were pulling out, too. Everybody was going. The orders were that we were to be out before the fifteenth of the month. That's today.'

'Why?' I asked.

'I don't know why. I think because things were getting too dangerous. There had been one or two near squeaks with American security patrols. Frederick heard from somewhere – I don't know where – that orders had gone out to check on ambulances and their crews. Anyone wearing a red-cross tab was having to show their papers.'

222

'Have you any idea why?'

She took a long time to reply. Her eyes searched my face, as if trying to read something there.

'No,' she said at last. 'But you do, don't you? It was because of something that happened in Paris . . . not here. Something went wrong . . . Something that brought you all the way from Paris. But it's Frederick you're after – not me. I'm not important. What was it led you to me? It wasn't that little bitch with the marked face . . . She didn't know enough . . .'

I wondered if I should tell her, and decided that there was no harm in doing so. Her reaction would be interesting.

'Your friend, Keitler, had a friend in Allied Head-quarters,' I said. 'Don't tell me you didn't know. Things got a little hot for him. He panicked.'

A look of comprehension dawned on her face.

'Cassius,' she said softly.

'Cassius?' I murmured. 'Him of the lean and hungry look. Tell me what you know about Cassius.'

Shakespeare's eloquent four-word cameo of Cassius – or rather, my allusion to it – seemed to pass right over her head. Perhaps it did not connect with the Cassius at the forefront of her thoughts.

'Tell me about Cassius,' I repeated, but the cat seemed to have got her tongue. She hesitated, as if weighing her words very carefully, before eventually replying.

'It . . . It was a code-name. I do not know his real name.'

'Have you bumped into him recently?' I asked casually.

Alarm flickered briefly in her eyes.

'No,' she said emphatically.

'But you have met him?'

'Yes,' she admitted, avoiding my eyes as she spoke. 'It was a long time ago. Nearly a year. Johann seemed to think he was a great prize – a gift from the gods.'

'Johann?' I queried.

223

'Johann Keitler. He was always conducting experiments psychological experiments... with captured officers. This one – he called him Cassius – fascinated him more than any other.'

'Why?'

She shrugged. 'I don't know. Johann said that he was as brave as a lion in battle... but a lion that could be tamed like a mouse.'

'You said you met him? How did this come about?'

Again, she hesitated before replying.

'I helped Johann conduct some... some experiments... with Cassius.'

'What kind of experiments?' The question seemed to fluster her.

'They were... Well, of a sexual nature. Johann wanted photographs...'

'Your job was to seduce this man for the camera – so that he could be shown in the act?'

She looked at me, surprised. 'No, it was not that,' she said, and I was given the impression that my question had struck her as naive. I treated her to a sweet smile.

'I had a sheltered upbringing,' I told her. 'You'll have to explain to me just what it was that you and Cassius got up to. Was he a voluntary partner in your... experiments? Or did he have to be forced to take part?'

Her lip curled contemptuously.

'He begged,' she exulted. 'The brave British lion begged...'

She broke off in mid-sentence as the door swung open and the gendarme, who had been posted outside, took a hesitant step into the room. He blinked at me apologetically.

'*Le téléphone, monsieur,*' he blurted out. '*Pour vous! Le Patron dit qu'il est tres important.*'

I was far from pleased at the interruption. However, I left the gendarme to keep Hilde Gronbach company and went to take the telephone call in the police chief's

224

office. It was Goldman on the line. He was at Army Headquarters.

'You'd better get your ass over here pretty damned fast,' he told me, and I got the impression that he was angry. 'Your boss, Colonel Hibberd, has been trying to raise you all day and he's all steamed up over what happened to your buddy, Thorn. He don't seem to realise that I got more to do than sit around here all day passin' messages between you two.'

'What does he want?' I asked.

'He wants words with you, buddy boy. That's what he wants. Now! At once! Immediately! If not sooner! He's callin' back in ten minutes and if you ain't here, you got more trouble than you know how to handle. He's gonna start nailing hides to the door, mine as well as yours! I ain't gonna be able to stall him a second time, so you'd better move your goddamned butt!'

He hung up. I cursed him and I cursed Hibberd. Neither seemed to appreciate that I had not exactly been loafing on the job. I reckoned that I had made more headway than they or I had any right to expect and it made me boil to have to suspend my interrogation of Hilde Gronbach just when I was getting to the nitty-gritty. There was nothing else for it, however. Hibberd was the boss and a man not given to histrionics. I wondered what was the cause of his agitation. There was only one way to find out, so – in Goldman's parlance – I moved my goddamned butt and got myself over to Army Headquarters in a hurry.

Danny – who seemed doomed to a perpetual existence of hanging around waiting for me – made no complaint at being left to twiddle her thumbs in the jeep while I sought out Goldman. I found him in the communications room, sitting at a long table with about a dozen telephones along its top. He was talking into one that had been daubed with red paint, denoting that it had been fitted with a scrambler. To be truthful, he was not doing much talking: his side of the conversation was confined to monosyllabic responses. His eyes lit up with relief when he saw me. He waved me over and nodded to an unoccupied seat next to his own.

'He has just arrived, sir,' I heard him say into the telephone, and he thrust the receiver into my hand: 'Colonel Hibberd.'

'Abernathy here,' I announced brightly into the mouthpiece, and waited for an explosion from the other end. It did not materialise. Hibberd sounded a lot more concerned than angry. The reason – it transpired – was that Goldman had just regaled him with an account of how I had narrowly escaped death at the Zinoniev mansion and how I had bravely soldiered on when I ought to have been in hospital. Hibberd seemed so relieved to discover that I was still in one piece that he omitted to bawl me out for not keeping him abreast of developments. He did demand to know, rather angrily, what the hell I had been doing, but that was as near as he came to giving me a round of the guns.

I told him briefly about Hilde Gronbach and her revelations about Frederick and Cassius – and I tried not to be too reproachful when I told him that I might have extracted more revelations if I had not had to curtail my interrogation and rush back to HQ in answer to his urgent summons. I said I gave his summons priority because I presumed its importance warranted it.

'You could say so,' he replied drily. 'Our guys have gotten hold of Cotter.' The thought of someone else running Cotter to earth had not crossed my mind. My surprise was total.

'Where, sir?' I asked. 'When . . .?'

'A night patrol brought him in about eighteen hours ago . . . near a German border town called Bleialf. That's only about twenty-five miles from where you are, John. It's only an hour's run from Spa.'

Bleialf! It was the place Hilde Gronbach had mentioned to me less than an hour ago. Until she had,

I had never heard of the town. Now here it was again! I quickly acquainted Hibberd with the context of the admission which had first brought Bleialf's existence to my notice. Had Cotter been captured trying to cross the German lines?

Hibberd did not know. He had only the scantiest details of the capture. But that was not what was bewildering me. What baffled me more than anything else was how Hibberd in Paris had got to hear about Cotter's capture before news of it had reached Spa. Here was something that had happened eighteen hours ago, right on the First Army's doorstep, and yet it had not been reported to First Army headquarters! In view of the previous night's operation and all the checkpoints that had been set up on roads in the region, it seemed absurd that Hibberd in Paris should learn of this prize catch before Goldman, me, or anyone else at Spa.

'You and the guys at First Army aren't the only ones who've been kept in the dark,' Hibberd revealed. 'Goddamn it, I only found out about it myself a couple of hours ago, and only then by accident! There was a report – but it went to Bradley's people in Luxembourg, not Spa. And it was passed on to SHAEF all right – first thing this morning – but through all the wrong channels. The first guy here who took any notice was your old chum Colonel Vardon. He got a call from Personnel Records about Cotter. Seems there was some confusion over the identity of the guy that the patrol brought in. Well, you know Vardon . . . That's all the excuse he needed to get in on the act.'

'That's bad news,' I observed. 'Vardon's trouble. He's the last person we want interfering. He could foul everything up.'

'My sentiments entirely,' Hibberd agreed, 'but that guy has a genius for sticking his nose in where it's not wanted. And this time, he's got the jump on us. He didn't stick around to discuss things. He took off up north with his new sidekick, like Custer heading for the Little Big Horn. He's got it in his head that Cotter is his very own personal pigeon and that he's going to be the guy that brings him back to Paris.'

'Can't he be stopped?'

'Maybe, if he had still been in Paris, I could have done something about it,' Hibberd said unhappily. 'Now, it's too goddamned late. You're the one who's going to have to head him off John. You got to get to Cotter first.'

'Me?' I choked.

'You're on the spot,' he said, and had the nerve to give a hoarse little laugh at the ambiguity of his phraseology. 'Get Goldman to write you an order that Cotter's to be given over to your custody and delivered by you to the First Army Interrogation Centre at Herbesthal. Get him to have the order countersigned by the Army Commander and anybody else up there who carries any rank. If you move your butt, John, you could have Cotter locked up in the stockade at Herbesthal in four or five hours from now!'

When, finally, I replaced the red-daubed telephone, I felt a little dazed. I was also tired and hungry – but sleep and food were low on my priorities. Top of my list was the recurring obligation to move my goddamned butt!

From Army HQ I drove to Kinneally's barracks, with the intention of dropping off Danny. She was having none of it and refused point-blank to be abandoned. Whithersoever I went, Danny was determined to go, too. She made it clear to me that only by having her forcibly removed from the jeep and chained up would I leave her behind in Spa for another night. So vociferously and with such pathetic pleading did she put her case that, for the sake of peace, I gave in to her.

I warned her that she could be in for an uncomfortable night but she was ready to face any discomfort

228

rather than be left on her own. We, therefore, delayed at the former school only long enough to collect bedding and rations, as a hedge against any eventuality.

Hibberd had advised me to head for a town called St Vith, in the first instance. The town was headquarters of the American 106th Division and, since it had been a reconnaissance patrol from one of the 106th's infantry regiments who had captured Cotter, Divisional HQ was the place to go to find out where the fugitive officer was being held.

Goldman had equipped me with all the document-ation I needed to have Cotter released to my custody for transfer to Herbesthal. He had also supplied a helpful route map along with my official 'trip ticket'.

Indeed, he had been so damned helpful, I'd got the impression that his eagerness was rooted in fervent hope that my absence from Spa might be of lengthy duration.

Once Danny and I were on the road to St Vith, my fatigue vanished and my spirits lifted. It was always a relief to escape from the pressure-cooker atmosphere of the Spa headquarters but that only partly explained my sudden uplift. I felt a new sense of purpose, a very real hope, that face-to-face with Cotter, I would finally get the answers to so much that was puzzling me. He was the key to the mystery, to so much that was baffling. I had no doubt that he was the Cassius, of whom Hilde Gronbach had spoken: the man whom Keitler had manipulated and subverted to serve the Nazi cause. I was confident that, confronted with my knowledge that Keitler had exploited some terrible weakness in him, Cotter would realise the hopelessness of not revealing all.

Perplexing me more than any other aspect of Cotter's treachery was the puzzle of what method Keitler had used to achieve it. How had it been done? What human weakness did Cotter possess to such a degree that Keitler had been able to prey on it so effectively that he – a patriot of proven bravery – had been induced to

229

betray all he held dear? The mind boggled. From what Hilde Gronbach had said, I reckoned that some kind of blackmail threat had been used. But I could think of no common blackmail threat potent enough to achieve such an end. Nor, for the life of me, could I imagine any *uncommon* blackmail format strong enough to bring about such an extraordinary *volte-face*. Blackmail only works where the price the victim pays is secondary to the price of exposure. I could not believe that this could be true in Cotter's case. What represented the greater enormity of shame: the admission of possibly unnatural sexual appetites or the selling out of country and comrades to a regime as loathsome as Hitler's National Socialism? It was no contest as far as I was concerned. Unlike Cotter, I was not a married man and I was not a war hero – but I reckoned I could live with the public stigma of being a sex freak a lot easier than even the private knowledge that I was a traitor and working for the Nazis.

I wasn't the only one in good spirits on the drive to St Vith. For no reason that I can explain, Danny seemed to think that I was the sun, the moon and the stars. I could be rude as hell to her – telling her frequently that she was a liability to me and, in general, the bane of my life – but it didn't dampen her enthusiasm to stick closer to me than the biblical Ruth. I think I was the security that she had never had in her life. All she asked was to be there, right at my side. I could tease her and swear at her all I liked; she could take it all. The only thing I couldn't do was send her away. The damnable thing was – and I realised it on that drive to St Vith – I was becoming very fond of her.

She taught me the words to a French song – *J'attendrai* – because, she said, she was always waiting for me. She had a pleasant husky contralto voice and I was a bathroom Gigli and the noise we made was probably awful, but our singing made that night-time trip through the Ardennes more fun that I'd had in a very long time.

When we weren't singing, we were joking: even making light of the buzz-bombs that winged overhead on their way to luckless Brussels. Maybe it wasn't very nice joking about such things but, later, I was to remember our amused conclusion that it would be hard to get lost in the Ardennes. You only had to look up in the sky and watch the fiery track of the buzz-bombs to find the direction of due west.

We were still singing songs when we rolled into St Vith at about 9 p.m. A passing GI directed us to the headquarters of the 106th Division. The building was a former hospital, the St Joseph's Kloster. Danny waited outside in the jeep while I made enquiries.

A lieutenant, with one of the closest crew-cuts I've ever seen, was detailed to take me in hand. He was on the G–2 strength and apologised for any signs of confusion at Headquarters. The 'Golden Lions' had just moved into the line and were still in the process of settling in. It had all been pretty hectic.

I assured him that everything at the Kloster looked all very orderly to me. His reference to the Division as the Golden Lions needed no explanation. The 106th's emblem – a lion's head – was much in evidence. The Lieutenant stared at me in surprise when I stated the business that had brought me to St Vith.

'Hey, ain't that funny? Somebody else was asking about the same thing, not two hours ago. He sure sounded English, too. Like the movie actor . . . what's his name . . . Aubrey Somebody . . . Yeah, Aubrey C. Smith.'

My heart sank. 'His name wasn't Vardon, was it? A Colonel Vardon, from SHAEF?'

The Lieutenant's face lit up. 'Yeah! That's the guy. You know him?'

'Unfortunately, yes,' I admitted. 'When was he here?'

'Oh, he wasn't here,' the Lieutenant explained. 'He was calling from Group, down in Luxembourg City.

Said he was on the way here, or at least he would be as soon as he'd eaten dinner.'

My heart rose again. 'Then I've beaten him to it?'

'Well, he ain't shown yet. That's for sure.'

My heart sank again when the Lieutenant provided me with details of Cotter's capture. Clearly, Hibberd had not got the full story.

A platoon from the 423rd Infantry Regiment had been on a routine patrol near Bleialf and had challenged two shadowy figures in woodland, near a river bridge. The pair had ignored the challenge and tried to run for it, whereupon the infantrymen had fired at them. One of the pair, a young woman, had died in the hail of bullets. The other – a man in the uniform of a British Army major – had been severely wounded. The only clue to his identity was an engraving inside the back of the gold watch on his wrist. It said: 'To Major H. Cotter, MC, on appointment SHAEF, Sept 1944.'

The infantry patrol feared that they might have inadvertently wounded an ally engaged on clandestine work and that they had killed the female agent whom he was trying to spirit into Germany or bring out.

'It was the first time these guys had been out on patrol,' the Lieutenant explained to me. 'They were edgy but they say they gave this guy and the woman every chance to show they were friendly.'

The patrol had brought the casualties back to a field dressing station, where the man had been patched up. The girl's body had been brought back to a morgue in St Vith. The British major had been taken to a hospital at Poteau, where he had been scheduled for further surgery that afternoon.

Suddenly, in view of the Lieutenant's information, I was presented with an entirely different situation from what I had been led to expect. What had tilted my perspective and roused nagging suspicions in me was the unexpected revelation of a woman being with Cotter. These suspicions and the fact that the hospital at Poteau was five or six miles away from St Vith dictated my immediate course of action. I wanted to get quickly to Poteau, but a short diversion to the morgue in St Vith was not going to take me much out of my way. I had a hunch that Danny might just have an idea who the dead girl was.

In the event, Danny didn't have to tell me who it was, laid out on a shelf in that cold temporary mortuary in St Vith. The crypt of an old church had been pressed into service to store the recent dead with the not-so-recent dead, and there I needed only a glance by flashlight to identify the corpse. I had been carrying her photograph about for days.

I knew I was staring at the chalky lifeless face of Violette Brochant.

Hating the need for her to go through the ordeal, I got Danny to accompany me a second time into the dank crypt. She confirmed my identification wordlessly, nodding her head in grim assent to my hoarse question.

Within minutes, we were speeding towards Poteau, saying little. An hour ago, we had been happy and singing. Now the night had gone sour.

The American military hospital in Poteau was a small unit: no more than a row of prefabricated huts, erected on a sports field. Yet the huts housed an impressive theatre facility and the surgical accoutrements to go with it. When the duty medical officer asked me to step inside the screened buckie that served as his office, I knew from his face that I had arrived too late.

He gravely imparted to me the news that the British officer I sought had died only half an hour previously. He had been brought in unconscious at ten that morning, had undergone surgery at two in the afternoon, and he had died a few minutes after nine without ever coming to or uttering a word. Would I like to see him?

The unit's mortuary was a canvas tent with trestles. It had a single occupant, already encased in a waterproof bag. The officer opened the bag, so that I could look at the face. I stared at the ashen features, grey with death beneath a shock of blond hair. The face was that of a stranger.

I did not know who he was. I knew only that he was not Major Henry Cotter.

TEN

Blitzkrieg

I don't know how long I stood gazing down at the dead stranger's face, trying not to give way to weariness and despair. All of a sudden, I felt drained. Perhaps I had built too much hope on coming face-to-face with Cotter, alive. Now that hope had evaporated. A confusion of thoughts whirled in my mind. I remembered that day – how distant it seemed now – when I had met Cal Thorn and had been scornful of the need for a gun to combat *Schatten Gruppe*. His words came echoing back to me as I stood over the corpse of the unknown man in the body bag.

'I've met up with *Schatten Gruppe* before,' Thorn had said on that distant day, 'and, like everybody else, I underestimated them. They don't play games,' he had warned me. 'Anybody who managed to get close to them had a nasty habit of winding up dead.'

Well, Cal Thorn had nearly wound up dead. And the trail that had led me from Paris to this mortuary tent in Poteau had been littered with corpses. How many now? Three men had perished in the Rue du Bourrelier. Poor Platt had died in the Zinoniev mansion blown to hell by a device attached to yet another corpse, that of an unknown girl. Then there had been the five murdered girls in the cellar. Now this unknown man and his companion, Violette Brochant. That made twelve dead.

It was more by good luck than judgement that I hadn't figured as the thirteenth corpse. I could say that, at the shuttered house in Paris and at the Zinoniev place, I had got close to *Schatten Gruppe*. Close enough to touch, almost. But how close is close? I felt no nearer unravelling the deadly skeins of their shadowy doings than I had been at the very beginning.

'Seen enough?' the Army doctor asked me, startling me from my sombre thoughts.

I blinked at him. 'Yes . . . Yes, I've seen enough.'

'You know him?'

I shook my head, wearily. 'No . . . All I know is who he's not. And that's no damned help.'

The doctor covered up the face. 'So, you can't identify him?' he said. 'That means a John Doe label.'

'Maybe you should label this one Johann Deutsch,' I suggested, and he threw me a sharp enquiring look. He waited for me to enlarge on the remark. I said, 'I think this John Doe is a member of the Master Race. One of theirs, not ours. One with strong SS connections.'

'Well, I'll be goddamned!' the doctor exclaimed. 'They told us he was a limey . . . a British major.'

'Me, too,' I said sadly. 'But he's not. Not the one I'm looking for, anyway.'

'What are you going to do? You got a place to bunk down for the night?'

'Nope. And I'm sick to my bloody teeth. I don't know what the hell I'm going to do. I seem to have come to a dead end.' No joke was intended in my last remark but the doctor read it as a comment on our immediate surroundings.

He laughed. 'This tent houses stores when we don't use it as a morgue,' he said. He studied me, his eyes warmly sympathetic. 'If you don't mind a professional opinion, Captain, you don't look to be in too good shape. You look bushed.'

'I always look like this,' I said, with an attempt at brightness. He was not deceived. He glanced at his watch.

'Look,' he said, 'I get relieved in ten minutes and I'm heading for some chow and a glass of very tolerable red vino . . . If you ain't in too much of a hurry, why don't you join me?'

I was tempted but declined. I explained that I was not alone. A young Frenchwoman, who was 'assisting' me in my work, was waiting for me out in my jeep.

'What the hell, bring her along!' he insisted, and clinched the argument by confiding that they were having steaks for supper. Their bountiful supply of meat was due to a crisis over starving cattle on farms from which the civil population had been evacuated. An arbitrary solution to the problem had provided the local market with an unexpected abundance of fresh beef.

The personnel attached to the mobile surgical unit at Poteau – including several army nurses – were all quartered in an old Belgian Army *caserne,* close to the field hospital. The barracks had at one time been occupied by Ardennes Chasseurs. I almost had to drag Danny into the forbidding-looking building. It was not its stark prison-like exterior that nourished her reluctance to enter. She was shy about accepting the medical staff's hospitality because of a continuing sensitivity over her short hair and scarred face and the silent hostility her appearance invariably provoked. Her anxiety fled, however, in the face of the concern and sympathy shown to her by the medics.

Our doctor host asked me, when she was not in earshot, what had happened to her.

'Parisian thugs,' I said, and cheerfully added the lie. 'A case of mistaken identity.' The medics did not ask for further elaboration and I offered none.

Although it was late in the evening, we were just in time to share the meal laid on for medical staff who – like our doctor friend – had just finished a fourteen-hour hospital shift. Oddly enough, despite their nearness to the battle front, their 'John Doe' had been the only firearms casualty in the theatre all day. Most of their surgical patients had been wheeled in for appendectomies or operations for perforated ulcers and the

237

like. While we ate, I was cheerfully regaled with staggering statistics of the number of non-battle casualties that any army in the field had to handle. I was given the impression that this small surgical team had to programme their theatre like workers on a conveyor belt and they were still hard-pressed to keep up with the constant stream of candidates for surgery.

The meal was over and we were lingering over strong black coffee when a blight was cast on the post-prandial proceedings. I was just beginning to feel like a civilised human being – having taken one puff on a cigar offered by my host – and was relaxing in well-fed bliss when the door of the mess-hall opened and Colonel Hubert Vardon walked in. His entry was anything but unobtrusive. He strode in with the proprietorial air of a feudal lord interrupting a conclave of vassals. He seemed to expect instant obsequious attention and when none was immediately forthcoming – a bemused silence greeted his arrival – he fretted impatiently for a moment before proclaiming his name, exalted rank and eminence at Supreme Headquarters.

The bewildered medics, occupying only three of the dozen tables, stared at him with a dazed astonishment that would have been no less if Mephistopheles himself had materialised in their midst. They continued to stare at him as he stood there, head averted from their gaze, pronouncing his authority and expectations to the four corners of the room. He talked over the company, rather than at anyone in particular.

Dancing close on Vardon's heels as he had made his entry had come an American Army captain: a tall man, with bright blue eyes and strikingly blond hair that curled from beneath his gold-piped overseas cap. As if Vardon had spoken in some incomprehensible tongue – which his plummy English may well have been to his audience – the captain translated the Colonel's comments, modifying the message for American ears and without resorting to Vardon's imperious tone. His

238

more temperate approach drew an immediate response from the senior medical officer, the doctor who had befriended me.

He acknowledged the captain's remarks and rose from the table to confront the braying apparition who had invaded his mess-hall. With careful courtesy, he greeted Vardon and gave him the unhappy news that the British major, whom he wished to see, was not a British major at all but a man whose identity was unknown. Further, the man in question had died from his wounds.

Vardon accepted this information, moustache twitching angrily, as if he found it difficult to believe what he was hearing.

'How can you possibly know that it's not Major Cotter?' he demanded.

'Because I told him, Colonel,' I said, piping up from my seat. Vardon, who had not seen me or had failed to recognise me until that moment, turned to stare at me. His face was a study. He could have shown no more acute dismay if he had suddenly realised that his bowels were about to become hyper-active.

'You!' he gasped.

'The same old bad penny, sir,' I said, enjoying his discomfiture. 'I'm sorry if you've come all the way from Versailles for nothing but you can take my word for it that the man who was shot by that patrol was not Major Cotter. There's not even a faint resemblance, except in build . . . I've seen the body.'

'Have you, by God!' He was clearly surprised. He sniffed petulantly. 'I have no intention of taking your word on anything. What the devil are you doing here?'

'Same as you, sir,' I said sweetly. 'Still looking for Major Cotter. It seems though that we both jumped to conclusions, or were misinformed. The man they've got here was wearing Cotter's watch . . . and possibly Cotter's uniform. But how he got them, I don't know.'

Vardon turned to his companion. 'What do you make of it, Trygverson?'

The blond-haired captain, who had been hovering attentively, frowned with uncertainty.

'Perhaps, sir,' he suggested diffidently, 'we should be thinking of getting back to Versailles. It looks like we've come on a wild-goose chase.'

'I'm damned if I'm going back empty-handed,' Vardon snapped. 'I certainly want to see this fellow for myself. We only have Abernethy's word for it that it's not Cotter.'

The American captain made a grimace in my direction, as if he, personally, regretted Vardon's unflattering reference to me.

'I suggest, sir, that once you have satisfied yourself one way or another on the man's identity, we go back to St Vith and see if the Divisional Commander can put us up for the night. It's getting very late.'

To my chagrin, my hospitable doctor friend butted in.

'We got plenty of room here,' he declared. 'You don't need to go trailing back to St Vith. Have you guys eaten?'

'We dined in Luxembourg,' Vardon said airily, dismissing that notion. He turned to the captain with the strange-sounding name, as if the offer of accommodation was worthy of serious consideration. 'What do you think, Trygverson? I wouldn't mind taking the weight off my legs for a couple of hours.'

'Whatever you say, sir,' said Trygverson.

'Then, that's settled,' Vardon said. He turned to the doctor. 'Your hospitality will be most acceptable. There are three of us, by the way. Captain Trygverson, myself and a driver outside in the car. I daresay you can accommodate other ranks somewhere?'

'That will be no problem, Colonel,' said the doctor.

'Jolly good show,' Vardon declared, with a clap of his hands. 'Now, if you would show us this man who

240

you say is not Major Cotter and then let us see our quarters, we shan't trouble you any more tonight.'

As they moved off, Vardon was saying in his loud voice: 'We shall be gone long before you're up in the morning, old chap, so there's no need to fuss about breakfast. Never eat it, myself – unless there are kippers on the go.' His voice continued to carry from the corridor. I heard him say: 'I don't intend to waste this journey. Damned if I will! I want to see something of the front while I'm up this way. One vegetates in a place like Versailles, what?'

God help the poor GIs up in the line, I thought. All they need is Vardon telling them how to fight the war!

Danny, whose language and conversation had been mercifully circumspect all evening, was accommodated in a dormitory block occupied by nurses and off-limits to other personnel. I bunked down all on my own in a room with five empty cots in addition to the one I chose. Where Vardon and Trygverson had been parked, I neither knew nor cared. It nettled me enough to know that Vardon was somewhere under the same roof.

I was in bed at midnight and slept like a dead man for four hours. I awakened so refreshed that I couldn't believe the time on my watch. I thought it must have stopped. Sleep eluded me then. Too many thoughts started spinning in my brain for me to settle again. I was also cold. My spacious room-for-six was like a refrigerator.

At quarter to five, I pulled on my trousers and smoked a cigarette, sitting on the edge of the bed with a couple of blankets wrapped round my shoulders. I tried to put into perspective the disappointment of not locating Cotter. All I had achieved in coming to St Vith and Poteau was that I now had two more meaningless jigsaw pieces to fit into a puzzle that had no recognisable picture. My guess was that Violette Brochant and the John Doe had been making for Germany, probably from

241

the Zinoniev mansion. Well, maybe Hilde Gronbach could tell me something about Violette Brochant. I had not had a chance to quiz Hilde about Violette but I intended to remedy that omission before another day passed.

In considering my immediate course of action, I quickly decided to waste no more time hanging around Poteau. Right after breakfast I would telephone St Vith and ascertain the whereabouts of the uniform and watch that the John Doe had been wearing. I would then arrange to take possession of them and also any effects belonging to Violette Brochant. It was inconceivable to me that the woman, for instance, had not been carrying a handbag containing money or means of identification, even false, and that the man's pockets had been empty. It was possible, of course, that the pair had jettisoned bags and anything else they had been carrying when they had run from the patrol. In that case, a search of the spot might be worth instituting. Other puzzles nagged.

If the uniform the John Doe had been wearing was Cotter's – and I meant to find out if it was – where the hell was Cotter? Had he ceased to be of value to the Third Reich in the same way as the girls found in the cellar? Certainly, his worth to his Nazi masters must have plummeted to next to nothing when he had been flushed out of SHAEF. The disturbing thought occurred to me: what if it had been Cotter who had been carried out of the house on the Rue du Bourrelier on a stretcher? What if he had never survived that fateful night in Paris?

Ever since that night, I had never doubted that, with my own eyes, I had seen Cotter emerge from the house. But what if I had been wrong? What if it had been the John Doe, wearing Cotter's coat and battered cap, and it had been Cotter who had been carried out feet first? The possibility shook and bewildered me.

The only tangible gain there was to show for all our

efforts since that night in Paris was the unmasking and placement under lock and key of Hilde Gronbach. She remained the single most likely source of new unexplored leads on the activities of *Schatten Gruppe*. Sitting on my bed in Poteau and reflecting on the fact, I was sorry that I had been deprived of the chance of milking her dry. The flap over Cotter had merely diverted me away from the most fruitful source of information. It was the old story of bird in the bush, but there was no point in lamenting it. The sooner I got back to Spa, the better.

I realised, too, that there was little more that Danny could do now to help our cause. Sooner or later, I would have to face up to the unpleasant necessity of sending her back to Paris. The thought of doing so made me strangely unhappy. She was not going to like it – and it worried me sick to think what might become of her.

I was about to light another cigarette when sounds from the washroom next door alerted me to the fact that I was not the only early waker. It surprised me that anyone else should be up and about at that hour of the morning but I was glad to know I wasn't the only insomniac. It meant that if I got dressed and ventured forth, the other early riser at large might know the way to a fresh brew of coffee. No American military establishments functioned without it.

As I left my room, with towel and shaving kit in hand, I encountered a bleary-eyed Trygverson in the corridor. He had been in the washroom. He yawned a greeting at me as he padded past in stocking soles then disappeared into a room at the end of the passageway.

It was not until I went into the washroom that I realised it was not unoccupied. Vardon was standing naked under one of the open showers, snorting like a grampus as water cascaded down on him. He ignored me and, deciding against turning back, I put my shaving tackle at the side of a washbasin and prepared to have

243

a quick scrape at my stubbly chin. It was not until I had run the hot tap for a couple of minutes that I realised there was no indication of steam from the shower stall behind me and that there should have been. The dreadful truth dawned slowly that there was no hot water in the tap I was running, nor anywhere else in the freezing washroom. Vardon was showering in water which was only a degree removed from ice!

It confirmed for me that his mind was unhinged. Only a galloping psychotic would subject his body to such prolonged torture. His skin was purple and I could see that his back and buttocks were marked by narrow weals. They were not livid enough to be called scars, but he was striped like a tiger. Of course! Cotter had told me that he had been tortured by the Gestapo. Was that the fading legacy?

Perhaps for the first and only time, I felt a pang of pity for him. Maybe harsh experience had made him the blinkered insensitive man he was. I tried to ignore that he was there, although this was not easy. The mirror into which I peered gave me a reflected picture of the showering Colonel. He finally emerged from the stall and proceeded to dry himself with a large towel, hopping about as he did so and grunting strange sounds. Then he wrapped the towel around his middle and commenced to perform callisthenics: running on the spot and making vigorous breast-stroke movements with his arms. He never once glanced in my direction nor made any acknowledgement of my presence. I had nearly completed my own shivering ablutions when he gathered his things and went out, still trotting. He did not close the door. I walked over and pushed it shut, thinking: bloody head-case! Not a word had passed between us.

It was still only 5.20 when, shaved and dressed, I quit my room and went in search of that much-needed cup of coffee. I was about to enter the mess-hall when I heard footsteps and voices from the lobby-hallway near the main entrance. Vardon and Trygverson appeared briefly at the far end of the corridor, crossing my line of vision, framed in the hallway light. I heard the bang of the big main door and the revving of a motor engine. The noise flared and then faded as the unseen vehicle moved away. It looked like Vardon had kept his promise to depart early. It was a promising start to the day. I hoped our paths would never cross again.

The mess-hall was deserted, but in the cook-house beyond I found a couple of fatigues-clad GIs. One of the stoves had been lit and a coffee jug steamed on its top. One of the men was sitting on an upturned box, cigarette in one hand and mug of coffee in the other. He was watching the other pile wood into a second stove. They overcame any surprise my appearance had provoked and assured me that, if I liked my coffee hot and strong, I had come to the right place. I was handed an enamel mug of their gloriously pungent brew and invited to find myself a crate to sit on.

Parked in front of the stove and thinking that the world was not such a bad old place after all, I was rudely wakened from that happy thought by what sounded like a distant roll of thunder. Only it wasn't thunder. The distant roll went on without end. It gathered in intensity of sound, clap upon clap, and rumbled on and on and on.

It took only dazed seconds to realise that it was gunfire: sustained gunfire and heavy stuff at that, on a scale greater than anything I had ever heard in my life.

'Jesus!' said one of the GIs to his buddy, in an awed voice. 'You ever hear anything like that before, Joe? We must be giving the Krauts hell!'

Joe was standing, his head cocked to one side, and a look of growing shock on his face.

'That shit ain't goin' out,' he said, his eyes wide. 'It's comin' in! There ain't a Kraut within ten, fifteen miles of here . . . And that stuff's burstin' this side of St Vith! Listen.' He winced as a sudden *crump-crump-crump* rent the morning air! It sounded very close. 'I'll be goddamned!' he exclaimed. 'That was just up the goddamned road!'

If I had known on the morning of 16 December 1944 what I know now, I would probably have bundled Danny into the jeep and taken off south out of Poteau like a bat out of hell. As it was, I was blissfully ignorant of the real significance of the German barrage that interrupted enjoyment of my early morning mug of coffee. If anyone had told me that the barrage was the prelude to a mighty offensive, aimed at splitting the Allied Armies in two and driving on Antwerp, I would have given him the horse laugh.

The trouble was that, in spite of Goldman's warnings of a big German push, I believed our own propaganda as much as the next man. Further proof if proof be needed, that I'm not very bright. I *knew* as well as the next man that the Germans had taken such a clobbering in France and Russia that they had neither the men nor resources to stage much more than token counterattacks of a local nature. I was wrong – but so was the next man and a hell of a lot of generals.

How the mad dictator in Berlin managed to gather together a quarter of a million troops, two thousand artillery pieces and close on eight hundred tanks, and concentrate them opposite the Ardennes without anyone knowing they were there, was something of a miracle. But that's what he did. And when he launched them against the eighty thousand Americans, stretched out paper-thin along seventy-five miles of front, I wasn't the only one taken by surprise.

Given these circumstances there were many worse places to be than Poteau, which was a good fifteen miles from the nearest gun in Hitler's west wall. At the time, however, I did not appreciate my good fortune. This unremarkable little Belgian village in the rear struck me as being a distinctly unhealthy place to linger. In my estimation, there was absolutely nothing there that warranted the Germans lobbing huge shells at the place from massive great railway guns, sited somewhere in the next county. I realise now, of course, that it was Poteau's location – rather than ammo dumps and the like – that attracted the brutal interest of the German gunners. The village was the meeting-place of three arterial roads and, with a railway line running through the middle, it was a junction of some military consequence: one which the enemy hoped to render unsafe.

As far as I was concerned, the enemy succeeded. Danny and I left hurriedly at breakfast-time. Two military policemen were erecting road signs – the old ones had just been destroyed – when we made our exit, left, down the St Vith road. It was not yet light on another raw and misty morning and the shelling had stopped – locally, that is. The big guns were still banging away in the distance, like a moving thunderstorm. The unbroken fury of the initial barrage was sustained for only half an hour. Since six, the noise of war had taken on a different character: rising and falling in volume, with cadences occurring in the patterns of sound. Whatever was happening – and nobody seemed to know what was happening – most of it was happening away to the east and south-east of St Vith.

I was determined not to let the early morning shelling interfere with my plan for the day and headed for St Vith, in the belief that it would be no less safe than Poteau. I was kidding myself. St Vith was six miles nearer the front and shells were dropping on the town with uncomfortable regularity. As I navigated through the narrow streets of the town, the thought kept recurring that I should have given the place a miss. The thought and its recurrence coincided with the sudden explosion of shells, which may have missed us by a mile but seemed to be almost right on top of us.

In an effort to avoid lumbering Army trucks, I took a narrow cobbled lane which I hoped was a short cut to the vicinity of the St Joseph's Kloster. It might have been if the rubble from a collapsed house had not fallen across the thoroughfare, effectively blocking it. I had to back a hundred yards towards the log-jam of trucks, from which I thought we had escaped. Rather than rejoin the jam, I ran the jeep up on to a tiny triangle of muddy yard that was just big enough to take it, and decided to make for the Divisional HQ on foot.

Danny was far from happy at being left to look after the jeep, but I promised her that I would be gone only half an hour at the most. It took me ten minutes at a steady jog-trot to reach the Kloster.

If, earlier, I had decided that that fateful Saturday morning was the wrong day to have come to St Vith, I soon realised that the same applied for a visit to the 'Golden Lions' HQ. With knobs on! Mild pandemonium reigned at the Kloster, with people running around in all directions.

All I wanted to find out was the whereabouts of the watch and uniform that the John Doe had been wearing and, also, what had happened to Violette Brochant's effects. It was information that I should have been able to obtain by telephone but I had been unable to raise HQ from Poteau earlier.

After waiting around like a whisky salesman at a prohibitionists' convention, I finally cornered the G–2 lieutenant to whom I had spoken the previous evening. Like everyone else he was not over-eager to be bothered by me and my particular problems. Everyone at Division had quite enough on their hands trying to assess the scale and penetration of the surprise German attack.

Nevertheless, he did tell me that the clothes worn by the John Doe and Violette Brochant had been destroyed, as unfit for further use. Other personal effects, including the watch, had been parcelled up and sent to Army Group in Luxembourg because – the lieutenant understood – of a request from there. He had thought the request may have originated from the British colonel

248

who had been in Luxembourg last night and had later called in at the St Vith HQ. The same colonel had been in St Vith before six that morning, although the lieutenant had not spoken to him. He understood – although he was not sure – that the colonel was returning to SHAEF via First Army Headquarters. If I was going back to Spa, I could probably catch up with him there and get everything clarified.

That was all the news I needed to cheer me up! Coming to St Vith had been a complete waste of time. I should have headed straight for Spa – not that I had the faintest desire to catch up with Vardon.

'Oh, there's one thing you should maybe know about,' the lieutenant said. 'You mentioned that this guy we thought was a British major is maybe a Kraut . . . Seems there could be Krauts knocking about in American uniforms, too.'

'I know,' I said, with some feeling. 'I've been chasing the bastards. They wounded my partner – and they keep leaving bodies all over the place. That's what brought me to St Vith in the first place!'

The lieutenant was taken aback. 'You know about them?' he said, with incredulity. 'I only got a call about them ten minutes ago.'

'A call?' It was my turn to show surprise.

'Sure. Some guy with the Four-two-fourth Infantry, out at Heckuscheid. They've been beating off Kraut attacks out there all morning. After one of them, they got themselves a wounded Kraut officer – a company commander with divisional orders in his pocket . . . There was something in the papers about an operation called GREIF . . .' The lieutenant spelled the word out. It meant nothing to me.

'What about this . . . GREIF?' I asked. He shrugged. 'I don't know the details. Only that the Krauts had some of their own guys operating in American uniforms and that there were special ways of identifying them.

Division didn't want their attack troops shooting up their own men.'

'This wounded officer . . . was he SS?'

'No. The guys at Heckuscheid named his outfit – but it wasn't SS. The Krauts hitting them were Volksgrenadiers. I'll know for sure by noon. The papers are being sent here by messenger.'

I toyed with the idea of hanging on at St Vith until the captured orders arrived, but decided not to do so. The thought of putting in time in the 106th's HQ, while it was such a bee-hive of frantic activity, did not enchant me. In any case, vital intelligence of this nature would surely be transmitted to Spa and other Army headquarters in the Group as a matter of urgency.

Yes, it would be passed on to Spa, the lieutenant confirmed. And he seemed relieved when I told him I would head there immediately.

'Be sure you check out your route with the traffic guys,' he warned me, in parting. 'Nearly every CP in the line has been screaming for reinforcements and, if they get them, the roads could be snarled up in no time. You don't want to be competing for road space with a couple of tank squadrons heading the other way!'

I promised I would check out our route.

If the lieutenant seemed indecently pleased to see the back of me, Danny's relief at my return to the jeep served as a small compensation. She was tearful with joy, having almost given me up for dead. Her charged emotions had been heightened by drama nearby. A monster shell had just demolished a house a few hundred yards up the road and given her a king-sized fright. I was touched that her thoughts had been centred on my safety, not her own.

I calculated that, even with delays, we could be in Spa in two to three hours at the most. This was to turn out to be a miscalculation of some magnitude. The route plan we had been directed to follow did not help, but was not entirely to blame. Understandably, we had rated a very low priority in traffic clearance compared with vehicles moving to and from the front. We were, therefore, given a route that avoided roads designated for the swift movement of essential traffic. And, by 'swift', they meant ten miles per hour: a positively breakneck speed for a military convoy.

'You'll miss all the known bottlenecks,' an officer at St Vith had assured me, extolling the elaborate scenic tour we had to take. He spoke the truth. Our route had all the *unknown* bottlenecks! The trouble was that, although the north-south traffic was far from heavy, the east-west flow was considerable and did not seem to be regulated. We were scarcely out of St Vith – the first cross-roads out of the town – when we were brought to a complete stop. On the junction, a huge earth-moving vehicle had become entangled with a big truck towing a gun and both were impossible to move because of tailbacks in all directions. It took three hours to clear the road.

We were arbitrarily re-routed east by military cops, who were having nervous breakdowns trying to untangle the jam. One of them, who seemed to know the neighbourhood and was not screaming and tearing his hair out like the sergeant who was with him, told me that detouring by the villages of Schoenberg and Andler would not take us too far off our prescribed northerly route. The alternative, he pointed out, was to sit where we were until our asses froze.

Eager to be moving, I was only too happy to back where he said 'back' and turn where he said 'turn' and, generally, extricate the jeep from the mess. We eventually reached the relative freedom of the Schoenberg road with his bellowed instructions ringing in my ears. I had to cross the river at Schoenberg, follow the river for a mile to Andler, come back across the river, and take the left fork for Herresbach and Amblève.

'You can't go wrong, he had shouted at me, as he had waved me through between two stalled trucks. I

251

would not have bet on it. The place names meant nothing to me and I doubted very much if I would have any memory of them five minutes later. I was past caring, however – so great was my joy to jockey the jeep out of that snarl-up and be moving *anywhere*.

As we neared what turned out to be Schoenberg, I was viewing things more soberly. Echoing from the mist-enshrouded valley came the sound of gunfire. I wasn't sure if we were getting nearer to it or it was getting nearer to us. Neither eventuality offered consolation. The racket of automatic and small-arms fire was loud enough for me to peg the distance at three or four miles. That was three or four miles too close for my peace of mind.

At the bridge over the River Our at Schoenberg, we had to wait to allow a convoy of towed artillery pieces to cross from the other side. I didn't like the look of this. They were going the wrong way to be of any help in the battle up ahead. I got out and asked a soldier guarding the bridge why the guns were pulling back.

'Maybe they feel safer this side of the river,' he said. 'If the Krauts take Bleialf, they're gonna come down that road over there.' He pointed towards the steep hill on the opposite bank and the road down which the artillery had come. 'That there's the road from Bleialf.'

An hour ago, I had not known of Schoenberg's existence, but at least the name of Bleialf was not new to me. I was able to nod wisely and contribute something to the conversation. The village was in Germany proper, wasn't it? On the other side of the border.

It sure was, the soldier told me. Schoenberg – where we were standing – was Belgian, but only just. The border was just a mile off, over the top of that hill on the far bank. Bleialf was another couple of miles further down the road.

'You ain't thinking of goin' there?' the soldier enquired, with an air of concern. He laughed when I told him we had not even meant to come to Schoenberg

252

– we were heading for Spa but had been diverted because of a traffic snarl-up near St Vith.

'It sure is one hell of a goddamned war,' he observed philosophically.

There was no answer to that. The GI had said it all. It sure was one hell of a goddamned war. And if proof of its perverse and unpredictable nature was required, the very next moment provided it.

Careering down the steep road on the far side of the river, horn blaring, came a dun-coloured car. It seemed to be having difficulty with its brakes – and a lot more besides – weaving down the gradient from side to side of the road. Ahead of it, almost on the bridge, was the last of the gun-towing trucks. The blare of the car's horn was accompanied by an abrasive metallic clanking, coming – it seemed – from a trailing exhaust pipe, all but shorn from its mountings. The appalling racket was further augmented by the roar of the car's unsilenced engine, which reverberated across the valley with the same kind of rasping splutter as a doodle-bug in flight. Black exhaust smoke trailed from underneath the vehicle.

The car continued its uncertain path towards the bridge, swerving wildly on the approach and then weaving across as if seeking a way past the tail truck and gun of the artillery convoy. There was none. The car skidded once, glancing into the towed gun before making a final swerve and crashing into the bridge parapet only a few yards from where I was standing with the soldier. We both ran forward to assist the driver, who had slumped forward over the wheel and was pressing on the horn with his bodyweight.

As we reached the car, the rear doors swung open and Vardon and the American captain, Trygverson, scrambled clear from opposite sides. Both seemed dazed and were staggering like drunks. I ignored them, not allowing my mind to dwell on my hope of several hours earlier, now forlorn, that our paths would never cross

253

again. My sole concern was for the driver, whose face was covered in blood.

The soldier and I, between us, disentangled him from the wheel and lifted him out of the car. We laid him on the ground, with me supporting his head. The man opened his eyes and groaned as I eased bloody hair off his forehead and tried to locate his injury. There was an angry cut above one eye and blood was seeping from a furrow like a whip-lash across his scalp. Neither wound looked too serious. The way the flesh was puffing up across the bridge of his nose suggested that he must have bumped his head hard when the car hit the parapet and the impact had nearly knocked him out. The scalp wound had not resulted from the collision, although it was recent. Blood from it had congealed and had matted the hair in its vicinity. The man looked up at me, trying to focus his eyes. I told him he was OK and to keep still.

Behind me, some distance away, I could hear Vardon's loud and complaining voice. He was going on bitterly about American incompetence and I heard him say 'damned disgraceful' at least three times. An officer and soldiers from the bridge detail had come dashing to the scene and there was now quite a mill of bodies around the car. I was glad to surrender my charge to a medic who, swab in hand, took the driver's head on his elbow and began his own expert examination.

'Looks like he got his hair parted with a bullet,' the medic said, looking up at the cluster around us. 'Anybody know what happened?'

It was Trygverson who answered. 'Some trigger-happy guys on the other side of that hill up there . . . they must have thought we were Krauts . . . Nearly shot us off the goddamned road.'

'Our guys?' one of the soldiers asked.

'As sure as I'm standing here,' Trygverson confirmed. 'We didn't stop to argue with them. We goddamn couldn't. We thought they'd killed the Corporal there but he managed to keep going. He saved our lives.'

I took a look at the car. It looked like it had been used for target practice. It was holed in several places, one window shot out. But bullets had not caused the obvious damage. The bodywork was crumpled along one side and there was the trailing exhaust pipe. All the way across the bridge, a track of oil marked the staff car's erratic path.

'How did they shoot away the exhaust pipe?' I asked Trygverson.

'They didn't,' he said. 'We ploughed up a line of wooden fence posts and went over some rocks when the Corporal got his skull creased. I thought the floor was falling out.' He shook his head in bemused wonder. 'God knows how we got back on the road and still had four wheels. Brakes were all to hell and bits and pieces kept falling off all the way down that hill. I don't want another ride like it if I live to be a hundred!'

I regarded the battered car, with its radiator buried in the bridge parapet.

'I don't think you'll be riding anywhere in that, anyway,' I commented.

Vardon didn't seem to give a damn about his injured driver. He was a little way off, having buttonholed the bridge control officer, and was still ranting on about trigger-happy Americans. The young officer's polite sympathy over what had happened had worn thinner as the tirade had gone on and on.

'Excuse me, sir,' I heard him say, with a definite edge to his voice, 'but, right now we're going to have to clear this bridge. I got a job to do.' He turned his back on Vardon and came towards us, calling for volunteers to manhandle the wrecked car off the bridge. The thunderous look on his face told me that Vardon had not made a friend.

I gave a hand to push the staff car off the bridge and clear of the roadway. So did Trygverson, at my elbow.

'Are you who I think you are?' he asked, as we applied our weight together.

'The name's Abernathy,' I said. 'We slept under the same roof last night . . . At Poteau.'

'I got you now,' he said. 'Sorry if I wasn't at my brightest last time I saw you. The Colonel should have been a milkman. He likes an early start.'

'The Colonel and I are old acquaintances,' I said.

'I know,' he said. 'I know all about you. He hates your guts.'

'It's mutual,' I told Trygverson.

He smiled. 'He sure ain't the most lovable character I've ever met. But don't tell him I said so. I'm kinda stuck with him.' He grinned. 'But I'm learning to bend with the wind.'

'You have my sympathy, Captain,' I said.

When the car was finally cleared off the bridge, Trygverson offered me a cigarette and we stood talking.

'How come you got landed with Vardon?' I asked him. The American grinned.

'He went to a whole lot of trouble to get me on the team at SHAEF after this other guy, Cotter, kinda let the side down. You know about him, of course. You've been trying to find him.' I nodded, and he went on: 'Well, Vardon had to take somebody from the US Army, which he didn't like much, but he agreed if he could pick his own man. He picked me. Asked for me by name. Wouldn't have anyone else.'

'You knew him before?'

'Briefly. He visited First Army back in October and I got the job of looking after him. I must have made a bigger impression than I realised.'

'I'm amazed,' I said. 'I always got the feeling from Vardon that he detested Yanks.'

Trygverson laughed. 'You could be right. But I'm only a Yank by adoption. I'm Norwegian by birth.'

The revelation surprised me. There was, perhaps, the faintest trace of European accent in his speech but it was

256

scarcely noticeable. It was not nearly so pronounced, for instance, as Goldman's back in Spa, but it was discernible in spite of a strong American twang and choice of idiom.

'How does a Norwegian come to be in the American Army?' I asked.

'Hell, I'm not the only one,' he replied, amused. 'You ask anyone at First Army about the Norwegian Ninetyninth. It's the finest infantry battalion they got – and Norwegian to a man. It's my old outfit.'

I would have liked to have learned more but Vardon arrived on the scene at that moment like the bad fairy. His face fell when he recognised me.

'Same old bad penny, Colonel,' I said with a smile. 'We really ought to stop meeting like this.' He was not amused.

'This is a bad enough show without your damned impertinence, Abernethy,' he snapped and, dismissing me, looked past me at Trygverson. 'These damned Americans say they have no spare transport. You'd better have a word with them, Trygverson. They don't seem to appreciate that a British colonel warrants rather more consideration than I've been shown so far.'

With an apologetic little nod to me, Trygverson went off to speak to the bridge control officer. Vardon was eyeing our jeep, parked thirty yards away. Danny, who had emerged to take an interest in the staff car's removal, was leaning against a door, smoking a cigarette. She gave a friendly wave.

'Is that creature a woman?' Vardon snorted, turning to me.

'That young lady,' I said, emphasising the words, 'happens to be with me.'

'Young lady!' he exclaimed. 'Dressed like that. What kind of hotch-potch of a uniform is that she's wearing? Has she any entitlement to go around like that?'

'She has every right in the world,' I said, needled by his sanctimonious attitude. 'She's on active service in a war zone. How do you expect her to dress – in silk stockings and high heels?'

'Is that your jeep?' Vardon demanded.

'Yes, it is,' I said, and I didn't like the look that came into his eyes. Facing me, he squared his shoulders and extended a hand, palm up.

'Ill take the keys, if you please, Abernethy. You're a civilian. You have no status here. And you won't be needing that jeep anymore. I'm commandeering it.'

'Over my dead body,' I growled. My anger was touching flash-point. It might have risen above it if Trygverson had not chosen that moment to return. He halted, eyes darting from Vardon to me as he sensed the two-way current of antagonism.

'It's no use, Colonel,' he said, deciding to intrude and say his piece. 'These people here don't have any transport to spare. They say it shouldn't be difficult to hitch a ride to St Vith.'

'I'm not going to St Vith,' Vardon said, 'And we don't need to scrounge lifts. Abernethy's got transport. I'm commandeering it.'

'He's bloody well not,' I said. 'He goes anywhere near my jeep and, so help me, I'll put a bullet in him.'

'Gentlemen,' Trygverson appealed, in a shocked voice, 'surely we can reach friendly agreement.' He looked me in the eyes, almost beseeching. 'Please, is there anything you can do?'

'I'm going to Spa,' I declared.

Trygverson's face brightened. 'But that's great! We're going there, too. Can't we all ride together? You'd be doing us a big favour.'

I said I wasn't doing Vardon any favours. As far as I was concerned, he could walk back to Versailles. Trygverson, however, was a persuasive advocate and he got me to back down. I had nothing against him and I made it clear that it was for his sake, not Vardon's, that I was prepared to let them ride in our jeep. I also made it clear that Vardon had no authority over me and that if he started coming the high-and-mighty with me again, he would be walking.

Me and my big mouth! Half an hour later, we were all walking! And the jeep, which had served me so faithfully, was left abandoned: up to its axles in a forest bog, miles from anywhere!

ELEVEN

Road to Nowhere

I blamed Vardon for the disaster. We were tootling along the road to Amblève – or so I believed – when we passed a road sign to which I paid scant attention. Vardon, however – sitting in the back of the jeep with Trygverson and their driver, who was sporting a turban bandage – gave out a great roar and told me that I had missed the turning for Amblève. I braked fiercely, my confidence in my navigation suddenly fragile. Only moments before, I had warned my passengers that we had to fork left for the village but, in my estimation, we still had several miles to travel to reach the junction I was talking about.

Under pressure from Vardon and the others, I backed the jeep to the signpost. Sure enough, the sign said: 'AMBLÈVE 11 km.' But the road it indicated was no more than a muddy lane.

'I've seen better farm roads,' I said. 'That can't possibly be the way.'

'You said we had to turn left,' Vardon twittered 'Why do you think they've got a sign there if it doesn't go where it says? For birds to roost on?'

Fear that I would be proved a proper idiot if I stuck to my guns made me swallow my misgivings. I gunned the jeep along the lane. It led up towards a wooded hill and its surface was every bit as bad as it had looked at first sight. Mud sprayed up from the wheels of the jeep as I negotiated the twists and turns of the looping ascent. Higher up, I was driving in slush.

As we reached the wood, the conviction grew that we were on the road to nowhere. Although the track straightened, it seemed to spear interminably into the heart of dark uncharted forest. It also narrowed perceptibly, with scarcely enough width to take the jeep. Little of the grey day's murky light penetrated the forest's depths and, with tree branches brushing the jeep on both sides, even Vardon and the others began to have doubts about our chosen course.

'Let's turn and go back,' suggested Trygverson.

That was easier said than done. It meant reversing nearly half a mile to a place where we could turn.

Leaning out above the driver's door, I did my best to steer the jeep backwards along the way we had come. It was tricky work. The tail section kept pushing back branches of trees that overhung the path and I had to pull my head back frequently to avoid being decapitated by them. They swung back unpredictably, slapping against my face and temporarily blinding me. It was possibly because I got one mouthful of pine needles too many that I over-compensated on the steering wheel.

As I corrected the steering, one of the front wheels climbed a boulder or other solid obstruction, a tree branch nearly knocked my head off, and I was thrown off balance. I lost my hold on the steering-wheel and, pushing out with my feet to save myself, tramped the gas pedal into the floor. The net result was that the jeep leapt backwards at an angle to the desired course and nearly capsized as the rear offside wheel plunged into black boggy turf and sank. I tried to steer out of the mess but succeeded only in getting the front offside wheel into the glutinous morass that skirted that side of the track. The jeep tilted steeply as both wheels sank deeper and deeper.

In the gathering dark, we tried for an hour to free the jeep. It was pitch black when, in the end, we were forced to admit defeat. If anything, the jeep was now even deeper in the mire than ever – and still slowly sinking. The only calm person was Danny. The rest of us, muddied and exhausted, were spitting with frustration.

Loaded with as much gear as we could carry, we began the long trek down through the woods to the road we should never have left. To add to our discomfort, it began to snow. Out of the forest, on lower ground, the squalls were of sleety rain, which reduced the track to a muddy slide.

As we approached the main road, we glimpsed traffic heading west: the way we wanted to go. There was traffic overhead too – buzz-bombs. Mostly, we heard them. Now and again, however, we saw the exhaust flames of the pilotless missiles crossing above, glimpsing them briefly in gaps in low thin cloud.

Watching their east-west passage confirmed for me that our diversion into the forest had taken us south, away from Amblève. I entertained dark thoughts of uprooting the signpost that had misled us as soon as we reached the road. In the event, I was saved the trouble. Others had beaten me to it.

A two-ton truck was parked at the junction and a group of poncho-draped soldiers had dug the four-by-four timber post out of the ground.

They were examining the sign and, at close quarters, it could be seen that an additional figure '1' had been painted on the original. One kilometre had been changed to read eleven kilometres. The soldiers suspended operations on our arrival.

They were surprised that anyone in their right minds had been fooled by the signpost into thinking that the logging trail we had been on was the Amblève road. There had been lots of west-bound traffic on the road that day but we were the only ones who had been taken in by it. The soldiers were from an engineer combat battalion, dispersed on a wide variety of duties along the length of the Amblève valley, and they had recognised the out-of-place signpost as one that had disappeared from a junction only a mile outside Amblève village. Some miles on from where we were, the Andler-Amblève road joined with the Amblève-Bütgenbach road and it was from this junction that the signpost had gone missing.

'We spotted the sign pointing up the track when we passed this morning,' one of the engineers explained. 'We knew it didn't belong.'

They had decided that if the sign was still in the wrong place at night, on their return to Amblève, they would uplift it and restore it to its rightful position.

'We didn't think anybody'd be stupid enough to go up that goddamned wood trail,' one GI declared to my blushing face. 'What bothers me is who would play a fool joke like that?'

'Probably one of them Kraut-speaking farmers that live around here,' another suggested. 'They may be Belgian but they ain't the same as the folks up around Liège and Namur. They ain't the least bit friendly.'

The likelier explanation is that the sign was moved the night before by one of Otto Skorzeny's commando teams, dressed in American uniforms. At the time, their mischief was unknown to me – but the activities of these marauders and their master-plan, code-named GREIF, ceased to be a secret from the Allied Command in the early days of the Ardennes battle. As it turned out, Skorzeny's commando operation had nothing to do with Keitler's gang of murderers and their activities, but ignorance of this fact was to confuse the issue for some time. It was unfortunate for me and those of us on the trail of *Schatten Gruppe* that Skorzeny's group happened to choose American uniforms and American vehicles to screen an operation in an area where Keitler's gang were already active and using similar ploys. I believe now that both SS groups were completely in the dark about each other's activities – so it's no surprise that we were confused by what was going on.

ObersturmbannFührer der Waffen SS Otto Skorzeny

and his specially mustered Panzer Brigade 150 were given an essentially military function in the Ardennes blitzkrieg. Their job was to create havoc behind the American lines ahead of the German offensive.

It is known now that forty jeeps, carrying four – and five-man teams of English-speaking Germans, infiltrated the American line. Their instructions were to range to the Meuse and beyond, sabotaging ammo and fuel dumps. They also had a reconnaissance role: pinpointing and identifying American armoured and artillery units. Road signs were to be switched and minefield markers removed and used to indicate false fields. Telephone lines were to be cut, radio signals intercepted and communications confused by the transmission of fake orders and counter-orders.

Skorzeny had thought of just about everything likely to make life difficult for troops reeling under an onslaught in which they were outnumbered thirty to one.

It was, perhaps, a small consolation, therefore, that the removal of one road sign near Amblève achieved no disruption worth talking about. All it did was inconvenience and embarrass me and my jeep-load of 'tourists', whose presence in the war zone was fortuitous and whose ability to influence the developing battle was negligible.

The squad of engineers, whom we had encountered, had been engaged on routine road-maintenance work and had been returning to their billet-quarters in and around Amblève. Vardon, as full of his own importance as ever, wanted them to take their truck up to the woods there and then to tow out our abandoned jeep. He was surprised when little enthusiasm was shown for the suggestion. The squad sergeant, a quietly spoken Oklahoman called Murdock, said he and his boys would be happy to oblige first thing in the morning, when there was some daylight to see by. He was not, however, about to take his truck in the dark up a forest trail that was running muddier than the Arkansas River. He very reasonably suggested that, if Vardon and the rest of us cared to ride with them into Ambléve, we could shelter in the dry and maybe do something about whistling up fresh transport from Spa or Malmedy. On the other hand, the Colonel might prefer to hang around in the wet and hope that somebody would chance along the road who might give him and his friends a ride all the way to Spa. Murdock reckoned that the Colonel might have a long and miserable wait if he chose this option. In his experience, goddamned little moved on that road after dark.

Murdock's quiet and reasonable manner – which fronted a firm steely resolve – seemed to take the bluster out of Vardon. He allowed Trygverson to step in with his more diplomatic approach. Trygverson suggested that Danny and I might be prepared to shelter in Amblève until morning, when our jeep could be recovered, but that he and the Colonel were anxious to get to Spa – that night, if possible. If it was all right with the Sergeant, they would come with him to Amblève and call First Army for help. I happily voiced my agreement. I wanted my jeep back and, if Vardon and Trygverson wanted to go their own way, that suited me fine. After what we had been through, I saw no point in breaking my neck to get to Spa that night at the expense of our jeep.

We all climbed aboard the 'deucer' – as the engineers called their two-tonner – and half an hour later Danny and I were feasting on corned-beef hash and coffee with Murdock's engineers in the warm kitchen of their farmhouse billet on the edge of Amblève. On our way through the village, we had dropped off Vardon, Trygverson and their driver at the schoolhouse – the engineers' command post – where they intended to send an SOS to Spa for relief transport.

Murdock told Danny and me to make ourselves at home anywhere we liked in the big farmhouse. He and

265

his boys stood on no ceremony and it was simply a case of finding a place on the floor to lay our bedrolls. If we wanted privacy, there was always the barn, which was dry but goddamned cold. He was clearly unsure just what kind of relationship Danny and I enjoyed and he seemed relieved when I let him know that it did not extend to us sharing a sleeping bag. He promptly ejected two of his men from a curtained recess in the kitchen and declared it 'off-limits' to his squad. Danny could sleep there.

The American soldiers accepted their displacement with commendable gallantry. Danny intrigued them and they were openly curious about our odd partnership. When I hinted vaguely at secret operations, they became almost laboriously discreet in the care they took to avoid any impression of seeming inquisitive.

Danny was a hit with them. For the second evening in succession, her shyness melted away in the face of uninhibited friendliness and generosity. The men were prepared to share what food and little comforts they had and Danny responded with all the vivacity and warmth that was so natural a part of her personality.

The soldiers loved her fractured English and, also, the occasional barrack-room expression which she slipped into her conversation with such innocence that the effect was comic rather than offensive. When she accepted a cigar and smoked it, wedged in the side of her mouth with the aplomb of a veteran dogface – as immortalised in the famous *Willie and Joe* cartoons of infantry life – her conquest was complete.

When, later in the evening, I left her to take a stroll to the village, she was still holding court: happily learning the intricacies of poker from a devoted entourage of GI tutors. It was Murdock's idea that we should walk down to the command post and meet his officers. No one, he said, was likely to raise any objections about a girl spending the night under the same roof as enlisted men – it was an emergency – but it was better to clear these things with the post commander. There was also the matter of recovering the abandoned jeep. Again, he foresaw no objection to his aim to haul the jeep out of the mud at first light but it would do no harm to get official blessing. Just in case the Army had different plans.

'Don't you worry none about the officers,' he said. 'I can handle them. Me and them get along just fine.'

To my surprise, Vardon and Trygverson were still at the command post when we got there. I thought they would have been long gone. Vardon was snoozing in a decrepit-looking armchair in front of a log fire. Trygverson was sitting at a table with a lieutenant and a captain, drinking coffee. I was introduced to the officers. They had heard all about me and the girl with the scarred face and they were just a little miffed that we had gone off with Murdock's squad without so much as a hello. What rankled, I think, was that Danny had not been paraded for their inspection. They didn't give a damn about me but they were filled with curiosity about the mysterious girl I had in tow.

The captain had no objection to Sergeant Murdock helping us to recover the jeep in the morning. Because of conflicting reports of what was happening at the front, he was not sending out a roads detail as usual the next day and he intended to keep his men nearer to home, in case of emergencies.

'Did you manage to get in touch with Spa?' I asked Trygverson.

He shook his head. 'We couldn't raise Spa – not direct anyway. But we got a message through via Malmedy, thanks to these gentlemen. Their battalion command is in Malmedy.'

'First Army's sending a staff wagon for the Colonel and Captain Trygverson,' the engineer captain said. 'But they couldn't say when it would get here. It could be on its way now . . . or it could be morning before it gets here. We just gotta wait.'

When Murdock and I left the schoolhouse, Trygverson came out with us saying he would catch a breath of fresh air.

'Do you still hope to find the elusive Major Cotter?' he asked me.

'Yes,' I told him. 'Cotter and a whole lot more.'

'You think you'll find him in Spa?'

'Maybe not,' I said. 'Maybe he's dead ... But the bird in the bush is not the important one. It's the bird in the hand.'

'I do not understand.'

'A canary in a cage,' I said darkly, running riot with ornithological aphorism. 'A canary who was only starting to sing before I went chasing off to St Vith on a wild-goose chase.'

'A canary?' He was mystified. Then the penny dropped. Comprehension dawned.

'Oh, yeah ... you mean a stool-pigeon!'

'A bird by any other name is still a bird,' I agreed. He laughed and stretched out a hand to grasp mine.

'In case we don't meet again, Captain Abernathy – good luck. And good hunting!'

He strode back into the schoolhouse. I ran to catch up with Murdock. He was looking up at the inky sky.

'I hope it don't snow before morning,' he said.

It did not snow before morning. I know because I got up a couple of times during the night and looked out through the heavy canvas flaps being used as window black-outs. On both occasions, I had been wakened by the noise of heavy traffic roaring through the village – although I saw none of it on the times I looked out. There was no view of the road from the side of the house where I had bedded down.

I could still hear traffic on the road at seven in the morning, as we sat around in the big stone-flagged kitchen, breakfasting on hot beans and coffee.

'I thought you said nothing moved on that road after dark,' I reminded Murdock.

He shrugged his shoulders, his mouth full of beans, and licked his spoon clean before replying.

'The road ain't never been that busy before. That stuff's pullin' back from further east.'

'Where is it going?'

'Most of it's headed in the Ondenval direction . . . up towards Malmedy. But the St Vith road's busy too.'

'St Vith?' I queried. 'How far are we from St Vith?'

'No more'n seven miles.'

I was astonished. After being on the road nearly all of the previous day, it was shattering to realise that we were still only a brisk two-hour walk from our starting point. I commented bitterly on the fact to Murdock.

'You sure picked a funny way to get from St Vith to Spa,' he said.

'I didn't pick it,' I pointed out.

'You'd no call to come through Amblève at all,' he said, ignoring my remark. 'Leastways, not the way you came.' He grinned.

'Thinkin' on it, you'd no call to go up that logging trail neither! Seems to me, Captain Abernathy, that you ain't been gettin' anywhere very fast.'

He was, of course, absolutely right. At our present rate of progress, we would be lucky to get to Spa before Christmas.

Murdock was taking no chances in getting bogged down in the woods where the jeep had come to grief. After a brief absence from the farmhouse he reappeared about eight o'clock and told Danny and me to get our things: our transport awaited. It was still not light as he led us out into the yard, where a big Ack-Ack half-track stood.

'Climb aboard,' Murdock invited Danny and me. 'Let's go an' haul that jalopy of yours back on the road.'

We piled our belongings into the armour-plated back,

beside the business-looking quad Browning, and clambered into the cab. Murdock took the wheel.

'Couldn't you find a Sherman?' I asked him.

He grinned. 'The Captain ordered me to take this baby,' he said. 'After I kinda put the idea in his mind.'

'In other words, you conned him?'

Murdock assumed a look of injured innocence.

'Would I do a thing like that?' he protested. 'The Captain's a worried man. The word is that the Krauts have broken through the Ninety-ninth Division line up near Losheim and they've been dropping paratroops all over the goddamned woods during the night. How bad it is, we don't know – but I volunteered to take the flak truck up the Andler road a piece an' see if there was any Krauts headed this way.'

'That's a cheerful thought,' I said, 'I thought we were going to get my jeep.'

'That's the unofficial part of the assignment,' Murdock said. 'Officially, we're looking for Krauts.'

We cruised down through the village and forked off the Bütgenbach road to Andler. When we reached the lane where we had been misled by the false signpost, Murdock turned and we lumbered up the twisting slope. On the breast of the hill – almost at the point where the track ahead speared into the forest – I shouted to Murdock to stop.

'What the hell's the matter?' he roared.

'I thought I saw something,' I said, and climbed up behind the cab to get a better view of the countryside below us: a vista of open snow-covered fields towards the main road, where it twisted towards Herresbach and Andler. Something had caught my eye. Murdock climbed up beside me, untangling binoculars from a case.

'What did you see?' he asked.

'Down there,' I said, pointing towards the distant road. 'What do you make of it?'

He raised the field-glasses and I heard his deep intake of breath.

'Jesus!' he exclaimed, and passed the binoculars to me. I adjusted the eye-pieces slightly as I sighted. Stretching along a straight in the distant roadway was a motorised column. It was halted. Right at the front was an open scout car. An officer was standing up on the seats, facing the line of vehicles behind and gesticulating as if he was bawling somebody out or giving orders of some sort. The vehicles immediately behind the leader were half-tracks and loaded to the gunwales with scuttle-helmeted soldiers.

'They're bloody Germans!' I yelled.

'They got half the goddamned Kraut Army down there!' Murdock confirmed. 'Count what you can see,' he ordered. 'The personnel carriers, the trucks, the lot!'

I counted seventeen vehicles before trees and a bend in the road hid the column. Beyond, where a gap in the trees allowed a further sight of the road, a view of five more trucks suggested that the convoy was nose-to-tail for miles. How far back it stretched was anybody's guess – all the way back to Herresbach, possibly.

'How bad do you want that jeep of yours?' Murdock asked, taking another look with the field-glasses.

'It was only on loan,' I said. 'It's not going to break my heart if we have to leave it and come back and pick it up after the war.'

Murdock lowered the glasses and grinned at me.

'Are you suggestin' we get the hell outa here?'

'Immediately,' I replied. 'Forthwith. With as much haste as our dignity allows. On second thoughts, never mind the dignity.'

We scrambled down opposite sides of the cab, to come face-to-face inside, with a startled Danny in between. Murdock still had that grin on his face.

'Dignity don't come into tactical decisions,' he declared. 'Let's go!'

He threw me a sideways look as we lurched forward down the lane.

'What did you say your outfit was?'

'The Psychological Warfare Department . . . They call it the PWE now – Political Warfare Executive – but new names take a long time to stick. Everybody still calls it the PWD.'

'You'd have to be pretty smart to get into an outfit like that' Murdock said, throwing the big flak wagon into a sharp bend.

'Not all that smart. Would I be here?'

Murdock laughed. 'The Captain's gonna throw a fit when he finds the Krauts are this close. I just hope we can warn him.'

We went careering down the twisting lane like a mammoth toboggan. Murdock slid the brute to a halt behind a screen of trees, just before we reached the road junction.

'Can you drive this thing?' he asked.

'There's a first time for everything,' I said. 'You want me to try?'

'Take it over,' he said. 'I'm getting in the back. I'll fly tail-gunner. When I give a smack on the cab, hit that road and put your foot down.'

He left us and I shrugged at Danny.

'Sorry I got you into this mess,' I apologised.

She fluttered a brave smile and put an encouraging hand on my wrist.

'*Avec toi, je n'ai pas peur.*'

Her touch and the tremulous smile made me feel like a giant. I cannot explain it.

Murdock thumped on the plated roof of the cab. I concentrated fiercely then on the controls of our flak wagon and the business of driving it. We lurched out on to the main road and, as we swung left, I saw two black specs approaching from the right. The bark of the quad Browning, somewhere behind and above my head, sounded deafening in the cab. Murdock, clearly, had wasted no time blasting off at the approaching motor-cyclists whom I had seen from the corner of my eye.

I wondered if the redoubtable sergeant had been able to get low enough elevation to fire at road-level. There was no wing mirror to give me a view of the road behind, so I had no idea what fate befell the two German outriders. A hail of .50 calibre bullets – even if passing overhead – must have made them think twice about pursuing us because, after a second short burst, Murdock did not fire again.

The field of vision from the driving seat was limited. There was a shut-in feeling, due partly to the low roof of the cab with its armoured visor projecting beyond the top of the squat windscreen. The latter was no more than eighteen inches high; not much more than a slit. One felt protected and yet, paradoxically, strangely vulnerable in the security one had. This arose from the restricted outlook, like wearing blinkers: never knowing what danger might be approaching from the flanks or behind. I was mentally braced for Murdock to open up again with the Browning and/or for a barrage of lethal projectiles to hit us from an unseen quarter. Neither occurred.

Our arrival at the engineers' command post with news of the German column threw the place into a tizzy. Murdock's CO had already decided that there was nothing at Amblève worth defending even if it could be held by a platoon of engineers. Battalion HQ in Malmedy had given him permission to fall back to more tenable positions at or near key bridges over the Salm and Amblève rivers. The general situation was still very confused but the possibility that the bridges in the Amblève valley would need to be destroyed to baulk German armoured thrusts was very real.

What had been planned as an orderly pull-out from Amblève became a frantic one when a six-by-six truck pulled up outside the schoolhouse and its driver yelled: 'The Germans are coming!'

There was general consternation when it was discovered that the Germans seen by the newcomer were a quite different lot from the column we had sighted. The soldier had been sent on a foraging expedition for gasoline – the engineers were desperately short of fuel for their trucks – and he had hoped to scrounge some from a TD company camped in Möderscheid, five miles away down the Bütgenbach road. He had not stayed in Möderscheid long enough to load a single jerrycan; turning tail and speeding out one side of the village as German tanks had entered the other. The unhappy conclusion that was drawn from the truck-driver's news was that the Germans were heading for Amblève from two directions, the south-east and the north-east. It was no place to linger.

Danny and I waited around nervously as engineers siphoned gasoline from two trucks, which were to be abandoned, and filled up the tanks of two reserved for evacuation. We were assigned to ride in the half-track, along with Murdock and some of his squad. Two more passengers were to make up the half-track's complement. I blinked in disbelief when Vardon and Trygverson emerged from the schoolhouse and were directed to join us in the back of the flak wagon.

'I thought you'd gone,' I said to Trygverson, as he threw me his carryall and climbed aboard.

'I don't know what the hell has happened to our car,' he said. 'Last we heard was that it was on the way from Malmedy. That was two hours ago. It still hasn't shown up. We sat up more than half the goddamned night waiting for it.'

Vardon seemed half-asleep. He didn't say much to anybody, just climbed into the back of the half-track, where he propped himself in a corner and sat as if he was having difficulty keeping his eyes open.

'Krauts!' a voice yelled. The warning came from the roof of the schoolhouse, where a couple of GIs had dismantled a radio mast and were about to lower it on a rope. One of the men was pointing to the north-east, where he could see something that was not visible to those of us nearer ground-level. 'Krauts!' he shouted again. 'Three half-tracks . . . About a mile up the road . . . at the fork!'

The radio aerial came down off the roof like a yo-yo on a string, to be grabbed and thrown into the back of one of the trucks. The men on the roof tied the rope to a chimney breast and came down only marginally slower.

Because the trucks were parked outside us, the half-track was the last to pull away. A couple of villagers came out from their houses to watch sullenly as our small convoy climbed away from the village with its river at the foot and headed out along the Ondenval road. Whether we brought up the rear by accident or design, I don't know, but Murdock immediately got one of his men to man the quad Browning and cover the road behind us. But it was not from behind that danger came.

The village of Ondenval is only about three miles from Amblève and the same distance from Möderscheid, where the six-by-six driver had seen the German tanks. The three villages form a rough isosceles triangle – with the five-mile stretch between Amblève and Möderscheid forming the base. This may seem superfluous information but I mention it to illustrate the predicament in which we quickly found ourselves.

The driver of the six-by-six – having seen Panzers coming into Möderscheid and done his quick about-turn – had raced back to Amblève in the belief that the Germans were in hot pursuit. The truth is that even if they had spotted his truck, they had not given it a passing thought and had not even expended an eighty-eight shell on it. They were heading west as fast as they could go and they were not about to detour to Amblève in pursuit of one miserable six-by-six. Their predetermined route was through Möderscheid and Ondenval and it was towards Ondenval that they kept going.

The leaders of the Panzer column – reputedly fifteen miles long – had passed through Ondenval while we were still thinking about leaving Ambléve. The result was that instead of running away from trouble, as we fondly believed, we were running slap bang into the middle of it. And we found out the hard way.

Our first indication that anything was wrong came when our lead truck passed under a railway bridge, less than half a mile from Ondenval, and suddenly stopped. We could not tell why it had stopped – but when there was an explosion and the truck went up in a roar of orange flame the presence of inhospitable elements in Ondenval became frighteningly apparent. We did not know it, but we had collided side-on with the notorious Kampfgruppe Peiper on its westward drive to the Meuse.

This was not a force to be trifled with. It numbered about a hundred tanks, two dozen assault guns, a battalion of howitzers, nearly a hundred half-tracks packed with Panzergrenadiers and paratroops, and God knows what else. The next few moments were among the most frightening of my life.

The loss of life in the lead truck must have been total. Two men, with their clothes on fire, did stagger from the blazing wreck but were immediately cut down by a torrent of machine-gun bullets which screamed and ricocheted from the walls of the railway underpass.

The truck in front of us started to back up, forcing us to do the same. We still could not see what had caused the death and destruction beyond the underpass and the sudden silence that followed the single explosion and the ensuing fusillade of bullets was almost as unnerving as the first shock of noise. Both vehicles somehow got turned and headed back towards Ambléve. We did not get far.

The truck behind us was the next to get the chop.

We felt the sudden blast of heat as it, too, erupted in a roar of black-tipped orange flame – only yards behind us. It careered off the road and went tumbling down a gully between the road and the railway embankment. Only moments before, we had been cruising comfortably down this road towards the underpass. Now the half-track was labouring painfully uphill in the reverse direction and we were all praying that it would reach a sharp bend and the salvation it offered from an enemy we had not yet seen.

That enemy did not remain unseen for long after the despatch of the second truck. Peering back over the armoured rim of the half-track, the sight that met my eyes stirred my insides with churning dread. A German Mark V Panther had nosed the blazing truck from its path through the railway underpass and was sitting in the tunnel mouth like a scorpion in a hole. The wicked spout of its gun was pointing uphill directly at us. It spat a drift of smoke and there was an echoing crack of deep resonance, even as I watched, mesmerised in numb fear. The gun's bark was followed almost instantly by a blast of the high-velocity shell exploding right underneath me – or so it seemed. I was sure my last moment had come.

Like the others in the back of the flak wagon, I was thrown violently in a heap as the half-track gave a terrifying lurch. My nostrils were filled with the stink of burning oil and there was a horrendous noise of metal grinding upon metal. The half-track shuddered to a stop.

The first to react was one of Murdock's men. He opened up with the quad Browning, pumping bullets at the monster peeping from the underpass. His action caused little visible damage to the Panther but it may have caused its gunner to lower his head, temporarily. It allowed Murdock seconds to take stock of the situation and burst into frenzied life. We needed little prompting to obey his screamed instruction to abandon ship and make for the bend in the road as fast as our legs would carry us. I was among the first down and waiting as Murdock bundled Danny unceremoniously after me into my outstretched arms.

Murdock was last to leave, having almost to pry the gunner away from the Browning and heave him over the side. They were no sooner landed and running when a second shell from the Panther ripped open the back of the half-track and blew the Browning apart. The first shell had shredded the track on one side of the flak wagon and started flickering oily fires in a black tangle of twisted metal below the hull. The second was the *coup de grâce*.

There had been nine of us in the half-track, including the two engineers who had been in the cab with Vardon's driver – and that, miraculously, was the number who arrived intact beyond the bend in the road: breathless and quivering with shock.

Although Vardon and Trygverson were the senior military men present, neither argued the point when Murdock – who had assumed leadership in the first instance – continued to issue orders. His first was that we get off the road. The second was that we moved like our tails were on fire. Obviously, he had concluded that, on the road, we would quickly be overtaken by the Panther that had blocked our way into Ondenval. And even if we ran all the way back to Amblève there was going to be no succour there. We would probably run into more Germans arriving from that direction.

When you are scared witless, the urge to debate what to do is not strong – so it is not surprising that Murdock's leadership was a godsend to the rest of us. We were only too willing to follow his leadership, because he was the only one who seemed able to comprehend what had happened to us and take instinctive control.

He ushered us down the tree-clad slope from the road. It was quite steep. We plunged down, stumbling frequently and running out of control of our limbs. Fear aided the headlong speed of our descent. The ground levelled out abruptly at the bottom, where the railway track offered an immediate goal. The line converged with the road we had left, to cross it at the tunnel where we had last seen the Panther. I remember thinking that if we could get across the railway line we might be safe. The girdered pillar of a railway signal, seen through the trees, drew me like a beacon over the last few yards. Danny was beginning to slow and I urged her to make for it, to keep going. We slithered, at last, through banks of brittle-crusted snow to reach the ballast-topped track of the permanent way. Beyond was another barrier – a river, which, I realised, must be the Amblève. No tank could follow us across that. But how did *we* get across?

The problem was not debated. When all nine of us were on the railway track, we paused to get our breath back and take our bearings. It was then that we realised that we were in full view of the bend in the road where we had abandoned the half-track. The Panther, whose whining metallic ascent of the hill had been audible to us, was shouldering the wreck off the road. Behind it was a half-track, with Panzergrenadiers spilling from its decks. We were not left in doubt about whether we had been seen. The Panther's gun belched and a shell blew the tops off a stand of trees nearby, as if a scythe had swished through at tree-top level. We scrambled hastily from the railway track, slithering down the embankment furthest from the gun. Heads kept down, we stayed with the embankment and tried to put distance between us and the Panther. The terrain between the railway track and the river was almost impassable. The riverbank was gorge-like, rocky and steep, and tangled with impenetrable vegetation in places where, otherwise, a passage might have been found. The railway line itself provided the only sure footing.

We kept below the level of the embankment until – sure that trees now hid us from the road – we returned to the track, where the sleepers measured our hurrying strides. The Panther sent several more shells screaming into the woods above the track but the shots were so dispersed and lacking in direction that I reckoned the gunner was either taking pot luck or unable to lower his gun sufficiently to do us damage.

Our fear, now, was the possibility of pursuit on foot. The sight of those Panzergrenadiers pouring off the half-track had been ominous. Had the soldiers followed us down from the road? Fear that they had seemed justified when a splutter of a burp-gun sent birds screeching from the trees, not far behind us. The gun had been fired at track-level, not somewhere above. But the rocky cut, through which the firing had echoed, described a curve that hid us from the trigger-happy perpetrator. He must have fired at shadows.

At Murdock's insistence, we hurried along the track. Its curving path, never very far from the river, offered us the means of unhampered movement and also scree-ned us from any soldiers pursuing on foot. At any one time, we had a clear view behind us of some three hundred yards of track, and by constantly looking back and seeing it empty we gained some reassurance. Our lead was, if not substantial, great enough to let us feel that we could take swift evasive action if the need arose.

After half an hour, we began to feel more secure – although Murdock did not allow us to slacken pace. We reasoned, wishfully, that the Germans must by now have given up the chase. My earlier conclusion that we would be safer on the other side of the river was given a fillip when I realised the reason why the railway suddenly looped away from the river and then turned back again towards it. There was a bridge ahead. The railway crossed the Amblève to maintain a due south-erly course in the direction of St Vith.

We approached the bridge cautiously. Murdock was hopeful that any Germans who had reached Amblève village two miles to the east of the bridge would – either have turned north-west towards Ondenval or kept heading south towards St Vith. In other words, that they had stuck to the roads. All the time we had been following the railway line, we had been moving steadily away from the Amblève-Ondenval road and we were now a healthy two miles from it at its Amblève end.

With no sign of life in the vicinity of the railway bridge, we ventured across. Danny and I kept close behind Murdock, who told us that if we followed the track for two more miles we would reach the village of Born which, two days before, had been packed with elements of the 106th Division. Our hopes rose.

We had gone no more than a few hundred yards down the track on the south side of the river, however, when Murdock suddenly signalled us to silence and motioned us off the track into cover. From somewhere ahead and below we heard voices and hammering sounds, like the chopping blows of axes into standing timber. The owners of the voices were making no attempt to keep their tones down. There was a kind of conversational shouting, as if workmen were engaged on a task that required many hands.

Murdock signalled me to accompany him and, together, we went forward at a crouch to take a look. We went through low spruce to a point where we were suddenly given a clear view of a river that ran parallel to the railway. It was not the Amblève but a tributary that joined it only a few hundred yards upstream of the bridge we had crossed. We could see the confluence of the streams to our left. But it was what we could see to our right that took our breath away. Camped in cleared woodland and among trees on the far bank of the narrow river, were what seemed to be thousands of German soldiers. The half-tracks, from which they had disembarked, were parked wherever space to do so had presented itself. There was a sprinkling of reconnaissance cars and light amphibian trucks with guns mounted on them. Opposite a muddy track that led back through the woods, and was thick with vehicles, a platoon of engineers were building a bridge over the river. And it was they who were shouting to each other and making most of the noise, as if they were on a training jaunt. The troops, who had dismounted from their carriers, were lounging around in groups, comparatively silent. Many were eating from mess-tins. The German Army was at lunch.

TWELVE

Survival

Murdock and I crept back to where we had left the others. Their faces reflected varying degrees of anxiety as they gathered round to learn the results of our reconnaissance. Without frills, Murdock told them of the large body of German infantry picnicking with apparent unconcern only half a mile away. Between the Germans and us was the thirty-feet-wide river that ran into the Amblève above the railway bridge.

'The river ain't gonna stop the Krauts for long,' Murdock said. 'That hammering you can hear is them building a bridge. They'll have it finished in no time. By the time their engineers are through, the rest will have eaten their chow and be ready to move. This side of the river's gonna be swarming with Krauts inside half an hour.'

'Where in hell's name are they all coming from?' It was the engineer who had manned the quad Browning who wanted to know. Murdock shrugged.

'My guess is they're the same bunch that Captain Abernathy and I spotted coming from Andler this morning. They must have come through Amblève, crossed the river there. But instead of hittin' south along the road to St Vith, they've turned west, across-country, along the south bank of the Amblève river . . .'

'So, what do we do now, Sarge?' asked the engineer. 'You think we can sneak past them outa sight along the railroad and get to Born?'

'That could be askin' for more trouble than we

283

already got,' Murdock said. 'For all we know, our people have maybe pulled back from Born. These Krauts down there don't seem too bothered meetin' any trouble. They're sittin' around like they're out on a hayride.'

'What do you reckon they aim to do?' asked the engineer. Again, Murdock shrugged.

'Could be they're crossin' the river here so's they can circle round the back of Born and hit our guys there from behind. That sure makes more sense than attackin' front-on across water. I reckon though that they ain't bothered about Born.'

Vardon, who had been quiet so far but had been listening to Murdock with a contemptuous smile on his face, chose that moment to offer his pennyworth.

'You've got it all worked out, Sergeant. Fancy yourself as a tactical analyst, do you? May I ask what you propose to do if we do not try to reach this village you mentioned?'

Murdock regarded Vardon coolly. 'I aim to keep what's left of my squad outa trouble, sir.'

'You intend to keep running away?'

Murdock's lips tightened. Otherwise, he showed no reaction.

'Yes, sir,' he said. 'All I'm thinkin' about right now is surviving . . . Stayin' alive long enough to get us somewhere where we can maybe do somethin' about hittin' back at them Kraut sons-of-bitches.'

'And how do you propose to do that?'

'We keep headin' west, Colonel,' Murdock said. He allowed the glimmer of a smile to play on his lips. 'Just like the old pioneers, sir. We keep headin' west. There's plenty of wood trails . . . places where we can move and keep outa sight if we have to.'

'And what if the Germans have the same idea? To head west, I mean?' Vardon's tone was supercilious.

Murdock smiled with his lips but not his eyes.

'I think, sir,' he drawled, 'that you can bet your last

pair of cotton socks that the Krauts are headin' west. This bust-out's a whole lot bigger than maybe any of us reckoned on. This ain't no powder-puff counterattack they're mountin'. I think they're goin' for broke. Last night, they musta bust our line like it never existed – and now our only chance of stayin' alive is stayin' ahead of them, no matter which ways they're goin'.'

Murdock made to turn away, but Vardon's voice stopped him.

'What if I disagree?' the Colonel asked loftily. 'Do I have to remind you that you are only a non-commissioned officer and that Captain Trygverson and I are your superiors?'

'You don't have to remind me nothin', sir,' Murdock replied. 'You're lookin' at the most respectful sergeant in the United States Army. I know better'n anybody that you and the Captain don't have to do a goddamned thing I say. But I'm still runnin' what's left of my squad and you'd better believe that what I say, they do. And I say we're movin' out. Right now. Some other time would be a good time to jaw about it.'

Again, Murdock made to turn away. Again, Vardon detained him, clearly disconcerted by the American sergeant's forthright manner.

'Just like that?' Vardon wanted to know. 'What about the rest of us?'

'You're welcome to come with us, sir. Or you can stay right here. That's your decision, sir. Not mine.' Murdock turned to me. 'Same goes for you and the girl, Captain Abernathy. I can't tell you what you gotta do.'

'We're sticking with you, Sergeant,' I assured him quickly. 'That is if you'll take us.'

'Gladly, sir,' Murdock replied, and his eyes met mine in a kind of silent accord. He turned to stare questioningly at Vardon and Trygverson. Indecision was written large on Vardon's face. While he hesitated, Trygverson spoke.

'I think we should all stick together, Colonel.'

'Do you, Trygverson? Do you, indeed?' Vardon glared at the other officer, eyes bright with anger at the absence of support from that quarter. The Norwegian-born captain met the glare without flinching, not giving way before it. To my surprise, it was Vardon who backed down.

'Very well,' he conceded, with a sniff. 'The Sergeant knows this country. We don't. That puts us at some disadvantage. I must say, however, that I don't like running away.'

'You been doin' it just fine, so far,' Murdock said with an edge to his voice, and did not wait for a reply. He marched past an astonished Vardon, indicating to the rest of us that he would lead us out in single file. He detailed one of his own men – one of two who still had their carbines – to bring up the rear. The second carbine-carrier was instructed to stick close to Murdock in the van.

'No more talk,' the Sergeant ordered and, without further ado, struck away from the railway track at right angles. We followed, with Danny a couple of paces in front of me.

The going was extremely tough for half an hour: uphill and through trackless forest. I was just beginning to have doubts about Murdock's sense of direction when we came on a grassy track, striking its path at an angle. It wound through the forest against the gradient we had been traversing and I guessed its starting point must be close to the place where the Germans were bridging the river. I wondered if Murdock had deduced from the Germans' choice of site for the crossing – that such a track existed. The alternatives were that he had a built-in navigation system like a homing pigeon or he was just plain lucky.

With a path to follow, the going immediately became easier: not good, because melting snow had made the track boggy, but easier. No longer did we have to contend with undergrowth and fallen timber and the impression that we were blazing a trail where no man had gone before. There was evidence that a vehicle of some kind had preceded us quite recently. Fresh wheel-marks had indented the snowy stretches and, elsewhere, had churned deep into boggy turf leaving muddy furrows into which water had oozed.

The forest itself was a silent place, eerily so: blanketing us from the sounds that reached us from somewhere beyond. We heard battle noise. It erupted at intervals, drifting to us like the mist that curled through the tops of the trees and swirled in aimless passage. Those sounds of battle perhaps some six or seven miles off – were a source of both comfort and nervous tension to us. The comfort – perhaps self-illusory came from the knowledge of distance between us and the furnace heat of battle. The tension came from the constant reminder, served on our senses by the roaring guns, that the tide of war was close and could catch us in its flood at any moment.

It was difficult to gauge the direction and flow of battle clamour. At times, the noise seemed to roll at us from the north and, at others, from the south-east. We hurried, enclosed by the shadowy gloom of the forest, but feeling pursued and encompassed by numberless hosts of an enemy we could not see.

We slogged on through the forest and had covered four, maybe five miles, when a distinctively different sound came to us through the trees. We heard it first as a steady whine, coming to us from somewhere ahead. Murdock stopped, halting the rest of us. Signalling for complete silence, he tilted his head to one side, listening intently. We all stood stock-still, straining our ears. I detected a metallic rattling noise embodied in the whine and edged forward to join Murdock, wondering if his interpretation of what we could hear was the same as mine.

Head still cocked, he acknowledged my presence with

a lift of his eyebrows. I mouthed one word in silent question:

'Tanks?'

He nodded. And he smiled. 'Ours,' he said. 'Lots of them. If that ain't Shermans on the move, I'll eat my goddamned helmet, chin-strap 'n' all!'

I don't know how he knew. Tanks on the move all sounded the same to me. I just hoped he was right. After our encounter with the Panther near Ondenval, the prospect of getting close to tanks of any description was not numbered among my ambitions.

The carbine-carrying engineer, who had been marching at Murdock's heels, confirmed his sergeant's identification of the noise up ahead.

'Definitely Shermans!' he proclaimed emphatically. His joy and optimism were quickly transmitted to the rest of our party. None was in any doubt that, now, salvation was at hand. I was less sure. The tanks did not seem to be coming our way. I suddenly realised why.

'There must be a road up ahead,' I said to Murdock. My brilliance failed to dazzle him.

'I sure as hell hope so,' he said. 'The one we've been makin' for. There's a highway runs south from Malmedy to St Vith... You shoulda been on it yesterday if they'd let you take the direct route to Spa.'

Yesterday! Was it only yesterday that the traffic-control officer in St Joseph's Kloster had told me that I could forget about taking the shortest route to Spa; that the road was closed to all north-bound traffic until further notice? Yesterday? It seemed years ago.

I said to Murdock: 'They did say something at St Vith about armour being moved south. From Faymonville? Everything else was being kept off the road, so they could get a clear run.'

'Could be the Seventh Armored,' Murdock said. 'They were round Faymonville... that's just a couple of miles the other side of Ondenval, where we ran into the Panther.' He seemed puzzled. 'If it is the Seventh we can hear, why the hell didn't they keep them where they were? That goddamned Panther wasn't on its own.'

If he now had doubts about the friendliness of the tanks we could hear, Murdock did not show them. He urged us forward as fast as we could go. We trotted, our orderly file forgotten in our eagerness to reach the road that we could not yet see. The slope of the ground was now in our favour: steadily downhill, although not dramatically steep. The track twisted and turned downward ahead of us and, at one point, we got a glimpse of the road – and tanks. Away to our left through a swatch of cut forest an elbow of roadway was visible. We paused only briefly to watch a succession of Shermans appear and disappear from view. They *were* Shermans – as Murdock had predicted – and the big white stars proclaiming their American identity was a joy to behold.

Danny and I were trotting a pace behind Murdock as we approached a curve in the track. We were taken by surprise when he suddenly veered to one side, colliding with us and knocking us off the trail. We all finished in a heap, sprawling in a bank of snow, to be joined immediately by the other leader, the engineer with the carbine. My first thought was that Murdock had lost his footing and that the collision was accidental, but the voluntary arrival in the same snow-bank of the engineer dispelled that notion. Murdock was quickly on his knees, hand covering his mouth in a warning to us to make no sound. Then he was frantically signalling to those following us to get off the track. I tried to catch the Sergeant's eye and, when I did, mimed puzzlement: seeking explanation for the sudden alarm. Making signs with his hands, he indicated to take a careful look beyond the bend in the path. It continued in easy curves all the way to the highway, which it met at right angles. The road was four hundred yards away, perhaps less, and traffic was streaming

289

along it, passing from right to left. Not a single tank crossed while I watched. The convoy stream was made up of heavy trucks, heading south. The engine roar of each one came up at me in waves as the trucks lumbered past, briefly filling the gap afforded by the trees. The smell of oil and exhaust smoke wafted up to me in the still winter air. The view of the road and the trucks had not been the cause of Murdock's alarm. Something much closer had prompted him to shoulder us unceremoniously off the path.

Less than a hundred yards from where I lay, belly-down, a squat open-topped vehicle – not much bigger than a jeep – had been run off the track, where it was screened from the road ahead by the lower branches of a tall standing pine. From my elevated vantage-point, I had an angled view of the dumpy boat-like vehicle. It was an ugly little duckling, with unfamiliar dark-grey and blue camouflage patterns. A slightly bulbous metal underskirt made it look a little like a walnut shell on wheels. It had two spare wheels: one bracketed to the back and a second mounted on the flat bonnet in front of the driver's seat. It had no windscreen.

The vehicle was empty, but leaning against a nearby tree and smoking a cigarette was the oddly-clad figure of the man whom I took to be the driver. He was wearing what looked like an anti-gas contamination suit: a mud-coloured waterproof coverall, with a tight-fitting rubber head-covering that enclosed head, ears and neck like a balaclava helmet. Only an oval of face showed. I was aware of Murdock edging up alongside me.

'That buggy's German,' I whispered.

'A Schwimmwagen,' he said softly. 'It swims – an amphibian. It must be scouting for them Krauts back at the river. That guy must be the driver. Can you see his buddies?'

I scanned the track and the trees below us. A movement caught my eye.

290

'Down there, to the right,' I whispered. 'Near the road . . . There's a fallen tree . . . this side of it. There's two of them!'

One of the Germans, sitting behind the natural hide provided by the fallen tree, watching the road, wore an officer's cap. The other was bare-headed, with ear-phones clasped across his blond hair, and he had what looked like his radio set between his knees. Both men wore the same kind of waterproof suiting as the driver of the amphibian.

'What do we do now?' I asked Murdock. He seemed not to hear me.

'Three of them,' he murmured, almost inaudibly. Then he turned, as if my question had just reached him. 'We take them out,' he said. 'We gotta get to the goddamned road.'

He slithered away and I heard him whispering terse instructions. I wriggled back to find out what was happening. The two engineers with carbines slipped off into the woods to the right of the trail. They had instructions to take care of the officer and the radio-man. I unsheathed my revolver and looked expectantly at Murdock.

'What about the driver?' I asked.

Murdock looked up at me, considering. He made a decision. 'Back me up,' he said. 'You know how to use that thing?'

I said I did. It satisfied him. We cut out into the woods to the left of the trail and circled towards the amphibious scout car and its driver. We crept to within ten yards of the unsuspecting German, not as silently as either Murdock or I would have wished – both of us stood on twigs that positively crackled under our weight – but the driver heard nothing. Perhaps the close-fitting rubber hood he wore had dulled his hearing to the point of deafness. He had finished his cigarette and was shuffling about like a bored schoolboy. By the youthfulness of his face, which I could now see with startling clarity, he was not much older than a schoolboy.

Four shots ringing out in sharp succession, from down near the road, caught both Murdock and myself by surprise, although it was the signal for which we had been waiting. They came as Murdock had made signs to me that he intended moving closer. Our intended victim got a bigger surprise than we did. He almost jumped out of his rubber suit, taking off like a startled partridge. It was his intention, possibly, to get to the track with the idea of discovering who had been firing at what – but he didn't reach it. His foot caught on a tree branch or exposed root and he tripped. He went all his length in a face-first dive. Murdock and I plunged forward, revolvers in hand. I reached the German first, having the benefit of an obstacle-free passage to reach him.

The fall must have winded the young driver. He did not get to his feet but was rolling dazedly over onto his back when he realised that the object pointed at him, three feet from his nose, was my revolver. A look of tragic acceptance filled his eyes as he waited for me to pull the trigger. His mouth fell half-open in surprise, almost disbelief, when I stepped back and lowered the weapon a fraction, indicating that he should remain lying on the ground. I had not reached a point where, in cold blood, I could take the life of an unarmed boy soldier. Especially one whose face was chalk-white with fright.

'We've got ourselves a prisoner,' I said to Murdock as he arrived.

'That's all we goddamned need,' he said. He went past me and collected the youth's automatic rifle, which was propped against the amphibian. Murdock holstered his own gun, examined the German Erma with an air of appreciation and then couched it in his right arm. Ignoring me, he disappeared beyond the tree that concealed the Schwimmwagen from the road. He was back almost immediately.

'Hanley and Kovac didn't take no prisoners,' he announced. I got the impression that Murdock was sore at me because I hadn't killed the boy at my feet.

'For Christ's sake,' I complained angrily. 'This one's just a kid and he was defenceless . . .'

Murdock's ill-tempered look softened. He acknowledged my protest with a conciliatory raising of one hand.

'I know, I know. I'm mad at myself, not you. I could have dropped him from back in the trees . . . I didn't . . . but I ain't paid for goin' soft. I shoulda done what I had to do.'

'There's hope for you yet, Sergeant,' I said. He snorted a comment that was unintelligible but may have been very rude. I grinned after him as he strode up the trail to tell the others that the way to the road was now clear. It proved unnecessary. They came running to meet him, in some agitation. The trail behind them was no longer empty. The Germans had, it appeared, not lingered long on the east bank of the river they had been bridging. The forest trail was now chockablock with half-tracks, loaded with infantry, heading for the road that we had seen as our salvation.

The grim news was sinking into my brain when I realised that the road in question was ominously silent. The whine of Sherman tanks had long since faded to the south and trucks were no longer lumbering across the gap at the track's end. The road was empty.

I was running again – like a geriatric mare that had strayed into a hurdles race. The trouble with this chase and the hurdles – was that I was carrying topweight. It was all Murdock's fault and I silently cursed him as I laboured to keep up with him and Danny. They were blundering through forest just ahead of me.

The fact that half the German Army was just out of

sight up the trail had not deterred Murdock from making a quick search of the Schwimmwagen before thinking of his immediate safety, and mine. He had directed the rest of the party into the woods on the north side of the track, telling them to avoid the highway but not to get too far from it. Trygverson had taken charge of our prisoner, while I had stayed with Murdock to plunder the amphibian.

The Sergeant had thrown me a back-pack that must have weighed fifty pounds and told me to sling it on my back and run. It did not occur to me to argue. I put my arms through the straps and ran like hell. The Germans had not yet reached the bend in the track above us – but I could hear those damned half-tracks and it put the fear of death in me. I had not gone ten steps when I began to think unkind thoughts of Murdock and the burden he had imposed on me. The pack felt like it was loaded with lead ingots. I was summoning up the breath to tell Murdock that it had been a crazy idea to waste time pillaging the amphibian, when he went panting past me, carrying as big a load. He was festooned with grenade pouches and in each hand was carrying haversack-like bags that rattled as if they were full of ball-bearings. He also had the amphibian-driver's rifle.

'Do we really need this bloody stuff?' I gasped at him.

'You got the food . . . I hope,' was his reply, between gasping breaths. 'I got us grenades, ammo. Don't slow down.'

Slow down? Every time I put a foot down, I was so heavily loaded that I nearly sank knee-deep into the soft ground. And he was telling me not to slow down! I made a brief comment that may have been impolite, but it greatly relieved my feelings. The whine and rattle of half-tracks was now so loud that I knew they must have reached the downhill stretch of the track where the amphibian was. I could hear voices shouting in German but I dared not look back. I concentrated all my mind

294

on forward movement and the hope that we were deep enough into the trees not to have been seen.

The hope was forlorn. There was a sudden crackle of automatic weapons and the air all around us became alive with bullets. Bark was gouged from trees; twigs and pieces of pine-branch leapt in all directions as lead from half a dozen guns sprayed the woodland about us. Something hit me in the face. With awe, I pulled a six-inch sliver of bark from my cheek, where it had lodged like a dart. Its removal left a trickle of blood and a nipping sensation.

Crouching low behind a bush, I looked back. Helmeted figures in grey were spilling from the deck of a personnel carrier. Some, already down, were advancing into the trees cautiously, firing as they came. I was sure they could not see us – but they had seen something, movement perhaps, and they were taking no chances. It would not take them long to discover the two dead Germans near the road, still warm. They had probably heard the shots that had killed them. Two infantrymen from the personnel carrier, bolder than their comrades, were moving directly towards me. Remaining low, but seeking cover when I moved, I hurried after Murdock and Danny. There was a shout from behind and another burst of fire peppered the patch of brush I had vacated and riddled the trunk of a tree behind it.

I made for another patch of thick brush and almost expired from shock when it parted and the black muzzle of a weapon poked through the screen. I threw myself flat and was crawling to one side when there was a blast of sound. Edging past the screen, I peered up and got a friendly nod from one of the engineers called Kovac or Hanley. Which of the pair it was, I did not know, but he was hefting a machine rifle of ugly proportions: acquired, no doubt, from the two Germans near the road. It was the size of a Bren, but with a twelve-inch magazine protruding laterally from the breech instead of vertically. He fired several bursts in the direction of the track, where I had seen the nearest Germans.

'What you waiting for?' he yelled at me. 'Keep going! I'll hold them sons-of-bitches off for a time!'

I nodded my thanks. My mouth was too dry to have uttered a sound. I crawled forward some distance and, then, abandoning caution, plunged deeper into the forest in the direction that I thought Murdock and Danny had taken. Behind me, I heard a fresh burst off fire. Kovac – or was it Hanley – was still discouraging close pursuit. I heard him shout a crude invitation, yelled at 'you Kraut bastards', to show themselves and eat some of their own lead. The response was a fresh and sustained outburst of rifle and machine-gun fire, followed by an eerie silence. It was broken by two sharp whistle blasts, some distance away, and a German voice shouting orders. I pushed further into the forest.

I glanced frequently behind but could see neither the engineer, who had stayed to fight, nor any sign of pursuit: only trees and deep shadow. That was all I could see ahead, too: trees and deep shadow. I tried not to panic but I did feel fear that I had lost the others; that I was now all on my own. My uneasiness was made worse by knowing how easy it would be to blunder round in circles in this forest and get hopelessly lost. I have a fairly good sense of direction but it needs guides, like remembered landmarks or the position of the sun. But there was no sun to glimpse, precious little sky even – only the Stygian gloom of the forest.

Then I heard Murdock call my name. With burgeoning relief, I made haste towards the sound: staggering under the accursed pack, which seemed to get heavier and heavier and was forever getting caught up in branches of trees and impeding easy progress at every turn. I broke through into a small clearing and there they were: all of our beleaguered little party, except one.

'I was beginning to think we'd lost you,' Murdock greeted me. 'Where's Kovac?'

So, it was Kovac back there, not Hanley. That was the matter of identity cleared up. Hanley was the one sitting on a log with a carbine slung round his shoulder and another cradled in one arm, trained on the driver of the amphibian. I took a couple of deep breaths to get my wind back before I replied to Murdock about Kovac.

'I saw him,' I said. 'He told me to keep going . . . A couple of Gerries were pretty close behind me . . . He said he would hold them off . . . He was blasting away good-oh . . .'

Murdock turned to the engineer who, I now knew, was Hanley.

'Ain't that Kovac's carbine you got there?'

'Yeah. Pete took the artillery belongin' to that Kraut officer we jumped. He was dyin' to try it out.'

'Dyin' coulda been the price of it,' said Murdock. 'If he don't come soon . . .' He left the rest unsaid but it was plain the way his mind was working. Murdock did not intend to wait indefinitely for Kovac to catch us up. If the missing engineer had sacrificed himself to buy us all a little time, that time was not to be squandered.

Murdock back-tracked a little way into the wood to look for Kovac. We waited.

A silence had descended on the forest that ate at the nerves. Flying from the bullets that had lacerated the woodland like an invisible scourge had generated a different fear: one that whipped the body into feverish physical effort. The mind's working was somehow suspended. Waiting in the silent forest the mind awoke and fear dripped into it as insidiously as acid: gnawing relentlessly with its corrosive bite. Murdock's return relieved the tension.

'There ain't no sign of Kovac,' he said. 'And if any Krauts followed us into the wood, they're keepin' hell

297

of a quiet.' He glanced at his watch. 'I'll give Kovac one more minute.'

At the end of it, he heaved a sigh.

'OK, let's move out!' he said, his face grim. 'I'll lead. Keep it quiet and keep the line closed up. Hanley, you bring up the rear with the Kraut. See he don't try nothin' and keep the line movin'. We don't want stragglers.'

The words were scarcely out of his mouth when there was a far-off pop, a whine, and then a clap of sound as, perhaps a hundred yards away, the treetops seemed to explode.

'Jesus!' Murdock groaned. 'Mortars!' The first was followed by more. It began to rain mortar bombs.

'Down! Get down!' The shriek emanated from Vardon. And he threw himself flat. Most of us showed little hesitation in following his example. I took Danny down with me and was trying to shield her when I realised that Murdock was still upright and screaming at us.

'Stay on your feet, goddamn you! All of you! Stand up straight! Get in close to a tree as close as you can go . . . But stay on your goddamned feet, as tall as you can stand!'

He was among us like a frenzied thing, hauling us off the ground and shouting at us to find trees and get against the trunks. It was ludicrous. Mortar bombs were raining down on the forest from the direction of the highway and, to add to the misery, what sounded like light howitzers were also lobbing shells into the woods – and there we were, playing hands-knees-and-boomps-a-daisy, as we tried to make up our minds whether to duck, dive or run like hell. I grabbed hold of Danny and pinned her against the stoutest tree I could find. Thankfully, she appreciated that I was trying to protect her and had not been seized by a sudden uncontrollable lust. She snuggled against me, head bowed against my chest. In the confusion, I had not hesitated in doing

298

exactly as Murdock had said. I reckoned he must know what he was talking about.

Vardon, clearly, did not have my faith in Murdock. To my utter disbelief, the Colonel got to his feet, almost apoplectic with rage, and, oblivious to the bombardment, started to engage Murdock in a heated slanging match.

With the forest seeming to be collapsing about our ears, I heard Vardon shout something about having seen more mortar attacks in the desert than Murdock had had pay-days and that Murdock was, like all Americans, a bloody imbecile who knew nothing about soldiering. Etc., etc. The Colonel was jumping up and down and waving his arms like a dervish.

Murdock, equally oblivious to the bombardment, gave not an inch. With the feet-apart stance of a Sumo wrestler, he thrust his face at the Colonel with the passion of one intent on homicide. His attack, however, was verbal and delivered at the top of his voice. He had – he screamed met some stupid limey sons-of-bitches in his ill-starred life but the Colonel was out and away the goddamn stupidest that he had ever encountered walking on two legs. He did not give a goddamn if the Colonel had been mortared all the way from Casablanca to Cairo, he, Murdock, had eaten his own basinful of sand from Kasserine to goddamned Sfax – but they weren't in the goddamned desert now. They were in the goddamned Ardennes and, although the Colonel might not know it, that was only a kick-in-the-ass down the road from the Huertgen Forest. And there the Krauts had dropped more shells and mortars on him, Murdock, than Heinz had put beans into cans. The one goddamned thing that he, Murdock, had learned from fighting in that ass-hole of a forest was that you stayed on your feet alongside a tree when the shit was coming down through the tree-tops. That way, you're a small target, no broader than your own fat head. Flatten yourself out on the ground and you get speared in fifty-seven different places with bits of timber coming down like goddamned assegais and lumps of shrapnel falling all over the place like goddamned hailstones.

Given the circumstances, it was a remarkable confrontation and, if my reportage of it is not a verbatim account, some allowance may be made for the crash of bursting shot and falling timber that served as a background accompaniment. The appalling encounter ended when Vardon, mindless with rage, aimed a blow at Murdock. The Sergeant evaded it with a shift of his head and replied with a short jab to the solar plexus, which floored the Colonel and left him gasping like a cod on a rock.

Trygverson, who had been crouching against a tree – as bewildered as the rest of us – ran to assist the fallen Colonel. As Vardon laboured for breath and gasped out threats of courts-martial and firing squads, Trygverson did no more than stare reproachfully at Murdock and offer the mild admonition: 'You shouldn't have done that, Sergeant.'

The Sergeant showed no repentance. 'You just keep that guy in order, Captain,' he warned Trygverson. 'Or, so help me, I'll put a bullet in him.' He suddenly seemed to become aware that the rain of mortar bombs had not slackened and, looking up, took evasive action when a twelve-foot length of pine-top – blown from some distance away – landed in the trees above us and made a slow descent, somersaulting from bough to bough, to crash into the clearing.

Murdock recovered his composure quickly. He made a quick check to ensure that there were no casualties and, ignoring both Vardon and Trygverson, jollied us with words of encouragement and told us to get ready to move out. We were in as much danger from a lucky shot where we were as we would be on the move.

'The Krauts are taking pot luck plastering the wood,' he said. 'They don't know there's just a handful of us and they ain't takin' no chances. For all they know, we got three companies of dogfaces stashed through the woods. There's no point in bein' around when they find out different.'

Leading the way, he tracked deeper into the wood and, although the Germans continued to lob mortar bombs into the forest from the road, we were never in great danger from them. They concentrated on an area away to our right, which seemed to confirm Murdock's contention that the Germans were trying to soften up an enemy whose strength they were grossly over-estimating and whose location could only be guessed. Their caution was our good luck. After half an hour's steady progress, we were trekking across woodland that undulated in deep folds. The only sounds were those of our own making: the suck of human breath, the brush of our bodies against needled boughs of fir and pine, the crack of fallen twigs underfoot. The silence of the forest encompassed us. The sky darkened, where it could be seen, and drizzled tiny snow-flakes: a token of winter, no more than that, and a reminder of the fast-approaching solstice.

Finding the logging trail, and later, a forester's shack was a matter of luck. Discovery of one led us to the other. It was almost black as night when we stumbled on the hut, although it was not yet four in the afternoon. With the absence of any sign that the Germans had ventured after us into the depths of the forest, Murdock suggested that we might as well take advantage of the hut's shelter until daylight. There were no dissenters. Even with the meagre light of day, progress had been difficult. As the light had failed, we had been groping and stumbling like the blind just to remain on the rough trail we had found.

The hut was a crude affair – what, in the Scottish highlands, would be called a bothie: log walls, log roof and an earthen floor. It was still a godsend. We had realised – ever since we had failed to intercept the American convoy passing along the highway – that we were probably going to have to spend the night in the open, and no one was exactly relishing the prospect of having to improvise shelter from sopping wet fir branches and the like. I, for one, had left my Boy Scout days behind.

Vardon, however, was far from happy about us all sharing the hut. At first he mumped and moaned about Danny being under the same roof as the eight men. He thought that it was highly improper and suggested that shelters be constructed for the nine of us in proper military fashion. Not even Trygverson seemed to take the suggestion too seriously, much to Vardon's annoyance. With scathing references to US Army practices, the Colonel revealed what he meant by 'proper military fashion'. He meant that the hut should house officers only – he did not class me in this category – and that the rest of us should build our own hides and dug-outs from the abundant natural materials of the forest.

Murdock did not argue the point with Vardon. He did not even engage him in direct conversation. He quietly took Trygverson aside and told him point-blank that if he didn't straighten the Colonel out, it would be the Colonel who would be sleeping in the open. We were all going to share the hut and, if anyone did not like that arrangement, they could clear out any time they liked.

Later Murdock sought me out to propound the belief that Vardon was certifiably insane.

'I've met some screwy officers in my time,' he said, 'but that guy's in a class of his own. He's a goddamned fruit-cake.'

'I hope you won't judge the whole of the British Army by what you've seen of him,' I said.

Murdock laughed. 'I think I maybe called him a stupid Limey son-of-a-bitch when the Krauts were throwin' that mortar shit at us . . . I hope you didn't take it too personal. Goddamn it, I was mad. I don't have nothin' against Limeys. I like them.'

'I'm glad to hear that,' I said. 'I wasn't offended. If a stupid Limey son-of-a-bitch is behaving like a stupid Limey son-of-a-bitch or, for that matter, like a stupid Yankee son-of-a-bitch, somebody should tell him.'

'You *did* take it personal,' Murdock insisted.

'No,' I assured him, laughing.

'But you wouldn't have said it,' he persisted.

'Maybe not,' I agreed. 'I try not to like or dislike people because of their nationality, so I would probably avoid bringing their nationality into the argument. It's what they are and how they behave to other human beings that matters to me.'

'That's exactly the way I feel,' he said.

'I know, you stupid American son-of-a-bitch,' I said. 'That's why I didn't take offence.'

Murdock stared at me for a moment, then burst out laughing.

'You're OK,' he said. On the strength of the happy bond we had established, he suddenly asked, 'What do you make of the Swede?'

'Trygverson? The Colonel's keeper? He's Norwegian, or was originally. He's OK. He seems able to hold the Colonel in check.'

'That's what bothers me about him,' Murdock said. 'One minute, he's crawling to him and kissing his ass. Next minute, he's telling him what to do.'

'Maybe that's the secret of how to succeed as a staff officer,' I said. 'Are you worried in case he reports you for clobbering the Colonel?'

Murdock shook his head. 'He can report me if he goddamned likes. I'd do the same thing again. Right now, I got only one worry. And that's getting out of these goddamned woods.'

The pack that I had carried through the forest turned out to be stuffed with tins of sardines. There were also some hard biscuits – the kind that sailors used to live

303

on in the days of sail – and some liver sausage. A tin contained ersatz coffee.

The rations had been wrapped in three white coats with attached hoods: snow camouflage suits. Murdock took one, I took another and we gave the third to Danny. She immediately put it on over her combat jacket because she was cold.

Deciding that the density of the woods was great enough to prevent it being seen, we built a fire near the hut so that we could boil water. The latter we obtained from the bottom of an irrigation ditch. The water was a muddy combination of seepage, rainwater and melted snow. It tasted brackish and the ersatz coffee, with which we laced it, made a revolting brew. But it was hot and wet and served its purpose. We boiled the stuff in an empty two-litre tin – the only useful item we found in the hut. It had served as a repository for cigarette ends and spent matches but we cleaned it as best we could and it, too, served its purpose.

Sardines and biscuits – the latter like a wedge of seasoned oak – made an unexciting menu, but we were all hungry enough to enjoy it. Even Vardon, who accepted his share sulkily and with some disdain, returned looking for more.

We spent half an hour interrogating the German driver of the amphibian, with Trygverson, who spoke fluent German, acting as an interpreter. We did not get much information from the youngster but he revealed that he and his two companions had been scouting for the 2nd SS Panzergrenadier Regiment. He was cockily confident that his captivity would be of short duration and said that the offensive, of which his regiment was part, was massive in size and would overwhelm the puny American forces in its path.

'By this time tomorrow,' he boasted, 'you will all be prisoners and I shall be back with my comrades.'

We all laughed at this, of course. But our laughter was a trifle forced. We were only too uncomfortably aware that our situation was precarious enough for his prophecy to be proved all too true.

Murdock was certainly of the opinion that great caution was going to be required before we made a break from the relative safety of the forest for the American lines. First, we had to be sure where the American lines were. And it was Murdock's pessimistic belief that, while it had been sensible to hole up for the night, the chances were that we were now well and truly cut off from friendly forces.

'We got nothing much to stop the Krauts this side of the Salm River,' he said. Not even the sight that day of the Seventh Armored's Shermans streaming towards St Vith gave him grounds for optimism.

'If they need Shermans in St Vith more than they need them up in the north, where that Panther hit us, we're in a godalmighty mess!' he concluded.

Murdock seemed to carry in his head a spatial conception of the entire region, with its roads and rivers and valleys. He tended to lose me when he spoke of the villages and natural features and expected me to comprehend without the benefit of an Ordnance Survey map in front of me.

When Trygverson joined our discussion, Murdock proposed that, next day, two of our number should make a reconnaissance sortie with the aim of scouting a route likely to bring contact with American troops. He reasoned that we were reasonably safe where we were and that it would be foolish to budge until an escape route had been found. Two men had less chance of being seen than a party of nine.

'That makes sense.' Trygverson agreed. 'Either that or we all split up into twos and threes . . . Not that I favour that. We could end up with everybody getting lost in these woods. Who do you have in mind for this scouting expedition?'

'I was thinkin' of going myself.' Murdock said. 'It's not that I don't trust anybody else – but I want to see for myself what's out there. And I'll find my way back. Maybe Captain Abernathy would come with me?'

I was flattered. And doing something appealed to me a lot more than sitting around doing nothing.

'When do we go?' I asked. 'Assuming that nobody's got any objections.' I looked at Trygverson.

'If you're willing, that's all that matters,' he said.

'Good,' said Murdock. He grinned at me. 'We go at first light.'

First light was a long time coming. Its arrival was protracted, reluctant. A thick blanket of fog cloaked the forest, obfuscating the division of night and day. Only a gradual greying of the impenetrable black of an hour before told us that, somewhere beyond the damp penumbral clouds, sunrise had occurred.

By nine in the morning there was light of a kind, but visibility was no more than a couple of hundred yards. The swirling fog was a mixed blessing to Murdock and me when we embarked on our scouting foray. It aided concealed movement and offered a ready means of undetected escape, if the need should arise. But it robbed us of the chance to observe from a distance. Any encounter with the enemy was likely to be sudden and at point-blank range.

Our first objective was the highway, on which we had seen the American tanks. We found it in less than an hour. Whether or not we arrived there by the shortest route, I cannot say, because the path we took from the hut crossed several forest trails – but Murdock seemed to have an uncanny instinct in deciding which fork to take. He just seemed to *know*. I have no reason to believe that his instinct ever erred.

The highway, he told me, had a name – or rather a number. It was Route N23. At its south end – maybe seven miles away – was St Vith. A couple of miles to the north, the road crossed the Amblève River at a village called Ligneuville. The problem exercising

Murdock's mind when we reached the road was: which way had the amphibian driver's Panzergrenadier chums taken when they had reached the road? Had they turned south to St Vith after the Shermans which their radio scouts must have told them about – or had they turned towards Ligneuville, to support the Panzers striking west along the Amblève valley?

There was a third possibility. Perhaps the Panzergrenadiers had turned neither right nor left but had gone straight on, due west. Somewhere very close to where we were was a side road that connected the highway with the little town of Recht. That might have been the Panzergrenadiers' immediate destination.

'So what do we do?' I asked Murdock.

'Our job,' he said, 'is to find out where the Krauts are . . . When we know where they are, then we go where we know they ain't!'

First, Murdock wanted to check out the side-road to Recht. So we started walking south along the deserted highway. The road junction, the Sergeant reckoned, must be close to where we had reached the highway the previous day.

'Maybe the place is still hotching with Panzergrenadiers,' I said.

'We'll soon find out,' he said.

It was strange, after so long in the forest, to be stepping out along a main highway. It induced a feeling of nakedness. The fog still reduced visibility to two hundred yards but that did not stop me feeling exposed and vulnerable on the roadway. I kept mentally measuring the distance I would have to dive to the cover of the nearest trees.

We heard the truck's engine behind us long before it came in view. By the time it did loom out of the mist, Murdock and I were lying flat on our bellies, peering from behind the broad trunk of a leafless elm. The truck materialised from the fog as a huge shadow and it was almost abreast of us before we could make out the white American star on its cab. We rose simultaneously, shouting and waving our arms, but the truck did not stop. We ran after it along the middle of the road, to no avail. The three-tonner accelerated away into the mist.

We were bitterly disappointed, but the mere presence of an American truck on the road was a sign of hope to us. We resumed walking at a brisker pace, optimistic that more American trucks might overtake us. Our optimism was short-lived. We had gone no distance when there was a sudden racket of cannon and small-arms fire from the mists ahead. We veered off the road at a fast run and we kept running until we were a good fifty yards into the woods. Then, carefully, we began to pick our way towards the continuing eruptions of gunfire. There was a series of dull explosions and then silence.

Keeping parallel to the road and moving with stealth, we had covered perhaps half a mile when we heard voices from the road. They were distinctly Germanic. Signalling extreme caution, Murdock began to belly towards the sounds. I followed him. When he stopped, I stopped. When he showed no sign of advancing further, I slithered cautiously abreast of him. We were some distance still from the road but twenty or more feet above its level, on a bank that afforded an excellent view of a long straight stretch of highway.

As I raised my head, the first thing to catch my eye was the bright yellow flicker of leaping flames. They snapped and crackled noisily, and little bubbles of explosion fountained upwards as the three-ton truck – so lately a source of hope to us – burned fiercely and emitted black oily clouds into the lowering mist. The truck was slewed at right angles across the road and, a short distance away, grey-coated German soldiers – who seemed to have emerged from camouflage-netted gun-posts on both sides of the road gesticulated and shouted across to one another like children enjoying some seasonal bonfire. They gave little excited shouts as geysers of flame spouted from the blazing wreck.

Beyond these soldiers, a signpost and a road opening were visible: the road to Recht. There was movement in the vicinity of the junction: two officers, holding open a map which they were studying; Panzergrenadiers unloading boxes of ammunition from a horse-drawn wagon. As we watched, a German officer strode towards the group watching the blazing truck and started shouting orders. The soldiers dispersed, retiring behind the screens of roadside dug-outs.

Murdock signed to me that we should go. With more silent signs, he drew my attention to a rudely-constructed roadside hide less than a hundred yards from where we lay, which the truck must have passed before it had come under fire. A helmet bobbed as I watched but its owner was looking away from us, up the road to the north: a look-out posted to warn of traffic from that direction. By going into the woods we had by-passed the position – which was lucky for us. If the truck hadn't passed we most certainly would have been seen and have walked straight into trouble.

Thanking our lucky stars for the escape, we slithered a long way into the woods before we deemed it safe to get to our feet. We made a wide circling sweep, to bring us back to the road at roughly the place where we had been overtaken by the truck. Remaining in the cover of the trees, we smoked a cigarette and held a brief council of war.

Our foray, so far, had confirmed one thing that we had previously suspected: that the road to St Vith was blocked to us. The way to Recht was dicey, too. The Germans controlled part, if not all, of it, which meant that if we headed west, it would have to be through the woods. That left us with one unexplored avenue of escape: the road north to Ligneuville.

Ligneuville, two miles away, was the only place the ambushed truck could have come from – and this gave us a crumb of hope that the crossroads village on the Amblève was still in American hands. The fact that the truck had been on its own and been in one hell of a hurry offset this hope somewhat. It raised the possibility that the lone vehicle was a straggler, fleeing from the German armour we had encountered in Ondenval. Well, there was only one way to find out – and that was to go and see for ourselves, and without delay. It was already well past eleven in the morning.

Sacrificing caution for speed, we returned to the road – heading north this time, instead of south – and blistered along at a marching pace that would have done credit to the Durham Light Infantry. It did not last. We stopped dead in our tracks when, for the second time that day, the still of the morning was shattered by heavy firing. The sounds came echoing up to us from low in the valley into which the road descended. Screeching *Nebelwerfers* added their blood-chilling signature tune to the din, which was of some intensity.

'Screaming Meemies,' Murdock said, as if unhappy memories were stirring. It was the apt American nickname for the fearsome *Nebelwerfers:* multi-barrelled 150 mm rocket-launchers that could loose off six rounds every ninety seconds. Their screech alone was enough to turn a strong man's bowels to water. Murdock and I stared at each other uneasily.

'How far off d'you reckon,' he murmured to me.

'Three miles,' I judged. 'Maybe four.'

'Three is what I figured,' he said. 'Somewhere the far side of the river.'

The clamour was far enough away for us not to be unduly panicked by it – but close enough, nevertheless, to instil new caution. That caution demanded that we get off the road and seek a vantage-point that might afford us a view of Ligneuville and the river and give us some idea of what was happening in the valley below. With this in mind, we angled across country, aiming for a breast of hill which – we reckoned – must look down on the village.

It was hard going: downhill to begin with and then a long steep climb as we worked our way round and upwards. The distance was deceptive and I was panting like an asthmatic goat long before we found a suitable observation point. These were few and far between because of trees getting in the way.

'Maybe we should climb a tree,' Murdock suggested. The idea had already occurred to me, but I had refrained from suggesting it. Most of the trees around looked eminently unclimbable, including the one that Murdock picked out as a likely candidate. It jutted out over a craggy drop, a fact that we did not fully appreciate until we had started to negotiate its slippery green boughs and got a glimpse of treetops some distance below us. I avoided looking down again as I ascended gingerly behind Murdock. To conceal the fact from him that I was almost sick with fear, I solemnly recited the Lord's Prayer out loud. He chortled above me, amused. Little did he know that I meant every word. When I finally dared to look away from the sturdy trunk I was embracing with fierce concentration, it was to be rewarded with a breath-taking view of the village and the river.

Most of Ligneuville was on the far bank of the river. There a road curved downhill into the village from the east, emerging on its western edge and looping away from the river. On our side of the river, the road we had been on joined with another that ran parallel with the river: merging before reaching a bridge at the low end of the village. These facts registered with me and, at any other time, the scenery encompassing the pictur-esque huddle of houses might have commanded ling-ering attention. The charm of the scene was rendered irrelevant, however, by a sight that made my blood run cold. The firing we had heard from the road had long since subsided, but as we had made our ascent of the

311

tree, the air had reverberated with two or three loud bangs. Now I saw the author of those explosions. A Panther tank straddled a bend in the road above the village's far side.

Its long barrelled gun belched out a puff of smoke as another shell went on its way. The target was on a hillside above the western edge of the village. There a tank-like vehicle with an artillery piece mounted on top was stationary in the lee of a large building that may have been a barn. The Panther scored a direct hit. A sheet of liquid flame spouted from the tank-like vehicle with a thunderous explosion. The wreck of another tracked vehicle blazed hereby, presumably an earlier victim of the German tank.

It seemed that we had witnessed the elimination of the only opposition delaying the Panther's descent into Ligneuville. Its motor whined and its tracks clattered tinnily as it swung round and came down the hill opposite with astonishing acceleration. More Panthers appeared behind it, filling the width of the road and dipping into the descent. They rumbled into the main street and it was only moments before the leader came into view on the road to the west of the village. There was a chatter of machine-guns but neither Murdock or I could see what was attracting these bursts of fire.

'Seen enough?' Murdock called down softly. He seemed anxious to vacate his perch above me, which was precarious.

'More than enough,' I called back. My fear of falling was nothing to the numbing dread that filled me at the sight of all those tanks. We returned to terra firma and our haste, as we made our way back round the hill, was almost indecent. One thing was appallingly certain to us. We could give Ligneuville a very wide berth. There would be no help for us there. Indeed, the gnawing fear had taken root that we were completely cut off.

We did not return to the road, convinced that it would be only minutes before Panzers would be streaming along it, but we kept it in sight because it alone could give us our bearings. We still had to find our way back to the hut in the forest and the road was the only directional aid we had.

Our only consolation as we made the long trek back was that nothing passed along the road, north or south, while we were in its immediate vicinity. But I wondered what our reception would be like when we told the others the grim facts of our predicament. Murdock tried to cheer me up.

'These woods stretch for miles,' he said. 'They're the one hope we got. If we keep heading west until we run outa trees and a place to hide, we can maybe still outrun the Krauts. Our guys gotta stop them somewhere.'

'I hope it's somewhere this side of Dunkirk,' I said gloomily. He grinned.

'You got the Yanks on your side this time.'

Murdock, with that uncanny sense of direction he had, found the forest trails along which he had led me in the morning. By two in the afternoon we did not have far to go, but as we neared the hut Murdock became edgy. He pointed to vehicle tracks on the soft ground.

'These weren't there this morning,' he said. 'You smell anything?'

I sniffed the air. 'Smoke?'

He wrinkled his nose. 'What the hell are they burnin'? Oily rags?'

His sudden unease made me nervous. He looked all around him, bristling almost, like a terrier that had got the scent of badger. Suddenly, he bundled me off the path and propelled me into a dense thicket of leafless canes that tore at my hands and face as they snapped under my weight. He flung himself down beside me. Then I heard the sound that had alerted Murdock: the rasping snarl of a motor-bike engine, so close that I marvelled that I had not heard it before. The forest must have blanketed the sound, because I have got good hearing. Murdock's must have been extraordinary. I swear he must have picked up vibrations. We peered up as a motor-cycle and side-car went tearing past along the trail, so close that we could almost have touched its passenger: an SS Panzergrenadier officer wearing goggles and sitting erect. He and his black-helmeted driver were past in a flash. The roar of the powerful engine faded and was gone from our hearing with the same bewildering speed as it had arrived. The forest just swallowed up the sound.

We remained where we were after the motor-cycle had passed – and we were wise to do so. It was followed along the track by a personnel carrier with a canvas top. We got a glimpse of German soldiers through the open flap at the back. The anxious minutes dragged by leadenly but nothing else appeared on the track.

Both Murdock and I were worried sick at the implications of what we had seen. The presence of Panzergrenadiers so near to the hut did not bode well for the rest of our party.

'Maybe they gave themselves away by building too big a fire,' Murdock said. 'Jesus, they got something burning up there that must stink all the way to St Vith!'

We decided not to approach the hut via the path but to circle towards it through the woods. Neither of us was prepared for what we found as we neared the clearing where the hut had stood. I say *had stood* advisedly. For it was no longer there. All that remained of it were some burning roof timbers, now no more than a heap of ashen logs on the ground. The walls had been incinerated and all round the rectangle site that the hut had occupied the earth was black and smouldering. Tiny flames flickered, emitting black oily smoke at their edges. The earth itself seemed to be spotted with sulphurous little blisters, speckled black and molten. The hut and the area around it seemed to have been visited by a phosphorus bomb. Or so I thought at the time. A later conclusion was that a flame-thrower had caused the devastation.

At first, I thought that the clearing was completely deserted, but Murdock tapped my shoulder and pointed. A short distance along the path, to one side, two German helmets were visible, a couple of feet above ground-level. They seemed to be sitting with their backs to us. As we watched, two more German soldiers came walking down the path towards them, along the way we should have come if we had not made our cautious circling approach.

The two sitting men stood up, still with their backs to us, and exchanged words with the newcomers. There was a querulous opener from one of the pair who had been sitting, as if he were reproaching his comrades. The reply was dismissive, scornful. I heard the word 'cigarette', or one just like it.

Murdock tapped me on the shoulder again. I gaped as he handed me a grenade from the pouch at his belt. I fingered it gingerly as he selected one for himself. With signs, he indicated that we should edge nearer and from different angles. I was to take my cue from him. Slowly, we converged on the four Germans, who were still arguing the toss about something. The argument stopped suddenly and one of the men shouted a warning. He may have seen me or he may have seen Murdock rise to launch his grenade – I don't know which – but his warning came too late. Murdock's grenade actually hit one of the men between the shoulder-blades and dropped at his heels. There was a flash, a thunderous blast and I retain an image of bits of tree and shrubbery flying in all directions.

My own grenade was on its way, perhaps five seconds later, but it was overkill. It landed with a dull sound in a clump of withered grass, like a golf bail plugging in deep rough. An age seemed to pass before it, too, went off with a roar, showering earth and twigs all over the place. Then there was a silence so total that I could hear my own heart beating. This may have been an illusion. The explosions had deafened me and left a buzzing in my ears which seemed to pulse like a pounding heart-beat within a hollowness that was my skull.

The carnage we had caused was awful to look upon. I had to force myself to do so because Murdock insisted that I see something that was puzzling him deeply. It was not the bloody remains of four Panzer-grenadiers that troubled him but the scant clues to what they had sought to accomplish by the siting of their path-side hide. Little remained of the spruce-branch hide but, six feet away, we found the tripod-mounted light machine-gun with which the soldiers had been covering the approach to the hut.

'It was a goddamned reception party!' Murdock declared, with awe. 'These sons-a-bitches were sittin' there waitin' to blow the daylights outa whoever came up the trail!'

I stared at him, wide-eyed.

'Us?' The word came out soprano. 'But they couldn't have known . . . What brought them here? Where are the others.? What happened here . . .?' I couldn't get the questions out fast enough. They were queuing up in my bewildered mind.

'Take a look around,' Murdock said, ignoring my questions because he was clearly as bewildered as I was. He drew his revolver. 'Take care,' he cautioned. 'If there were any more Krauts about, they woulda come running but . . .' He didn't finish what he was saying, as if the complete thought he had meant to articulate had drifted away like a cloud. He scarcely seemed to be aware of me, eyes darting here and there, searching for answers to the mystery. He started moving back towards the burning embers of the hut. He was absorbed and yet wary.

Murdock poked around in the remains of the hut with a stick. I went on past him, searching both sides

316

of the trail but unsure what it was I should be looking for. Thirty yards past the clearing, I stopped – and I knew that my uncertainty was a form of self-delusion. My mind had refused to accept that the object of our search was bodies. Now I had to admit it. Because I had found one.

It was Kovac's buddy, Hanley. He lay face-down, close to the path, in a grotesque sprawl. I called out to Murdock, who came at a run. Before he reached me, I had stumbled across a second body. Vardon's driver – easily recognisable with his bandaged head – was lolled against the trunk of a tree, head sagging as if he were asleep. He was quite dead.

Murdock, grim-faced, had turned Hanley over and was staring at the wound in the dead engineer's chest. Both dead men had been stripped of their outer jackets and boots.

'He's been knifed,' Murdock announced as he bent over Hanley. 'There ain't no bullet wound.'

I took a closer look at Vardon's driver. Blood had congealed around a wound near his heart. I detected an inch-long tear in his khaki pullover and the shirt underneath. It was located above the seat of the wound and the bloody flesh around the wound was unbroken. No bullet had caused this wound. I told Murdock.

'Bayonet, maybe?' I suggested.

It was a possibility, he said. He just did not know. We were baffled. From the stiffness of the bodies, the two men had been dead for several hours. We searched around to see if there were more bodies. We found one. I made the discovery, having first found the two-litre can in which we had brewed the ersatz coffee. The blackened tin lay discarded near the irrigation ditch from which we had scooped muddy water. Lying in the ditch, staring at the sky, was Danny. She was still wearing the snow camouflage suit and hood. It lay open beneath her, spread out like a bridal train. Around the

317

neck it was dark with her blood. Her throat had been cut.

I stared at the nightmare image with a rage of emotions: horror, grief, guilt and a loathing revulsion for whoever had committed this final barbarity upon her. The mixing emotions fused, leaving me in the grip of a consuming anger such as I had never known.

THIRTEEN

No Way Out

The forty-eight hours following our discovery of the three bodies near the burnt-out hut are blurred in my memory. More than anything else I remember pain: the pain of acute hunger, the pain of bodily cold, the pain of fatigue, the pain of utter despair.

Murdock and I were reduced to living like animals — creatures of the wild, whose every sense is subservient to a single instinct: survival. Every waking moment was vibrant with the expectation of danger. Every movement was furtive, our cunning honed sharp by the fear of the predatory forces whose ravaging presence we often heard and sometimes glimpsed.

The cold inhospitable forest was our refuge and, simultaneously, the source of much of our wretchedness. It hid us from our enemies and sheltered us — but on its own harsh terms.

The mystery of what had happened at the burnt-out hut, during our absence from it, continued to baffle and perplex us. What had happened to Trygverson and Vardon? Had they escaped into the forest and become its prisoners, as we were? Had they been captured by the Germans? Or had they perished inside the hut? Had their bodies been incinerated as pressurised blasts of clinging liquid flame had reduced the tiny wooden cabin to oily ash? Murdock — who was more familiar with these things than I — was certain that the hut and its environs had been hosed by a flame-throwing weapon.

Most perplexing of all was the manner of Danny's

death, and that of Vardon's driver and Hanley. This added a bizarre and inexplicable dimension to the puzzle.

I had wanted to bury the bodies. But it was a wholly impracticable idea, prompted possibly by guilt I felt that I had failed to protect Danny. I was unwilling just to leave her lying there. Murdock pointed out, however, that we had no tools to hollow out graves in the muddy floor of the forest. Nor did we have time to perform such a task. Every minute that we spent at the scene of the horror increased the risk of our own discovery by the Germans. So we covered the bodies with brushwood and concentrated on saving our own skins.

We tracked back through the forest to Highway N23, crossing it into the hilly woodlands beyond as darkness fell. Thus began our futile wanderings of the next forty-eight hours.

In the forested hills, we were relatively safe. Only when we approached roads or habitation did we run into trouble. There were Germans everywhere. I lost count of the times that we went scurrying back to the sheltering gloom of deep forest like rabbits to a burrow.

The winter dark – more than sixteen hours out of every twenty-four – was both a blessing and a curse. We thought we would be able to use its cover to infiltrate the concentrations of German soldiery who stood between us and the American lines – but it merely hid every landmark and sign that could have told us where we were. The darkness not only concealed every village, hill and river that might have a friendly presence, it hid every obstacle and enemy entrenchment between.

At night in the forest, with not a star visible in the inky overhead where patches of sky might otherwise have been seen, navigation was impossible. There were trails to follow but, without precognition of where they led, using them was a lottery. Even Murdock's uncanny sense of direction could not be relied on at night. The dark was as effective as a blindfold and the signs which, by day, fed his instinct for direction, were hidden from his sight.

We were thus compelled to move by day, when we could see where we were going. What we saw drove us back to the forest and reinforced the belief that it had no safe exits without the cover of night.

The day after we had crossed to the west of Highway N23, the sound of fighting drew us through the woods in the hope that where the Germans were encountering stiff opposition, we would somehow be able to worm our way round the battle area and make contact with the friendly forces supplying that opposition. It seemed a good idea at the time.

The action seemed to be concentrated to the north and west, along the Amblève valley from Ligneuville. There, the next place of any size was the small town of Stavelot – which I remembered passing through on the journey from Spa to St Vith. It lay in a particularly precipitous stretch of the valley, with road gradients in and out that had tested the jeep and me, as its driver. I reckoned if that was the place the Americans had chosen to stop the Panzer column which we had seen in Ligneuville, they could not have picked a better spot. It was the last place on earth to lend itself to a tank battle.

Although Murdock and I buoyed ourselves up on hopes that the German Panzers had run into a bottle-neck at Stavelot and were being cut to ribbons, getting anywhere near the town to see what was happening was far from easy. Using the heavy firing as a guide, we set off towards it across the forest where we had spent a miserable night. Half a mile on, we found a good secondary road athwart our line of travel and deduced that this must be the road that converged with Highway N23 near the bridge over the Amblève at Ligneuville – but we made no attempt to verify that likelihood. The only traffic we saw on the road was German – several trucks towing artillery pieces – and that was enough to end our speculation on where the road led. As soon as the trucks had passed, we dashed across the road and kept on through rolling forest towards the distant guns.

Overhead buzz-bombs told us we were travelling west, but we must have edged north at the same time. The up-hill-and-down-dale terrain did not allow us the luxury of maintaining a straight course like the rasping missiles above us. We tended to work our way round the contours of the steeper slopes rather than across the tops. As a result, we struck the Amblève valley much sooner than we anticipated. We were aware of a gorge-like drop to our right and could hear rushing water before we saw the river. Another sound reached us: the now-unmistakable metallic rattle of tanks and other traffic on a road. A bridge spanned the river below us. Lumbering slowly across to our side of the river came a succession of Tiger tanks, most with infantrymen riding on them. Trucks towing field guns and *Nebelwerfers* made up the rest of the procession, followed by troop-carriers: squat wagons packed with troopers clad in distinctive para blouses and egg-shaped helmets.

The tail-back stretched out of sight on the far bank of the river. On our side, the road angled sharply away from us and the bridge to follow the westward course of the river. Here, too, the German column stretched out of view, a monstrous crawling centipede whose head we could not see. The sight was depressing enough, but what made our high hopes sink like a stone was the fact that this great armed caravan was *moving*, albeit slowly. It meant that the Panzers had not been halted at Stavelot, only three or four miles distant. We wondered if it was worth attempting to get any closer to the little town. We decided to try.

There had been no respite in the heavy firing along the valley. The noise was continuous – and it drew us like moths towards a flame. Not until the heat singed our wings were we to admit that its beckoning lure offered only destruction.

In order to avoid the considerable forces on and around the road into Stavelot, Murdock and I had to make a wide detour that would have tested the toughest commando. We waded through bogs, crawled on our bellies, we climbed up and down cliff-faced gullies – and we finally emerged on a shrubby crag that gave us a spectacular view of the precipitous valley in which Stavelot sits. It seemed to be full of German tanks, guns and soldiers. Below us, the land dropped dramatically. To our right, the Ligneuville road descended from the heights to a bridge over the Amblève at the south end of the town, which nestled against the steep face of the narrow valley's far side.

A huge pillar of black smoke rose from behind the valley-top opposite, and north-west of the town, the steady *crump-crump* of light field pieces and the whining blast of mortars kept up a steady din. Small-arms fire racketed from amid the quaintly-beamed buildings of the town itself some of which were burning. A German tank demolished one house with a single shell as I tried to identify any demarcation of the sides contesting the town. There was no doubt that American units were still holding out but, from the preponderance of German armour and mobile guns moving about without let or hindrance, it seemed that the few defenders remaining were hopelessly beleaguered. German tanks were streaming out of the town on its west side on a road I knew – the road to Spa. Immediately below us, south of the river, more German armour was racketing westwards.

'Looks like we're too late,' I said to Murdock. He nodded grimly.

'I wonder if our guys over there know they haven't a hope in hell.'

'They're still fighting,' I said.

'Maybe we shoulda stopped and fought, too,'

323

Murdock growled. 'All we done is run and keep running. I'm sick of it.'

'We're alive. You're no good to anybody dead.'

He smiled sadly. 'What keeps you going, Captain Abernathy?'

'The thought of dying on an empty stomach,' I said. 'I want one good meal before I die.'

'You'll be goddamned lucky if you get it,' he said.

We were dodging Germans for most of the day and night that followed but, throughout that time, the thought of food was uppermost in my mind; superseding even the fear of stopping a bullet. The near squeaks with the Germans were not without anxiety, but the crises came and went. The hunger pangs did not come and go. They stayed with me like a gnawing cramp and it was impossible to ignore the painful emptiness of my stomach. It was more distracting than severe toothache.

On account of the large numbers of Germans around Stavelot, we decided to head well away from the Amblève valley. It was back to the woods. We climbed uphill through thick forest and were daring enough to take advantage of a logging trail which we struck by chance. As a result, we nearly ran straight into a Panzergrenadier foot patrol near the village of Wanne. Fortunately for us, they were chattering like schoolkids on a nature ramble and we were able to take evasive action. They went noisily past while Murdock and I were sprawled motionless, not daring to breathe, only twelve feet off the track.

It was the first of several such brushes before we reached the River Salm, late the following afternoon. The Salm is a tributary of the Amblève and flows north to join the Amblève at a place known as Trois Ponts, so-called because there are three bridges there. Murdock reckoned that all the Panzers we had seen the previous day would be heading for Trois Ponts and its bridges

324

because, once there, they would have to cross to open tank country beyond. For that reason, we decided to steer well clear of Trois Ponts. It seemed inconceivable to Murdock that the American Army would not try to stop any westward drive by the Germans at the natural barrier which the Salm presented. So if we could get across the river we had a good chance of being home and dry.

Perhaps he should have said home and wet – because, spying out the land from a distance, it looked like we might have to swim the river. This was not a prospect I viewed with any pleasure, but we were both so desperate that neither of us saw it as an impediment. A greater impediment was the road that ran parallel to the river. It lay between us and the river and, on its own, presented no barrier. It was the German soldiery using the road who posed the problem.

There were two separate roadside camps of Panzer-grenadiers, perhaps a mile apart, and there was a steady trickle of traffic between the two. From the amount of men and vehicles we could see, we reckoned that each was about company strength. They seemed to us to be digging in for the night.

We watched from a distance, frustrated at having got so close to the river only to find our access to it denied. We were reluctant to retreat to the high woods for another night of misery, and were so weak from lack of sleep and food that we lacked the will and energy to scout out a safer crossing-place. We would wait until dark and, one way or another, we intended to get over the river that night.

In the failing light of late afternoon, we belly-crawled to within thirty feet of the road, at a point precisely midway between the two German camps. Thirty minutes had passed since we had last seen any move-ment on the road. The absence of traffic filled us with hope. Then we made an astonishing discovery. Right opposite us, a track, twenty feet wide, ran down to the river. At its end – perhaps two hundred yards away – was what remained of a timbered bridge. It had been hidden from our previous observation points by a copse of trees and, possibly, by the fact that the weathered supports had collapsed below the banks to river-level.

We could not believe our eyes. The bridge had obviously been destroyed and made impassable to vehicular traffic, *but a man could climb across*. I could have shouted with joy. Not least because the torment of swimming an icy river no longer loomed as a dread prospect. With luck we could get across without wetting our feet.

'Funny the Krauts are ignoring it,' Murdock said. 'They could throw a new bridge across there in an hour if they wanted to. They ain't even guardin' the place.'

'Maybe they're not so efficient as you give them credit for,' I said. 'Why should we worry? There's not a Jerry in sight and there's been nothing on the road in half an hour. Let's make a dash for it. We could be on the other side of the river inside five minutes.'

Murdock grinned at me. 'What are we waiting for? C'mon, let's go.'

We scrambled down the bank and sprinted for the road. We were halfway across when Murdock called: 'There's something coming! Hurry!'

I had heard it, too. I did not slacken my stride.

'Make for them trees,' Murdock shouted.

We reached them and were diving for cover when the first of two lumbering trucks reached the junction of the track and road. To our dismay, they turned into the bridge approach and halted, motors still running, halfway between us and the junction. Scuttle-helmeted troops, less than a dozen in all, baled out from the backs of the trucks and stood about chatting, their guttural German voices harsh on our ears. We sweated, not daring to move as much as an eyelid.

Our horror grew when the men started unloading things from the trucks and we realised they were setting up camp for the night. One lit a small spirit-stove and, pouring water out of a jerry-can into a dixie, got a brew going. Another came down the track and urinated, twenty feet from where we lay. A voice shouted what sounded like a warning to the man. He made a jocular reply.

Like me, Murdock had been alerted by the warning voice to something that resembled English in the terminology. One word in particular had rung in my ears – *Minen*.

Murdock made a movement with his head, nodding towards the track close to us. White tape had been pegged to the ground marking an area of track and its immediate environs. The copse of trees where we lay was just inside the marked-off area. The tape effectively sealed off the entire track for its last fifty yards to the fallen bridge. A wooden notice, emblazoned with a skull and crossbones, had been hammered into the muddy path close to our hiding place. Its message – *Achtung – Minen* – needed no translation. We were lying within the perimeter of a minefield that stretched all the way to the demolished bridge.

The sickening realisation dawned on me that, earlier, these German soldiers had pegged off the bridge approach and posted notices that the area was mined. Now they had returned, probably to disarm the mines and clear the way to the bridge – a task they were unlikely to undertake in darkness. And now it was getting very dark.

In the meantime, there was no way we could move. The mines barred our way to the river. The Germans barred our way to the road. And the trees where we lay provided the only cover there was on the river side of the road. We were well and truly trapped.

While the Germans made themselves at home on both sides of the track, almost within spitting distance, Murdock and I lay doggo in the trees, shivering with

327

cold. Our enemy seemed to be in good spirits: eating and smoking and joking with each other with the confidence of men in an area they knew to be safe. They were so close that Murdock and I were denied the opportunity of even discussing our monstrous predicament. We had no choice but to endure it, not daring to utter a word.

We were in a walk-the-plank situation – right out there at the end of the plank. Did we throw ourselves on the swords of the pirates or take the one step that led to oblivion? Short of divine intervention – and I discounted that probability – we were doomed, whatever we did.

As the minutes and then the hours passed and the night got colder, the conviction grew within me that neither German bullets nor American land-mines would end my life. Instead, the Ardennes winter would simplify matters and freeze me to death where I lay. The temperature dropped so quickly that it must have gone through zero like an elevator with a snapped cable: straight to the basement.

I did not know I could be so cold and remain alive. I lost all feeling in my hands and feet, other than a numbing deadness, and my face felt as if it had been sand-papered raw. Murdock, too, was suffering and we devised ways of silently moving our limbs and changing our bodily position in an attempt to keep the blood moving in our veins. We timed these exercises to coincide with the absence from our immediate vicinity of two patrolling sentries posted by the Germans. The two men were patrolling singly but, every so often, they stopped near the road for a chat and, I suspect, a cigarette. They, too, were feeling the cold because we heard them blowing on their hands and beating their bodies for warmth. By this time the rest of the encampment had gone quiet.

The silence from the trucks, where the Germans had – I assumed – bedded down, was what I had been waiting for. If we were to try to slip away, we clearly had to do it when most of the opposition was asleep. We had to take our chance when the two on guard were up near the road. Murdock was of the same mind, although our guarded communications were terse to say the least. We were daring, now, to indulge in single-syllable conversations:

'Go?' From me.

'Wait!' From him.

He was much the more patient of the two of us. But the cold was such that the moment came when I knew that I had to do something or I would never get off the ground. It must have been nearly midnight by then. I could not take the cold anymore. I was in agony with it. With neither of the guards particularly close, I got to my feet. The effort was almost beyond me. It was as if *rigor mortis* had already set in. My muscles had solidified.

I had only intended to stretch my suffering limbs but Murdock must have thought I intended to make a break for it there and then. He grabbed at my trouser-leg, possibly to restrain me, but I was closer to him than he may have realised. His arm struck me just below the knee when I was completely off-balance. It was no more than a glancing blow, but enough to topple me. I went staggering out from our little island of trees, seeking desperately to keep my footing. But my legs wouldn't support me and I went sprawling with considerable momentum. There was a pronounced down-slope at that point of the track and I found myself sliding help-lessly with it. I got back on my feet at the third attempt to rise but it was not until I was on my feet and desper-ately trying to remain upright that I realised how far I had slithered from the trees. I was in the minefield. I stood petrified with sudden fear, not daring to move a muscle.

I cannot describe the horror of the moment, which was made worse when I heard the footsteps of one of the German guards and realised he was just beyond the silent trucks. He must have heard my fall and was coming to investigate.

Stars were shining out of a clear sky – the first stars I had seen in weeks – and the ground all around me glistened. I could see Murdock crouched beside a tree so plainly that I knew the approaching guard would have no difficulty seeing me. There was no time to think about what I should do – I just did it.

Six quick paces – I expected each one to be my last – took me to Murdock's side. I fell on my knees beside him, almost a nervous wreck.

My heart was pumping away like a diesel engine that had gone berserk.

The guard must have heard something. He advanced cautiously down the track, his gun cradled expectantly, and he stopped twenty feet away, peering towards the river. We could see him so clearly that it seemed impossible that he could not see us with equal clarity. He seemed to look right through us as Murdock and I played statues and pretended we were invisible. Perhaps, with the trees and the dark trench of the river behind us, we were invisible to him. At any rate, he satisfied himself that nothing threatened and turned to trudge back towards the road.

Murdock kept staring at the glistening ground that I had crossed to reach him. He tapped my shoulder and put his mouth close to my ear.

'The ground's like rock. It's frozen.'

It dawned on me then why I hadn't gone up in smoke. The earthen track was as unyielding as granite and coated with ice. The minefielld was frozen over so solid that a road-roller could have crossed it without making an impression on its surface. Hope exploded in me that the Ardennes winter was not, after all, to be my executioner but our saviour. Only a flicker of doubt tempered that hope. It looked a betting certainty that the sub-zero temperature had frozen the detonating mechanism of the mines to impotence in the earth where they were buried – but did I have the courage to test the odds against that likelihood? Murdock and I did not debate the choice before us.

We saw the flare of a match up near the road. The guards were taking time out for a smoke.

'It's now or never,' I whispered.

Together we took a few tentative steps from the trees. Ground that had been muddy was now like flint. It was also slippery. Surface water had become sheet ice. We joined hands, like schoolkids, to give each other support, and stumbled forward as fast as we dared. We did not look back, both of us concentrating on where we placed our feet.

With Murdock's huge paw in mine, I derived a strange glow of comfort from the thought that, if this was where it all ended and the lights went out, then it was appropriate – after we had been through so much – that we shared the moment. The words of an old mission hymn came hack to me: something about walking hand-in-hand to glory. Well, so be it, I thought – one big bang and we won't know another thing.

We reached the bridge. Crossing it was not the simple task that it had looked from the road. In fact, clambering across was almost as nerve-racking as crossing the minefield. Only now we were not afraid of being blown all over the landscape; we were terrified of slipping into the icy water below. The fallen and disordered bridge spars were slippery and insecure, moving under our weight and with wide gaps that had to be negotiated. However, we made it to the other side. We clambered up the steep bank and collapsed, spent, on the freezing ground. We had done it!

Bereft of breath and nervous energy, I experienced, nevertheless, a sense of joyous elation. Neither hunger nor cold nor fatigue could dampen the euphoric feeling of deliverance. We lay there, savouring the moment and gasping air into our lungs.

When I struggled on to one knee, it was to break the skin of my nose on the muzzle of a gun that was thrust into my face. The shock nearly stopped my heart. The man who held the gun was a dark shadow above it. I could see only legs. Another shadow hovered over Murdock, who had also been immobilised by a gun, inches from his face.

Not a word was spoken. Prodded by rifles, we were propelled on hands and knees away from the riverbank. The prods were applied like commands, so that we were steered like cattle in obedience to the drover's stick. This treatment went on until we were over a railway embankment and tumbling down its far side. I tried to rise but a booted foot pushed me flat and kept me pinned there by the shoulder. The gun muzzle was poked firmly into my neck.

'Do you know the password, buddy?' drawled a voice above me. I had not the faintest idea what the password was, but relief drained through me at the sound of that American voice. I still had to get a view of our captors above knee-level and it was some time before we found out who they were.

In fact, they numbered twelve in all and their ugly cork-blackened faces were a sight to warm the cockles of the heart. We had encountered a forward patrol of the US 82nd Airborne.

Two starving fugitives, unwashed and unshaven, were a poor haul for that paratroop patrol, who were a long way from their base. However, our value to them soared when we gave them details of the two companies of Panzergrenadiers who were camped a mile apart south of the river, in addition to what we presumed was an engineer squad near the bridge. The paras had embarked on their night patrol to scout any German presence north of the Salm and the river crossing had been the most southerly point of the sweep. They had known that the bridge was down and that the far approach had been mined.

Although they had been specifically warned to be on the look-out for German infiltrators in American uniforms – Skorzeny's jeep-riding commandos had caused a monumental spy scare – I think we satisfied them that we were not Nazis in disguise. The sorry state we were in, plus the fact that Murdock knew the name of President Roosevelt's dog, helped to allay their suspicions. They quizzed us thoroughly, because of our ignorance of the password, and I was little help to Murdock in establishing our credentials. If he had not had an intimate knowledge of American baseball and known that Roosevelt had a dog called Fara, I don't think they would have believed a word of our stories.

Meeting up with the Americans was not quite the end of our misery. Although the sergeant in charge of the patrol believed we were genuine, it was not up to him to make a judgement one way or another on our identities. In the meantime, we were his prisoners and would be treated as such until the patrol had returned to the security of the American line. This was no hardship to Murdock or me. The bad news was that the paras' command post was five miles back from the river. Murdock accepted it philosophically with the observation that there was nothing like a five-mile hike to keep the circulation going.

The paratroops were no slouches. They moved carefully – we were deep in no man's land as far as they were concerned but they moved fast. I was tottering and ready to drop when we were challenged and passed through a perimeter guard before being led towards a darkened farmhouse. We were ushered into a room, lit by a storm lantern, where a sleepy-eyed captain bade us approach the light so that he could see us. He surveyed our dirty hirsute faces and mud-stained clothes with curiosity.

'What the hell you got here, Sergeant?' he asked. The

sergeant recited the details, telling the captain that we had crossed the Salm at the downed bridge: the bridge he had been told to make for to scout for Kraut activity.

'You say these guys crossed the bridge?' the captain queried. 'How about the minefield that's supposed to be on the other side? Are you telling me the Krauts have cleared it already?'

'No, sir. The Krauts ain't got round to clearing the minefield. These guys walked across it.'

The captain digested the sergeant's words and looked at us with new interest.

'Did you, by God!' he said, staring at us. His gaze settled on me and he smiled. 'You're just the kind of guys we could use in the Airborne. We wouldn't have to issue you with 'chutes . . . You wouldn't need the goddamned things!'

At the time, we did not know where it was that we were taken. We were fed, we got some sleep and we were interrogated three times. Then there was a long journey in a closed truck in the presence of two taciturn 'snowdrops', who regarded us with stony suspicion until we reached our destination. It was the First Army Interrogation Centre at Herbesthal.

Murdock's debriefing was completed ahead of mine. He was permitted to visit me to say farewell. In a freshly issued uniform, bathed and shaved, I scarcely recognised him at first. He looked a different person. It was an emotional farewell, inasmuch that the atmosphere was charged with feelings that neither of us could put into words. What was said was almost banal. What was unsaid had a profundity of bonded understanding and communication that went beyond words. Deep friendship needs no words. The depth is known in the heart and that knowledge is enough.

'So, you're going back?' I said.

'There's a truck heading for Malmedy in fifteen minutes. I'll be on it.'

334

I shook his hand. 'I'm going to miss having somebody to tell me what to do.'

'It wasn't that way – and you know it. You're the one that kept me going. We made a good team.'

'One of the best.'

We wished each other luck. Then he was gone. And my world felt emptier.

Ahead of me lay further interrogation. When it came, I detected a less aggressive approach by the American major who conducted it. He was painstakingly polite, sympathetic to the hardships with which I had contended, and was anxious to stress that the questioning was a necessary formality. When it was over, he led me to the room that I took to be his office and invited me to take a seat and help myself from the cigarette pack on his desk. He busied himself on the telephone.

I was smoking one of the major's cigarettes and staring out of the window at snowflakes drifting out of a leaden sky when he suddenly pushed the telephone across to me.

'Colonel Hibberd,' he said, handing me the receiver. 'I'll take a walk and leave you to it.'

I had to tell Hibberd all that had happened. His relief that I was alive was considerable. It had been impossible in Paris to get a clear picture of what had been happening in the Ardennes but, from what he had heard, he had given me up for dead after four days had passed and I had failed to report. With Thorn out of action and me missing, the *Schatten Gruppe* investigation had become stalled – and confused, too, by reports from the Ardennes of Germans in American uniforms operating behind the American lines.

Hibberd had been on the point of flying north to do some investigating himself when he had been notified that I was being held at Herbesthal. Whether he now did so or not depended on me. Was I in any shape to carry on? I told him that I had no intention of quitting.

As far as I was concerned, I had been side-tracked and lost the best part of a week, but I had no intention of giving up because of that. All I needed was a ticket of authority to get past First Army red tape, a new set of wheels, and I was back in business. There was the matter of my unfinished interview with Fabienne Lans, alias Hilde Gronbach, who – I insisted – knew a great deal more than she had so far told me. That was a state of affairs I intended to remedy without delay.

Hibberd, relieved and happy that I had no desire to quit, assured me that I would have all the backing I wanted. My authority to pursue the investigation would be endorsed by the Supreme Commander himself. It would be in Herbesthal by morning. With it would come documents which would allow me to requisition transport and fuel where and when I needed them. In the meantime, there was something I could do in Herbesthal, because it might have a bearing on *Schatten Gruppe*. A number of German prisoners were being held at the Interrogation Centre who had been caught wearing American uniforms. One of them, an SS lieutenant called Gunther Schultz, had boasted under questioning that he was part of a team heading for Paris. The team's objective was Supreme Headquarters, he had said, and its aim: the assassination of General Eisenhower.

What influence Hibberd exerted from Paris over the authorities at Herbesthal, I do not know, but it was certainly effective. The change of my status at the establishment underwent a transformation that was one to savour. One minute I was in a room like a cell and being treated like a suspected criminal and the next I was in comfortable officers' quarters, enjoying the most deferential respect. That respect was tinged, I admit, with a certain amount of unspoken doubt concerning my eligibility for favoured treatment, but it was enjoyable nonetheless.

When I enquired about being given an early opportunity to speak to the German lieutenant called Schultz,
I was told that it would be arranged. I was given the
impression that I was being awarded a privilege given
to few. The concession was granted with the grudging
reluctance of bureaucrats who have wangled a personal
audience with the Pope for a heretic with good connections. Just before entering the interrogation room to
which Schultz had been brought, I was shaken to be
told that he was under sentence of death. His execution
by firing squad was likely to take place on the morning
of Christmas Eve.

I faced the condemned prisoner while I was still trying
to absorb the shock revelation that his death was only
hours away. He was much less perturbed about his
approaching end than I was. I felt at an enormous
disadvantage and he was quick to realise it. He was
confident to the point of arrogance.

'They say you have more questions to ask of me,' he
said, in accented English. 'You had better be quick. I
have not so very much time.' When I did not reply
immediately, he added: 'You look as if it is you they're
going to shoot, not me.'

I found myself apologising to him. I told him that,
until a moment ago, I'd no idea that he had been
sentenced to death. It had come as a surprise.

'A surprise to you perhaps, but not to me,' he said.
'I expected no more from American military justice than
what I have received . . . a joke of a trial and a verdict
that was decided beforehand. One does not expect
justice from barbarians with no military tradition.'

'You were wearing American uniform,' I reminded
him. 'Is that in keeping with German military tradition?'

'It was a *ruse de guerre*,' he replied haughtily. 'Below
the American coat, I wore the uniform of a German
officer. I am a soldier, not a terrorist – although it is as
a terrorist that I have been judged.'

'You have admitted that the purpose of your mission

337

was the assassination of the Allied Supreme Commander?'

'He is a legitimate military target. And the destruction of your High Command is surely a legitimate military aim. I do not like the word you used, 'assassination'. It suggests that we would have killed like murderers, without revealing our true colours. That is an insult. The clothes we wore were only a means of deception . . . a ruse to enable us to pierce your most closely guarded stronghold. There, we would have fought and killed as soldiers – honourably. Unfortunately, the word 'honour' has no meaning to you Americans.'

'I happen to be British, not American, but we'll let that pass,' I said. 'I want to know more about this *military* operation of yours. If you are prepared to co-operate, there may still be time to save you from that firing squad.'

He regarded me, mockingly. 'You are wasting your time. I do not want your mercy and there is no need to beg on my behalf. From the day I took my oath of allegiance, I knew the day would come when I would die for the Führer and the Fatherland – and I am not afraid. Tomorrow, the next day . . . it does not matter. I am ready.'

'You won't answer my questions?'

'I did not say that. If it humours me to give you answers, I shall give you answers. But I make no bargains in exchange for my life. I want to let the Amis see that a German officer knows how to die.'

'All right,' I said. 'No bargains.' I was coming to the conclusion that there was more than a glimmer of the fanatic in this man. He was a fanatic through and through. A fool. A brave fool, perhaps – but a fool nevertheless. He was liable to tell me anything that suited his hunger for martyrdom. It would not necessarily be the truth: just something consistent with the heroic image he sought to project. I started throwing questions anyway.

'You are a member of the SS Special Forces – the group known as Panzer Brigade One-Fifty, whose commanding officer is Obersturmbannführer Otto Skorzeny?'

'And proud of it,' Schultz said defiantly.

'You've been with Special Forces for some time?'

'Long enough.'

'Was this your first operation?'

'Certainly not,' he retorted, offended: as if I had implied he was a rookie.

'You have a good record in the field, do you? Where have you seen action?'

'In western Bosnia. You have not heard of Operation Rosselsprung? Tito only got away by the skin of his teeth. We took his headquarters in Drvar. He left six thousand dead behind. That really was a battle.' His tone was boastful.

'You specialise in attacking headquarters, do you? When was this?'

'In May.'

'Was that before or after you joined *Schatten Gruppe*?'

The look of complete mystification on his face told me that my sudden arrow had missed the target. His puzzlement was not feigned. He had never heard of *Schatten Gruppe*, he said, and I knew he was telling the truth. I returned to a previous tack.

'I asked you if you specialised in attacks on headquarters . . . First, Tito's headquarters and now General Eisenhower's.'

He held his head up arrogantly. 'The idea to attack Eisenhower's headquarters in Paris was mine. This is something that I did not tell the Americans, but I am telling you now. It was my idea. I drafted the plan and sent copies to both Sturmbannführer Skorzeny and to the Führer himself. The Führer took the trouble to write to me personally to say that it was a good plan and would be implemented.'

'And you were given the leading role, of course?'

'Naturally,' he said, in a miffed tone. Something in the way he said it gave me the impression he was lying. As if it were unthinkable that the author of such a plan might be excluded from its implementation. Somewhere behind the facade he presented, I detected hurt pride. It was betrayed in that one word, 'Naturally'. Had Schultz really concocted a master plan – one that had been accepted – and then been handed something much less dazzling than the starring role? Was that what hurt? And was he now putting in a bid to go on record as the genius who plotted Eisenhower's demise?

'How many of you were to stage the raid on Eisenhower's headquarters?' I asked.

'Forty picked men,' Schultz said boastfully. 'We were to meet in the Café de la Paix in Paris. That was the rendezvous. All of us had to pass for Americans. That deception was necessary until we were in Paris and ready to strike. We had to be bold . . .'

'Until you were caught,' I suggested, interrupting. 'You must realise that by telling us all about your plan, you have doomed it to failure. All your friends will be caught . . . Because you betrayed them.'

His face darkened with anger at the suggestion.

'I have betrayed no one. I got no further than the Meuse, but there was a fall-back plan if I failed to reach Paris by the eighteenth of December. That is already under way and there is nothing that you or anyone can do to stop it.'

It sounded like bravado to me. I honestly could not tell whether he was telling the truth or lying his head off. He seemed to believe what he was saying. But his fervour and his frank admission that he had set out to kill Eisenhower didn't make sense. Why hadn't he just kept his mouth shut? Surely that would have been the hero's course: to have said nothing.

I talked with Schultz for another fifteen minutes or so but his answers to my questions were oblique, tauntingly so. He tried to tease me by implying that there was a great deal more he could tell me, if he chose to do so, but there was a hollowness about his claims. His performance lacked conviction, in a way that was rather sad. He did not seem to realise it but it told me a great deal about himself. In different circumstances, I would have found it difficult to have liked the man on the evidence of his personality. Modesty was not one of his outstanding characteristics. Exaggeration came easily to him, especially when he was trying to impress me with his own importance. I felt a strange pity for him, roused possibly by the imminence of the clinical ritual that would extinguish his life. He had an almost pathological need to occupy centre stage and, for a minute or more in a cold December dawn, he would. But his glory would be brief – and there would be no encores, no curtain calls.

Later in the day, I called Hibberd in Paris to report on my meeting with Schultz. I voiced the view that the young SS officer had been seeking notoriety in claiming to be part of a plan to kill Eisenhower. I had read the interrogation transcripts of all the Skorzeny men, caught in similar circumstances to Schultz, and none of these prisoners substantiated Schultz's story. Most had claimed that their mission had been to disrupt communications behind American lines as part of the German offensive, and this is what they seemed to have been doing.

'Why in hell would Schultz concoct such a story?' Hibberd asked. 'What's the point in telling us about an attack on Ike if it's all baloney?'

'That's the puzzle,' I admitted. 'If there is going to be an attack on Ike, why should he warn us? And if there isn't, what reason has Schultz got for saying there will be? He's bound to know it's the sort of thing we can't just ignore.'

'We haven't ignored it – that's for sure.' Hibberd said. 'Ike's kicking up hell, we got so many guards around him. We got him locked up in a cottage in the woods near Headquarters and we got a guy doubling for him in his house in St Germain . . .'

'You've got a double for Ike?'

'If *Schatten Gruppe* can do it, we can do it, too,' Hibberd said. 'Fact is, we got this lieutenant-colonel, name of Baldwin Smith, who'd pass as a dead ringer for Ike at twenty paces. We got him dressed up in a general's uniform and driving along Ike's usual route to the office every day. I sure as hell hope no Kraut sniper takes a pot at him. He's a nice guy' There was a pause. 'John, you've seen Schultz. You got any theories on the guy? Is he a nut?'

I did have a theory about Schultz – but that's all it was, a theory.

'He's a nut, all right,' I told Hibberd. 'A Nazi fanatic nut. The kind who sits down and writes a letter to Hitler telling him how the enemy Supreme Commander should be eliminated . . .'

'I didn't hear about any letter to Hitler,' Hibberd interrupted. 'Is this something Schultz told you?'

'This very day,' I confirmed. 'He claimed he dreamt up a plan to wipe out Ike and then sent copies to Hitler and his Group Commander, Skorzeny. And he says he got a nice little letter back from Hitler, saying the plan would be implemented.'

'So . . .?'

'Seeing for myself what kind of man Schultz is . . . has given me a theory. It may be nonsense . . .'

'Try me,' Hibberd invited.

'I thought Schultz was romanticising when he said he was part of a plan to kill Ike. All that stuff about forty picked men rendezvousing in Paris at the Café de la Paix . . .'

'We got the Cafe staked out,' Hibberd put in. 'Go on, John. You thought Schultz was romanticising?'

'He made out that the whole plan somehow revolved around him . . . That if he didn't reach Paris on the eighteenth, the whole thing would be scrubbed and some other plan would be put into effect . . .'

'Well?'

I groped for words to describe the feeling that Schultz had given me.

'It wasn't so much what Schultz said, sir . . . More his attitude of mind. I got the impression that he was piqued. I'm sorry to be so vague . . . I think Schultz did submit a plan to Hitler. But he didn't get the leading role he saw for himself . . . Because the plan, or something like it, was high-jacked from Schultz by another branch of the SS – a much more clandestine branch, one with an agent already planted at Allied Supreme Headquarters . . ..'

'*Schatten Gruppe?*' Hibberd almost shouted the words.

'I'm sorry if it sounds daft, sir,' I apologised. 'But you did ask me if I had any theories. It's crazy I know but . . .'

'Crazy? Damn you, John, it's the first I've heard in this goddamned affair that makes any sense. You got any more theories?'

I had several: things that had been playing on my mind, tormenting me in the hours that had passed since I had been freed of the necessity of thinking only of my survival. I unburdened my thoughts on Hibberd, who heard me out patiently and promised to seek particular information which I requested.

He said that the sooner I got back to Paris, the better. I agreed, but first there were things I had to do in Belgium. Top of the list was a trip to Spa and the continuation of my tête-à-tête with Hilde Gronbach. And I wanted to catch up with Thorn, whom I had left in the military hospital in Spa. I wondered what his reaction would be to my news of what had happened to Danny.

That evening, the sound of Christmas carols being sung in German drew me towards the windowless cement structures of the detention blocks. The singers were women and a guard told me they were nurses imprisoned in one of the drab single-storey blocks. They were serenading the prisoners in another block, where Schultz and other members of Skorzeny's brigade were awaiting execution. In due course, eighteen of Skorzeny's marauders would die before American firing squads.

I found the carol-singing hauntingly sad, but the guard to whom I spoke confessed no pity for the Germans awaiting death.

'Not after what happened at Malmedy,' he told me in no uncertain terms. I had to tell him that I did not know what had happened at Malmedy, although I had been trying hard to catch up with the details of the great land battle being fought not so many miles away.

The incident to which the soldier had alluded had not actually happened at Malmedy but at the Baugnez crossroads, a few miles from the town. I was to hear a great deal about it in the following days because it had incensed every American soldier. Eighty-six captured Americans had been gunned down by SS Panzer troops in a field near the crossroads, in what was talked about as the Malmedy Massacre. The perpetrators had been members of the Panzer column we had encountered at Ondenval and which Murdock and I had later seen at Ligneuville and Stavelot.

I went to sleep that night trying not to connect carols and the approach of Christmas with the festival of killing that held all Europe in its thrall. I dreamt of Danny, lying bloody in a forest ditch, and I awoke in a frenzy of weeping rage. An anger and a bitterness remained with me that was alien to the person I had been. I welcomed this hardening of the soul, this change that I knew had taken place within me. It was the shedding of a kind of innocence. My war was not the game it had been. It had become real. And only one thing mattered now – winning. All my life I had taken the soft option. I had let people and events push me around and always come up smiling. Now the smile did not come so easily. I wanted blood.

I wanted blood for Danny. I wanted blood for Kovac and Hanley and for all the others who had died. The path of my own survival was a trail of death marked by their broken bodies, and I had only to look back to feel the sharp goad of obligation from which I could not escape. If their deaths were to have any meaning or my own charmed life to have any purpose, it was incumbent on me to square the account at whatever cost to myself.

Next morning, I had breakfasted and was returning to the quarters I had been given when I recognised a familiar figure striding towards me. It was Major Goldman, the C-I Corps officer attached to First Army. He had been to my quarters looking for me.

'I got you a jeep,' he said. 'The driver who brought it up from Liège is topping up the tank and he'll put a couple of jerry-cans aboard. I got some papers for you, too.'

Hibberd had kept his promise. I was back in business.

'I hear you had a rough time,' Goldman said. 'Glad you made it out.'

'I was lucky,' I told him.

'You sure were. It looks like we've lost St Vith. And Middleton's only hanging on at Bastogne by his finger-nails. Things look bad.'

'The darkest hour's before the dawn,' I said, aware of the banality. I was anxious to be off. I knew I wasn't one of Goldman's favourite people and, although he was doing his best not to show it, I got the impression that he resented having to busy himself on my behalf on orders from Paris.

Fifteen minutes later, I was on my way to Spa. The journey took me an hour. The proximity of the resort town to the battle zone was brought home to me by the continuous thunder of artillery from the south and west. Spa itself seemed strangely deserted. The Army traffic on the road was going right through without stopping. I made straight for the gendarmerie where Hilde Gronbach was being held. A uniformed policeman showed me to the office of the red-necked overweight officer whom I had encountered on my previous visit to the station. On that occasion, I had had to come over all high-powered to prod cooperation from him, so I expected him to fall over himself in his anxiety to keep in my good graces. Instead, my welcome was positively surly.

He asked me what I wanted, in a tone that suggested I would be damned lucky if I got it. His whole attitude was one of calculated insolence.

'I want to see your prisoner again – the one you know as Sonya Zinoniev.'

'You're out of luck. She is not here.'

'Not here?' I was rocked back on my heels.

'You heard me. She is not here.'

'Where is she?' I demanded.

'How should I know? She was released, the same as the others.'

'What others?'

'The ones they called collaborators. The Mayor himself gave the orders. They were all to be freed. I just do what I'm told.'

'But that's preposterous! You'd no damned right . . . why?'

The mean little eyes gleamed with anger.

'No right? Were you going to protect us? We have been abandoned. The Americans cleared out a week ago and left us to the Germans. What kind of friends are they? The General and his lackeys left in such a hurry that they even left their war maps pinned on the walls at the Grande Britannique. They did not care what happened to us. Tomorrow, or the day after, the Nazis will be back in the Grande Britannique and it will be their flag flying from the town hall. Will you be here then to tell me who should be locked in our jail and who shouldn't? It will be like nineteen-forty all over again.'

I had no words to answer the scowling policeman. Perplexed and angry, I could only stare at him. For two pins, I would have landed my fist in his ugly face. I emerged from the police station trembling with anger and sheer frustration. There was murder in my heart.

FOURTEEN

Operation Sun King

Back at the wheel of my jeep, I nearly killed a woman walking her dog as I made a fierce U-turn in the Place du Monument and accelerated away with screaming tyres. I did not even look back to see if the dog-walker was all right. I had other things on my mind.

There was – I reckoned – just one person in Spa who might know the whereabouts of Hilde Gronbach, alias Fabienne Lans, alias Sonya Zinoniev. That person was her besotted admirer, Theo Bech, the lawyer. It was a long shot, perhaps, but I was desperate. I knew of no one else in Spa to whom Hilde Gronbach might have turned to for help and, I reasoned, she must have needed help. Thorn and I had taken possession of her cash funds and identity documents, so what had she done when she had suddenly been given her freedom? My guess was that she had run, eyes a-fluttering, to her little lapdog of a lawyer.

I was at Bech's office inside five minutes. His aged clerk looked up, startled, at my sudden entry, and tried to bar my way into the inner sanctum. I did not wait to be announced but pushed past the bewildered Methuselah and barged right in on his boss.

Bech rose from behind his desk with a face like thunder and advanced on me as if he intended to throw me out bodily. I hoped he would try. I had not forgotten that, after our first meeting, he had tipped off his Nazi-loving ladyfriend that we were on our way to see her. Bech thought better of laying a finger on me. Instead, he started shouting the odds about this unforgivable intrusion of private premises. I told him to shut up. When he did not do so instantly, I unsheathed my .45 Colt automatic and pointed it at his face. I told him that if he didn't quieten down and do as he was told, it would give me a lot of pleasure to blow his brains all over the ceiling.

His complaining died in mid-yelp and the sudden chalkiness of his face seemed to indicate that he took my threat seriously. I reinforced it by telling him that by shooting him dead I would be saving the State the trouble and expense of putting him away for the rest of his natural days. Because that was as lenient a reward as he could expect for aiding and abetting a woman whom he knew to be the agent of Nazi murderers.

Bech started to make what sounded like a denial, but I advanced the Colt a little nearer to his nose.

'I'm talking about your girlfriend, Sonya,' I said, 'only her name isn't Sonya and she is not the virgin goddess you seem to think she is. She is a one-time con artist, prostitute and procuress who has worked for Hitler's SS since before the war. She is the accessory, before and after the fact, to at least a dozen murders, and if there are any crimes she hasn't got round to committing it's only because there wasn't a big enough profit to make them worth her while. I only want you to tell me one thing about her, Monsieur Bech, and you'd better tell me quick. Where is she? Where is she hiding?'

'I don't know,' the lawyer stammered. 'I swear I would tell you if I knew – but I don't know where she is.'

'You know the Mayor emptied the jail. Weren't you there? Damn it, you were trying to get her freed long before the Mayor came on the scene!'

'It happened when I was in Liège. I knew nothing about the Mayor's order until the day after Sonya . . . the prisoners . . . were released.'

349

'But you've seen her . . . She had no money. You're the one she would have come to.'

'She got money . . . She was one of the bank's richest customers . . . She withdrew a very large sum.'

'How do you know this?'

'There were papers to sign. She wanted money transferred to Switzerland. There are regulations. I was called to the bank the day after she had gone, as her guarantor. There was nothing illegal . . .'

'When did you see her?'

'I told you, I have not seen her. She came to this office but I wasn't here. I was in Liège the whole day. My clerk saw her . . .'

'The old man? What did she tell him?'

'She wanted some personal documents from the strong-room. She was very angry because my clerk could not let her have them. He is not authorised, you understand. And, in any case, I had the only keys.'

'You still have the documents?'

Bech looked perplexed. 'Yes, but . . .'

'But what?'

'I do not know what they contain. And there is a sacred obligation . . .' He stared at me unhappily. Then he walked to his desk and picked up a letter. He handed it to me. 'This came this morning.'

I stared at the blue envelope. It was franked 'Bruxelles' and dated the previous day. I took a single blue sheet out of the envelope and read the brief message it contained. It was written in French, and, translated, it read:

Theo Darling,

We shall never meet again. I am leaving Belgium for good. I am sorry that I could not become your wife but it is for the best. I could never have given you the happiness you deserve. Do one last service for me. You have a deed-box of mine in your safe deposit. It contains only some personal things of sentimental value and some insurance deeds that I no longer require. PLEASE DESTROY THE BOX UNOPENED AS SOON AS YOU RECEIVE THIS LETTER.

Do this service for me WITHOUT DELAY. It is important to me that the box and its contents are COMPLETELY DESTROYED. I would be embarrassed if these old letters etc. fell into the wrong hands. I know I can rely on you. You will always have a place in my heart.

Love always, Sonya Z.

I looked at Bech, who had sat down behind his desk and was staring at his clasped hands, head bowed like a man in prayer.

'Well, Monsieur Bech, have you done what she asked?'

'Not yet,' he said unhappily. 'One can incinerate papers. but a . . . metal box . . . how do you destroy that? Do I throw it in the lake?'

'Not if you know what's good for you,' I said, with a note of warning in my voice. 'What you do is you go to your strong-room, you get that box, and you give it to me.'

He looked at me, shocked. 'But I cannot breach a client's trust. It would be most unethical to . . .'

I cut him short. 'Get it!' I ordered, and waggled the automatic menacingly. 'I'll worry about the ethics. Just treat this gun in my hand with the same respect as you would treat a court order.'

He smiled wanly. 'I accept the authority of the court,' he said, surprising me with unexpected humour.

He opened the door of what I had thought was a closet. In fact, it was a passage, about eighteen feet long and shelved on both sides: a document store. At its end was a heavy steel door, which Bech unlocked with two keys. The interior was shelved, like the passageway. From one of the shelves Bech retrieved a black metal deed-box. He carried it into his office and laid it on the desk.

'What are you going to do with it?' he asked.

'Open it,' I said.

'We do not keep a key for our clients' boxes. It is just a safe storage facility, you understand.'

'Then we'll have to break the lock,' I said.

Bech managed to looked shocked at the suggestion, but I think he was as curious as I to see the contents of the box. He fetched a stout screwdriver from the outer office and it took me only seconds to prise open the flimsy lock. I gasped at the treasure trove within.

I was reminded of a bottom bureau drawer in my late grandmother's house: one into which she cast holiday snaps, old wedding invitations, radio licences, household receipts, things she couldn't bear to throw away. Hilde Gronbach's box was crammed untidily with mementoes of a rather different character. Some of them may have been of sentimental value to her but a quick rifling examination suggested that the collector's heart was pretty close to the cash register.

There were a number of notebooks with detailed inked entries: cash books that clearly recorded daily takings and wages paid. The employees had no surnames. Entries were marked against Yvette, Denise, Mimi, Gabrielle, and so on. All girls' names. It took me a moment to realise that I was looking at what some would label 'the wages of sin'. The books contained the carefully recorded accounts of a brothel.

There were also dozens off photographs. Hilde Gronbach figured in most of them. There she was with a Nazi officer at a terrace café. She was wearing an enormous sun-hat and they were toasting each other in champagne. There they were again, this time on a beach: Hilde in a fetching swimsuit and him in shorts, his torso tanned. There were lots of photos of the twosome, some with the man in uniform and some with him wearing civilian clothes. Were these sentimental, I wondered? They must have been rare. The archives of the Western Allies had failed to yield one single photograph of Colonel-Doctor Johann Keitler and yet here I was sure – were dozens of this most shadowy of men.

A brown envelope contained more photographs of Hilde Gronbach. And if the photographs were wrapped, that was more than can be said of the lady they revealed or the male companions with whom she frolicked. I must say that, naked, Hilde was quite an eyeful.

One photograph in particular took my interest. In it, Hilde wore a leather cap and leather knee-boots – and nothing else. In her hand she held a riding crop, with which she was playfully teasing the genitals of a sexually roused naked man. Hilde's voluptuous body, brazenly displayed, interested me much less than the face of her drooling companion. It was a face I instantly recognised.

I searched for more photographs of the man. There were several. Another pornographic pose with Hilde showed him on all fours, looking round with entreaty as Hilde guided him like a performing dog with the riding crop across his buttocks. The remaining photographs showed the man in British military uniform. One showed him shaking hands with a black-uniformed SS officer, with the Eiffel Tower in the backgroundd. Both men looked very jovial. The same camaraderie was evident in the pictures of the British officer with other Nazis: being shown what looked like a gun emplacement in the Atlantic Wall; studying war maps in a room that could have been one in a great palace; posing cheerfully in front of a portrait of Adolf Hitler.

Bech was standing opposite me, gasping with curiosity about the contents of the box. I show him one of a naked man astride his beloved Sonya.

'You weren't the first man in your client's life,' I said. 'More like the thousand and first. This is the kind of thing she went in for.'

He stared in horror at the offending photograph.

'But why?' he cried. 'Why should she keep such filth . . .? To blackmail?'

'Maybe,' I said. 'Extortion was her trade. They're the nearest things to insurance policies we're likely to find in her box.'

The lawyer was shattered. 'All the things you said about her are true,' he said, his face a torment. 'I've been a fool.'

'And not the first, as far as she's concerned,' I agreed.

I retrieved the photo from Bech, put it in the box, closed it and tucked it under my arm.

'I'll relieve you of this,' I said. 'Do you want a receipt?'

'No, no,' he said distractedly. 'What is to become of me, my practice . . .? Will you prosecute?'

'For your stupidity, Monsieur Bech? No, I'm not interested in you.' And I wasn't interested in him. I wanted knaves, not fools. That said, I have to confess I felt a lot more sympathetically disposed towards the lawyer than I had done earlier. He had led me to Cassius.

My next stop in Spa was the military hospital where I had left Thorn. I wanted him to share in my discovery. I found the hospital without difficulty but I wondered what had happened to all the road signs leading to it. I soon discovered the reason for their removal: the hospital was shuttered up and empty; staff and patients had gone.

I drove on to the Hotel Britannique with the hope that somebody at First Army HQ would be able to tell me where the patients from the hospital had been moved but was shocked to find the hotel as shuttered and deserted as the hospital. The entire Headquarters staff had moved out. It dawned on me then that this was what the police chief must have meant when he said that the Americans had abandoned Spa. I was flummoxed.

I flagged down a passing jeep. Its driver was a weary-looking infantry officer who was impressed by the identification documents I showed him.

'What the hell has happened to First Army Headquarters?' I asked him.

'You been looking for them, too?' he said. He expressed considerable disgust at the speed with which his Army Commander and staff had scuttled to the rear at the first rumbles of the German offensive. They had cleared out on the day after the German breakthrough at Losheim and set up house nearer Liège, at Chaudfontaine, another spa resort.

'They didn't stay there no more than a night,' the infantry officer informed me. 'Seems the General couldn't sleep for the traffic noise outside his hotel. That and the doodlebugs going over all the time. On Tuesday, they loaded up and moved to Tongrès.' He pronounced the name Tongers, which didn't mean a thing to me.

'Where's that?' I asked.

'Fifteen goddamned miles the other side of Liège!' he said forcefully. 'End of next week, they'll be back in goddamned Normandy and we'll need to get a seven-day leave ticket to go and see them!'

Before he went on his way and I went on mine, the disillusioned officer warned me to steer clear of Headquarters if I had any sense because the German penetration had cut off First Army from Bradley's Headquarters in the south. As a result, Montgomery had been given command of the forces in the north. The British general – whom the Americans called 'the biggest mouth in the West' – had descended on First Army like Moses from the mountain and, in his usual tactless way, had set back Anglo-American relations 169 years. Indeed, my informant believed, Britain had enjoyed greater popularity with Americans in 1775 than was the case at the moment. The atmosphere at First Army HQ at any rate, was something to be avoided. Everyone was going around spitting bile and fury.

I headed for Liège, where one of the first things I saw

was a military signpost directing traffic to the hospital unit to which I had delivered Thorn as a casualty. I followed the arrows for ambulances and drew up in the courtyard of a grey, forbidding building on a hill above the Meuse. The reception area was going like a fair, handling an intake of wounded, and it wasn't until the furore had died that I got the chance to ask about Thorn. A harassed noncom consulted a mountain of papers heaped on his desk before informing me that Captain Calvin T. Thorn had been discharged only a short time ago. If I hurried, I could maybe catch him at the railway depot because Thorn had been issued with a travel warrant to take him to Paris.

In fact, it didn't come to that. As I emerged from the hospital's main door, who should appear from a side exit further along the building but Calvin T. Thorn. It was not he who took my eye but the fetching blonde nursing captain at his side.

'John!' he roared and came shuffling towards me. I think he would have hugged me if his arm had not been in a sling. 'Where the hell have you been?' he wanted to know. 'They told me you were dead.' The pretty nursing captain waited patiently while we went through the long-lost-brother routine. I confess it did my heart good to see him looking so well, considering the sorry state in which I had left him.

'Doreen . . .' He corrected himself. 'Captain Swanson here was gonna run me down to the depot for the Brussels train. She's been a real angel to me . . .'

'Looks like you won't need me now,' the smiling blonde said. 'That is . . .?' She threw me a questioning look.

'I've got transport,' I confirmed. 'If Captain Thorn wants to get back to Paris, I can take him all the way. That's where I'm heading.'

It was all arranged swiftly and amicably. The nursing captain went off, after wishing Thorn a deccorous good-bye and warning him to take good care of himself. I voiced the hope to Thorn that I wasn't breaking anything up by taking him off the blonde nurse's hands. He assured me that I wasn't.

'She's a real sweetheart that one and no mistake,' he said, 'but she was only doing me a good turn. There ain't nothing between us. She's too goddamned bossy for me. I reckon she nagged me into getting better.'

We walked towards the jeep. He was still strapped up underneath his clothes and could only walk slowly. He stared at the jeep, realising it was a different one — but that wasn't what was on his mind.

'Where's Danny?' he asked. 'Ain't she with you?'

'No, Cal,' I said. I sighed unhappily. Telling him about Danny was something I was not looking forward to. There was so much to tell him that I scarcely knew where to begin.

It was getting on for midnight when we reached the Château Beauséjours, Hibberd's base to the north of Paris. Long before we did, I had brought Thorn up to date with all that had happened to me. As much as he was saddened by Danny's death, he was perplexed by the manner of it. He wondered, too, why the Germans had troubled too prepare an ambush for Murdock and me at the scene of the crime.

'We thought our German prisoner must have tipped off his pals about the Sergeant and me,' I had told Thorn.

'But now you know different,' Thorn had replied grimly.

'Now I'm not sure what to think,' I had confessed.

In Bech's office in Spa, I had been elated with the discovery I had made. There was no doubt in my mind that the British officer — so clearly identifiable in Hilde Gronbach's photographs — was Cassius, *Schatten Gruppe's* inside man at SHAEF. But knowing the traitor's identity posed almost as many questions as it answered.

There was a vengeful satisfaction in having proof that

Cassius was none other than Colonel Hubert Macaulay Vardon, MC and bar. I had disliked the man from my very first encounter with him. But that did not make me unique. He was a thoroughly detestable man. That fact aalone did not account for the monumental treachery he had committed. What had made him – a man who had distinguished himself in the field, fighting Germans – so compliant an ally of the Nazis? A taste for kinky sex seemed insufficient basis for conversion to the Nazi cause. As a blackmail lever, it was a means whereby Vardon might have been persuaded to do the bidding of the Nazis but I was sure this could not have been the entire explanation. From what Hilde Gronbach had said, the infamous Keitler had earmarked Vardon as an easy victim so readily that I was sure there had to be much more to it. What had made Vardon so obvious a candidate for Keitler's methods of manipulation?

Had Keitler detected a latent Nazism in Vardon? From a behavioural pattern, it was possible. Vardon had the intolerance and bullying characteristics of a Nazi. But this argument had weaknesses, too. Vardon did not strike me as a person who would hhave acted from political motive or ideal. He was not idealist material: too short-sighted, in an intellectual sense, and too obsessed with himself to embrace a cause that espoused any authority other than his own.

Knowing that Vardon was a traitor cast a different light on the destruction of the forest hut and the fate of its occupants. That remained a mystery. For the life of me, I could not picture Vardon in the role of knife-in-hand murderer. It seemed strangely out of character. I could imagine him beating somebody to death in a rage or blasting somebody's head off with a shot-gun or automatic weapon, but stabbing Hanley in the chest or cutting Danny's throat did not seem his style. In short, he seemed more the hot-blooded killer than the type who could employ stealth and calculation to ruth-less effect.

I knew I could be wrong, off course. He was a soldier, trained to kill. I was perhaps creating niceties of division that did not exist. A man capable of his treachery was capable of anything. And tempering my satisfaction at unearthing proof of that treachery was some uncertainty on what use that proof would now be. My last sight of him had been in an Ardennes forest. Had he revealed his Nazi associations to the Panzergrenadiers who had fired the hut and was he now safely restored to the bosom of his German friends, deep in the Fatherland?

These and other questions occupied Thorn and me on the drive through France. The journey exhausted Thorn, who was still very weak from his wound and the surgery it had required. He made no protest on our arrival at the chateau when I bundled him off to bed as a matter of priority.

Hibberd, who had been in bed, was dressed and waiting for me when I had seen Thorn safely tucked up for the night. I presented him with Hilde Gronbach's deed-box and its pot-pourri of souvenirs. He examined the box's contents with awe, giving voice to monosyllabic expletives every so often as he studied one photograph after another.

'I wonder how Vardon's going to explain this little lot,' he said, when he had seen enough.

'If we ever see him again,' I said. Hibberd stared at me, eyebrows arched.

'Of course, you weren't to know. I should have mentioned it to you when you were on the line from Herbesthal. He's back in Versailles, John.'

'He's what!' I was staggered. Quite apart from anything else, I dearly wanted to know his version of escaping from the Germans in the Ardennes and how he explained the shambles we had found in the forest near Born.

'He was picked up by our guys near a place called Poteau, this side of St Vith,' Hibberd told me. 'Both him and the captain that was with him – the guy with the funny name.'

'Trygverson?'

'Yeah, that's it.'

'I hope they had a good story,' I said. 'What did they say happened to them?'

'Said their camp in the woods had been jumped by a German patrol and they had run for it. They blamed a German prisoner for giving away their position. You said the guys you were with had taken a prisoner, John . . .?'

'An amphibian driver, just a kid. How the hell could he have given their position away?'

'I'm only telling you what I've been told,' Hibberd said. 'It's all on the record now. We can check it out. It seems though that this Kraut prisoner got away and must have come back with his buddies . . .They sneaked up on your camp.'

'But Vardon and Trygverson got away?'

'Only as far as some highway or other. Some Krauts caught them on the road. They said they were taken down the road a piece and made to sit in a ditch with other prisoners. Then, when they were being marched off somewhere, Vardon and this guy, Trygverson, or whatever you said, sneaked out of the line into the woods. They said the Krauts only had two guys guarding more than thirty prisoners and it was a piece of cake sneaking off when they weren't looking.'

'It's all lies, of course,' I commented bitterly. 'Vardon must have told the Germans who he was and they probably fixed it for him to reach the American line without getting his head shot off.'

'You're forgetting Triggerson. His story backs Vardon's.'

'Trygverson,' I corrected Hibberd. 'If his story backs up Vardon, that means one of two things. It means that Trygverson is in this up to his neck as far as Vardon or the Jerries have let Trygverson go deliberately, in order to give Vardon's story a bit of window-dressing.'

Hibberd gave a low appreciative whistle. The possibility that Trygverson might be involved had not occurred to him.

'Which is it, John?' he asked. 'Which is it?'

'I don't know,' I said. I had had nagging little doubts about Trygverson but, until that moment, I cannot honestly say that I had him figured for a traitor. Now I considered that possibility in the light of all the homework I had done about *Schatten Gruppe* and their method of operation.

In the past, *Schatten Gruppe* had successfully infiltrated civilian and military agents to the Allied side by supplying them with almost watertight anti-Nazi identities, mixing them with genuine escapers from Nazi tyranny. One agent, German-born and possibly their most efficient operative, had operated successfully over a period of years as a Norwegian national serving as a seaman in the British Merchant Navy. It was, therefore, not beyond the bounds of possibility that Trygverson was a long-term 'sleeper' with similarly manufactured credentials. He claimed to be Norwegian by birth and, indeed, to satisfy American immigration officers his supporting documentation must have been very authentic. But had it been genuine? Had the young man with the real title to the name of Trygverson long since perished in a Nazi prison or concentration camp?

I voiced these thoughts to Hibberd and suggested that maybe it was time that both Vardon and Trygverson were placed under lock and key and asked some very searching questions. Hibberd agreed that perhaps it was, but a niggling doubt made him wonder if such a move would produce the answers we needed, particularly in the light of an intelligence intercept passed to him only that day.

He took great pains to impress upon me the necessity of seeking no elucidation from him on the source of his information, because of its extreme sensitivity. I could, however, take his word for it that it was one hundred per cent authentic. An exchange of messages – he said – had taken place between KG 200, the secret wing of the Luftwaffe, and an unidentified department in Hitler's High Command.

The text of the message from KG 200 headquarters in Western Germany was: 'In state of readiness Operation Sun King. Request revised date.'

The reply from Hitler's headquarters stated: 'Cassius advises conditions favourable for twenty-sixth December. Proceed as planned unless notified to suspend before 12.00 hours, twenty-fifth.'

I felt a stab of excitement as I read the terse message and watched while Hibberd carefully locked the copies of the intercepts in his briefcase.

'Am I supposed to read Vardon for Cassius?' I asked. Hibberd gave me a meaningful look.

'What do you think? When I got this in the afternoon, I didn't know that Vardon was Cassius. I have you to thank for giving Cassius a face. I still figured it was Cotter.'

My mind was leaping about on something else.

'Operation Sun King,' I said, quoting from the KG 200 missive. 'Can that be as corny as I think it is? I would have credited the Germans with being a little more imaginative.

'What would you say it refers to?' Hibberd cut in.

'The original Sun King reigned in Versailles,' I said. 'The man who's running things from Versailles now is Dwight D. Eisenhower . . .' I shook my head. 'It's too simple. Surely it's not as simple as that.'

'Why shouldn't it be?' Hibberd countered. 'Remember that we're not supposed to know anything about this. The Krauts don't know we're reading their top secret mail. And they sure as hell don't know we got Cassius's number.'

'So, you read this the same way as I do?' I said.

'They're going to spring on the day after Christmas. And the target is General Eisenhower . . .' I quoted again from the intercept: 'Cassius advises conditions favourable for the twenty-sixth . . . That's three days from now – which is too far away for him to have been talking about the weather. That means he was probably talking about the opportunity to attack Eisenhower, maybe something they've been waiting for . . .'

'You could be right,' Hibberd agreed. 'They talked about a revised date, which means that perhaps an opportunity has occurred already but they missed it . . . had to postpone.'

'Vardon was traipsing about in Luxembourg and then got caught up in the Ardennes, same as me. Maybe they postponed because he wasn't at base to give the word. Where the hell do the Luftwaffe come into it? Do they intend to drop paratroops all over the park at Versailles?'

Hibberd shook his head, doubtfully.

'If they tried that by day, they'd be shot out of the sky long before they got to Versailles. By night, they'd never find the place without a hell of a lot of luck running for them. No, John, it would be too dicey. They'd be crazy to try it.'

'If we don't run in Vardon and Trygverson and beat the truth out of them, what do we do?' I asked.

'We watch them twenty-four hours a day. We got two days to find out what they're up to.'

'This is where I came in,' I said, uncomfortably aware that my watch on Cotter had ended disastrously. 'Isn't that just a bit risky? For all we know, Vardon has done his dirty work by setting things up. Maybe all he has to do now is sit back and let some marksman take a pot shot at Eisenhower.'

'It's taking one hell of a risk,' Hibberd agreed, 'but it's one I gotta take. Even if we moved in on Vardon tonight, there's no guarantee it'll stop Operation Sun

King going ahead on schedule just as the Krauts planned it.'

'We can always lock Ike up in a dungeon until the twenty-sixth has come and gone. That would foul up their plans.'

'Ike wouldn't wear it,' Hibberd said emphatically. 'And even if we did take him out of circulation on the twenty-sixth, we'd be tipping our hands to the Krauts that we knew their operation date. That's something we can't let happen . . . because they'd *know* then that we were reading their mail. And them not knowing is even more important than the worst happening to Ike.'

'Is he still under round-the-clock guard?'

'He is,' Hibberd confirmed, 'and still kicking up hell about all the fuss. We got him stowed away in that house in the woods and we still got Baldwin Smith doubling for him between St Germain and Versailles.'

'And what plans does the General have for the twenty-sixth of December? Do you know?'

Hibberd did not know, but he wasted no time in finding out. He put a call through to Versailles there and then. A few minutes later he returned from the communications room, looking very thoughtful.

'Well, sir?' I enquired.

'He ain't making things easy for us. He's set on making a trip.' 'By road?'

'By train. He's going up to Belgium to meet Monty.'

'Then the train must be the target. Does Vardon know about this, do you think?'

'He goddamned should, or his office should!' Hibberd declared, worriedly. 'They keep tabs on everything that moves by road or rail. Contingency planning, they call it – the movement of mobile reserves and replacements so's they're always in the right place at the right time. The General's train couldn't go anywhere without Vardon's office being involved.'

If the nature of the problem facing Hibberd had seemed daunting before, it now seemed monumentally so. Neither of us were in any doubt that the outcome of the wrong decision now could be the death of the Allied Supreme Commander: an event that could alter the course of the war, on which history could hinge. It was an awesome responsibility and the weight of it showed on Hibberd's strained face.

'It changes nothing,' he said. 'We give Vardon rope but we don't pull him in yet. It must be the train they're planning to hit, but where and how, I don't know. It could be anywhere along a hundred miles of track – and we've got forty-eight hours to find out exactly where and when.'

The surveillance operation that Hibberd mounted on both Vardon and Trygverson was a great deal more elaborate than the watch that Thorn and I had kept on Cotter. Where he got all the men, I have no idea, but the team was two-dozen strong and equipped with radio trucks, walkie-talkies and a variety of transport. Some of the men were installed in Vardon's offices, ostensibly to install new electrical wiring. Simultaneously a painting and decorating squad desscended on the Pension Charleroi to refurbish the entire interior. It seemed to me that Vardon and Trygverson were being spied upon from so many different quarters that they must surely be alerted by the sheer numbers involved. Hibberd declared otherwise, however; insisting that by constant switching of personnel and by instructing the men to create as much disruption and inconvenience as possible, the entire operation was given the air of a typical military snarl-up. The Army, he said, had a reputation for organising things so that the maximum inconvenience was caused to the greatest number of people and so chaotic was the upheaval his men caused that no suspicion was roused of the careful planning behind it.

To the best of Hibberd's knowledge, Vardon did not know that I had come out of the Ardennes alive. So that he should remain in the dark on that score, it was decided that I should take no part in the surveillance operation. Hibberd did not want us meeting face to face. He wanted Vardon to feel secure. With Thorn also on the sidelines, we both felt suddenly redundant and we were most unhappy about it. At precisely the moment when the case was about to be blown right open, we were being denied the chance of being where the action was.

Hibberd, of course, would have none of this. We would get our chance to be in at the kill, he promised. In the meantime, we could do worse than familiarise ourselves with the French railway system and the route which Ike's train would take. Why didn't we take ourselves off to the Gare du Nord and talk to the US Army's railroad experts about the normal security involved in getting the Supreme Commander around the country by rail?

In consequence, Thorn and I spent most of Christmas Eve bumming around the Gare du Nord, talking to men who spent most of their waking hours organising the enormous movement of military traffic along France's thousands of miles of railway track. It was an education. So complex and so overworked was the system that we could only marvel at the fact that it kept on going day after day without ever snarling up and coming to a dead stop.

Special coaches were retained at the Parisian depot for the use of top military men and government VIPs. We were shown the coach that had been reserved to take General Eisenhower to the Belgian town of Hasalt, where he was to meet up with Montgomery.

'Will the General board the train here or at the main-line station?' I asked the American major who was showing us around.

'Neither,' he replied. 'Sometime tomorrow, we'll move the coach out of here and park it at a siding in St Germain-en-Laye. It's handy for the General's villa there. He ain't due to travel until the day after Christmas, so we'll leave the coach in the siding overnight. If everything goes to schedule, the General will come aboard at nine o'clock, Tuesday night. He'll have plenty of time to settle down and make himself comfortable, because it'll be midnight before we move him out.'

'What route will you take?'

The major pushed back his cap and scratched at his head, as if he had been asked the sixty-four-thousand-dollar question.

'Gee, don't hold me down on that one,' he appealed. 'We like to keep plenty of options open and a hell of a lot will depend on other traffic further north. This end is more straightforward. The General's train will take the up line through Beauvais and Pois . . . Then it begins to get tricky. We could take him on all the way to Abbeville or we might route him through Amiens for Cambrai, Mons and points north. But, like I say, it all depends on the traffic in that part of the world.'

I found his answer encouraging.

'That means, Major, that no one planning to do the General harm could know in advance what the precise route of his train will be?'

'Like the Krauts?' he replied. 'There's absolutely no way they could know for certain. It ain't as if the General gets the right of track or anything like that. Other trains got more priority and it's a case of the General taking his turn like any other unscheduled loco. The only place where I know the train will be at a particular time is the place it starts from on Tuesday night. After that, your guess is as good as mine. I can't even tell you to within twelve hours when the goddamned thing will arrive in Hasalt!'

We spent some time looking around the coach. It was far from luxurious: sleeping quarters, bathroom, a small kitchen, and a large compartment which could be used as lounge, conference room or operations room. The furnishings were utilitarian. Thorn and I came away from the big sheds where the coach was kept with one phrase of our guide's harangue preoccupying us both. It had registered with us independently and with such impact that we concluded we werre either telepathic or had one-track minds. It provided our sole topic of conversation on the drive back to the château because of its significance to the place and timing of any attack upon General Eisenhower's train. Without realising it, our guide had surely pinpointed the location and timing of Operation Sun King for us.

'The only place where I know that train will be at a particular time,' he said, *'is the place it starts from on Tuesday night.'* So it had to be there – the siding at St Germain and it had to be carried out sometime between 9 p.m., when Eisenhower boarded the train, and midnight, the train's departure time.

Hibberd was impressed with our reasoning that, if there was going to be aa German strike against Eisenhower, the St Germain railway siding was where it would take place. Our problem was: what form would it take? The possibilities were limitless. We could not ignore that strange confession of Gunther Schultz of Skorzeny's commando brigade, whether it was true or a fairy tale. So we had to take precautions against the possibility that a German commando team was already lying low in Paris and intended to storm the train with grenades and automatic weapons. It was decided, therefore, that two companies from the Headquarters defence force should cut off all access to the railway siding. They were to be in position twenty-four hours before the General's train was scheduled to leave and would mount road-blocks on every thoroughfare within half a mile of the siding.

There was also a chance that saboteurs might try to plant a bomb on the General's coach so an anti-sabotage watch would be mounted on the coach itself and a bomb disposal team would be kept in readiness nearby on twenty-four-hour alert. With the aid of the Security Forces commander at Versailles, Hibberd mounted a shield of steel to encompass the General's movements: so comprehensive that it seemed every contingency had been covered. In spite of this, we still had moments of fluttering panic that the measures to defend Ike were inadequate.

One occurred just before midnight, as Christmas Day approached. An incident was reported from Dinant, a town on the Meuse to the west of the Ardennes. A jeep containing four 'Americans' had burst through a road-block, manned by soldiers of the British Tank Corps, and tried to force its way across the Meuse bridge. It had failed to make it. The jeep had hit a mine necklace laid on the road specifically to thwart such a break-through. All four occupants of the jeep had died. All four were found to be wearing German uniforms beneath their American topcoats.

'Skorzeny's men,' said Hibberd, but we wondered. Were they? And although this jeep-load had failed to pierce our last line of defences, how many had succeeded?

When midnight came, we all wwished each other a happy Christmas but that was as near as we got to any kind of celebration. We had other things to think about and all of us were only too aware of the critical battle being fought not so very far away in the north. Snow had come with a vengeance to the Ardennes and my thoughts were, for much of the time, with the foot soldiers and tank crews fighting for survival in the forests of Belgium.

The places mentioned in the communiqués were no longer just meaningless dots on a map to me and I felt a deep sense of identity with the men holding the line at Malmedy and Stavelot. Elsewhere, the battle was precariously poised. Bastogne was encircled and Patton's tanks were not having things all their own way as they battled to reach the beleaguered garrison in the town. The 'Bulge', as some of the commentators were calling the German salient, had now ballooned well to the west of Bastogne and German armour had been reported only six miles from the Meuse. That was at Dinant, where the jeep-load of Germans had unsuccessfully tried to cross the river. I thought a lot about Murdock and the kind of Christmas he was having, north of the Amblève valley, and I put any thoughts of festive celebration to the back of my mind. Next year might be different but, as far as I was concerned, Christmas Day 1944 was going to be just another day in a long war.

Appropriately – or perhaps inappropriately – Hibberd styled his operation to protect the Supreme Commander *'Operation Father Christmas'*. For the purposes of communication, Ike was to be referred to as Father Christmas. Hibberd himself adopted the code-name, Scrooge. Thorn and I were saddled with the call-signs Rudolf and Blitzen. Vardon and Trygverson, for coded identification, were to be known as Plum Pudding and Roast Turkey respectively. It was all rather puerile, but it served a purpose.

Hibberd set up his control in a big communications pantechnicon in the grounds of the Palace of Versailles. Thorn was allocated a mobile radio truck to patrol in the vicinity of the railway siding in St Germain-en-Laye. I was assigned to the General's railway coach and was to remain with it until the Supreme Commander boarded it the following night. I would have the anti-sabotage squad for company and a two-way radio was to be installed to keep me in touch with Hibberd's Control.

I joined the coach in the railway sheds which we had visited the day before. The big cabinet was already in place when I arrived and an Army technician was there to show me how to operate it. We were testing the radio when six combat engineers with battle-packs arrived and took up residence in the far end of the coach: the anti-sabotage guard. They were followed by an officer from Transport Control, who had news of a change of plan. The General's coach was not going to be moved on Christmas Day, after all, because too many of the French locomotive drivers had been given the day off. The coach would not now be moved to St Germain until noon on the 26th.

I cannot say that the prospect of spending twenty-four hours cooped up in a railway shed was one I found enchanting, but I had come prepared to sit things out. It turned out to be extremely cold in the coach and there was not much I could do to keep myself warm. The anti-sabotage detail had three men constantly on watch outside the coach, while the rest camped in the kitchen, where they lost no time in firing up the coal cooking stove. I was tempted to camp in the kitchen, too, but it was overcrowded without me adding to the jam and I think that the engineers would have taken it amiss if I had intruded on their privacy. I was invited to avail myself of their constant supply of hot coffee, which I did, but they regarded the kitchen as their territory and the General's day compartment as mine.

Hibberd called me up at regular intervals to ask if there was anything to report. There was not. It seemed to be quiet all over. The only event of note was that Vardon had left his office after only a token morning appearance and attended a Christmas Day church parade for serving personnel. Trygverson had worked until noon and then gone for a long walk. According to Hibberd's watchers, both men had been very irritable and on edge, but this may have been the result of the disruption caused by the workmen's presence at Head-quarters and the Pension Charleroi on what might otherwise have been a holiday.

I napped during the night and, next morning, life returned to the railway sheds with the bustle of rolling stock being shunted. The juddering cacophony of wagons buffering into one another and the toot-toot-tooting calls of steam locos signalling rent the air. At eleven, preparations began to move the General's coach out of the sheds. A guard cabin was hooked to the back and a passenger coach to the front before the loco that was to pull us to St Germain arrived. The slow journey out of the marshalling yards, with frequent stops and starts and waiting for signals, proceeded uneventfully and ended at St Germain when we were shunted along a spur line backwards.

The single-track spur ended in a wide yard, with a series of points from the in-track leading to four parallel sets of tracks. One of these tracks was occupied by a string of freight wagons which stood near a bunkering and water point. The loco that had pulled us into the yard was detached, ran some distance up the spur line, waited for the points to be changed, then reversed into the yard to hook up with the freight wagons. It steamed out to leave our section of train in sole occupation of the yard.

We were sitting there, alone in all our glory, when a jeep came charging down the earth track that seemed to be the only road access to the yard, which was encompassed by a steep grassy slope all the way round. The high surrounding bank formed a natural amphitheatre and blotted out all view of what lay beyond.

A heavily built Army captain climbed out of the jeep whilst his driver remained at the wheel with the motor running. I got down from the railway coach and walked to meet him as the sergeant in charge of the anti-sabotage guard jumped down from the far end and also made for the jeep. The captain was from the HQ defence force and checking up that all was well.

'Where have you got your men?' I asked him

'We got this whole place sealed off,' he said. 'Don't you worry.' He made a sweep with his arm. 'We got our guys all the way round, just the back of that hill. There ain't nobody gonna get in or out without our say-so.'

Satisfied, he went off in his jeep the way he had come.

The sergeant posted his three men to patrol outside and went off to check that the two French railwaymen in the caboose did not have time-bombs in their lunch haversacks. I called up Hibberd at Control to report that the train was at St Germain.

'We've stalled Father Christmas,' he told me. 'So he won't be coming aboard at the time you expect him. I don't want him walking into anything.'

'It's all very quiet and peaceful here,' I assured him.

'It's too damned peaceful,' he said. 'That's why I'm going to stir the deck a bit. I don't like playing the cards I've been dealt. I'm going to shuffle them up and deal out some of my own.'

'Can I ask what you have in mind, sir?' I asked.

'Sure. You'll have to handle it if it goes wrong.'

I didn't much like the sound of that.

He explained. 'You wanted me to run in Plum Duff and Roast Turkey, right? Well, I ain't gonna run them in. I'm gonna get them to run themselves in. I'm gonna make goddamn sure that if the balloon bursts, it's gonna burst in their faces!'

His plan had a certain grim logic. If Vardon and Trygverson were at the back of some dastardly scheme to attack Eisenhower on the train and intended to be conveniently elsewhere when it happened, Hibberd was going to scupper their game. Without consulting the Supreme Commander, who was blissfully unaware of the precautions being taken to safeguard his life, Hibberd had issued written orders to Vardon and Trygverson in Eisenhower's name instructing them to join his party travelling to Belgium for a meeting with Montgomery. A car would call for the two officers at 8 p.m. at the Pension Charleroi and would take them to the Supreme Commander's train. They were instructed to take overnight bags in anticipation of being absent from Versailles for three days.

'What happens when they show up here and find

that Father Christmas isn't here, only me?' I wanted to know.

'You'll have company before they get there,' said Hibberd. 'And you can expect more pretty soon afterwards. Father Christmas's schedule is going to be followed to the minute, although it may not be the old guy with the white beard who shows up at twenty-one hundred hours . . . Just somebody like him.'

Hibberd did not elaborate further. I was left to work out for myself what he had in mind. I did not think for a minute that I was going to get a visit from a white-bearded man in a red coat and hood, carrying a sack of toys.

It was getting dark when I heard the toot of a steam whistle and the slow approach of a train on the spur line. I watched from an open window as the train backed along the track furthest from us across the yard. There were five carriages of the wagon-lit type and a sixth that looked like a kitchen-cum-restaurant car. All had their liveries painted out and the sides adorned with big red crosses on white backgrounds. There was no visible sign of life aboard.

The locomotive that had backed the hospital train in did not linger. It puffed out again along the spur. Ten minutes later, another line of wagons came clanking up the spur and were shunted on to one of the tracks between our train and the hospital train, partially hiding it from view. I was enjoying the activity when the sergeant of the anti-sabotage detail hailed me from the track.

'You know we were getting this stuff alongside?' he asked. I confessed that I did not. 'I'll check it out,' he promised.

I watched him clamber from wagon to wagon, two lines away. Most were open-topped but, here and there, was a closed goods car. The sergeant gave me a wave. 'All empty,' he shouted. He disappeared round the last wagon, heading towards the hospital train. At that moment, the high floodlights on masts at the four corners of the yard were switched out, leaving the yard to the shadows of the winter twilight. The sky was clear, with the promise of frost. It was going to be another cold night.

I closed the window and went round the coach lowering the blinds and drawing the black-out curtains – more to keep out the cold than anything else, because the cumbersome battery lamp that was my only source of light was not much brighter than a penny candle. I had no sooner finished when I heard a truck outside. It was the kitchen and stewarding staff come to get the coach ready for the General. They turfed the anti-sabotage crew out of the kitchen, but the small squad were on their way out anyway. From now until the train's departure, there was to be no splitting of duties. All would be out on the trackside, guarding the train.

I got myself something to eat but kept getting in the way of the stewarding staff. The latter kept moaning about the absence of heat and light. They could not see to stack away the stores that had been dumped at the side of the track and they kept complaining about the mess in which the kitchen had been left.

At eight, the radio bleeped and I went to answer it. I heard the word 'Control' on the phone-piece and then got nothing but crackling atmospherics. I tried to let the other end know that I was getting nothing but had no way of knowing if I was being heard. After ten or more minutes, I gave up, in a very ill-humour. All the waiting had made me edgy and now, without a means of communication with Hibberd, I felt decidedly rattled.

Rather than leave the communication problem unresolved, I went in search of the guard sergeant. I was going to suggest that he spared one of his men to go up the hill and contact the troops guarding the road access to the railway yard. They could surely get a message back to Hibberd to say the radio was u/s. He was bound to know anyway, through his failure to make contact, but I felt the need to do something.

I met the sergeant coming along the spur track from the signal-box at the yard's entry. He greeted me with his mouth full and revealed that he was eating a leg of chicken.

'I got it from one of the medics,' he said. 'I could've had a bottle of brandy, too, if I'd wanted it.'

'What medics?' I almost screamed the words.

'The guys in the hospital train. They're quartered up the front.

Been living on the train for more than two weeks, waiting to ship up north. They're finally on their way . . .' He broke off disconcerted perhaps by the fact that I was paying little attention and showing some agitation. I was thinking aloud and my mind was in a ferment.

'That's it, don't you see! Medics! The hospital train! Jesus! How many of them are there?'

'You ain't makin' any sense, sir,' the sergeant said, bewildered.

I was about to enlighten him in no uncertain terms when there was a shout from along the track, near the train.

'You there, Sergeant? Car comin' down the road. Looks like the General's arrivin' early!'

FIFTEEN

The Strike

As I ran back along the track, I could see the headlights of vehicles coming down the hill into the yard. They had pulled up alongside the train before I reached the front coach. A big staff car was flanked, fore and aft, by two guard jeeps. Soldiers from the two jeeps leapt out and, tommy-guns in hand, formed an outward-facing lane as two figures walked from the staff car to mount the steps of the General's coach.

One of the anti-sabotage guards came smartly to attention as the two from the staff car boarded the train. The sergeant and I were restrained from passing through the lane of bodyguards until an officer, who had remained near the staff car, came forward and satisfied himself that I was 'Blitzen'.

'Shouldn't you be aboard the train?' he asked me, rather severely.

'The radio's gone on the blink,' I told him. 'I only stepped off to get somebody to pass a message to Control . . . pardon . . . to Scrooge.'

'Is it important – the message?'

'It is now,' I almost screamed at him. 'There's a hospital train at the other side of the yard, on the far track, and it's full of bloody Nazis. They're wearing American uniforms . . . medics . . .'

'You gotta be kidding,' he replied. His tone was scornful, trying my temper to snapping point.

'Don't take my word for it,' I snapped. 'Why don't

you go and find out? But take plenty of men . . . You'll need them!'

He seemed, at last, to realise that I was deadly serious.

'OK, Blitzen, I'll check it out. But if this is some kind of joke . . .'

'It's no joke,' I assured him vehemently. 'Have you got radios in those jeeps? I want to get word to Scrooge . . .'

'You won't need no radio for that. Maybe we both better have a word with him. He's aboard the train.'

I moved towards the coach door and was about to pull myself on the the step when the sergeant of the anti-sabotage detail called out:

'A word with you, sir.'

I stopped with my hand on the hand-rail, but the sergeant had not called out to me. It was the officer that he wanted. I hauled myself up on to the step and caught what was meant to be an aside, *sotto voce,* to the officer.

'That guy's a fruit-cake,' I heard the sergeant say. 'The medics on that train over there are OK. I checked them out myself.'

'Goddamn you, Sergeant, I heard that!' I shouted down at him. 'You'd better come and repeat it to the officer who's running this operation . . . And in front of my face . . . not behind my back!'

'I'll go along with that, Blitzen,' the officer said. 'You'd better come with us, soldier. You can tell your tale to the Colonel.'

The pair followed me aboard the train. Hibberd and another officer, a stranger, were in the General's day compartment.

'Where the hell have you been, John?' Hibberd greeted me. 'Can't we get any heat and a bit of light in this caboose? It's like an ice-box!'

'There won't be any heat until the engine's hooked on and we get some steam,' I said. 'Sir, can we worry about that later? We've got trouble.' I told him about

378

the hospital train across the siding, and its reported occupants. Hibberd grilled the A-S sergeant about what he had seen. He nearly blew his top when he discovered that the sergeant's visit to the hospital train had taken place just after dark, more than four hours ago. The sergeant's admission surprised me, too.

'That chicken-leg you were eating . . . you hadn't just got it?' I threw the question in. The sergeant stared at me unhappily.

'No, sir. I'd just had my chow. The guys over there wrapped it and told me to keep it for later. I just stuck it in the pocket of my coat . . .'

Hibberd cut him short and addressed the officer who had been on the track-side.

'Captain Foley . . . I want men round that hospital train now. Get your own guys across there right away and get Anderson on the radio and tell him we want his stand-by platoon down here on the double. If they don't make it down the hill in three minutes flat, I'm going to have somebody's head on a spike! Got that?'

Foley was aware now that it was not all some kind of joke. He almost fell out of the door in his haste to do Hibberd's bidding.

Hibberd turned to me and grinned. 'I'm beginning to sound like a goddamned general,' he confided. 'Don't look so worried, John. How do you like my hat?' He retrieved a helmet from its resting place on a chair and turned it so that I could see the full general's stars emblazoned thereon. 'I hope,' he said, 'that Ike don't get too mad if he finds out about this. Impersonating a general is a serious offence. I could spend the next ten years breaking rocks.' He didn't seem too worried about it.

He introduced me to his companion, a Major Lindhurst from HQ Security.

'We came earlier than I said,' Hibberd explained, 'as we thought it might be a good idea to be here when Vardon and Trygverson showed up. Maybe it's a good job we did.' He glanced at his watch. 'Where the hell are Plum Pudding and Roast Turkey? They shoulda got here by now.'

The sound of vehicles outside sent us scurrying to check on the new arrivals. Two trucks were disgorging combat-ready GIs on to the track-side. Foley sent them off in squads of ten in the direction of the hospital train. They disappeared into the darkness of the yard.

Then a jeep came roaring down the hill and halted a few feet from Hibberd. Four 'snowdrops' baled out and one of them came smartly to attention in front of the Colonel.

'Subjects on their way, sir. We came through Checkpoint Abel ahead of them. The guys on their tail radioed to say there was nothing to report. Subjects left Versailles right on schedule.'

'You know what to do when they get here?' Hibberd asked.

'Yes, sir,' the military policeman replied.

'OK, stand by,' Hibberd ordered.

There was not long to wait. A staff car came down the hill and glided to a halt opposite the railway coaches. Vardon and Trygverson alighted. I heard Vardon tell the driver to bring his and the Captain's bags. The two officers peered across to our little group and Trygverson had taken a tentative step towards us when the 'snowdrops' moved. Before the pair realised what was happening, they were seized, quickly relieved of their side-arms and hand-cuffed.

'Take them aboard the train,' Hibberd ordered.

'This is an outrage,' Vardon protested as he was bundled up the high step. Trygverson remained silent.

We followed. As Hibberd pulled himself up on the step, however, a noise came wailing out of the darkness beyond the amphitheatre of the yard. We heard distant replicas of the same wailing sound as air-raid sirens from Versailles to St Ouen caterwauled across Paris. Hibberd stopped and looked down at me.

'The Luftwaffe connection, John,' he said. 'They've timed an air raid to cover their dirty work on the ground.'

The observation made sense. With bombs dropping and anti-aircraft guns banging away all over the place, what better way to distract ground forces while a small group of trained assassins went into action to eliminate the Allies' Supreme Commander?

'Let's see what Colonel Plum Duff has to say about it,' Hibberd said, and swung himself into the railway carriage.

Vardon was spitting fire: threatening dire retribution on the heads of whoever was responsible for him being man-handled and chained like a common criminal.

'You can save your breath for your court-martial,' Hibberd told him flatly. 'We got enough on you to hang you ten times over.' But Vardon was not so easily silenced.

'Damn you, man, don't you know who I am?' he shouted. 'Have you no respect for the uniform I wear?'

'I have no respect for a goddamned traitor!' Hibberd snapped back icily. 'As for your uniform, sir, you're not fit to have it on your back. You dishonour it.'

Vardon exploded with fury, screaming with rage and struggling, so that two of the MPs had to force him down in a chair and hold him there. He ranted about imbecile Americans and Yankee conspiracies and upstart colonials, who should have been put in their place. Hitler was right about one thing: the Americans were a mongrel race, polluted with Jews and niggers, and had no right to impose their half-baked ideas on the rest of humanity and, particularly, the thoroughbred nations of the world.

It was painful to have to listen to his outpourings — a claptrap of bile and bigotry that made me ashamed to acknowledge Vardon as a fellow-countryman. Hibberd soon tired of it.

'If he doesn't shut up, gag him,' he told the MPs. He

turned to Trygverson. 'You're pretty quiet, Captain,' he said. 'You got nothing to say?'

Trygverson looked up at Hibberd nervously. 'All I've got to say, sir, is that you're making a big mistake if you think I've done anything wrong.'

'You like to enlarge on that, Captain?' Hibberd asked.

'I know that Colonel Vardon's been up to something,' Trygverson said. 'He keeps going on about how much he hates Americans and how Montgomery ought to be running things. He says Montgomery's a better general than Eisenhower, Patton, Bradley and Marshall all rolled into one. He's crazy, sir. I got the idea he wanted to harm General Eisenhower in some way . . . I've been real worried.'

'Have you, Captain? Have you, indeed?'

'Yes, sir. And I aimed to do something about it. I was going to make a report . . . It's all written out in my desk at SHAEF – all my suspicions . . . I was going to pass it in to the Commandant's office in the morning. You let me go up there right now, under escort, and I'll bring it back and show you I'm telling the truth. I got no part in what the Colonel's been up to, I swear it.'

Vardon had gone silent. Now he was staring at Trygverson with bulging eyes, his mouth working.

'He's a liar!' he screamed. 'He's the traitor you want! He's the one that wants Eisenhower dead. He'll do anything, say anything! You mustn't believe him!'

'I'm telling you the gospel truth,' Trygverson insisted, ignoring Vardon, his eyes fixed steadily on Hibberd. 'If there's anything I can tell you that'll convince you . . . anything at all . . . you just ask it.'

'I've got some questions I'd like answered,' I said. I had been standing in the shadows, behind Hibberd. Now I stepped forward, where Trygverson and Vardon could see me. Both men looked at me as if they were seeing a ghost. Trygverson was first to recover.

'Captain Abernathy . . .?' There seemed to be more

382

uncertainty and fear written on his face than any relief at seeing me. Yet it was relief he sought to convey. 'Captain Abernathy... Thank God! We... I... thought you were dead ... Captain, you know Colonel Vardon and you know me. You must know that what I've been saying is true ... that I'm on the level. . .'

'Are you?' I asked softly. 'Are you also handy with a knife? Or is Colonel Vardon the trained butcher? The question seems to surprise you ... Or do you always twitch like that when you're trying to think of a snappy answer?'

Trygverson started to say something but he was drowned out by Vardon's shouted accusation: 'He killed the girl! I saw him do it — after he'd killed the others! He held her by the head and slaughtered her like a goat!'

The hate-filled look that Trygverson threw at his accuser told me all that I wanted to know. It was as good as a confession. Perhaps if Trygverson had not been so ready to rat on Vardon in the first place, Vardon would have remembered that neither he nor Trygverson were supposed to know what fate had befallen Danny and the others in that benighted Belgian forest, or he might not have been so free with his mouth. At any rate, Trygverson now seemed to accept that further mendacity would be futile. He looked up at me with a resigned little smile on his lips. His shrug of hopelessness was an acknowledgement of defeat.

'That's what comes of having to work with amateurs,' he said, meaning Vardon.

'I wouldn't know,' I said. 'I'm an amateur myself.'

Hibberd had listened silently. Now his gentle tap on my shoulder indicated that I should step aside and let him take over the questioning. We exchanged looks and he gave a little nod of appreciation.

'John, you go and see if you can find Foley, will you,' he said. 'Tell him I'd appreciate it if he'd send somebody back here to report on what's happening across the

383

yard. If anything's happening over there, they're keeping mighty quiet.'

I paused in the doorway. Hibberd eyed me, aware of my hesitation.

'Anything bothering you, John?'

I looked at my watch and then at Hibberd.

'Yes, sir. It's gone nine and we don't have an engine for this train yet. Shouldn't it be here? Or doesn't the General mind travelling in an ice-box? I would have thought the place would have been heated up before he was due.'

'Check it out after you've seen Foley,' Hibberd said. 'The French railroad guys in the rear van ought to know when the loco's due to hook up.'

I did not have to go far to meet Foley. I almost knocked him down when I jumped from the coach step to the track-side. He was on his way to report to Hibberd in person.

'The Colonel's beginning to twitch,' I told him. 'He wants to know what you've been doing over there.'

'If there's anybody on that goddamned hospital train, they're either dead or they've taken sleeping pills,' he said. 'There ain't a sign of life. We got men all the way round it – in the wagons on the next line, on the hill above it. We waited for somebody to show but nobody did. Now we got guys stomping all over the roof and rattling all the doors but the thing is shuttered up tighter than an Ay-rab's billfold. We're gonna have to break a few windows to get inside.'

'No medics with guns and German accents?' I asked, alarmed at the implications.

'Not a goddamned one,' Foley confirmed.

I walked from sleeper to sleeper along the track of the spur line, guided by a white pinhead of light. The Frenchmen in the tail van had told me that their loco-motive was long overdue but they were sure they had heard it along the spur. If it had been stopped there, they were unaware of the reason for the delay. Perhaps it had something to do with the air-raid alert.

Anti-aircraft guns were popping away in the distance, to the north of Paris: far enough away not to cause too much concern in St Germain. The pinhead of light towards which I was heading turned out to be the partially blacked-out headlamp of a large railway loco-motive. It loomed up as a huge black shadow across my path, but hissing steam identified the monster for what it was.

I hailed the driver in my best French, asking why the loco was stopped where it was. There was a subdued glow from the area of the cab: furnace reflection perhaps, or maybe only the panel lighting of dials. It was plain, however, that the head thrust from the cab could not see me, whereas I could see the head.

'What do you want? Where are you?' a voice demanded. It was not the only voice I heard. There seemed to be a lot of low muttering going on in the background, up there in the cab.

'Have you got a convention up there?' I asked.

'Go away,' the voice shouted down. 'You shouldn't be on the track at night.'

'I'm from the train up the line,' I shouted back. 'We're waiting for you. You're late.'

There was an unnaturally long silence before the voice came again: 'We can't proceed against the signal. We must wait for it to change. We'll be along as soon as it does.'

There was something terribly strained in the way that the man in the cab was delivering his contributions to the conversation. And a possible reason hit me with some shock. The echo-like muttering, the silence preceding each reply. It was as if the driver was checking with an unseen companion on what he should say. And maybe he was. The dread realisation hit me like a douche of cold water that the 'medics' from the hospital train had to be somewhere in the vicinity and the answer

385

was in front of me. Had they flagged down the locomotive and taken it over? Finding out was something I
had no intention of undertaking on my own.

I acknowledged the driver's explanation about the
stop signal and said we would just have to be patient
and wait for him, or words to that effect. I turned and
made my way back along the track, passing the signal
exhibiting a single red light, and the high signal box
that overlooked the spur and the railway yard.

I found Hibberd and Foley in conversation on the
track-side, outside the General's coach. Foley had forced
entry into the front carriage of the hospital train but,
apart from evidence of recent occupation, all he had
found was a heap of discarded medical corps uniforms;
more than twenty of them. I interrupted the confab
to report my suspicions about the locomotive being
hijacked.

It all began happening at once then. From inside
the General's coach, a succession of shots rang out.
Lindhurst, who was nearest to the coach door, leapt up
to go inside but fell back, knocked down by one of the
'snowdrops', who was trying to get out. We ran to
disentangle the fallen bodies. Lindhurst was only
winded but blood was pouring from a wound in the
military policeman's neck. He had difficulty speaking
but he gasped out:

'The fair-haired guy . . . the captain . . . he must have
had a gun in his sock . . . down his leg. He shot Bryant
and Spasski before I knew what was happening . . .
Then he got the Sergeant and me . . . Don't go in
there . . . Spasski's tommy-gun . . .'

The warning about the tommy-gun came too late for
Foley, who had already ventured up into the doorway.
Crouched there, he was hit by a spray of bullets from
inside the coach. His body thudded on to the ground
beside me, only inches from where I cradled the
wounded MP.

Hibberd was running around shouting orders, organising the thirty or more men who had returned from the hospital train with Foley and directing them to cover the doors and windows of the coach but not to fire.

'I want these bastards alive!' he yelled several times and ordered a couple of soldiers to unhook the front coach and get help to push it along towards the spur line. He wanted to isolate the General's coach, as far as it could be done. The two Frenchmen in the brake van were quick to realise his intentions and, with the aid of a small gang of railway workers who had just arrived on the scene in a military truck, they separated the tail car and pushed it towards buffers at the end of the track.

While this was happening, Lindhurst – who had recovered – gave me a hand to carry the wounded MP to the safety of a hangar-like storage shed, where a couple of medics took charge of him. We returned to Hibberd's side. He was angry at himself for not having ordered a body-search, which would have revealed Trygverson's concealed gun.

'Did you get any more out of him?' I asked.

'Not a goddamned thing!' he replied. Trygverson had clammed up and Vardon had gone into something approaching shock, as if it had just sunk through to him that he could not bluster his way out of the predicament he was in. 'The guy just doesn't seem to understand that he has done anything wrong,' Hibberd commented. 'There's no way through to him. You'd need a pneumatic drill!'

I reminded Hibberd of the locomotive along the spur.

'Shouldn't we do something about it?' I asked.

'Jesus, yes!' he exclaimed. 'But you'll need some fire-power, John . . . Just in case your theory's right. There's plenty of men over by that hospital train. Get over there and get hold of Foley's Number Two . . . what the hell's his name . . .? Harvey. Yeah, Captain Harvey . . . Tell him what you told me and get him to take some men down the line. We could use that loco . . . get it to tow those freight wagons out of here. They're shutting up one side of the General's coach and Trygverson could use them as cover if he's fool enough to make a bolt for it.'

Hibberd detailed Major Lindhurst to go along with me, just in case the unknown Captain Harvey wondered who I was, to be passing on orders. Harvey, in the event, was eager to go. He had been disappointed to find the hospital train empty, having expected to shoot his way aboard. It had all been an anti-climax, although he was bursting with curiosity about the shooting he had heard from across the yard.

We told him and broke the news to him that Foley was dead. This merely whetted his hope that we would find the railway engine awash with Nazis.

'Just what did the Colonel say we had to do?' he asked me.

'We take the engine. With such force as may be required. But we need the driver and the fireman intact.'

Lindhurst said he would get back to the Colonel but there was no way I was going to miss out on ascertaining if my hunch about the engine was correct. I tagged along with Harvey. He took two squads of men and, after a brief conference with the squad-leaders, we set off. Harvey was happy to have me as a guide, on the strength of my previous excursion along the spur.

When we saw the pinhead of light from the engine's headlamp, Harvey directed his men on to the steep grassy banks on either side of the track and told them to wait and keep the train covered. Detailing two men to follow us, he whispered to me:

'Let's see if we can sneak by and come at it from the back.'

We took to the grassy bank for silent movement and wormed our way past the steam-hissing monster. The noisy discharge from the locomotive's box-glands helped to drown any sounds we made as we slithered along the bank. We were further aided by the racket of anti-aircraft fire, which was erupting near at hand. We heard the drone of aircraft overhead. The pencil-like beams of searchlights stabbed up at the heavens from beyond our dark canyon of rail track.

There was no sign of movement in the glowing area of the engine cab as we slid quietly down the bank to step on to the track in the shadow of the high-backed tender. A steel ladder led upwards and Harvey was quickly on to it. He climbed up out of sight. I took a deep breath and followed. Revolver in hand, he was trying to negotiate a way across a hillock of coal to the front of the tender. I followed him, Colt in hand. Silent progress was impossible. Both of us started noisy slides of coal – just gravel trickles really, but they sounded like avalanches.

A head appeared above the far end of the tender as a canvas black-out awning was pushed aside. Against the light from the cab, I saw head, shoulders and an arm holding a gun. Harvey fired. The head and shoulders disappeared and the falling body made a din like sauce-pans being knocked off a stove. I don't know what the man had fallen on.

Harvey and I scrambled quickly over the coal to the cab. I drew back sharply as a shot fired at close range came up from the cab and nearly parted my hair. I'd had a flashing glimpse of a black-clad figure aiming a pistol at me. I made for the side of the tender, wondering if a more indirect route to the cab was available. As I looked over the side, a black-clad figure emerged back-wards from the cab, in the act of climbing down. He looked up and his shoulders jerked in surprise as he saw me. I saw his gun come up as I pulled the Colt's trigger. The black-clad figure went backwards as if he had been kicked. There was a sickening thud as his body hit the track-side.

From the cab came frantic shouts of 'Ne tirez pas!' Harvey and I clambered down into the cab to find the engine crew in a state of nervous anxiety but otherwise

389

intact. They excitedly told us that there had been about ten Boches, all dressed from head to foot in black, although only the two we had killed had boarded the loco. The others had gone down the track towards St Germain, carrying large canisters, each weighing about sixty pounds. The railmen also pointed out something that, in my stupidity, I had not realised before. In order to stop the train, the high-jackers must have taken over the signal box that overlooked the yard and the spur line. Why else had the signal remained so long at red?

The dead German in the cab had fallen on a coal-shovel – the clatter I had heard – and I helped Harvey haul the body clear of the cab door. For no particular reason, I pulled off the black balaclava-type helmet he was wearing. He was not a pretty sight. Harvey's bullet had gone clean through his throat. But, even in death, the face of the dead German was disturbingly familiar. Then it dawned. I had seen the man before. Only the last time I had seen him he had been wearing American officer's uniform. It was the same man Thorn and I had encountered in front of the Zinoniev mansion, near Spa, and who had told us that his outfit was an advance hospital unit attached to the US 75th Division.

While I explained to the engine-driver that we wanted his loco to pull some freight cars out of the yard, Harvey whistled up his men to tell them that he wanted the spur line searched all the way to St Germain station. He wanted the Germans with their mysterious canisters found.

In the event, the object of the canister-carrying marauders became abundantly clear while Harvey was still giving out his orders, although things happened so suddenly that there was not much we could do about it. The racket of the flak barrage was now considerable and the drone of a low-flying aircraft was so close that it was quite a distraction to the work in hand. For some reason, it did not occur to us that the railway yard might be the target. I certainly did not doubt for a minute that the attacking planes were staging a token raid as a diversionary tactic.

I was disabused of that notion in the space of a few minutes. And it all happened so quickly that the bewildering shock of it all is like a blur on the memory. The initial shock occurred when the rail-yard at the end of the spur was suddenly lit up like the White City dog track. The clustered lights, atop the pylons in the four corners of the yard, came on to festoon the area in bright light.

We were still goggling at the spectacle when a shout caused us to direct our attention to the long straight of spur line behind us. A series of brilliant flaring lights burst forth, like roman candles, illuminating the straight path of the railway. The flaming magenta flares burned in a line, marking the track towards the yard like an arrow. The nearest was a mere two hundred yards from the stationary locomotive.

Even as Harvey ordered his men along the track after the unseen marauders who had ignited the flares, the intention of the low circling aircraft suddenly became apparent. A searchlight beam caught the raider as it approached from the direction of the St Germain railway station. It was coming straight for us, following the flares towards the floodlit yard.

Exploding shells burst like stars all round the plunging aircraft, which seemed grotesque and misshapen. The explanation of the strange shape flashed in my mind as I watched in horror. Before the war, at Southampton, I had covered a story about the pick-a-back flying boats, *Maia* and *Mercury,* and I realised I was witnessing a similar phenomenon: a mother aircraft with a second and smaller machine riding on her back.

Sure enough, the smaller craft on the bomber's back lifted suddenly and I marvelled at the pilot's nerve in delaying separation so late. At such a low height, the manoeuvre seemed suicidal and – although I didn't know it at the time – it proved to be. The fighter aircraft,

391

from which the flight of the mother-and-child combination had been controlled, crashed into a house three miles away. But it was the pilotless bomber that held us rooted in terror as it hurtled towards us. It vanished from the searchlight's beam at the moment of separation and only its screaming descent announced its inexorable passage like a meteor towards us.

It passed over the stationary engine as a swooping shadow, wings darkening the sky like a giant vulture's as it falls on its prey. There was a thunderous rending crash as it bellied in the railway yard and a continuing dissonance of grinding metallic shrieks and bangs until its meteoric momentum was spent. I waited, eyes closed and teeth ground together, for the explosion that I felt must come. But none did and I could not quite comprehend. I was sure that the bomber must have been loaded from nose to tail with enough explosive to blow several square miles of Paris off the map, but the big bang did not come. Instead, a succession of stuttering little explosions eddied from the direction of the yard. In the same instant, the floodlights blinked out and left a darkness that was only broken by the flicker of leaping flames from the far end of the railway yard.

Harvey and I raced along the track from the spur, not daring to contemplate what sight of devastation might meet our eyes. Suddenly, there were bullets flying all over the place. Hibberd, or someone else, had twigged that the signal box had been occupied by hostile elements — the box was where the overhead lighting switches were located — and he had sent in troops to investigate

Fewer than a dozen black-clad Germans had occupied the signal box and — it later became clear — had intended to escape along the spur in the hijacked engine when their work was done, picking up their fellows who had lit the flares as they went. Harvey and I almost ran straight into the escaping Germans on the track. Fortunately, one of his squads was right behind us, or we might have been in trouble. The Germans found themselves between two lots of Americans looking for blood and the ensuing firefight was of short duration.

It ended with ten dead Germans on the track and four seriously wounded American soldiers. Regrettably, the Americans seemed to have been victims of compatriots' bullets: a consequence of the pig-in-the-middle situation.

The rail-yard, when we eventually got there, was like a corner of Dante's hell. Illuminating the scene were flames licking up from the wrecked German bomber and a series of smaller fires that it had started. The bomber had bellied on to the separated front coach of the General's train, overturning it, and had continued, hitting the General's coach and simultaneously becoming entangled in the line of freight wagons on the parallel track. It had ploughed through the yard like the blade of a harrow, throwing wagons in all directions.

The General's coach had finished up standing on end, like a toy discarded on to a junk heap. The aircraft's nose was buried deep in its base and the tail area was necklaced by overturned freight cars, which were still hooked together.

There were dead and dying everywhere. Survivors, in a state of shock, wandered about aimlessly. Others sought frantically for comrades in the wreckage. A sulphurous smell hung over all and the ground was covered with small pieces of rock-like substance, which burned with a blue-edged flame and dissolved oilily. It had been shed by the breaking aircraft and strewn along its fiery wake.

'What the hell is it?' I asked Harvey.

He kicked a piece of burning rock with his foot and sniffed its distinctive odour.

'Smells like gelignite,' he said.

Later, a bomb-disposal expert, who arrived on the scene, told me that it was in fact TNT and that there must have been about a ton of it on the bomber. The aircraft had indeed been a king-sized flying bomb — but why it had failed to detonate remained an unsolved mystery. The plane and its lethal load burned for the rest of the night, but it did not explode.

The fear that it would explode provided a nervous urgency to the task of removing the dead and injured from the devastated yard. Most of the casualties were those soldiers whom Hibberd had deployed to besiege Trygverson in the General's coach. The mangled bodies of Trygverson and Vardon were found and I made the identification. They were recovered with the bodies of the MPs whom Trygverson had shot. The French railmen in the tail van were also brought out, both dead. It was nearly dawn before we found Hibberd, almost decapitated beneath an overturned freight wagon,

I have no idea what time of night it was when Thorn had arrived to join in the search, but it was he and I who found Hibberd's body. By then there must have been about three hundred carrying out the search and rescue operation. As Hibberd's body was carried away in a blanket, Thorn put an arm round my shoulder.

'Come on, old buddy,' he said. 'Let's go. There's nothing more we can do here.'

'We failed, Cal,' I said miserably. 'We should have stopped it and we didn't.'

'They didn't get Ike,' Thorn said. 'We stopped them getting Ike . . . you more than anybody. So no more of this about failing. We won.'

'If this is winning,' I said, 'I'd hate like hell to lose.'

My participation in the fight against *Schatten Gruppe* virtually came to an end with the death of Hibberd and the failure of Operation Sun King to claim the life of Dwight D. Eisenhower. Both Thorn and I took part in the SHAEF inquest into the damage done by Vardon and Trygverson to the security of the base. The ease with which Vardon had abused the system was an eye-opener, but it stemmed mainly from the trust placed in an officer of his seniority. One can take precautions against a senior man's ineptitude or slackness in security but it is almost impossible to budget for a senior man's total betrayal of the trust he enjoys.

It was particularly important to us to discover the precise nature of Vardon's co-operation with *Schatten Gruppe*. How, for instance, had the German infiltrators managed to stay at large in Belgium and France for so long? How had they managed to acquire a hospital train and actually move it about on the railway network in a way that dovetailed perfectly with their planned attack on Eisenhower?

The simple answer is that when an order comes down from Headquarters be it in a multi-national corporation or a two-million-strong assembly of armies – the order is usually obeyed if the paperwork is in order. The paper bureaucracy that supported SHAEF was essential to the armies' needs but its sheer size offered endless opportunities for a mischief-maker and abundant protection for his activities. It occurred to me that keeping track of the components of several armies is like trying to keep check on the shelved stocks of a thousand and one busy stores all at once. Six months later – when all the invoices have been returned and all the sales accounted for – one could say roughly how many of this commodity and how many of that happened to be on the shelves at a thousand and one outlets on a particular day. But coming up with an instant answer or even an accurate estimate when sales are brisk and all those shelves are being emptied and refilled is next to impossible.

Bearing this in mind, it was startlingly easy for Vardon at headquarters to create a phantom American unit of doctors and medics, give it the tab of a division that was actually in the process of moving from England to the Continent, and locate it here, there or anywhere. The fact that the phantom unit was staffed entirely by

Germans was not likely to come to light at Headquarters where it was identified by a paper flag on a map and a reference file that was permanently mislaid. The main danger to such a unit's discovery lay in its personnel: their ability to carry off the deception without attracting attention to themselves and, more generally, the extent of their familiarity with American military custom and habit.

The well-trained *Schatten Gruppe* operatives made mistakes. They had obviously been hand-picked for their command of American idiom — much more carefully than Skorzeny's men had been — but they had slipped up badly by wearing side-arms, when it was not the practice of American medical personnel to ddo so. Nor were their attacks on medics for the purpose of acquiring uniforms all that clever, if only because the high rate of incidence aroused suspicion. They could not have anticipated that their ambulance mode of transport would be noted by me but, at the end of the day, it was their medic-orientated choice of ruse that proved their undoing.

The hand of Trygverson, or whatever his real name was, was evident in the acquisition and deployment of the hospital train as part of the German plan. How much luck, opportunism or calculation went into the move of installing him at SHAEF it is impossible to tell, but his arrival undoubtedly gave impetus to Operation Sun King and stiffened Vardon's contribution to the German cause. Possibly, the Germans feared that Vardon would bungle things if left to his own devices and could not be relied on without one of their own pushing him from behind.

One of the successful outcomes of the affair from the Allied point of view was the closure of the hijacked Allied escape route, the Sapphire Line. During the Occupation of France and Belgium, the Sapphire Line had been penetrated along its length by German agents and used to catch Allied escapers. After the Occupation, the

Germans had continued to use its chain of safe houses and sympathetic cells as a means of ferrying their agents from Germany to Paris, and vice versa. *Schatten Gruppe* had taken part in the original penetration of the various cells and had used it to smuggle their operatives to and from the Fatherland. Unlike Skorzeny's teams, they had not been compelled to burst through Allied road-blocks but had employed subtler tactics. Now, thanks to Vardon's elimination and, not least, Thorn's intuition, we were able to fold up the entire German operation and close it down permanently.

Early in the New Year, I was sent back to the Prof in Paris to carry on where I had left off in the PWD or the Political Warfare Executive as, increasingly, the powers-that-be insisted on calling the Department. Thorn seemed genuinely sorry to see me go. He did not relent in the fight against *Schatten Gruppe* and his pursuit of Keitler and his shadowy associates was to continue throughout the death throes of Nazi Germany and beyond, when the hunt began for those war criminals who had survived the war and gone to earth.

I never did find out what happened to Hilde Gronbach, or if she ever made it to Switzerland to live out her days on the ill-gotten gains of her murky career. The file on her remained open. For all I know, it remains open to the present day.

It seemed, too, that the open file on Major Cotter would gather dust indefinitely. And it might have done, but for the chance discovery of a shallow grave after the spring sunshine had melted the Ardennes snows. The body it contained was taken to Spa for a post-mortem and to await identification. The dead man had been shot through the back of the head at close range. A dog tag, attached to a cord round his neck, bore Cotter's identity number, and a check of Army dental records confirmed that it was the missing officer from SHAEF.

Cotter had officially been posted as a deserter, but

the more that Thorn and I had delved into the activities of Hubert Vardon the more convinced we became that the Major had simply been used. Cotter may even have covered up for his treacherous boss during the first flap over missing documents, attracting suspicion to himself because he could not bring himself to believe that Vardon was actually dealing with the enemy. In this Cotter may have shown an excess of loyalty to Vardon, but if he did he was simply adhering to an old Army tradition that the No. 2 does not rat on the No. 1. He stands by him. Thus, when missing docuuments were traced to Cotter at SHAEF he may well have been telling the plain truth when he said he had no memory of borrowing them. It would have been gross disloyalty in his eyes to have explained away his seeming incompetence by saying that his chief had borrowed the papers and must have stuck them in his desk instead of returning them.

Vardon, at any rate, had repaid his junior's loyalty by allowing him to take all the flak that was going and continuing to use him as a messenger, with the hint that he was merely passing Headquarters tittle-tattle to Montgomery. By the time I arrived on the scene at Versailles, Vardon and his German paymasters may have already decided on Cotter's fate. If the Allies wanted a hare to chase, Cotter would be given to them. Vardon despatched him to the house in Rue du Bourrelier with another load of secret documents and thereby consigned him to death. With Cotter's 'defection' Vardon must have been confident that he was removing the heat from himself. Unfortunately I had given credence to the belief that Cotter was the traitor by reporting Cotter's departure from the house in Rue du Bourrelier on his own two feet. But that was before I had been fully acquainted with *Schatten Gruppe*'s penchant for acquiring Allied uniforms. Cotter, dead or doped, had been the man in the stretcher and had been removed to the north for disposal. It would not have done if the 'defector' had been found in or near Paris.

Vardon must have had the shock of his life when Cotter had been reported captured up near the German border. By then, Cotter's place at SHAEF had been filled with *Schatten Gruppe*'s 'sleeper' the professional Trygverson, and I have no doubt that the pair's hurried excursion to the Ardennes was to silence, permanently, the man they thought was dead. Fortunately for them, death claimed the 'John Doe' before they or I got to him. The secret of how he came to be in possession of Cotter's watch died with the man. Perhaps, if I had not reached St Vith before Vardon, he would have identified the John Doe as Cotter, arranged a quick burial, and successfully put the seal on the myth that the Major was a traitor and had died fleeing into Germany.

I am glad to say that submissions by Thorn and myself, that Cotter was in all probability innocent of treason or desertion, were instrumental in persuading the War Office that pay and pension rights should not be withheld from his widow. In preparing my written submission, I owed much to the help of the Prof. He advised me to stress the absence of hard evidence to support the view that Cotter had any voluntary dealings with the enemy. With equal emphasis, he said, I should point out that Cotter's unswerving loyalty to a senior officer, whom he disliked, might have been unwise but was totally in keeping with the code of conduct which the Army demanded from its officers. At any rate, I received a stiff letter of thanks and the hint that my helpful deposition had gone some way to convincing the Board of Enquiry that Major Cotter had not betrayed his country.

It was the Prof, too – with his knowledge of the human psyche in general and the working of military minds in particular – who gave me some insight into what had bewildered me most about the Vardon affair. That was Hubert Vardon's own monstrous treachery:

its manner and motivation. Here was a man from the same proud military tradition as Cotter, but a man who had betrayed it without any visible sign of guilt or regret.

It did not surprise the Prof when I told him that Keitler had apparently swooped on Vardon as ideal material for subversion to the Nazi cause. The Prof said that from what he had heard about Vardon, any competent psychiatrist would have picked the Colonel's psyche clean in five minutes.

'Some people,' the Prof said, 'are so complex inside that a mining expedition is required to dig out the secrets of their subconscious. Vardon, as far as I can tell, was the opposite. To a person who can read the signs, he advertised his subconscious every time he opened his mouth. He was a walking billboard of his own inadequacies.'

The Prof and I discussed Vardon endlessly, mainly on the basis of details which we acquired of his family background and Army career. Gradually, we pieced together a picture of the course of his subversion by Keitler.

It is possible that Keitler may have known something about Vardon before he was taken prisoner by the Germans in Italy in late 1943. Both the Abwehr and the SD kept extensivve files on prominent British military families, so the chances are that the name Vardon rang a bell with Keitler. Was he any relation to the General Vardon, who had been labelled a butcher in the 1914 war? A phone-call would have supplied the answer. Yes, there was an only son, Hubert Macaulay Vardon. Perhaps the file gave a couple of lines about the son: date of entry to Sandhurst, date of commissioning, name of regiment he joined.

News of Vardon's capture in Italy – and the rather bizarre circumstances – must have reached Keitler very soon after it happened. Because he acted quickly to begin the subverting process.

As the Prof and I unearthed facts one by one of Vardon's time in German hands, a picture emerged of that period that was vastly different from the one that Vardon had provided to debriefing after his 'heroic' escape into Switzerland in April 1944.

It appears that Vardon was fêted by the Germans as a gallant enemy – at Keitler's instigation, of course. He was given luxurious accommodation and lavish dinners; invited to discuss battles lost and won with high-ranking officers who treated him as a brother-in-arms – a respected adversary whose only misfortune was to be on the wrong side in the game called war. Vardon – a major at the time, but one who probably adjudged himself deserving of at least brigadier's rank – accepted the adulation and respect of his enemies as no less than his due. He had gloried in it and swallowed whole the confidential assurances that, if he had been on Rommel's side in Africa, a man of his experience and talent would have been commanding a division.

Perhaps, when Keitler had brought Vardon to Paris in order to probe the depth of the British officer's sado-masochistic tendencies and suppressed sexuality, Vardon may have begun to have some doubts about his hosts' orchestrated benevolence. But there is no evidence to show that he did. The photographs of his sex games with Hilde Gronbach testified to his final debasement and the last step in his surrender to Keitler's will.

The scars on his back were not – as he had claimed – the work of Gestapo torturers but were the marks of his own depravity. He had exulted, writhing, at the fall of Hilde Gronbach's whip on his flesh; begging to be punished for the blackness of his sin. That sin was not the betrayal of his country or his class but the sin of knowing the shameful carnality of the desires within him: devils, whose existence could never be revealed nor released.

The Prof, whose expositions on mental disturbance overflowed with psychiatric jargon, tried to explain to me some of the confusion that was Vardon's mind. He believed, for instance, that a psychiatric interview with the Colonel when he was younger – if it had been Army practice to indulge in such things – would have revealed a man totally unsuited for a military career. Indeed, the same might have been said for Vardon's father before him. Vardon Senior had not died from shock because of any newspaper article – as his son had suggested to me – but from choking on a fish-bone in the private hospital where he spent the last two years of his life. It is unlikely that he ever saw the offending article. His hospitalisation was 'voluntary', the outcome of a violent unprovoked attack with a walking stick on a postman he had accused of being sloppily dressed. A court trial would have followed but the General was said to be 'unfit to plead' and undergoing treatment. It was said that the General's outbursts of violence and frequent irrational behaviour had been the talk of the neighbourhood for years and that it had caused no great surprise when he had to be 'put away'.

The Prof, who was apolitical and more anti-militaristic than anti-military, had pungent things to say about the shortcomings of the military caste into which both Vardon and his father before him had been born. He was not blind to the praiseworthy aspects: the tradition to serve king and country, the value placed on valour and honour. What the Prof disliked were the false values that had grown up with the true and had flourished in the system: perpetuating taboos and prejudices that had no place in an enlightened society. He abhorred the military elite who had fought to retain flogging and the death penalty as a means of enforcing military discipline. It was an indictment on their thinking that, as recently as 1914–1918, the British Army had been putting its own soldiers in front of firing squads at the rate of twenty a month not only for desertion but for offences such as striking an officer, cowardice, sleeping on duty and casting away arms. No mercy had been shown to many who had endured the slaughter of the trenches for years and had simply buckled under intolerable mental stress.

Many fine men, the Prof contended, had been born into the system that had evolved Vardon and his father. But the system had also thrown up its freaks and monsters and misfits and completely failed to recognise them as such. Indeed, it had often singled them out as the natural successors to power and influence and advanced them at the expense of more gifted and more natural leaders.

Vardon had been born with all the natural advantages with which to succeed in a military career but none of the mental attributes which might have guaranteed it. Fear of his father and an undue emotional dependence on his mother had marked his early years and separation from his mother for schooling at an all-male establishment had been traumatic for the boy.

Later, as a military cadet at Sandhurst, both parents had influenced Vardon's continuation of a career for which he showed little talent and the odd sign that he was quite unsuited. His father's reputation and eminence as a soldier earned him the benefit of the doubt when his own soldiering qualities were assessed as borderline. His mother's intervention and advocacy won the day when his behaviour failed to measure up to accepted standards.

On one occasion, Vardon and a fellow-cadet came close to expulsion for their bullying of a younger trainee, the son of an Indian maharajah, who they nicknamed 'Prince Wog'. Their bullying of the youth got out of hand one day and ended with the pair throwing him in a canal and laughing when he got into difficulties. They ran off when other cadets chanced on the scene. The new arrivals rescued the Indian from drowning and reported the matter.

Only the pleading of Vardon's mother and the Indian cadet's wish to forgive and forget the unsavoury episode saved Vardon from being kicked out of the Academy. Commissioned in due course, Vardon entered the Army in peacetime and found that promotion in wartime did not come as rapidly as he might have expected. Conspicuous acts of bravery earned him a greater reputation for recklessness than for inspired leadership, and his superiors had shown a longer memory for acts of incompetence that had cost his Division hard-won positions and the ill-afforded loss of men and equipment.

The Vardon I had briefly known was a man awash with prejudices. He despised all ethnic groups but his own, and only a small section of that met with his approval. He distrusted innovation or anyone who was creative or artistic. He abstained from alcohol, possibly because he feared its power. He professed Christianity and went to church – but from habit and the need to conform rather than from profound belief. He was insensitive to the suffering of others. He took no interest in the welfare of the men under him, regarding them as inferior beings. He was a vindictive man, who never forgave a wrong – real or imagined. He was in every respect a ready-made candidate for high office in the Nazi Party and exalted rank in its military arm.

And yet . . . And yet . . . Was that what had turned him from service of his country and the flag and made him the servant of his country's sworn enemy? An enemy, to boot, which sought to involve him in the destruction of the man commanding the combined armies of the nation to whom he had sworn allegiance and of the nation who was her greatest ally. I could not fully accept it. Given Vardon's latent Nazism, given the fact that he disliked Americans intensely, there must have been some other motivating factor to account for Vardon's one-hundred-and-eighty-degree about-face.

'He must really have hated Eisenhower,' I said to the Prof as I wrestled to identify the elusive factor which would make me comprehend his treachery. 'It must have been an obsession, a madness.'

'No, John,' the Prof said. 'There was a lot of hate in him – for people whose skins had a different colour to his, for foreigners, for Americans, for things he could not understand, for people like you who had the ability to *think*. He probably resented Eisenhower, envied his power and his position – but I doubt if that was what drove him. It was more likely fear.'

'Fear?'

'Yes, John – fear. Not physical fear – of bullets or pain. Not fear of discovery and being branded a traitor or a murderer. Because he was the kind of man who could always justify himself and find reasons to excuse behaviour that would overwhelm the likes of you or me with remorse and guilt. The knowledge that we were doing something wrong or despicable would weigh us down with guilt. But Vardon could do wrong and convince himself that he was doing right. His mother was to blame for that.'

'Why, for God's sake?'

'Because his mother brought him up to believe he could do no wrong. When he did wrong, whenever he did do something that the rest of us would class as unacceptable, his mother was always there ... to condone it, to excuse it, to say that it was everybody else's fault but not little Hubert's. It was this nasty person to blame or that nasty person to blame ... but never little Hubert ... not her own darling child. And when Mother wasn't there in later life to soothe her little darling and make up excuses for Hubert's misdemeanours, he made up the excuses himself ... And he believed them passionately ...'

'But you said he was driven by fear. Fear of what?'

'Fear of the one thing his mother made him repress all his life – his sexuality. That was the one thing that he could never admit. Because to have done so would have meant that his emotional need for his mother was

405

sexual, not filial . . . So the black beast had to be kept down, suppressed within him.' The Prof said this as if the conclusion must be patently obvious to the humblest intellect. He went on: 'You must understand the potency of Vardon's fear, its power to destroy him. He had to deny the existence of his sexuality from himself but, most of all, he had to hide it from the mother who worshipped him and cosseted him. This deep subconscious fear was the lever that Keitler used to make Vardon do his bidding. Keitler could have made him do anything – anything he commanded! Vardon could have turned back somersaults through hips for Keitler at the slightest prompting. Just a gentle threat was needed. Those naughty photographs you unearthed up in Belgium . . . they were Keitler's prod. They kept Vardon's fear alive. He wasn't afraid that Keitler would send them to the British embassy in Lisbon or that he would parachute copies down on Versailles addressed to Eisenhower. He was afraid that they would find their way to his mother. Vardon would do *anything* to prevent that – and Keitler knew it. That was Keitler's secret.'

'Then Vardon was mad,' I said.

The Prof shrugged. 'That depends on your definition of madness,' he said. 'If that kind of mother-fixation is madness, it afflicts quite a number of military careerists. I suppose it depends entirely on how the madness manifests itself that the career develops. Things could have been worse, you know. Vardon could have made general, like his father, and there's no saying what the results of that might have been.'

'I shudder to think,' I said. 'God knows we've got enough generals whose sanity I wonder about. They all seem a bit nutty. Look at Monty, with his vanity and insufferable conceit . . . Or Patton, with his pearl-handled revolvers and the way he struts around like a circus barker. He and Monty are two of a kind. One thinks he's Joshua, sent by the Lord, and the other thinks he's Julius Caesar. Am I being unduly cynical?'

'No more than usual, John. No more than usual. Maybe we need a madman or two like Monty and Patton to win wars. At least we have a down-to-earth farmer's boy to keep them under control. Ike is one of the sanest persons I have ever met and that's one hell of a comfort. Especially when you look at who's bossing the show on the other side.'

'Adolf? I won't argue with you over that. For galloping insanity, he wins by the length of a street. We've got nobody in his league. For that, I suppose we should count our lucky stars.'

The Prof smiled. 'Adolf puts a lot of faith in his lucky stars.'

'He should,' I said. 'He came through the last war in one piece, which is our bad luck. It's preposterous when you come to think of it. Heaven knows how many millions died, fighting the war to end all wars . . . Good men, like my own Dad, who didn't want to turn the world upside down but just wanted to live ordinary humdrum lives in peace with their neighbours. They died by the tens of thousand, but for what? Just so that this tiinpot madman could come along and start the same idiotic carnage all over again. I say: damn his stars!'

Our discussion had started over coffee at ten on a cold February night. It was now midnight and I still had work to do. I returned to my desk and discovered that I had not crossed off the day on my calendar, as I usually did in the morning. With vicious strokes of a blue pencil, I crossed off the day that had gone. Then I crossed off another. I felt better. Another day nearer peace. Another day nearer that blissful dawn. Peace, perfect peace. Oh, Lord, will it come in my time? Will it ever come?

Epilogue

The place was the City of London. The occasion was the granting of the City's freedom to the man who led the Allied armies to Victory in Europe, Dwight D. Eisenhower. He was no great orator — not in the Churchill league — but he was inspired that day. He gave a speech that deserves to be remembered on equal terms with the Gettysburg Address and the American Declaration of Independence.

Considering the claims on Ike's time that day by many notable people, I was flattered when one of his staff approached me, ascertained that I was John Abernathy, and told me that the General wanted to speak to me before he left. I was conducted to an ante-room, where the General had availed himself of the facilities and was freshening himself up.

He greeted me warmly. 'We have a mutual acquaintance,' he said. 'Major Thorn said you'd be here. I've been wanting to meet you for a long time. Did you know Major Thorn was getting married in London — an English girl he met a couple of years back?'

'I'm going to be his best man,' I said. 'Is anything wrong?'

Ike shook his head. 'The Major's in Frankfurt right now. He's flying over next week. I hope the wedding goes well but that's not what I wanted to talk to you about. You remember Christmas, forty-four?'

'Vividly.'

'I want to thank you for what you did then. You did

a good job. But for you, I maybe wouldn't have been around to see the end of the war. You know that they never told me the full story of what happened that Christmas?'

'I didn't know that, sir,' I said.

'I've always had a very protective staff,' he said. 'I used to get mad as hell at them at times. The guys around me were so goddamned intent on wrapping me in cotton wool like some priceless china ornament that I had to kick up all hell just to go for a walk in the rain. Maybe they thought I would shrink.'

'You were . . . You are . . . A very important person.'

'In a pig's eye! I had a job to do – and if anything had happened to me, some other guy would have had to step up and do it. But I will say this, goddamn it! If anybody had a right to know what was going on, it was me!'

'What was it they kept back from you, sir?'

'Too damned much! Things they thought I might worry about – embarrassing things like having a parcel of Germans running round Paris like they were part of the US Army. Goddamn it, they were even drawing rations! Wouldn't have surprised me to find they were on the pay-roll and drawing their pay, too!'

'At least they didn't get away with it for too long, sir.'

'Maybe not, but it frightens me to think just how many outfits this man's army has got that we've just lost track of . . . Guys who are sitting around somewhere, doing something that was maybe important when they were sent here but doesn't matter a cuss now. They probably don't even know the Army's forgotten them, lost all record of them . . .'

'It's as bad as that, sir?'

'I don't know how bad it is but I reckon that out of every million men enlisted, the Army loses fifty thousand – in the goddamned files! When I get home I'm going to push for an Army Census . . .' He broke off and, eyes twinkling, apologised for getting carried away on one of his pet hobby-horses. He wanted to talk about Christmas 1944 and the train trip he should have taken on December 26th.

'All they told me that night,' he said, 'was that I'd have to postpone going to Belgium for at least a day on account of the train I should have gone on getting bombed. And that's the way it happened. They got a new train and I went the following night. Took us a day to get up to Hasalt.'

'You didn't know you were supposed to go up with the first train? In little pieces, I mean?'

'I just thought I was lucky,' Ike confessed. 'I didn't know they were after me until we got an intelligence report about two months later – about Mistels. I didn't know what the hell Mistels were, so I asked to see every scrap of information we had on them.'

'What are Mistels?' I asked. He gazed at me in astonishment.

'You don't know? According to what I was told, you were mighty lucky you weren't killed by the first one the Germans threw at us. It was a Mistel hit that train I should have been on.'

'The pick-a-back planes? Small one on top, big one underneath – with the big plane playing the part of the bomb?'

'The Luftwaffe called them Mistels. They trained up whole squadrons of them. Our own bombers took most of them out on the ground – but the first one they made operational was the one that was meant for me. And nobody even thought of telling me. I'm afraid my temper wasn't too good when I found out. I made a few people jump, I can tell you. I wanted to know what else they were holding back. That's when I found out about John Abernathy and a hell of a lot more.'

He paused, smiling at me as if he were enjoying a private joke.

'I've got a good memory for names,' he said, and

grinned, 'well, most of the time. I knew I'd heard the name Abernathy before . . . It's a name that sticks in the mind . . . I'd heard it before I'd heard of Mistels.'

'In what connection, sir?'

'You're the guy who wrote some pretty interesting things about generals being blundering incompetents – idiots, most of them.'

I shuffled uncomfortably. 'There have been some generals who did idiotic things,' I said defensively. 'I've never classified you in that bracket.'

The eyes twinkled some more. 'Oh, is that so?' He thrust his jaw out pugnaciously. 'What's so special about me?'

I stared him straight in the eye and smiled right back at him.

'You have a weakness, sir, that I find very reassuring. I don't think your ego will ever get out of hand.'

'This is where I get it in the eye,' he said. 'Keep talking. I want to know about this weakness. Maybe I can do something about it.'

'It's too late, sir. From what I hear, you're well and truly hooked. You are, I am told, addicted to that most humbling of pastimes, golf.'

'I've been known to cuss a bit on the golf course. You wouldn't find that too reassuring.'

'But I do, sir,' I said. 'You've managed to keep your sense of humour. And I find that very reassuring. I've always been of the opinion that anyone who plays golf and still has a sense of humour can't be all bad.'

Ike roared with laughter. And that's how I'll remember him – a big man, in every sense of the word, with twinkling eyes.

Bestselling War Fiction and Non-Fiction

☐ Passage to Mutiny	Alexander Kent	£2.95
☐ Colours Aloft	Alexander Kent	£2.95
☐ Winged Escort	Douglas Reeman	£2.95
☐ Army of Shadows	John Harris	£2.50
☐ Decoy	Dudley Pope	£2.95
☐ Gestapo	Rupert Butler	£4.50
☐ Johnny Gurkha	E.D. Smith	£2.95
☐ Typhoon Pilot	Desmond Scott	£2.95
☐ The Rommel Papers	B.H. Liddel Hart	£5.95
☐ Hour of the Lily	John Kruse	£3.50
☐ Duel in the Dark	Peter Townsend	£3.95
☐ The Spoils of War	Douglas Scott	£2.99
☐ The Wild Blue	Walter J. Boyne & Steven L. Thompson	£3.95
☐ The Bombers	Norman Longmate	£4.99

Prices and other details are liable to change

ARROW BOOKS, BOOKSERVICE BY POST, PO BOX 29, DOUGLAS, ISLE OF MAN, BRITISH ISLES

NAME..

ADDRESS..

....

....

Please enclose a cheque or postal order made out to Arrow Books Ltd. for the amount due and allow the following for postage and packing.

U.K. CUSTOMERS: Please allow 22p per book to a maximum of £3.00.

B.F.P.O. & EIRE: Please allow 22p per book to a maximum of £3.00

OVERSEAS CUSTOMERS: Please allow 22p per book.

A Selection of Arrow Bestsellers

☐ The Lilac Bus	Maeve Binchy	£2.50
☐ 500 Mile Walkies	Mark Wallington	£2.50
☐ Staying Off the Beaten Track	Elizabeth Gundrey	£5.95
☐ A Better World Than This	Marie Joseph	£2.95
☐ No Enemy But Time	Evelyn Anthony	£2.95
☐ Rates of Exchange	Malcolm Bradbury	£3.50
☐ Colours Aloft	Alexander Kent	£2.95
☐ Speaker for the Dead	Orson Scott Card	£2.95
☐ Eon	Greg Bear	£4.95
☐ Talking to Strange Men	Ruth Rendell	£5.95
☐ Heartstones	Ruth Rendell	£2.50
☐ Rosemary Conley's Hip and Thigh Diet	Rosemary Conley	£2.50
☐ Communion	Whitley Strieber	£3.50
☐ The Ladies of Missalonghi	Colleen McCullough	£2.50
☐ Erin's Child	Sheelagh Kelly	£3.99
☐ Sarum	Edward Rutherfurd	£4.50

Prices and other details are liable to change

ARROW BOOKS, BOOKSERVICE BY POST, PO BOX 29, DOUGLAS, ISLE OF MAN, BRITISH ISLES

NAME...

ADDRESS...

....

....

Please enclose a cheque or postal order made out to Arrow Books Ltd. for the amount due and allow the following for postage and packing.

U.K. CUSTOMERS: Please allow 22p per book to a maximum of £3.00.

B.F.P.O. & EIRE: Please allow 22p per book to a maximum of £3.00

OVERSEAS CUSTOMERS: Please allow 22p per book.

Whilst every effort is made to keep prices low it is sometimes necessary to increase cover prices at short notice. Arrow Books reserve the right to show new retail prices on covers which may differ from those previously advertised in the text or elsewhere.

Bestselling Thriller/Suspense

☐ Hell is Always Today	Jack Higgins	£2.50
☐ Brought in Dead	Harry Patterson	£1.99
☐ Russian Spring	Dennis Jones	£2.50
☐ Fletch	Gregory Mcdonald	£1.95
☐ Black Ice	Colin Dunne	£2.50
☐ Blind Run	Brian Freemantle	£2.50
☐ The Proteus Operation	James P. Hogan	£3.50
☐ Miami One Way	Mike Winters	£2.50
☐ Skydancer	Geoffrey Archer	£2.50
☐ Hour of the Lily	John Kruse	£3.50
☐ The Tunnel	Stanley Johnson	£2.50
☐ The Albatross Run	Douglas Scott	£2.50
☐ Dragonfire	Andrew Kaplan	£2.99

Prices and other details are liable to change

ARROW BOOKS. BOOKSERVICE BY POST. PO BOX 29. DOUGLAS. ISLE
OF MAN. BRITISH ISLES

NAME...

ADDRESS...

....

....

Please enclose a cheque or postal order made out to Arrow Books Ltd. for the amount
due and allow the following for postage and packing.

U.K. CUSTOMERS: Please allow 22p per book to a maximum of £3.00.

B.F.P.O. & EIRE: Please allow 22p per book to a maximum of £3.00

OVERSEAS CUSTOMERS: Please allow 22p per book.

Whilst every effort is made to keep prices low it is sometimes necessary to increase cover
prices at short notice. Arrow Books reserve the right to show new retail prices on covers
which may differ from those previously advertised in the text or elsewhere.

Bestselling Fiction

☐ Hiroshmia Joe	Martin Booth	£2.95
☐ The Pianoplayers	Anthony Burgess	£2.50
☐ Queen's Play	Dorothy Dunnett	£3.95
☐ Colours Aloft	Alexander Kent	£2.95
☐ Contact	Carl Sagan	£3.50
☐ Talking to Strange Men	Ruth Rendell	£5.95
☐ Heartstones	Ruth Rendell	£2.50
☐ The Ladies of Missalonghi	Colleen McCullough	£2.50
☐ No Enemy But Time	Evelyn Anthony	£2.95
☐ The Heart of the Country	Fay Weldon	£2.50
☐ The Stationmaster's Daughter	Pamela Oldfield	£2.95
☐ Erin's Child	Sheelagh Kelly	£3.99
☐ The Lilac Bus	Maeve Binchy	£2.50

Prices and other details are liable to change

ARROW BOOKS, BOOKSERVICE BY POST, PO BOX 29, DOUGLAS, ISLE OF MAN, BRITISH ISLES

NAME...

ADDRESS...

....

....

Please enclose a cheque or postal order made out to Arrow Books Ltd. for the amount due and allow the following for postage and packing.

U.K. CUSTOMERS: Please allow 22p per book to a maximum of £3.00.

B.F.P.O. & EIRE: Please allow 22p per book to a maximum of £3.00

OVERSEAS CUSTOMERS: Please allow 22p per book.

Whilst every effort is made to keep prices low it is sometimes necessary to increase cover prices at short notice. Arrow Books reserve the right to show new retail prices on covers which may differ from those previously advertised in the text or elsewhere.